WITH THE LIGHTS ON

JACKIE ASHENDEN

MILLS & BOON

To all my dirty, dark DARE heroes.
Thanks for everything, guys.
It's been quite a ride. ;-)

Jackie Ashenden writes dark, emotional stories, with alpha heroes who've just got the world to their liking only to have it blown wide apart by their kick-ass heroines. She lives in Auckland, New Zealand, with her husband, the inimitable Dr Jax, two kids and two rats. When she's not torturing alpha males and their gutsy heroines she can be found drinking chocolate martinis, reading anything she can lay her hands on, wasting time on social media or being forced to go mountain biking with her husband. To keep up to date with Jackie's new releases and other news, sign up to her newsletter at jackieashenden.com.

A.C. Arthur is an award-winning author who lives in Baltimore, Maryland, with her husband, three children, grandson, and an English bulldog named Vader. An active imagination and a love for reading encouraged her to begin writing in high school, and she hasn't stopped since.

If you liked
With the Lights On and *Give Me More*
why not try

Hold Me by Anne Marsh
Skin Deep by Lauren Hawkeye

Also by Jackie Ashenden

Kings of Sydney

King's Price
King's Rule
King's Ransom

The Billionaires Club

The Debt

Billion $ Bastards

Dirty Devil
Sexy Beast
Bad Boss

Playing for Pleasure

In the Dark

Also by A.C. Arthur

The Fabulous Golds

A Private Affair
At Your Service
The Last Affair

Discover more at millsandboon.co.uk

WITH THE LIGHTS ON

JACKIE ASHENDEN

GIVE ME MORE

A.C. ARTHUR

MILLS & BOON

First Published in Great Britain 2021
by Mills & Boon, an imprint of HarperCollins*Publishers*
1 London Bridge Street, London, SE1 9GF

With the Lights On © 2021 Jackie Ashenden

Give Me More © 2021 Artist C. Arthur

ISBN: 978-0-263-29795-9

MIX
Paper from
responsible sources
FSC C007454

Printed and bound in Spain
by CPI, Barcelona

CHAPTER ONE

Magdalen

IT WAS DIFFERENT tonight and I knew it the moment I walked in the door.

Normally when I had an evening with Trajan, the lights would be dimmed and he'd have music playing in the background. Sometimes it was a woman singing, low and husky and sad, sometimes dark and dirty blues. He liked classical and opera as well, and occasionally there'd be something electronic and dreamy.

Music to fill the silence, I'd thought initially. But then after I'd got to know him better, and he'd got to know me, he'd put on music that we both enjoyed and that he wanted to share with me.

Tonight, though, there was no music.

And, tonight, all the lights were on.

I stopped just inside the door, letting it shut with a heavy thump behind me, my heart beating far too fast for comfort. I'd never actually seen Trajan's apartment fully lit before—he was a fan of 'diffuse' lighting, as in so diffuse that it was sometimes difficult to see—but right now I was too distracted to take a proper look around.

I worked for Company of Strangers, which I'd heard some call a glorified escort agency, and to some extent they were right. But sex wasn't its only purpose. Or, rather, it was only one aspect of its purpose, which was essentially to provide people with company. That company might be sex, if both parties agreed, or it could be simply dinner and conversation. A friend to have a drink with in a bar. A casual coffee and a gossip.

Clients tended to be mostly lonely business people who didn't have either the time or the inclination to forge friendships and who were willing to pay someone to keep them company for a couple of hours. Sex could be included if that was desired, but only if the Strangers employee was willing. And it was, of course, extra.

From an employee perspective, Strangers was an excellent company to work for, since all clients were heavily vetted before they could access the services provided, and there were lots of systems put in place for the safety of both clients and employees. I'd never felt unsafe, not once in the years I'd been working for them.

However, that had changed over the last two months, though it wasn't my physical safety I was worried about. It was my heart I was afraid for, especially since that last meeting with Trajan, where I'd exploded everything…

I took a slow, deep breath, trying to calm myself. My palms were damp, though I knew better than to wipe them on the red satin of my dress.

Honey; I had to be Honey. That was my persona, the warm, nurturing, sensual woman who was Strangers' best and most highly paid employee. The most sought after, the most booked. She was expert at putting a client at ease, at figuring out what they wanted, and providing them with the best experience possible. She was never shocked or surprised. She always knew what to say and she always knew what to do.

But I was having a hard time holding on to Honey right now, because whenever I was around Trajan I always found it difficult to hold onto her. Especially now. Especially after what had happened between us two weeks earlier.

Never get involved. That was the motto everyone in my industry tried to stick to and it had never been a problem for me. Never, ever.

Not until now. Not until him.

Feeling slightly calmer, I walked slowly down the short hallway and into the big, open-plan space that was the penthouse apartment proper.

It was unusual for a client to invite me into their home. Normally meetings were in hotel rooms, bars or restaurants. But even from the first Trajan had been different.

He'd invited me to his private residence, a gorgeous penthouse that looked out over Central Park in Manhattan. It was decorated in a very minimalist fashion, with white walls and dark carpet and low, soft couches upholstered in textured white linen. The coffee tables and shelves were all of sleek powder-coated black metal, the only colour the rich, silk antique Persian rugs dotted at intervals on the floor and the velvet cushions scattered here and there.

There was no art on the walls, no photos. He'd told me he didn't want anything to compete with the floor-to-ceiling views of the park, which made sense. Though, I suppose he could have hidden any personal decorative touches when I was there in order to keep his identity secret.

That was usual for Strangers. For the protection of both employee and client, no real names were used. Trajan was the name he'd given me and he knew me as Honey. But over the course of our meetings we'd gradually come to know more about each other than just our names, and then two weeks ago we'd crossed a boundary we couldn't come back from. The boundary that separated pretend from real…and real was the one thing I could never be, not with anyone…

I frowned around the room, trying to figure out why the lights were all on, and where Trajan was, because he didn't seem to be here.

Normally he either greeted me in the hallway or he called me through into the living area or the kitchen; if he'd called, I hadn't heard.

The room was empty.

I moved over to the big windows, looking out over Central Park, a long rectangle of darkness dotted here and there with lights like tiny sequins.

My heart was beating faster now and I felt jittery, though I tried to tell myself it was less about facing Trajan again after our last meeting and more about the fact that I shouldn't have been meeting him at all tonight.

My evening had been booked by someone else, a guy who wanted only sex and who paid outrageously well to get it. He was a black-star client—which meant he was on Strangers' trusted clients list—and every woman who'd ever been hired by him had nothing but good things to say about his bedroom skills. I should have been with him tonight, but Trajan's request had come through and I couldn't not see him.

So I'd let my best friend Vesta convince me to let her have the black-star client while I spent the evening with Trajan. It was an extremely bad move, as Vesta wasn't actually employed by Strangers. But I hadn't been able to find a Strangers employee who was either free or willing to fill in, and I just couldn't turn down a chance to see Trajan.

There were things he and I had to talk about.

The bright light of the room threw my reflection back at me in the glass: small and curvy, my extremely tight red, silk dress glowing in the light. My curly blonde hair—gone even more curly in the summer humidity outside and impossible to do anything with—I'd left loose down my back. I'd kept my make-up to a minimum, except for my lipstick, which was bright red to match my dress and red stilettos.

I was very definitely Honey tonight, not Maggie, but then I had to be. I had to put some distance between us, and being Honey was the only way I could do that.

Staring at the glass, I lifted a hand to adjust my hair and then froze. Reflected in the window was Trajan, his tall figure motionless behind me, standing near one of the low sofas, so still I'd almost missed him.

My breath caught as the hard punch of desire came, the way it always did when I saw him, and had from that first day.

He was the most beautiful man I'd ever seen, and I'd seen a lot of men.

Over six-two at the very least, he had wide, heavily muscled shoulders and a broad chest tapering to narrow hips and long, powerful thighs. He embodied strength, radiating it like the sun radiated warmth, and I found it incredibly attractive. It was a patient strength, and solid too, like a mountain. The kind of strength you could lean on, trusting totally that it would hold you up.

He wasn't pretty—his features were too strongly carved for that, with a sharp jaw, cheekbones to die for, a high forehead and a straight nose. His was an intensely masculine, compelling face. Fierce, uncompromising and absolutely mesmerising.

He'd never spoken about what he did for a job, but it had to be something high-powered—not only because the penthouse must have cost millions, but because he exuded the kind of self-confidence and arrogance that heads of companies did. And I should know; I'd met quite a few in my line of work.

His hair was black and shorn close to his skull, and he had the most startlingly clear dark-blue eyes.

Right from the first night when he'd opened the door to me and I'd looked into those eyes, I'd felt dizzy. And breathless and excited and hungry, everything a highly paid escort shouldn't feel for her client. But, since I hadn't been attracted to anyone in years, I dismissed the feeling as an aberration.

I shouldn't have. Because then I wouldn't be where I was now, with something immense and heavy sitting in the air between us, squeezing the life out of the atmosphere and making it hard to breathe.

Sometimes he wore a suit, which always made me dry-mouthed with desire, because he was all kinds of hot in one. Tonight, though, he was in jeans, worn and faded, sitting low on his hips, and a black T-shirt that clung to his chest in a way that sent desire spiralling through my veins.

God, I was stupid to be here, especially after last time, when I'd run from him as if the hounds of hell were on my tail. But maybe that was what I was. Stupid.

Stupid to have put my livelihood at risk by letting my best friend take my other client for the night. Stupid to meet again the client standing in front of me, the client I'd already been warned off.

Stupid to let my heart get involved in the mix.

Well, as of tonight, I wasn't going to be stupid any more.

He said nothing. I said nothing. The memory of us on the couch, sipping expensive brandy and talking, lay between us.

It had been so late, and I'd already had a couple of glasses of wine and was more relaxed than I should have been. We'd been talking about something innocuous—I couldn't even remember what—and then somehow the conversation had strayed onto more personal topics. Topics that I'd never talked about with anyone before. About growing up with my grandmother, and my mom's stints in jail, and how bullying at school had scarred me. And then he'd poured us more brandy and told me about his own cold upbringing and the car accident he'd had at seventeen that had involved his girlfriend and that had nearly killed both of them.

It had been two a.m. and I'd forgotten myself. Forgotten that the contract Trajan had with me was a 'friendship only' contract and was not for sex. Which meant touching wasn't allowed. But, as he'd told me about the accident and how his girlfriend had been injured, I'd put my hand on his hard thigh in instinctive comfort. He'd gone utterly still, then had looked at me.

And, before I knew what I was doing, I'd leaned in slowly and kissed him.

I'd kissed lots of men. But I'd kissed all of them because they were my clients, and if they wanted a kiss I gave it to them, since making them happy was an important part of my job. I'd never actually kissed a man because I'd wanted to, not even the guy I'd lost my virginity to in the back of his car after prom. I'd only kissed him because the situation had seemed to demand it rather than out of any personal need.

Yet I'd kissed Trajan. And that was when I realised what was happening. I was falling for him, pure and simple, and it couldn't happen. It just couldn't.

Terrified at my own feelings, I'd jerked away and left the apartment before he'd been able to protest. I hadn't seen him since. Part of me had been hoping he'd never book me again, while another part had been dreading that he wouldn't, that that night was the last I'd see of him.

Then I'd received the booking notification and

I hadn't been able to stay away. I had to see him one last time, if only to tell him face to face that he couldn't book me ever again.

The silence sat heavily, the bright light around us an intrusion.

His intense gaze focused on my reflection in the glass, black brows drawing down as if he'd seen something in it he didn't like. 'Are you okay?'

I wasn't expecting either the question or the soft note in his familiar deep, rich voice, and it sent a hot stab of longing through me.

Unlike every other client I'd ever had, Trajan had always been solicitous of me. He always made sure I had a drink or something to eat, and it was always something I liked. And he always seemed to notice if I was too cold or too hot, either adjusting the AC for me or wrapping a throw around my shoulders. He was never hard to talk to and I never had to work for conversation.

Sometimes it was almost as if I was the client and he was paid to look after me, and maybe that was partly why I'd started to feel things I shouldn't for him. I didn't know why the question made my heart constrict painfully in my chest, even now when I knew it was wrong.

I liked the way he always thought about me. I liked it far too much.

But it wasn't what I was paid for.

I took a silent breath and turned from the window,

pasting on my best Honey smile. 'Yes, of course. Were you worried about what happened last time?'

He stood so still, entirely motionless, his gaze riveted to my face as if he'd never seen it before in his entire life. 'You left very suddenly. I wondered if I'd hurt you.'

Oh God, I hadn't thought of that. The only thing in my head was the need to get away, to put some distance between us, because that kiss should never have happened.

'No,' I said, because I couldn't let him think it was his fault. 'It wasn't that.'

'Then what was it?' The expression on his beautiful face was oddly intense, different from the cool, charming man who'd greeted me that first day, whose cold blue eyes had been guarded and whose smile had been slight and impersonal.

Slowly that had changed, though. Slowly his smiles had become deeper, warmer, and those blue eyes had lit up with rare amusement and even rarer laughter as I'd learned the kind of man he was beneath that cool, controlled exterior.

But there were no smiles for me today, only a strange, glittering heat in his eyes that made my pulse beat even faster.

'Trajan,' I began, wanting to say it quickly, because the quicker I said it the quicker I could leave, and that would be better for both of us. 'I need to talk to you about—'

'Our contract?' he interrupted. 'Yes, I changed it.'

I blinked, not understanding what he was talking about, too caught up in what I'd been going to say. 'Our contract?' I echoed.

His gaze remained riveted to mine, his tall, powerful figure radiating a curious leashed tension. 'Yes. I called them about it this morning. Did they not tell you?'

I'd been busy today, running around after my grandmother, and there had been a couple of missed calls from Strangers. But I hadn't had a moment to call them back, not with Gran and getting Vesta up to speed for her own meeting tonight, and besides, I'd assumed it wasn't urgent.

I swallowed. 'I had a couple of missed calls on my phone, but I didn't have a moment today to call them back. So, what did you change?'

His focus was absolute. 'I don't want a friendship-only contract any more. Tonight, I want to have sex.' He paused then added, as if I hadn't understood, 'With you.'

CHAPTER TWO

Trajan

I COULD SEE her face clearly for the first time in the bright light and it stole all the breath from my body. The rest of her—the entire rest of the room—was just a blurry smear of colour, but I didn't give a shit about that.

All I wanted was to see her and I still had enough central vision for that at least.

She stood against the windows and, given that some of the blurry colour was red, I assumed she was wearing a red dress. Her face was perfect and heart-shaped with straight, golden, silky brows, a wide, generous mouth and a pointed, determined chin. Her eyes were very dark, which was unusual, given the riot of thick golden curls that framed her features.

She looked exactly like her photo on the Company of Strangers website, but a photo couldn't capture the expressiveness of her features or the sheer warmth of her presence. She had a light inside her and I could see it; she just fucking glowed.

I'd caught glimpses of her every time she arrived on my doorstep for our evenings together, but never for long, because I kept the lights in the apartment low at night so I could practise not having any vision at all—I was night-blind—but of course that meant not seeing her.

Tonight, though, was different.

Tonight, I wanted to see her.

I'd had months of her warm presence, her husky, sweet voice, her expensive floral perfume and the much simpler coconut and vanilla scent that lay underneath it.

That scent had been taunting me at every meeting, a hint of a different woman beneath the polished responses of the highly paid, professional escort. A woman I'd slowly uncovered over the course of months. A woman who'd kissed me at our last meeting two weeks ago, before escaping my penthouse as though it had been on fire.

I shouldn't have been surprised, though. Not when that kiss had changed everything.

That kiss had changed me.

Sex hadn't been the point of our contract when I'd initially booked her—all I'd wanted was someone to practise not being able to see on—someone who didn't know me, who I could spend a social evening with and discover if I could adapt enough that they wouldn't be able to guess.

I was the CEO of Howard and Hart, a company that my best friend Eli Hart and I had started and subsequently grown into a multi-billion-dollar business off the back of a patented material used in the making of specialised body armour. We'd initially targeted the military, but had soon branched out into commercial applications, and that had sent the company into the stratosphere. And I absolutely refused to let my blindness get in the way of its success.

Reading people's faces was important when it came to managing meetings and dealing with people, so I would have to learn how to read them without sight. From the way they spoke, their intonations and inflections. Learn to be alert to the sounds of movement too, since fidgeting could betray someone just as sitting still could.

My meetings with Honey were supposed to help me with that. As I learned how to read her, so I learned how to read other people. It was also important to me that no one guessed that I was losing my sight. Of course, I knew I wouldn't be able to hide it for ever, but up until then I wanted to remain in full control of the process.

Remaining in full control of every aspect of my life had always been imperative and it was even more so now.

At first I'd simply wanted to see if I could get

through one evening without giving myself away, and when I hadn't that evening had become two, then three and then more. Then she'd kissed me, and practising being blind was the last thing on my mind. Now, all I could think about was sex.

I wasn't sure why she'd run out, but I'd thought that maybe it had something to do with our existing contract, by which even touch wasn't permitted. She was a good girl at heart—I'd learned that much about her—and I knew she took her job and her contracts very seriously. The kiss had been a major breach and perhaps that had worried her.

So, since I was the one who'd hired her in the first place, I'd decided to change the contract. I was going to lose my vision—my ophthalmologist had been very clear about that—but before I lost it I wanted a night with the woman whose presence was starting to consume my every waking thought.

A relationship would never be an option for me—not with her, not with anyone—but one night would be enough. One night, no holds barred. Indulging in everything I'd fantasised about in the silence of the apartment after she'd gone, her scent lingering in the air.

One night when there would be no other clients and no contracts. Where she was mine and mine only.

I kept very still, not wanting to move in case she ran again, because I could sense her tension. I'd sensed it the moment she'd stepped into the apartment.

In the small circle of my vision, I could see expressions ripple over that beautiful face of hers—shock, mainly—and then she turned slightly away, the bright gold of her curls obscuring her features.

I gritted my teeth at the loss. I could take a couple of steps to the side to keep her face in view, but even so it would remain in shadow, and therefore I wouldn't be able to see it.

Shit.

I stared hard at the mass of golden curls, trying to get a sense of what she was feeling. She was so expressive I could almost always tell her mood the moment she arrived, and really, this was no different.

Tension filled the air around her and the space between us, and I could feel it getting tighter and tighter.

'You don't want this,' I said, my voice on the edge of a growl, a sharp and bitter disappointment collecting inside me. It wasn't a question; her feelings on the subject were leaking into the air around us, making it very obvious.

She didn't reply immediately and I concentrated on the sound of her breathing. It was faster than normal, agitated. 'Trajan…' Her sweet voice was huskier than usual, a thread of distress running through it.

I knew every inch of my apartment. I knew the measurements of every room, the exact distances between the door and the bed. From the couch to the table. From the stove to the counter. Every single one. I knew every object and where it had been placed. The bowl of fruit on the counter. The pile of magazines on the coffee table.

I kept the lights low at night on purpose so I could practise navigating it with no sight, so when I took a couple of steps towards her, wanting to get a clearer picture of what was she was thinking and feeling, I didn't hesitate or stumble because I knew exactly where I was in relation to everything else.

I hadn't meant this little experiment to last for longer than a couple of weeks. A few meetings to enable me to adapt to interacting with people without sight, and then that was supposed to have been it.

Yet I'd found myself booking more evenings with her, and a couple of weeks had stretched into months, and instead of focussing on how to read people, I found myself obsessed with how to read *her*.

And, yes, she was definitely distressed now; I could almost feel it in the air around me.

'It's not as simple as that,' she murmured at last, her head turning once again so she was looking at me. Her dark eyes widened slightly when she realised I was closer than before, but the aching regret in her expression didn't change. 'I can't, Trajan. I can't.'

The bitter disappointment coiled inside me, squeezing tight, and I tried to ignore it. Because it shouldn't matter. What did I care if she didn't want to have sex with me? There were plenty of women who did; I had no shortage of takers.

But of course, it wasn't just sex that was the issue. It had never been the issue.

The issue was that I wanted sex with *her*.

I shoved my hands into the pockets of my jeans, my fingers curling into fists. Normally I had no problem keeping my emotions buried, but Honey always seemed to find them. I didn't know why and I still didn't. There was just something about the warmth of her presence and the sweet note in her voice that dragged them to the surface again and again, and had done since the day I'd first met her.

'You're Honey?' I'd asked the first night she'd arrived at my doorstep. The lights in the hallway had been low so I hadn't been able to see her. She'd been only a faint blur in the darkness.

'That's me,' she'd replied, the sweet, textured sound of her voice enveloping me in warmth. 'And what should I call you?'

'Trajan,' I'd said without thinking, giving her my real name.

'A Roman emperor, huh?' Amusement had coloured her tone. 'I like it. Pleased to meet you, Trajan.'

I'd heard the chime of bracelets and knew she'd lifted her hand and was presenting it to me to take. My first challenge and I'd already fucked up by giving her my real name, too mesmerised by the sound of her voice.

However, I wasn't going to fuck up again, so I levelled my gaze to where I estimated her face was and I put out my hand, my fingers connecting with a soft, warm palm. 'Pleased to meet you, Honey,' I'd said, and as I'd wrapped my fingers around her small hand I'd felt the lightning strike of sexual attraction hit.

Right then, my fate had been sealed.

'Explain, then,' I demanded now, the authoritative control freak in me asserting itself. 'Because it seemed like you might want it two weeks ago.'

'I know.' Silky lashes lowered, veiling her gaze. 'That was…a mistake.'

The disappointment bit deeper, even though I tried not to let it, the memory of that kiss seared into my brain. Sitting on the couch in this very room sipping brandy with her beside me, with Billie Holiday crooning softly in the background. She'd taken her shoes off—I'd heard the thump as they'd hit the carpet—and she'd curled up. The subtle tension that I'd sensed when I'd met her must have been nerves because, the more we'd seen of each other, it had eased, until it was completely gone.

She'd been utterly relaxed as she'd sat beside me, the warmth of her body tantalising as the conversation had turned to more personal topics. She'd told me about her shitty upbringing after her mother had gone to jail on drugs charges and she'd had to go and live with her grandmother—who, from the sounds of it, had been very grudging with her care. And so I'd found myself reciprocating, talking about my exacting father, who'd always expected excellence, and how I'd delivered on a regular basis, arrogantly sure of myself and my abilities, believing myself to be bulletproof, until the car accident that had nearly killed me and Susannah, my girlfriend at the time.

I hadn't gone into detail, but she'd picked up on the horror of it all the same. And that was when I'd felt her hand on my thigh, a reassuring touch that had seemed to short-circuit my brain. I hadn't sensed her move, too busy absorbing every aspect of that light touch; but then had come the lightest brush of her mouth on mine, a searing moment of contact that had changed everything.

Because she wasn't supposed to touch me. She wasn't supposed to kiss me. That was in the contract she and I had both signed, and which she'd explained that first night as we'd dealt with what she'd termed 'housekeeping details'; she'd made it clear that she viewed that contract as sacrosanct.

But she'd broken it that night. She'd shattered it completely, and with it the leash I'd kept on my own control.

'That wasn't a mistake.' My voice was too sharp, but I didn't care. 'You must know that I've wanted you from the moment you turned up on my doorstep.'

'But we can't let that—'

'And you wanted me too; don't deny it.' Disappointment had turned to anger and I had to fight to lock it down.

You're letting this mean too much. Get it together.

I couldn't allow the emotion curdling in my gut to take control. Besides, her wanting me or me wanting her made no difference. If she didn't want it, she didn't want it, and that was the end of the story.

'Okay, so I did,' she said quietly. 'But...' I heard her take a little breath. 'But I can't take it any further. *We* can't take it any further.'

'It's just one night,' I bit out. 'That's all I'm asking for. One last night together. So don't you want it to be something special?'

CHAPTER THREE

Magdalen

HE STOOD UNDERNEATH another spotlight, the light glossing his inky-black hair, the starkly masculine planes and angles of his face thrown into sharp relief. His whole posture vibrated with tension, the intensity in his expression catching me by the throat and squeezing tight.

He wanted me, and he wanted me badly.

The longing that gripped me was so strong that for a moment I could hardly breathe. Because he wasn't wrong: I *did* want him, and every bit as badly as he wanted me, probably from that very first moment when his long fingers had closed around my hand. I'd felt his heat and strength, and something had told me that I would be safe with him. I hadn't felt that with a client before.

I'd never felt that with *anyone* before.

I should have realised then that meeting with him

might be dangerous, but I'd dismissed the thought. I'd told myself it was nothing, that being attracted to a client would be a good test for me at staying professional.

I hadn't known just how much of a test it would be and how badly I'd fail in the end.

My hands clutched onto each other—a habit from back in my school days that I'd tried to get rid of, because no one liked a nervous escort—and I tried to loosen them as what he'd said finally penetrated.

'I see.' I struggled to get my thoughts in order, my heartbeat thumping loudly in my head.

One last booking. One last night.

Don't you want it to be something special?

'Well?' His voice was sharp with an edge of demand that was new to me.

He hadn't been like that the last time we'd met. He'd been lounging on the couch cushions beside me, one arm along the back of the couch, his other hand resting on his thigh. His deep voice had been soft, and there had been a note of pain in it as he'd told me about the car accident that had ended up with his girlfriend being in hospital for a year, and how guilty he'd felt because he'd been driving. I'd watched his face as he'd told me, had seen his dark-blue eyes stare off into the distance, and there had been a vulnerability to him that had tugged at my heart. I'd been able to sense that there was more to that story, but I hadn't pushed.

When we'd first met I'd thought him a little cold, because he was so precise about things and so in control of himself. He'd been perfectly charming, and yet I'd sensed in him a deep reserve that had slowly melted over the weeks. I'd been thrilled when he'd relaxed with me, smiled with me, revealing himself to be a much warmer and genuine man than I'd thought. Helplessly, I'd been drawn in.

A man of deep feeling, that was what I'd sensed about him, and I tended to be right in my impressions of people. That was what made me so good at my job.

I could see that feeling now, burning in the midnight-blue of his eyes—anger and disappointment and desire. And all for me.

God, I was such an idiot. I should never have kissed him. Should never have crossed that boundary and put us both in this position.

I swallowed. 'That's kind of the problem. In fact, that's why I'm here.'

'Why?' His head tilted, the force of his gaze almost palpable. 'Because of the sex?'

'No. It's…the opposite.' My hands had found each other again, clutching on tight. 'I came because I have to tell you something.'

'Tell me what?'

I let out a breath, trying to force down my nervousness and the stab of pain that went with it. Because ending it with a client shouldn't make me nervous and it shouldn't cause me pain. It shouldn't make any difference to my feelings at all. But Trajan had always been different, right from the start.

'I can't see you any more,' I said baldly. 'I can't get involved with a client.'

He was so still, his midnight eyes on mine, staring at me as if he could read all the thoughts in my head. 'But we're not involved.' His voice had cooled, yet the edge in it was still apparent. 'I hire you for the evening, and presumably that money goes into your back account, and that is the extent of our involvement.'

I studied the lines of his harshly beautiful face. Did he really believe that? Surely not? Surely he wouldn't have told just anyone what he'd told me a couple of weeks earlier as we'd sat there together? About his cold father, who only valued him for his success, and his shallow mother, who only competed for his attention to get back at his father. About his younger sister, who always got lost in the mix, and about how he felt guilty for not being there for her.

No, he wouldn't have told just anyone that. Not a man as reserved as he was.

'That's not true,' I said quietly. 'It's become more than that and you know it.'

An expression I couldn't read shifted across his face then was gone. 'Like I said, I'm not asking you for anything more than one night, Honey. That's all.'

It shouldn't have hurt me that he didn't demand more, that one night was all he wanted. Because I wasn't in a position to give him a relationship any more than he was in a position to give me one. And yet it did hurt. Which was another reason—if I'd needed one—why breaking it off now and walking out the door was what I should do.

I couldn't risk it, not even one night. Because what if it was good? What if being with him ruined me? How could I go back to my job, to being with other men, after a night with him?

And it will *ruin you; you know that.*

I looked away from him, unable to bear the pressure of his gaze any more, staring down at the thick, dense pile of the carpet instead. 'I can't,' I repeated. 'Not even one night. It would…make going back to work far too difficult and it wouldn't be fair to my other clients.'

'Fuck your other clients.' The edge in Trajan's voice got sharper. 'I'm the one who's paying for you now. Tonight, you're mine.'

He'd never asked about my other clients, and I'd never discussed my job with him, so I'd had no idea how he'd felt about it. The subject just hadn't come up.

But I was very clear on how he felt about it now; the possessiveness in his tone sent lightning humming through my veins.

'You don't get a say.' I tried to stay cool, longing and desire simmering inside me, along with a building anger at him for making this so difficult.

'A change in the terms of our contract requires my consent and I didn't give it.'

'Why not? What the fuck is so wrong with having one night with me?'

'There's nothing wrong with it.' I caught my breath as everything I felt for him constricted in my chest, gathering in a tight, heavy, aching ball. 'And you may not care about my clients, but I do. They pay my bills. And I'll never be able to give them what they need, what they damn well pay for, if all I'm thinking about is you.'

Something leapt in his gaze, a kind of heat, and the air between us shivered.

Then suddenly he strode towards me with loose, predatory grace, setting my heart racing.

I should have moved. I should have walked straight out of the door.

I shouldn't have stood against the window, waiting for him to come to me, my heart in my mouth, part of me wanting this desperately. Wanting him to get close and to take the decision from me so I didn't have to make it. So I didn't have a choice. So I didn't have to say goodbye.

I didn't want this to be the end. I didn't want never to see him again. I didn't want to be left wondering what his mouth tasted like or how it would feel to have him touch me, kiss me. How it would feel to have him inside me.

Sex was a job for me; it had never been a pleasure. I'd never had a real partner, and all this time I'd never thought I'd wanted one.

Until Trajan.

He'd changed everything.

Cold glass hit my spine and I realised I'd taken a step back against the window as he came for me, stopping in front of me bare inches away.

The light of the city shone through the window at my back, illuminating the harsh angles of his face, his midnight-blue eyes burning into mine.

He was so very tall, his shoulders wide, the cotton of his T-shirt stretching over the hard plane of his chest. And now he was so close I could see the sheer perfection of his body—not that I hadn't noticed it in the past two months we'd been seeing each other; I just hadn't seen it up this close.

God, he was incredible.

His familiar scent wrapped itself around me, fresh and clean, like pine trees and the sea. Like a place I desperately wanted to visit. There had been times over the past couple of months when all I'd wanted to do was to get close to him and breathe him in.

'But I want you thinking about me, Honey.' His deep voice had become deeper, gravelly almost, his blue gaze raking over my face. 'Because I can't fucking stop thinking about you.'

A shudder rippled down my spine at the intensity in his voice and the heat in his eyes as he said it. Clients had wanted me before; that was nothing new. Yet it wasn't really me they wanted, it was Honey: the beautiful escort who made all their fantasies come true. Which was fine, because that was what they paid me for. It was all about them, not me, after all.

But the mask of Honey had slipped when I'd been with Trajan. Slowly and by degrees, I'd become more and more myself. More and more Maggie, who liked talking about the books she'd read, and strange facts she'd looked up on the Internet, and all about new scientific discoveries that she was interested in and following, and how they could make the world a better place.

He'd listened to me, encouraged me, and had then joined in, his own thinking processes apparently as quirky and left-field as mine.

'You shouldn't,' I said hoarsely, trying to ignore the warmth that confession had made unfurl in my chest.

'I know I shouldn't but I can't help it. Thinking about you is all I've been able to do for the past two weeks.'

I wanted desperately to touch him. To put my hand on the hard plane of his chest, feel his heat. Or brush my fingertips over the smooth, tanned skin of his cheekbones. Ease the desperation I could see in his eyes, ease it for us both.

But it was impossible and I couldn't allow it.

'Then you need to stop.' I tried to find Honey

again, pull her on like armour, put some distance between us. 'You'll only make this difficult for the both of us, darling, and I—'

'Don't darling me,' he interrupted forcefully. 'And stop it with the Honey bullshit you give everyone else. Those are excuses and you know it. Give me the truth.' The expression on his uncompromising features was fierce and there was something equally fierce burning in his eyes: his considerable force of will.

I'd sensed that before in our meetings, in the arguments we'd had about various different topics. He liked to be right and he liked to argue to prove his point. And, although he'd always been playful with it, I'd felt the edge of that will of his.

Now, though, it was as if a sword had been taken out of its scabbard and I could see the naked blade shining and sharp.

He was ready to do battle whether I liked it or not.

My heartbeat was an aching pressure in my chest. I liked the fierce way he wanted me; I liked it far too much. He was so beautiful, the kind of man I'd always fantasised about but who I knew would never want me—because I was stupid Maggie, and no one had ever wanted stupid Maggie. Not my grandmother, who'd been forced to take me in after my mother went to jail, and not the kids at school I'd never managed to make friends with. Weird Maggie, with her strange fixation on science, who hunted bugs and did messy experiments in the kitchen that her grandmother hated.

I'd told him all of that. Had shared with him my most private self—the self I'd never shared with anyone, and he'd shared his with me. How he'd been a nerdy kid, obsessed with computers and computer games, who'd once spent an evening taking apart the new computer his father had bought him so he could see how it worked. And then figuring out how to put it together again before his father could find out.

He deserved the truth. He deserved to know why I couldn't do this with him. Because he was right— my job, the other clients, they were just excuses.

I took a shaky breath. His dark blue eyes burned, straight black brows drawn together. His chiselled jaw was tense and his finely carved mouth hard.

'You want the truth?' I managed to force out. 'Fine. Here's the truth. I'm falling for you, Trajan. Which makes anything between us impossible, and most especially sex.'

CHAPTER FOUR

Trajan

SHE WAS RIGHT against the glass, the pale oval of her face taking up the entirety of my vision. There was a desperate look in those beautiful dark-chocolate eyes, and I could hear the echo of it in her voice too, along with the soft note of anguish.

I shouldn't have got so close to her, but I was tired of the distance between us. Tired of the way she kept turning her head away so I couldn't see her. I'd come close to get a better view, but now she was only inches away and I could feel the tantalising warmth of her body, smell the layered scent of orchids and sweet coconut, and… Yeah, getting this close was a mistake.

I'd never been territorial and possessive over a woman before—I preferred to stay in control when it came to my relationships with people—so the intense need to have Honey all to myself should have been a warning.

But I didn't listen.

And most especially not now. Not now she'd said she was falling for me.

The need to touch her, to see her face, was almost overwhelming and I'd reached out and taken her chin between my fingers and thumb before I'd even realised what I was doing, tipping her head back so her face was fully in the light and I could see her clearly.

She stiffened as I touched her; the sharp sound of her breath catching filled the space between us. And then, as I watched, a fiery blush spread over the fine-grained skin of her cheeks.

It was beautiful. *She* was beautiful.

Christ, I wanted her. Wanted to see that blush move all over her naked body. Wanted to actually *see* her naked body, as even over the couple of months I'd spent with her I hadn't been able to get an impression of her figure. Small and curvy, according to the description on the company's website. But that wasn't a substitute for the measurement I could make with my own hands if they traced her body. And I wanted that. I wanted it badly.

Her skin felt soft and silky beneath my fingertips and there was a subtle tension in her jaw, as if she wanted to pull away but couldn't bring herself to do it. As her pupils contracted in the light, I saw the threads of gold running through the darkness of her iris that grew brighter as I gripped her—sparks of heat.

'What are you doing?' Her voice had become huskier and I could hear a note of challenge in her tone. 'Touching isn't—'

'Permitted?' I finished for her. 'It is now. I changed the contract, remember?'

'But I haven't signed it yet.'

'I'm not holding you very tightly. You could get away easily enough if you wanted to.'

She said nothing, just stared at me, her whole body vibrating with tension.

I still didn't let her go.

'But you don't want to,' I went on softly. 'Do you?'

She swallowed and my gaze was drawn by the movement of her throat down to the hollow where her pulse beat frantically. My peripheral vision was nothing but shades of light and dark with bits of colour but, for the first time since my sight had begun to deteriorate six months earlier, I didn't care. Because all I wanted to see was her.

'Let me go, Trajan.' There was a soft plea in the words this time. 'Please.'

I should have. But I didn't.

'No, I don't think I will.' I let my thumb stroke along the skin of her jawline and, Jesus, she felt good. Warm and silky and soft. A fucking delight. There had been brief moments of touch over the past couple of months—that initial handshake, the brush of her fingertips against mine when I'd handed her a glass of wine, the occasional slip-up when I misjudged where she'd positioned herself in relation to me and had brushed soft fabric, silky curls or warm skin.

Those moments had had the power to stop me in my tracks, even though I hadn't let it show. I was good at hiding my feelings, good at hiding everything, but right now I didn't want to hide this. I wanted her to see how much I liked touching her, how badly I wanted her. What she did to me.

She shivered at the stroke of my thumb but still didn't pull away. Instead, her lashes lowered, hiding those beautiful dark eyes, gold glinting where mascara hadn't covered the lashes properly. I could see that. I could see the freckles on her face beneath the light covering of her foundation. I could see the line of gold eye-shadow she'd put on her lids. I could see the glossy red slick of lipstick on her beautiful mouth.

I could see so many things in the light. I wanted to see so many more.

'Trajan…' My name was a whisper on those plush red lips, sounding like a prayer; but whether to let her go or keep hold of her, I wasn't sure.

No, I did know.

She wanted me to keep hold of her.

'One night,' I murmured, stroking her again. 'Just one. What are you afraid of?

The gold threads in her eyes glowed. 'I… I told you.'

'You're falling for me. Yes, I heard that.' I lifted

my other hand, cupping her lovely face, feeling the warmth of her cheeks against my palm. Her body was so close. All it would take for me to close the gap was one small step and then I'd finally know what she felt like against me. Finally know the real shape of her. 'Perhaps the feeling is mutual. Ever think of that?'

It was true. I hadn't wanted to fall for someone; that hadn't been the point of hiring someone like her. But all the same every meeting we'd had, every time she'd stepped over my threshold and into my home, I'd felt something inside me relax. Felt a tightness in my chest ease. She was like the first breath of oxygen in a drowning person's lungs. A cool breeze on a sweltering summer day. A bright light in my darkness.

She was interesting, with a quick, incisive intelligence, and she liked the same science stuff I did. It had been a natural meeting of minds. And then she'd opened up to me, revealing personal things about herself, things I sensed she didn't usually talk about with a client. That she'd trusted me with them made me feel good, made me remember what it was like just to enjoy someone's company, not to have every waking minute consumed by work.

Nothing real could ever happen between us, but maybe we could have real for a single night.

'I can't do it, Trajan.' Her dark eyes met mine and this time she didn't look away. 'It's hard enough having to end this now, let alone having to do it after sex. It's easier this way.'

I hated that look in her eyes, I hated her distress—mainly because I couldn't solve it. 'Honey, I can't—'

'I know,' she interrupted quickly. 'And I'm not asking for anything from you. I couldn't give it to you even if you did. I can't get involved with anyone, not right now. Not with my situation the way it is.'

Of course she couldn't. She was looking after the grandmother who'd taken her in after her mother had gone to jail. The grandmother who from the sounds of it hadn't wanted her and hadn't appreciated her. And still didn't.

'You know you don't owe your grandmother anything,' I couldn't help saying. 'She didn't give you—'

'She brought me up. She fed me and clothed me. I can't leave her alone.' Honey lifted her hands to my wrists, gripping them. 'You shouldn't argue with me about this anyway. Unless of course you're offering me more.'

It was a throwaway line, but I saw the expression in her eyes as she said it, the flickers of half-fearful hope. It made something tight in my chest get even tighter, because what could I say? That I wanted a relationship? That I wanted her in my life?

She was lovely, and I enjoyed being with her, and, yes, I wanted to sleep with her. But a relationship was a bridge too far for me. I had my company to think about and I was still wrestling with the implications of my most recent vision loss; I had no room in my life for the extra demands a relationship would entail.

So I said nothing, letting my silence speak for me.

Abruptly, her fingers tightened, and she pulled my hands away. 'I didn't think so,' she murmured, turning her head, her face disappearing into the shadowed blurriness of my peripheral vision.

I'd hurt her and I knew it. I could hear it in the note of pain in her voice and the dull acceptance with which she'd said the words. And that tightness in my chest constricted even more.

I should have let her go then. Should have stood back and waited for her to walk out through the door. But something in me refused; she was hurt and I wanted to give her something to make her feel better.

She was already turning away from me, but before I could stop myself I'd reached out and taken her face between my palms, turning the pale oval of it back towards me once more.

Her eyes widened slightly. 'Trajan? What are you...?'

I didn't let her finish.

I bent my head and covered her mouth with mine.

She froze and I could feel the shock vibrate through her. But sensation had hit me and I was already drowning in it. The give and the heat of her soft lips. The warm scent of her body rising all around me. The catch of her breath and that subtle pulse of shock.

I didn't let go and she didn't move, both of us caught in the intensity of the moment.

Fuck, for so many weeks I'd been dreaming of what her mouth would feel like beneath mine. How I would taste it, find the shape of it, explore the hot, silken depths when she finally let me in. And she would let me in, because she was as hungry for this as I was.

I touched my tongue to the plush curve of her bottom lip, tracing it gently, going slowly because it was the only way I could stay in control. My heartbeat accelerated, my cock hardened in response, and the need to shove her against the glass and hike her dress up and get into all that soft, wet heat was almost overwhelming.

She made a helpless sound that nearly undid me, her lips getting softer under mine. I felt her fingers close around my wrists again but she didn't pull them away this time, only held on, as if she needed something to ground her.

My heartbeat thumped like a fucking drum in my ears, desire flooding through me, but I ignored the urgency of it, instead learning the shape of her mouth—the full curve of her bottom lip, the perfect cupid's bow of her top lip—and relishing how they softened even further.

Gently I teased the seam of her lips, pushing, nipping lightly, until she opened for me, letting me inside. As the heat of her mouth hit me, her nails dug into my wrists, a shudder coursing the length of her body.

Fuck. She tasted so good. She tasted incredible.

I could feel my control slipping and a surging hunger rising inside me. A hunger for light and warmth, for heat to melt the darkness. It was gathering around me and it was familiar, this feeling. There was danger associated with it and I shouldn't be giving in to it.

Yet I couldn't stop.

I tipped her head back, pushing my tongue deeper into her mouth, tasting the sweetness of her, because she really did taste sweet. Of melted honey, just like her name. God, so good. I couldn't get enough.

I kissed her deeper, harder, electric shocks of intense pleasure hitting me as she began to respond, her tongue against mine tentative at first, as if she didn't quite know what to do—which couldn't be right, since she must have kissed a lot of men before.

Yet she was kissing me as though I was her first.

I slid my hands into her hair, loving the brush of silky curls against my skin. And then I cradled the back of her head, feeling the delicate, vulnerable shape of her skull.

She was so sweet, the heat of her body and the scent of her skin filling my senses. The taste of her mouth, just a hint of tartness, made me desperate. But desperation was always dangerous. It led to a loss of control, and that was something I could never allow myself.

Perhaps she was right. Perhaps this was a bad idea after all. Perhaps we needed to end this now, before we didn't have the strength to do so.

It took everything I had but I managed, forcing myself to lift my head, to take my mouth from hers. Her head was cradled in my palms, the light shining in her face. And I could see the bright seams of gold in her dark eyes, the flush of heat in her cheeks. Her mouth was full and red and slick from my kiss, and everything in me was urging me to cover it again, taste her again.

But I didn't.

Instead I made myself release her. 'Okay,' I said, my voice little more than a growl. 'Have it your way. Maybe it is better if you go.' I stepped back, putting some distance between us. 'Goodbye, Honey.'

CHAPTER FIVE

Magdalen

I STRUGGLED TO process what was happening. One minute I'd been drowning in pleasure and heat, his hands cradling me so gently, his mouth on mine kissing me with such devastating skill that I couldn't even remember why I was supposed to be refusing this. Then the next minute he was gone, the warm strength of him withdrawn, leaving my entire body flushed with heat, my mouth throbbing, seared from the effects of his kiss.

I'd always thought that talking of a kiss making your knees weak was being overly dramatic. Apparently it was not.

Trajan's face had been wiped clean of expression, yet nothing could disguise the burning blue of his eyes. He looked like a man with a fire inside him, blazing hot and bright while he fought to keep it contained.

God, all of that was for me, wasn't it?

He was burning for *me*.

I swallowed the taste of him, a dark, decadent flavour like cocoa-rich chocolate mixed with expensive brandy lingering in my mouth. I could still feel his palms against my cheeks, the press of his fingers against the back of my head, his lips on mine…

I didn't do a lot of kissing. Sometimes clients wanted it, and naturally I gave them what they wanted, but I didn't like it. With a lot of men, the kiss ended up being wet and unpleasant, so I usually tried to avoid it. And when I couldn't avoid it I usually ended up being the one in charge, showing them what to do to make it good for both of us.

But I hadn't needed to do that with Trajan. And I hadn't realised how good a kiss could be from someone I wanted and who knew what they were doing.

Your first kiss…

The thought wound dizzily through my head as I tried not to sag against the window behind me, my breathing fast and hard.

My first kiss from someone I wanted. My first kiss from someone who wanted me… Except he'd stopped. He'd let me go and he'd put some distance between us, and now I was the one struggling to process the fact that he'd told me to leave.

Desperately, I pulled myself together, smoothing my dress with shaking hands, my brain concentrating on inanities such as how I'd have to redo my lipstick, because no doubt that kiss had smudged it all to hell, and how I'd probably need to do something with my hair too, since he'd had his fingers all through it.

Anything to distract from the aching pressure in my chest that shouldn't be there in the first place. I couldn't think what I'd been hoping for when I'd refused him again, or why I'd made it sound as if I was hoping he'd offer me something, because it wasn't as if I wanted a relationship or anything. We might have revealed secrets to each other that we'd never told another person, but we were still essentially strangers. I didn't even know his real name and he didn't know mine. And besides, how could I have anything more with anyone, given my job and the necessity behind it?

No, a relationship was out of the question, and I knew that. So why I'd felt a ripple of hurt go through me at his silence, I had no idea. Even if he'd suggested we keep seeing each other, I would have refused. I simply wasn't at a place in my life where I had room for anything more.

'Okay,' I said, my voice gone thick and husky. 'Okay, then.' I smoothed my dress yet again, everything inside me chaos, and looked blankly around the room, though for what I had no idea. I just didn't want to look at him. 'Well… I guess this is it, then.'

He stood in front of me, his face an expressionless mask. Yet his hands had curled into fists, the cotton of his T-shirt pulling tight over his broad chest in time with his quickened breathing.

The fire inside him was burning higher. If I put my hands out towards him, I would probably feel its heat against my palms.

Don't look at him. Don't look into his eyes.

I dragged my gaze away, my heart shuddering in my chest. This was such a bad move. I shouldn't have come back. I should have refused the booking. It would have made things so much easier on both of us. We would simply not have seen each other ever again, and eventually the two months we'd had together would have faded from our minds.

'Yes.' His voice was a harsh scrape of sound. 'Get out, Honey. Now.'

'Okay,' I repeated for the second time. 'I'm going.' Yet I didn't move. I stood there, rooted to the spot, a strange pressure gathering in the air between us.

'Honey...'

God help me... I looked at him, the impact of his gaze clashing with mine echoing throughout my entire body, setting every cell vibrating.

He's right. Get out now. This can only end badly for both of you.

It was true. Staying wasn't the answer. Because if I stayed there was only one thing that would happen and, even though I wanted it more than I wanted my next breath, it would be a disaster. How could I go back to my job after I'd been with Trajan? How could I convincingly look at another man as if I wanted him? As if I were desperate for his touch?

As if he were important to me? How could I give myself to someone else when there was only one man I wanted?

You can pretend. Isn't that what your entire job is based on?

It was a dangerous thought. Because, yes, it was true. The whole of my job was pretence. Being someone I wasn't for someone else, pretending I wanted them, pretending I liked being with them. Pretending they were handsome, that they were the most interesting and complicated man in the universe.

God, what would it be like to have one night where all of it was real? Where I was with someone *I* wanted for a change? Just one night…

'Honey,' he growled again, demanding this time, blue fire leaping in his eyes.

Still I didn't move and I didn't look away.

And I watched as something inside him snapped and he moved, no hesitating, no uncertainty. He closed the distance between us and he didn't stop. And then I was being pushed up against the glass as he caged me with his body, his forearms pressed to the window on either side of my head, the hard length of his body on mine. He ducked his head, his mouth against the side of my neck just below my ear. 'You should have left,' he said in a raw, gravelly voice. 'Why didn't you?'

I closed my eyes, letting my head fall back against the glass, my entire body alive and aware of the feel of him against me, of his heat, the fresh salty scent of pine undercut with the warmer, darker spice of male arousal.

His breath was hot against my neck, the brush of his lips on my skin making me shiver. Words formed in my head, only to fracture and scatter as his teeth found the sensitive tendons on the side of my neck and bit down.

'Why did you kiss me?' My breath was coming in short, hard pants. 'You shouldn't have.'

'No, I shouldn't.' His mouth moved down to the place where my neck met my shoulder, another piercingly sensitive spot, nuzzling gently. 'But I did. Because I wanted to. Just like I want to do this.' Then he bit down again, slightly harder this time, sending an electric burst of pleasure that arrowed straight between my thighs.

I gasped, my entire body shuddering, and I reached for him, my hands settling on his hips. He made a low, raw sound and I felt a shiver of tension course through the hard, hot body pressing against mine.

This was insane. How had we got to this so quickly? How had everything ignited with so much heat and so fast? I felt as if I was burning up, as if I was dying of thirst, dying of hunger, just dying…

'Trajan…' His name escaped on a soft groan as he bit me yet again, his teeth a gentle, insistent pressure at that sensitive place on my neck.

'Don't say no to me.' There was the soft brush of his mouth along my collarbone, goose bumps everywhere, and then heat at the base of my throat, the press of his lips there. 'I want this with you. Let me have it. Let us both have it.'

The reasons I'd had for refusing were still there and my situation hadn't changed. It was still a bad idea. And yet, the more his mouth travelled over my skin, the less those reasons mattered.

I couldn't think now why it would be so terrible to have this. Sex was a job for me, never a pleasure, and I was always giving other people what they wanted. Why couldn't I have what I wanted for a change? Why did I always have to deny myself?

I never got to have anything I wanted. My life was all about endlessly fulfilling someone else's needs. My grandmother's, as she began the long slide into dementia. My mother's, as she demanded a response to the letters she sent me from prison. The clients and their demands, which were never onerous and yet took something from me every time.

All wells ran dry eventually, and the water in mine barely covered the bottom these days. And I was tired. Tired of looking after people. Tired of making decisions for people. Tired of being someone I wasn't. Honey was great, but being her was exhausting. And there were times when I wanted someone who knew me, and knew what I liked, just to…take charge. To handle all the crap I had to do myself, to look after me so that I didn't have to. Someone I didn't have to be Honey with.

There was only one person who could give me all of that.

Him.

My hands squeezed convulsively on his hips as he pressed burning kisses to my throat, the long, hard ridge of his cock nudging between my thighs. I wanted to rock against him, to ease the ache inside me, the unbearable pressure. It had been a long time since I'd felt this turned on, a long time since another person had given me pleasure.

'Yes,' I said thickly as his mouth travelled back up the side of my neck, nuzzling beneath my ear again. 'Yes, okay. But…' I took a shaky breath. 'I want this to be real.'

He went still then slowly lifted his head, the flame in his eyes flickering like lightning. He stared at me fiercely, as though he was trying to see inside my head. 'Real? What do you mean real?'

'Sex is always a transaction for me. I'm never myself when I have it because the clients want Honey, not me. And I'm…tired of being Honey, Trajan. I don't want to be her tonight.'

He shifted, cupping my face in his big, warm palms, turning it up towards the light, his deep-blue eyes narrowing as he studied me.

My heart beat even faster, even harder. I could have pushed him away if I'd wanted. One shove and he'd let me go; I was sure of it. But…he was so warm. And the way he held my face was so gentle, even as he towered over me, making me feel so very small and feminine and delicate. It was intoxicating.

'I'm not asking you to be,' he murmured, the rough, warm timbre of his voice hitting me like sunshine on a cold winter's day. 'I want the woman you are with me, not the woman you are with your other clients.'

Me. He wanted *me.* Maggie, not Honey.

I leaned into his hands, into his strength, staring up into his eyes. 'In that case… Honey isn't my name,' I whispered. 'My name is Maggie.'

CHAPTER SIX

Trajan

SHE STOOD BENEATH the spotlight, her eyes wide and dark, looking up into mine. She was all flushed cheeks and red mouth, the scent of her skin in the air along with the sweet, feminine musk of an aroused woman.

Maggie. Her name was Maggie.

A strange, heavy feeling gathered in my chest, as if I'd been given a precious gift I didn't deserve. Because that was what it was. She wasn't supposed to tell me her real name and yet she had, offering it up to me without hesitation.

I want this to be real...

Hell, I could understand that. Nothing she had with anyone was real except the pleasure she gave to her clients, and if she got any pleasure in return it wasn't from anyone doing something real for her. No, they wanted Honey, which meant she had to get that pleasure alone.

'Hi, Maggie.' I drank my fill of her lovely face, watching heat shift in her eyes as I said her name. 'I like it. It's beautiful.'

She flushed. 'It's short for Magdalen.'

'I like that too.' And I did. I meant every word.

Her cheeks were rosy and I wished I could see how far down the flush went, but the rest of her was nothing but a dark blur. I could feel it, though, the shape of her against me, as small as I'd thought and deliciously curvy. I could feel the soft give of her breasts against my chest, the press of her rounded hips and thighs against mine.

I shifted, lifting my forearms from the window and trailing my fingers down her sides, following the outline of her body, the graceful indent of her waist and the flare of those hips.

She shivered under my touch, her gaze drifting to my mouth. I should give her something in return. She'd wanted real and so she'd given me her real name, but I couldn't return the favour. Not when she'd had my real name all along. But I could let her know that at least.

'My name is Trajan,' I said, stroking back up her glorious figure.

'Trajan... But...' Her silky golden brows drew together. 'You mean that's your real name?'

'Yes.' I gave her a faint smile. 'I wasn't supposed to say it, but when I met you, you basically left me unable to think of anything else.'

She blinked. 'So...all this time I've had your real name?'

'You have.' I settled my hands on her sides, just below her breasts, my thumbs tracing the soft underside of them through the material of her dress. It felt like silk and it seemed to be close fitting; all I wanted to do in that moment was to strip it from her body so I could get at the warm skin beneath it.

Her breath caught as I stroked her, her back arching slightly, lifting her breasts against my chest. I could feel the hard little points of her nipples through the cotton of my T-shirt, and just like that the desperation was back.

I bent my head to her throat again, nuzzling the fragile dips and hollows of her collar bone, touching my tongue to her skin, tasting sweetness. 'How do you want this?' My voice had roughened and become even deeper. 'What does real mean for you?'

'I don't know, I just...don't want to pretend tonight. I want to feel as if...' She trailed off.

I lifted my head and looked into her face, angling so I wasn't blocking the light from above, so I could see. 'As if what?'

Emotion shifted in her eyes, deep currents of it, so complicated I couldn't tell what they were. 'I want to feel as if you haven't paid me for the night. As if I was someone you met in a bar, someone you wanted, and so you flirted with me. Seduced me. Not...picked me out of a catalogue.'

I touched her face gently, watching those deep currents. 'Has anyone ever seduced you, sweetheart?' Even as I asked the question, I thought I knew the answer already. So when she shook her head I wasn't surprised.

'No.' The word was husky. 'I haven't ever been out on a date even.'

But that…that *did* surprise me.

I frowned. 'Not even one?'

The flush in her cheeks deepened. 'I don't meet people, not these days. Dating is difficult with my job being what it is. And before… Well, I wasn't exactly a hot-date ticket.'

She'd told me about her childhood, about how her grandmother's indifference had led to crippling shyness that had blighted her teenage years. She'd retreated into books and study, which had only alienated her even more from her peers.

She reminded me so much of myself at that age that it was almost painful. Except my father's relentless insistence on success, and his absolute refusal even to acknowledge failure, hadn't made me retreat into shyness. No, I'd become arrogant instead, not to mention over-confident. I'd had no insecurities, and I'd been certain of my own abilities because I was good at everything I attempted. I'd excelled academically and at sports—the two things my father valued highly—and, as far as I was concerned, my future as his heir in the company he'd founded had been assured.

And look what happened.

Oh, yeah, I knew all too well what had happened.

As soon as I'd turned out to be not as perfect as my father had expected, he'd dropped me without a single word. Of course, I'd proved him wrong in the years since then, but even so I hadn't forgotten his abandonment. I hadn't forgiven him, either.

Caring too much—that had been the problem. Wanting too much, expecting too much, too. So these days I didn't allow myself to care, and I definitely shouldn't care about wanting this night with Maggie.

Then again, this wasn't emotional; this was physical. Plus, I was older, wiser. I wasn't seventeen any more. I was in control of myself and I sure as hell wouldn't let it become anything deeper.

One night of being real worked for me, because it was only that—one night. In one night I could have her and then move on.

'Okay,' I said, and released her.

Surprised, she stared at me. 'What are you…?'

'We've been out,' I said. 'I took you to dinner and we enjoyed it and now we're back at my place. And I'm going to offer you a drink.'

The colour ebbed and flowed in her cheeks, and then, clearly understanding what I was going for, she said, 'Oh… Oh, okay. Uh…yes, I think I would like a drink.' Her hands flicked to her hair, touching her curls in an adorably self-conscious way, clearly playing along. Which definitely wasn't Honey.

'Good.' I gestured to the couch. 'Please, sit. What can I get you?'

She took a step then stopped. 'What are we pretending—?'

'We're not pretending,' I interrupted, holding her gaze so she could see the truth in mine. 'This is us, Maggie and Trajan, on a date.' I paused, adding, 'And, just so you know, I fully intend to seduce you.'

'I see.' She looked flustered, which for some reason pleased me a great deal. Then she moved over to the couch, giving me a look from beneath her lashes as she did so. 'Well, I do like a man who knows what he wants.'

A Honey look. And a very Honey statement—I could tell by the practised sensuality in her voice.

'No,' I said. 'I don't want Honey tonight, Maggie. I want you.'

She was in the process of sitting down, arranging herself on one end of the long leather couch, and the statement made her pause. 'Wow,' she murmured. 'Was that Honey? I didn't even realise.'

She sat down, her face still in focus. I got the impression of movement from the rest of her, though, as she settled herself, but the way she was sitting was unclear. There was an angled light on a side table at the other end of the couch, which was good, because I had plans.

Desire pumped hard in my veins as I turned towards the drinks cabinet, orienting myself in the room. I strode over to it and opened it. 'What will it be?' I asked, automatically running my fingertips over the neatly shelved bottles, noting their shapes and the feel of the labels.

'I… Oh…brandy, I think.'

She sounded nervous and I liked that. I wanted to make her nervous. I wanted her off-balance and uncertain. I wanted her to think of me as dangerous. God knew, it would be the last time before I lost the rest of my sight.

And then you won't be dangerous. You'll be helpless.

A cold thread tightened in my gut, but I ignored it. No, fuck that. I wasn't going to be helpless. I'd put all the necessary precautions in place, learned the things I'd needed to learn. I could move around in my apartment as easily as someone sighted, and even after two months Maggie hadn't guessed that I couldn't see.

Outside the apartment, I knew every inch of my office and the attached meeting room. And I had Eli. He did most of the necessary face-to-face stuff, all the while helping me cultivate my reputation for inaccessibility to limit contact with people.

It was all working well. No one would be able to

guess, and that was just the way I wanted it. I refused to let it limit my existence, refused to let it influence other people's opinions of me.

I would have control over it; it would not control me.

I grabbed the bottle and then found the brandy balloons. I didn't need sight for this, since I'd been fixing drinks without vision over all the months we'd been meeting without any issues. I poured, listening to the sound of the liquid going into the glass in order to gauge how much was going in. I could have used a measuring jigger but, as I wouldn't have if I'd been sighted, I didn't now.

Glasses poured, I took them both and moved over to the couch where the angled light was. It was sitting on a small table beside the arm of the couch, and I bent, putting both glasses down on the table. Then I sat down, the angled light just above my head. I looked at Maggie, sitting at the other end. The light was more diffuse where she was, her face indistinct.

'If you want a drink, you'll have to sit over here,' I said softly.

She opened her mouth then shut it. I couldn't see the expression on her face, but I got a sense that I'd flustered her again, which made something raw and demanding turn over inside me.

Yes, I wanted to fluster her. I wanted to set her off-balance. I wanted her unsure and affected by me.

For months I'd been forcing our chemistry aside, trying to ignore it, and now I didn't have to. I wasn't going to pretend it wasn't there.

I wanted her to feel it.

Slowly she moved, shifting over to where I sat at the other end. The light was much better and her face was clearer; her hair fell over it, momentarily veiling her features, before she pushed the cloud of golden curls back once more. She sat next to me, close enough for me to feel her heat. Certainly close enough to touch, and that was good, because touching was definitely going to be happening.

'There,' she said, settling in next to me, touching her hair and then smoothing her dress in nervous movements. 'Happy now?'

I picked up her brandy glass and held it out to her. 'Oh, yes. Very happy.'

She took it, the tips of her fingers brushing mine, sending small electric shocks through my entire central nervous system. I was very tempted to snatch the glass from her, put it back on the table and push her down onto the couch before ripping that dress from her body.

But no. This was a date and I wanted to take this slow, seduce her. Lay her across my lap with the light on her, watch her face as I touched her, giving her pleasure as I examined every inch of her body and made her come.

Tonight it would be about her, because if she was

going to give me her body then she deserved to have what she wanted too. One night of being real. I could give her that.

She lifted the glass and sipped, her dark eyes studying me from over the rim.

I hoped it hadn't escaped her notice that we'd been sitting like this two weeks ago when she'd put her hand on my thigh and leaned forward to kiss me.

If she did it again, I wouldn't let her run. This time I'd grab her wrist and hold her, keep her here with me.

'Did you enjoy dinner?' I asked, keeping up with the pretence.

'Yes. It was delicious.' She gave me a shy smile, her hand drifting once more to her hair. 'The company was even better, though.'

Pleasure uncurled in my chest at the genuine warmth in her eyes. 'I agree.' I reached out to where a tendril of gold lay across her forehead, pushing it back from her face and then back behind her ear, letting my fingers graze against the soft fragile skin.

Her breath hitched, her dark eyes widening.

I let my hand move gently through all those silky curls to settle on the vulnerable warmth of her nape. Then I took her brandy glass from her, putting it down on the table beside mine.

'Come here,' I murmured.

Another soft hitch of breath and then she moved closer. Once she was near, I pulled her into my arms and across my lap, settling her head on my shoulder, her back against the arm of the sofa. She didn't protest, but her muscles had tightened.

Then I took her chin in one hand and gently tipped her head back even further, lifting that gorgeous face to the light so I could see her.

'Now,' I said quietly. 'Let's start this date properly.'

CHAPTER SEVEN

Magdalen

I SAT IN his lap, his body hard and hot under mine, my heartbeat going into overdrive. All my muscles had tightened and I felt breathless, nerves fluttering in my gut.

So stupid. He was just a man, and it wasn't as if I was a virgin. I'd been with a lot of men. It wasn't as if I hadn't been held in someone's lap before.

Then again, I hadn't been held this carefully, and I hadn't had a man tilt my face into the light, examining me intently, as if he was memorising every aspect of me.

Trajan's gaze narrowed as he tilted my head slightly, as if I were a difficult line of text in a book whose meaning he was desperate to understand.

His eyes were so blue. I felt as though I was falling into them.

'What are you doing?' I asked, my voice shaky.

'Looking at you.' He tilted my face the other way, frowning.

I was acutely conscious of his body beneath mine. It felt as though I was lying on sun-warmed rock. His shoulder cushioned my head, his fingers on my jaw firm yet not hard enough to be painful, more like little points of fire against my skin.

'Why?' I asked, not sure what he was doing. The way he was examining me made me feel exposed and not a little vulnerable. 'Surely you've got a good look at me already?'

'Hush.' His gaze raked over my face. 'This is part of my seduction technique.'

The trace of dry humour in his voice made the tightness in my muscles ease. I'd thought, when we first met, that he was humourless, but he wasn't. I'd slowly discovered that dry humour of his over the course of our meetings. It had always delighted me and it did so now.

'Staring at my face is a seduction technique?'

'Of course.' His thumb traced along my jawline. 'You have the most beautiful skin. It feels like silk. Has anyone ever told you that?'

A shiver chased over me, the tension in my muscles easing even more as I relaxed against him. He was so warm and he smelled so good, of pine and warm earth with a hint of salty sea.

'No,' I answered huskily. And they hadn't. No one had ever looked at me like that either.

'There are tiny gold threads in your eyes and I think they glow when you're aroused.' His beautiful mouth curved. 'They're glowing now.'

I sucked in a breath, shivering in his arms, falling into all that blue. I'd never felt this way with a man—not once. Had never lain in a man's arms and let him look at me with so much intent. It was confronting.

'You're trembling,' he murmured. 'Am I making you nervous?'

'Yes. A little.' There wasn't any point in hiding my discomfort. He knew. 'I'm not used to being looked at.'

'Surely you must be by now?'

'Not…not as Maggie.'

Gently he turned my head to the side, cocking his head to examine my jaw and the side of my neck. 'Maggie is beautiful. Maggie is the most beautiful woman I've ever seen.'

I wanted to tell him that was a lie, but then all the words vanished from my brain as he leaned in, and I felt his breath at the side of my neck, his mouth and nose nuzzling at the soft skin beneath my ear.

I shuddered, my breath catching, the slight contact sending a wave of delicious sensation flooding through me.

'You smell so fucking sexy,' he said softly. 'Orchids on the top, coconut and vanilla underneath.'

I shut my eyes. 'It's just some cheap body lotion from the local pharmacy. I should have splashed out—'

'It's fucking delicious.' His mouth brushed down the side of my neck. 'Just like you.'

I swallowed, heat prickling all over my body, a heavy ache gathering between my thighs. 'Is this more seduction technique?' I had to force the words out, going automatically into Honey mode to cover my nerves. 'If so then you're—'

'Quiet.' Trajan cut me off softly. 'Just lie still.'

My breathing accelerated. It was rare for me to feel like this, nervous and uncertain and yet turned on at the same time. So turned on. And it made me feel vulnerable. It was always me directing everything and the client who was getting off. It was never the other way round.

I kept my eyes closed, feeling his breath against the side of my neck. 'It's never like this,' I said hoarsely, wanting to explain. 'It's never me feeling this and the client in control. I'm not the one usually—'

'Hush,' he murmured, one hand keeping my head turned firmly to one side, the other gripping one hip to keep me secured in his lap. 'You're not Honey now, remember? It's just us, Trajan and Maggie on a date. And I'm trying to seduce you. Which, I may add, is proving very difficult because you keep talking.'

I used to talk a lot as a kid, something my grandmother had hated. She'd preferred silence to 'chatter', and had made sure I knew it, so I'd spent my childhood biting my lip and then my teenage years second-guessing everything I said, because I didn't want to annoy people. Until I'd finally found Honey in a fit of rebellion.

Trajan's gentle reproof should have irritated me, but there was humour in his voice again, and it was warm. I found myself relaxing again, huffing out a laugh.

'I'm sorry,' I said huskily. 'I always talk when I'm nervous.'

'Really? I didn't notice at all that first night we met when I couldn't get a word in edgewise.' More humour laced his tone.

I gave a mock groan. 'Oh, God, did I?'

'Yes, and don't apologise.' His fingers traced my collarbone gently. 'All I want you to do is relax and let me look at you, because you're beautiful. We only have one night so I want to see every part of you, memorise you.'

The light pressed against my closed lids.

'Why?' I asked, even though I hadn't meant to. 'What's so special about me?'

There was a silence and I could feel the tension in his body, though why I had no idea. I could have opened my eyes to look at his face but I didn't want to. For some reason I felt safer in the dark.

His fingers moved on my skin, stroking lightly over my collarbone. 'What did that grandmother of yours do to you, sweetheart?'

The question was light, casual, the endearment

sending a shiver of pleasure through me, because no one had ever called me sweetheart before. At least, not when I wasn't being paid.

He's still paying you, don't forget.

No, I wasn't forgetting. But we were being real now, that was the deal. And the way he said it was as if it was something he'd call me if we were seeing each other properly, as if this was an actual date…

I shouldn't tell him about my childhood. Who wanted to know about that boring crap?

'I thought I was supposed to be quiet.' My tone was probably too acidic, but I couldn't help it.

'You don't have to answer. I won't force you.' His fingers stroked lightly to the hollow of my throat, as if measuring my pulse, and I felt the warmth of his breath against the side of my neck as he leaned in once more. 'I just think it's a tragedy you even have to ask me that question. Especially when there's so much that's special about you.' His mouth burned on the skin beneath my ear as he pressed a kiss there. 'I wanted you the moment you took my hand that first night, did you know? I thought you were special then and I didn't even know you. There was such a warmth to you, like there was a light inside you.'

I let out a breath, something catching in my chest. 'Trajan. I'm not—'

'You were putting on an act that first night and I could tell you were trying to read me. Trying to be what I wanted you to be. So I gave you nothing back, just to see what you'd do. I don't think you expected that, did you?'

His lips moved further down, finding the sensitive spot where my neck met my shoulder. 'But then you started talking about travel, about how you'd been to Paris, and your voice was full of genuine excitement and wonder. You talked about the Eiffel Tower, about the Louvre, about how amazing they were, and then you asked me questions, gradually drawing me into your enthusiasm.'

He breathed softly over my skin, causing goose-bumps to rise, my own breath to catch hard. 'You were genuinely interested in me. It wasn't an act—I could sense it. I hadn't talked to anyone the way I talked to you that night. I hadn't enjoyed being with anyone the way I enjoyed being with you.' His fingers stroked my jaw, moving in soft circles. 'I'm not an easy person to get to know. I'm not an easy person to talk to, but you managed it. You made me smile and I couldn't remember the last time I smiled.'

There was a note in his voice that sounded a little like pain and it made my throat tighten. Because I remembered that first night. His handsome face had been expressionless, his blue eyes guarded; he wasn't lying. That night I'd tried to do my usual thing of figuring out what a client wanted from me based on body language, expression and speech. But Trajan had given me nothing but a blank wall.

I'd never encountered anything like it from a cli-

ent before. Nervousness, yes. And reserve, yes. But
nothing to what Trajan had given me. We'd sat in
this very room, sipping wine, and I'd started to feel
things becoming awkward, which I prided myself on
never letting happen. And I'd had to do something.
I'd been so flustered by him and my own reaction
to him that I'd fallen back into the way I'd used to
chatter back when I'd been a kid, going on about a
visit I'd made with some client to Paris.

I didn't mention the client—it was bad form—but
I'd found myself going on and on about Paris and
how much I'd loved it, because I had. I had never
done that in front of a client before, become Maggie when I should have been Honey, and I was sure
I was going to disappoint him, because he'd looked
away from me, barely making eye contact.

Then, strangely, as I was wittering on about some
of the art I'd seen in the Louvre just to fill up the silence, he'd asked me whether the room that held the
Mona Lisa was still packed with people. And then
he'd asked about the other art there, and whether
I'd visited the Pompidou Centre and other places.
He'd been there a couple of years earlier and, before I'd known it, we'd been sharing experiences,
talking about the places we'd been to and the things
we'd seen.

I actually hadn't been to many places, given that
most of my jobs for Strangers were based in New
York, but I'd been out of the country a couple of

times on all-expenses-paid trips with clients. Paris. London. And once to Singapore.

I'd loved talking about my experiences to someone, as I didn't have anyone interested to hear about them, except Vesta. And she hadn't been anywhere herself. But to share it with someone who had and who'd loved what I'd loved…

Why had that hurt him?

I opened my eyes and turned my head, blinking in the light from the lamp above. He lifted his head, his gaze darkening as he looked at me.

'I made you smile, did I?' My voice sounded a bit rusty. 'So why do you make that sound like a bad thing?'

CHAPTER EIGHT

Trajan

SHE LAY ACROSS my lap, her head on my shoulder, her face fully in the light. The delicious flush in her cheeks made her dark eyes ever darker as they searched mine.

I didn't know how I'd given myself away, but I had. She was so sensitive when it came to picking up mood, and if there was one thing I should have remembered about her it was that. Clearly she'd heard something in my voice as I'd mentioned how she'd got me to smile, though I thought I'd managed to keep the bittersweet aspect to that memory out of it.

Bittersweet, because I hadn't realised until that night that I hadn't smiled in too long. That my life up until then had been consumed with getting Howard and Hart off the ground with Eli. It had been a serious business, and Eli and I had worked hard. He'd been battling with his own issues—he'd been horrifically scarred in a house fire—and then, with my sight loss suddenly starting to accelerate, everything had felt like darkness and shadow.

Until Honey had turned up, bringing with her the promise of light and warmth. Of smiles and laughter. Making me remember what it was like to sit with someone, sipping wine and casually talking about nothing, just enjoying someone's company.

I'd deliberately kept the lights low, so I hadn't been able to see, but her voice had been like a balm I hadn't even realised I needed. There had been laughter in her voice and I'd found myself smiling in return, wishing I could see her face…

'It wasn't a bad thing.' I wasn't going to tell her about my sight, but I could give her some of the truth. 'I just hadn't realised how serious my life had become until you turned up.'

Her brow wrinkled in concern. 'Too serious?'

'Yeah, far too serious.' I touched her mouth, drinking in the lovely shape. 'The past couple of years I've been building up my company and, even though it's doing well now, it was hard work. Not enough time to play.'

I felt her body shift as her arm lifted, and then came the light touch of her fingers in my hair. 'You looked serious,' she said. 'And so very stern. I kept wittering on about all this crap and I couldn't shut myself up. I thought you'd never book another night with me but…well, you did.'

Letting go of one silk-clad hip, I ran my hand up her arm to where she was touching my hair, closing my fingers around her wrist and drawing her hand away. Her touch was already insanely distracting, and I didn't want to be distracted, not now she was lying across my lap and I had seduction in mind.

'I did,' I agreed, lifting her hand to my mouth and brushing a kiss across the backs of her knuckles. 'And I didn't find your wittering crap. Now, are you going to let me continue with this seduction or not?'

Her mouth curved and I felt the soft weight of her body relax. There was a curious light feeling in my chest, a fizzy excitement in my blood, like champagne. It felt good. It felt as if there had been a lump of granite pressing down on me, as if I were slowly being crushed, for months now, and the only relief I had from it was when she visited me.

Yeah, everything had been too serious, too grey and too dark, and right now I could have this lightness. The sunlight of her in my hands. And so why the fuck not? Why shouldn't I tease her a little? Flirt with her a little? Make her smile?

Why couldn't I have the memory of fun and pleasure to take with me when she left and I lost the rest of my sight?

Sure, maybe I didn't deserve it—but, fuck, I was going to take it anyway. If I was going to endure a lifetime of penance for the accident that had nearly killed Susannah, then surely a few hours of pleasure wouldn't make that penance less effective?

'I suppose so.' Maggie's voice was full of warmth. 'Though, it has to be said, you're taking your time.'

'Taking my time is the whole point.' I placed her hand down in her lap. 'You've had very little experience of this, have you?'

She wrinkled her nose. 'I don't know if I'd want to put a number on my experience but...'

'I'm talking about being seduced.' I let my fingers trail over the warm, silky skin of her collar bone again, brushing over the fast beat of her pulse. 'As well you know.'

'Technically I don't need to be seduced,' she said with a trace of dry humour. 'Not given a man's best seduction technique is the money that turns up in my bank account.'

I laid a finger over that plush mouth. 'Quiet, Honey. Let Maggie speak.'

Her breath was warm against my skin as she sighed, no doubt preparing to protest.

But I went on before she could. 'Don't be nervous, sweetheart. This is for you, remember?' I knew it would be hard for her to give up control, to let me take the lead instead of being Honey and subtly directing me.

Honey, I was rapidly discovering, was the mask she wore when she was nervous, and she was definitely nervous being Maggie.

It made me wonder why. Something to do with that grandmother of hers, no doubt, and that seemed especially certain since she hadn't answered when I'd straight out asked her. Part of me wanted to push, but that wasn't the mood I wanted to build right now. I didn't want her upset or angry, not when what I wanted to give her was pleasure.

'Okay,' she whispered after a moment. 'It's just… difficult not to be Honey sometimes.'

'I get that. But you don't have to do anything, remember? All you have to do is lie here and let me do all the work.' I turned my hand over, brushing the backs of my knuckles across her skin, gliding down to the neckline of her silky red dress. 'Tell me, Maggie. What do you like?'

She shifted on me, arching into my hand. I couldn't see anything more than her face filling the small circle of my central vision. But, for the first time since I could remember, I felt no need to see anything more. To wish I could see the wider world.

For once, everything I wanted to see was right here in front of me.

Her breathing was coming faster now, and her voice, when she spoke, was huskier. 'I…don't know.' She let out a soft laugh, even though there was no amusement in it. 'I really don't know. Crazy, huh? I'm twenty-five and I don't even know what I like.'

I was surprised. I couldn't deny it. Had she really not thought about this? Surely she must fantasise with her clients?

I didn't want to get into thinking about her with other men—the thought made something dark and possessive coil inside me—but seduction was about doing something the other person enjoyed, and if I didn't know what she enjoyed how could I seduce her?

'Not at all?' I asked, the thought that she really might not know making my chest go tight.

'I lost my virginity at eighteen in the back of a guy's car after prom. And since then I haven't had a relationship so, no.'

Shit. She really hadn't.

'What about your clients?'

'That's a job. And it's not about me, it's about them.'

I stroked down over the curve of her breast, letting my fingertips lightly graze the soft point of her nipple. She shivered in response, the tip hardening almost immediately.

Fuck, she was responsive. Sensitive too. A soft, sensual woman…

'Do you get any pleasure from them?'

'I don't fake it, so…' She stopped, sighing as I let my fingertip circle her nipple lightly through the fabric of her dress. 'I suppose…what I think about is…being with someone who cares about me. Who wants to please me.'

'I can understand that.' I looked down into her flushed face. She'd closed her eyes again, gold lashes lying still on her cheeks. 'Do you want to tell me what to do?' It wasn't my thing, but I'd do it for her if that was what got her off.

'No.' She gave another soft laugh. 'God, no. I tell clients what to do all the time, even when they're not aware of it. I'm always controlling things. I don't want to do that now.'

'Then will you trust me to do it? To be in control?'

There was a silence, and I could hear the beat of my heart suddenly loud in my head. I hadn't realised how important her answer was to me until this moment.

Her lashes lifted and her dark eyes looked into mine. 'Yes,' she said quietly. 'I trust you.'

She shouldn't. Not when I'd essentially been lying to her all this time. But then that was why I'd hired her. Why I'd paid money for this. So I could lie.

Was that why she'd said she trusted me? Because of my money? Or was it me?

But I wasn't here to second-guess. Whatever she was trusting, it was enough that I believed her. And, besides, it was only her pleasure she was trusting me with, and that I could certainly provide.

There was something warm in my chest, though, an easing of something tight. As if I'd wanted her to give me this on some level, as if I'd been waiting for it.

You need it.

Maybe I did. It was certainly the last time I'd ever have anyone trust me to look out for them. Not when it was soon going to be vice versa. Which meant I was going to take this opportunity and enjoy every fucking minute of it.

'You won't regret it.' I let her see what her trust meant to me, because if she could give me something then I wanted to give her something back. 'I'll make it good for you, Maggie. I promise.'

An expression I couldn't interpret rippled over her face as I said her name. 'Okay.' Her voice sounded much more breathless now.

I circled the hard point of her nipple with one finger, keeping my touch light and delicate, watching her face. 'Do you like that?'

Her throat moved, her body quivering slightly as I grazed over the hard tip of her breast. 'Yes. That's... good.'

I did it again, brushing my finger back and forth over her nipple, feeling it get even harder. 'What about this?'

Her lashes fell closed and she shuddered. 'Oh, yes... Don't stop.'

I took my hand away.

Instantly her eyes flicked open again and her brows drew together, an aggrieved look on her face. 'You stopped.'

I smiled, because she wasn't the only one who was

going to get immense pleasure out of this. I was too. And I couldn't fucking wait. 'I'm proving a point.'

'What point? Isn't this supposed to be about what I want?'

'Sure it is. But I'm the one in control, which means I get to decide how to give you the most pleasure. And sometimes that won't be what you want in that moment.' I raised a brow. 'You still okay with that?

'This conversation sounds horribly familiar.' She sounded so annoyed and flustered. It was adorable.

'Feel free to say no.' I eased the tip of my finger over her nipple again. 'At any time.'

She shifted restlessly on my lap. 'Fine. Got any other points you want to prove?'

'Possibly. But let's see how things go.'

'I suppose telling you to get on with it won't make any difference?'

Slowly, I spread my hand out beneath the curve of one silk-covered breast, my fingers lightly pressing down and squeezing gently, testing the weight of it against my palm and moulding it carefully. Then I dragged my thumb over the hard little tip of her nipple once more.

Her breath hitched as she caught her upper lip between her teeth, her lashes fluttering.

'No,' I said softly. 'No difference at all.'

CHAPTER NINE

Magdalen

THINKING WAS GRADUALLY becoming difficult. The movement of Trajan's thumb over my achingly hard nipple was sending hot, bright shocks of pleasure along all my nerve endings. It was so strange that just that touch, just his thumb teasing my nipple, could get me so hot and so desperate, when I'd felt next to nothing with other clients doing things far more intense and sexual to me.

God, he hadn't touched me anywhere else and already I could feel the building pressure between my thighs, that dragging ache. What could he do to me with more?

Perhaps I should have been afraid. The intensity of all the sensations was so new to me, and sex had never been anything more than a job.

And it was also strange how weird I'd felt when he'd asked me about my clients. I didn't discuss them with anyone, period, but I'd felt compelled to answer. Because I didn't fake my orgasms. Strangers didn't have a policy about faking, but they advised employees not to do it, and I never did. I wanted to give clients the best possible experience, and most of them wanted it to feel real, even when it wasn't. Many of them were lonely and most often the sex was simply about having another warm human body to hold and to be held in return, to have a moment of connection. An orgasm with them felt like I was giving them a gift, a moment when it was as real as it could be between us.

It was important to me that I gave them that, mainly because I knew what it was to be lonely. In fact, though I'd never admit it to anyone, in my secret heart of hearts the encounters I had with my clients satisfied me on some level too. I could share in that moment of closeness and connection, and even though we both knew it wasn't real we had a facsimile of it at least.

Despite that, the sex was never all that sexy—or at least not for me…not when it was work. I controlled the interactions and they were all focused on the client's needs, so if I wanted to come I had to fantasise. My fantasies weren't very pornographic, and most people would probably think them mundane; but my most private, most erotic one was to be touched slowly, with sensuality and care, by a beautiful man who loved me. Who thought I was precious and worth taking the time over, worth making sure my needs were met. Who looked at me as though I was the most gorgeous woman on earth and who didn't just have sex with me or fuck me. He *made love* to me, in the most literal sense.

I'd never told anyone about that fantasy. It was too personal and said too much about me. Because, really, what a sad individual I was that my most private sexual fantasy wasn't whips or ball gags or blindfolds. It wasn't exhibitionism or voyeurism. It was just to be touched by someone who cared.

Yet I'd told Trajan. He'd been touching me carefully, gently, in the way I wanted, and he'd asked me what I liked, and…it had just…fallen out. And, as soon as I'd said it, I'd realised that, actually, my most private fantasy was happening right now, with him. Because of the way he touched me and the way he looked at me.

As if I mattered to him. As if I was important.

Me. Not Honey.

It was the most erotic thing I'd ever experienced.

I could feel his hand now spread out over my breast, his thumb teasing my nipple in a slow back-and-forth, and the electric pleasure of his touch was so acute I could hardly stand it.

This was for me. *He* was for me. Finally, after so long giving everything to everyone else, I had something for myself.

I couldn't believe I'd wanted to walk out on this earlier, that I'd been so afraid of taking it. Perhaps this wouldn't break me after all. Perhaps this would mean I could give people an even better experience now I knew what it was like myself.

I pressed myself into his hand, wanting more of the flickering lightning that was striking all over my skin. Wanting more of his touch.

He shifted his hold, lifting me to the light that was angled over the back of the couch, lowering his head, as if he wanted to get a really good look, that deep-blue gaze of his raking down my entire body—and not quickly, either. He stared hard, as if memorising each specific feature, examining it closely, like a miner sifting for gold going through a pan full of gravel, trying to find that one bright spark.

No one else had ever looked at me that way before and it made my heart beat harder, my pulse go into overdrive.

'You're so lovely.' His fingers stroked down my chest and over the silk of my dress. 'You feel so soft.' His gaze moved down to the curve of my breast and he leaned down for a closer look. I could feel the warmth of his breath through the fabric and a gasp caught in my throat as the edge of his nail flicked over the tip of my nipple, another bright burst of sensation rocketing through me.

'You like that, hmm? So sensitive.' His thumb moved again in slow, tight circles around the tip of my breast, hardening it even further. And then he bent over me, and the gasp became a moan as I felt his tongue touch the fabric, hot and wet, dampening the silk and moulding it around my tight, aching nipple.

I shuddered, arching up again. 'Oh…yes… More…'

But he ignored me, lifting his head and looking down at the damp spot on my dress where his mouth had been. The hard, masculine lines of his face had pulled taut with concentration, his eyes gone pure midnight. I felt suddenly surrounded by him, his powerful body rock-hard beneath mine, one arm cradling me, his other hand cupping my by now acutely sensitive breast. I loved it. Sometimes with a client who wanted to hold me I felt suffocated or impatient, but not with Trajan.

With Trajan I wanted to lie there all day.

'Pretty,' he murmured, examining his handiwork. He made a soft humming sound and then bent again and this time the wet heat of his mouth covered my nipple entirely.

I bit my lip as another electric jolt of pleasure hit, getting more intense as he began to suck. 'Trajan…' I lifted my hands instinctively, wanting to touch him, but I'd barely grazed his hair with my fingertips before he straightened up suddenly.

His gaze caught mine, authoritative and intense. 'No touching, sweetheart. This is about you, not me.'

'I…know. But what if I want to touch you?' I felt desperate. The hard expanse of his chest and the firm muscle of his shoulder beneath my head were warm, and I wanted to stroke him the way he was stroking me. Strip away the cotton of his T-shirt, see what his skin felt like under my hands. 'This is supposed to be about me, right? So what if touching you is what I want?'

'I'm assuming you know all about topping from the bottom?' His deep voice was gravelly and stern, and yet there was a hint of amusement in his eyes.

Of course I did. That was what I did with my clients, subtly directing things while making it seem as if it was all their idea.

I pulled a face. 'I'm not…'

'You are.' He gave me a speculative look. 'How do you feel about restraints?'

'I mean, I—'

'Because, if you feel that would help you guard against temptation, I'm happy to oblige.'

I wasn't sure it was possible to blush even more, but I did anyway, my cheeks burning. 'You say that like I haven't been tied up before,' I said tartly. 'Which, FYI, I have. Many times.'

'Not by me you haven't.'

The arrogance in his voice was, for some reason, incredibly endearing. 'Trajan…' I began.

'This is a pretty dress.' One hand slipped beneath my back, finding the zipper and drawing it down. At the same time, the fingers of his free hand curled into the front of my bodice. 'But right now, it's in my way.' Then, with one smooth movement, he jerked the bodice down to my waist.

I gave a soft gasp as he bared me, the cool air of the apartment raising goose bumps all over my skin, moving over my sensitive nipples.

I'd been naked in front of a lot of men, so it had long since ceased to be an issue. But now, as Trajan's dark gaze moved over me, examining me in the same close way as he had a minute ago, I felt an inexplicable shyness creeping over me.

Shifting in his lap, I made a half-hearted attempt to cover myself, only to have him catch my hands in his. Then he circled my wrists, gripping them in one hand and drawing my arms slowly over my head and back slightly, holding me fast. My spine arched with the movement, my breasts lifting.

'No,' he murmured. 'I don't want you hiding. I want to see you.'

I shivered, the restraint of his hands both maddening and arousing at the same time. 'I don't know why you would,' I said thickly.

'Because you're beautiful. And because I've been fantasising about you for weeks now.'

Holding tightly to my wrists, he let his other hand drift down my body, the backs of his fingers grazing my skin, the touch so light and maddening that I shivered yet again.

Every part of me seemed to be alive and aware, acutely conscious of all the places he was touching and all the places he wasn't. His hard thighs against my butt, his chest against my back, his hands around my wrists holding on tight. And the agonising drift of his fingers over my skin.

'Close your eyes, sweetheart,' he murmured, and so I did.

And when I did I relaxed, the darkness allowing me to concentrate only on the feel of him tracing me, every line and curve. My shoulders and throat and chest. My breasts…his fingertips brushing over each nipple in a light touch before moving on, down over my stomach, that wasn't as flat as I would have liked it to be, to circle around my belly button.

'You like this?' His voice had become soft as velvet and yet rough. 'You like me touching you?'

'Yes.' My own voice sounded cracked.

'Not so shy any more?'

'No.' I swallowed. 'Not that I was shy before, but you know…'

'Of course.' Again, a warm thread of amusement ran through the words. 'Not that you being shy is a problem. Or you not being shy. You can be any way you want, as long as it's good for you.'

I kept my eyes closed, the breath hissing in my throat as I felt his fingers and warm palm spread out and cup one breast. They were slightly rough and the rasp of them on my bare skin sent the most delicious shivers through me.

'And is it good for you?' He sounded so calm, and somehow that made it hotter.

'Yes,' I gasped hoarsely as I felt the pad of his thumb rub over one nipple. 'It's good for me.'

He didn't reply to that, but his hand disappeared. For a second all I could feel was cool air before wet heat closed around the throbbing tip of my breast once again, searing me.

'Oh, my God,' I groaned. 'Oh… Trajan…'

His mouth was so hot it burned, and then came a slight pressure as he began to suck, and I was arching helplessly into him, pulling against his grip on me, wanting more, my thighs pressing together to control the deepening ache in my sex.

I'd never thought my breasts were particularly sensitive, but the way he touched them and touched me, lightly and sensually, layering sensation on sensation, building up each caress until it culminated into this one, intense moment…

God. I might even come from his mouth on my breasts alone.

He didn't rush. He took his time. Mapping the curves of me with his mouth. Light kisses and little licks that turned into harder, deeper kisses and nips, the edge of his teeth against my tender flesh. And then his mouth closed around the sensitive tips of my breasts once again, sucking lightly at first, and then harder.

I was shaking, lights exploding and reforming behind my closed lids.

Then I felt a warm pressure between my thighs; his hand rested there lightly, the heel of his palm pressing on my clit. Then he exerted some pressure at the same time as he bit my nipple. 'Scream for me, Maggie,' he whispered against my damp skin as the pleasure detonated like a bomb inside me. 'Scream for me now.'

And I did. I screamed his name as the climax hit me, broke me, shattered me into a thousand white-hot pieces and left me drifting in the air.

CHAPTER TEN

Trajan

SHE WAS TREMBLING against me, giving little breathy pants as I nuzzled against one bare breast, the delicious creaminess of her skin lying heavy in my mouth. The echo of her scream was still resounding in the air and I realised I hadn't known what satisfaction was until this moment. Until I made her scream my name.

My cock ached. And holding her soft weight in my arms tested the control I had on myself. But I wasn't going to break—not when I'd barely even started.

Fuck, she was responsive. I could have made her come without even touching her clit; I was sure of it. Maybe I'd even try that later. Right now, though, I still hadn't seen all of her and I wanted to.

I glanced down at her stretched out in my lap, her head resting against my shoulder. All I could see was a mass of golden curls shielding her face, the rest of her nothing but a blur. But that was okay, especially as an image of the rest of her had been burned into my brain. Hard, red nipples. The flush of colour that ebbed and flowed beneath her soft, pale skin. The tantalising contrast between that skin and the red fabric of her dress bunched at her waist. The glisten of moisture left from my mouth on the tips of her breasts. The curve of them. The way they looked as I held them in my hands…

Beautiful. The memory was going to remain in my head for years to come. Now, I was desperate to see the rest.

I checked the angle of the light on the table next to the couch, then I shifted her in my arms, easing myself out from underneath her.

She made a soft murmur of protest, but I ignored her, arranging her so she was sitting upright on the couch and leaning against the back of it while I knelt on the floor in front of her.

Taking hold of her dress, I pulled it down over her hips and thighs, easing it off. Then I gripped the waistband of her panties and did the same, pulling the material down and off, leaving her naked.

She shifted on the couch as I discarded her panties then put my hands on her knees and pressed them apart. A soft hiss of breath came from her, but she didn't resist. I glanced up, narrowing my gaze on her face, the glorious pale expanse of her body now a blur.

Her cheeks were deeply flushed, her eyes very dark. Her mouth was full and red and I wanted to feast on it for days. She looked dazed, which made the satisfaction inside me deepen. Apparently even she hadn't known how responsive she was.

'You okay?' I asked, stroking the satiny skin of her thighs. The scent of her body, warm and sweetly musky, was intoxicating. I couldn't wait to see her perfect little pussy, but I wanted to make sure she was with me.

'Yes.' The rough huskiness of her voice damn well thrilled me. 'I mean, I think you just blew my mind. But apart from that, yes.'

I smiled, unable to help myself. Jesus; I thought I was above taking an adolescent pride in making a woman come, but apparently not. 'Well, that was the general idea.' I eased her thighs wider, letting my gaze drop down the beautiful body in front of me. Those pretty breasts, full and round and topped with button-hard red nipples. The graceful indent of her waist and soft roundness of her stomach. Down further, to more pale skin. It didn't surprise me that her pussy was shaved, but the fleeting regret that I wouldn't see soft, golden curls did. Not that it mattered. She was so pretty, her sensitive flesh glistening with wetness and all flushed pink.

Because of me.

An unexpected surge of possessiveness gripped me, a growl collecting in my throat. She was wet and flushed and panting because of me. Because I'd made her come with only the attention I'd paid to her breasts and the lightest touch of my hand on her clit. She hadn't had to fantasise about something else to get off—no, that had been all me.

I was her fantasy and so this was mine.

She was mine.

Not that you deserve any of that.

But I forced the thought from my head. I might not deserve it, but I was going to take it nonetheless.

I leaned forward, kneeling between her spread thighs, sliding my hands up all that silky, warm skin to the crease where hip and thigh met, and then inward. Her body stiffened and she gasped as I let my fingers drift lightly over the slick folds of her pussy. The shadows were wrong, though, and I couldn't see as well as I would have liked, so I slid one hand beneath her ass, lifting her into the light.

Pink skin. Glistening moisture. A musky, sweet-salty scent. My mouth watered. My cock was so hard it was difficult to think. It was so fucking pretty and I was desperate for a taste. But I wasn't going to rush this. I wanted to see every part of her, commit her to memory, so, keeping one hand on her ass to keep her raised, I used my free hand to part the delicate folds of her pussy, exploring her gently.

'Oh, my God…' she whispered, sounding almost shocked, her body quivering, her hips jerking as my fingers eased her open. 'What are you doing?'

'I told you I wanted to see you.' Gently, I uncovered her clit, swollen and hard and rising proud to my fingertip. 'All of you.' I touched her, the lightest of brushes, and she jerked again in my grip.

'T-Trajan…'

I tightened my hold on her, exploring her, spreading her wider so I could see. Her pink flesh filled my narrowing vision, unbelievably erotic, the shivering of her body as I mapped the soft dips and valleys letting me know how much my touch was affecting her.

She shifted restlessly, her hips bucking as I stroked and teased her. The soft, gasping whispers gradually became more and more inarticulate, her muscles tightening and going stiff as I played with her.

It was mesmerising. I was drunk on the feel of her slickness under my fingertips and the scent of aroused woman filled my senses, clouding my brain. Nothing could have dragged me away from her in that moment. Nothing. I nuzzled against the soft skin of her inner thigh, focusing as I eased a finger inside her. The sight of her sensitive flesh closing around me and the feel of her muscles clamping tight was the most intensely erotic thing I'd ever experienced.

She groaned, her hips shaking, and I could sense that she was desperate to move, to ride my hand. But I held her tight. I was in control of this and I wanted her to come and come hard. And it wasn't going to be fast. I would draw this out as long as I could to give her the most pleasure.

I used my fingers to push her higher, easing another into the tight, wet heat of her pussy as I pressed kisses along her inner thigh, making her gasp and cry out. I took her almost to the brink, her body trembling, before easing off, making her groan in protest. I toyed with her some more and played with her slowly and carefully until she was writhing in my grip.

And I could feel my own control begin to slip, my hunger for her almost suffocating in its intensity. My cock pressed painfully against the fly of my jeans. Jesus, if I held off any longer, I was going to embarrass myself.

I slid my fingers out of her, licking the honeyed sweetness from my skin. Then I slid my hands beneath her thighs, lifting first one and then the other over my shoulder, before gripping tightly to her ass as I buried my face in her pussy.

She cried out, her hips jack-knifing under me, her whole body stiffening, and I felt my control snap. I'd wanted to take this slowly, to explore her delicately with my tongue, to rain kisses down on her, lick her and nip her, pay attention to her. But I'd pushed myself too far and I was too fucking hungry.

I pushed my tongue deep inside her, ripping another scream from her throat. I tasted her climax, drinking it down, and I didn't stop. I feasted on her, gorged on her, filled my mouth with the taste of her.

She bucked against me, her whole body writhing

as I ate her out, and she sobbed as I made her come again. I couldn't get enough of her, and I probably wouldn't have stopped if I hadn't felt her fingers in my hair, pulling hard.

'Stop,' she gasped hoarsely. 'Trajan, stop. I can't… I can't…'

What the fuck are you doing? You're going to lose it if you're not careful.

My pulse was loud in my head, the most intense lust pumping hard in my veins. I'd never been so hungry and, maybe if it had been at any other time, I would have stopped this in its tracks.

But it was just one night and I'd promised her real. So real I'd give her. I let her pull my head up as I eased my grip, stroking her thighs to soothe her. My vision was blurry and I realised I'd closed my eyes as I'd feasted on her, which hadn't been my intention at all.

Gritting my teeth, I tried to focus, and her face slowly became more distinct. I couldn't see the rest of her now, but I could smell her arousal which hung heavy in the air—musk mixed with coconut and vanilla and orchids. A complicated scent for a complicated woman.

Perspiration gleamed on her forehead, golden curls stuck to her skin. Her mouth was red and bitten-looking, and her eyes were as black as space. She looked wrecked, ruined. She looked fucked, and fucked hard, and I was the cause. This beautiful woman had been destroyed by me and I wanted to do it again. And again. I wanted to do this all night until I'd been burned into her brain the way she'd burned herself into mine.

Until she couldn't look at another man without seeing me. Until the fantasies she got herself off to when someone else touched her were about me. My hands. My mouth. And my fucking cock.

I let her go and slowly rose to my feet, holding her black, shocked gaze with mine. Then I reached for the hem of my T-shirt and pulled it off and over my head, dropping it on the floor.

I reached for the fly of my jeans and flicked open the first button. 'My turn,' I growled.

CHAPTER ELEVEN

Magdalen

I SAGGED AGAINST the back of the couch, half-stunned and barely with it. My whole body was suffused with heat and I felt boneless and sated and heavy. The remains of the orgasms Trajan had given me pulsed in the background, small electric shocks sparking along all my nerve-endings.

I'd never felt so good in my entire life.

I didn't think I could move—perhaps I'd never move again, as Trajan seemed to have stolen not only my ability to think coherently and breathe normally, but also the strength in my arms and legs.

My God, that man had wrecked me. He needed to come with a public health warning.

The long fingers that had played with me so delicately and carefully, that had stroked me and teased me into incoherence, now flicked open the button on his jeans.

I couldn't drag my gaze away from him.

I thought my libido would definitely need a break after what he'd done to me with his mouth and tongue, but apparently all he needed to do was take off his shirt and I was desperate once again.

He was the most beautiful man I'd ever seen. The light outlined every definition of every muscle, the broad expanse of his pecs and the hard corrugation of his abs, each one chiselled and sharp. He looked as though he'd been carved by some masterful Renaissance sculptor who'd been obsessed with him, every line lovingly shaped with great skill.

His skin was smooth and velvety and tanned, and there was a scattering of crisp black hair on his chest. I'd never wanted to touch a man more. In fact, the level of want inside me was disturbing. I'd seen men built like he was, cut like he was, but I'd never felt the need for them that I felt for him.

My fingers itched, wanting to touch him.

He said nothing as he looked down at me, a ferocious hunger burning in his blue eyes that thrilled me down to the bone. He'd been very careful with me before, going slowly and insistently, examining me intently. The sight of him bent over my sex, his fingers exploring me, watching what he was doing so fixedly it was clear wild horses weren't going to pull him away, was incredibly erotic.

And then he glanced up at my face and his eyes narrowed. I had the strangest sense that he was squinting at me because he couldn't see me. It reminded me a little of my grandmother peering intently at things because of her cataracts. But then I forgot all about my grandmother as he rose to his feet and took his shirt off.

My turn, he said, and I was more than happy with that. I was desperate to taste him, desperate to touch him.

I leaned forward on the couch, reaching for him, but he gave a sharp shake of his head. 'Not yet.' His voice was pure gravel, sending a thread of excitement through me.

I took pride in getting my clients off, and I was good at it, though the sex was only a part of the service I provided. Yet I'd never felt the same thrill at getting them worked up as I felt with Trajan.

And that was probably because I hadn't done a thing. I'd just lain there and let him touch me, taste me, and he'd lost it simply doing that. It filled me with pleasure, made me flush with heat, and now I wanted to return the favour.

'Please.' I looked up at him. 'You gave me two orgasms in a row. I think you deserve some attention.'

'Yeah, I'm not about keeping score.' Those long, capable fingers grabbed the tab of his zipper and began to ease it down. 'And what I deserve doesn't matter. This is about you, Maggie; I told you that.'

I found myself staring at the movement of his hand, my mouth going dry. I wanted to see him. Taste him. I wanted to give him all the intense pleasure he'd given me. 'If this is for me, then I want that to be for me too,' I murmured, reaching out yet again.

'Maybe.' He brushed away my hand. 'If you're very good.'

I shivered, slipping down off the couch and kneeling in front of him. 'Oh, I'm very good. I'll be your good girl, just watch me.'

Instantly a hand gripped my chin and I found my head being tipped back, his dark gaze on mine. And it hit me again just how intent his focus was on my face, how narrow. Like Gran trying to read the newspaper, holding it close, frowning in concentration just as Trajan was doing right now…

'Don't,' he said flatly. 'I'm not a client tonight, remember? And I don't want you to be anything but you.'

My thoughts fractured at the hard note in his beautiful voice. The good-girl thing was Honey, it was true, and it had slipped out before I'd been able to stop it. A rote response.

I stared up at him and gave him bare honesty. 'I want to taste you and I want to touch you. I want to do all the things you did to me, because you're not the only one who's been fantasising the past two weeks.'

His thumb moved to my mouth, dragging the pad of it over my bottom lip, his touch scattering sparks and lighting little fires everywhere. He didn't say anything for a long moment. Then his mouth curved. 'Well, I can hardly refuse that, can I?' He dropped his hand and stepped back. 'But not until I say. You're so fucking sexy, Maggie, that I'm in danger of disappointing us both.'

A shiver of sheer pleasure went through me. 'Then you'd better hurry, hadn't you?'

One dark brow rose. 'Didn't I say I was going to take this slow?'

'You weren't going slow just now,' I pointed out. 'I don't think I ever came so hard or so quickly, twice in a row.'

The curve of his mouth deepened, taking on a hungry, wicked edge that I felt deep in my sex, making me breathless. 'No, that's true. I hadn't realised how delicious that pussy of yours would be.'

My mouth dried. A lot of clients talked dirty to me but, although I made sure that I was into it with them, I didn't have to work for the flood of heat that washed through me at the sound of Trajan's voice.

He is going to ruin you. You know this, don't you?

I shoved the thought away. Hard. I'd deal with that later. Right now, this was for me.

Trajan was still looking down at me and I thought I saw a flicker of frustration cross his face, though why he'd be frustrated I couldn't tell. Then he lifted a finger and brushed my cheek, running the tip over my skin. 'You're blushing,' he murmured. 'Your cheeks are all hot. What? No one ever told you that your pussy tastes delicious?'

'Yes,' I said, because they had.

His hand cupped the side of my cheek. 'You blush with them too?'

'No.' I turned my face into his palm. 'Just you.'

I heard him let out a breath and then his hand dropped away. 'Stay where you are, sweetheart. Don't move.' And then he tugged his zipper down the rest of the way and, in a series of smooth, economic movements, he got rid of the rest of his clothes.

I wanted him to go slower. I wanted to touch him as he revealed himself, take some time to trace the outline of his magnificent cock beneath the cotton of his boxers, stroke him, squeeze him, make him growl. But he'd told me to stay still and so I did, watching the play of his muscles as he divested himself of his clothes, the light falling over smooth velvety skin, tracing the dips and hollows of sinew and bone.

He was a beautiful, beautiful man. Every bit as spectacular as I thought he'd be.

And then he was naked, standing in front of me, his cock long and thick and hard, curving to brush against his flat stomach. He was incredibly aroused and the sight of it made me even more hungry.

Dimly, a warning bell dimly went off in my head—that my response was too intense, that I needed to keep myself separate—but I ignored it. I'd kept myself separate with everyone else, and I didn't want to do that with him.

With him it was as if I were feeling this for the first time. As if all this were new to me.

It is new to you.

God, maybe it was. Sex didn't touch me because I'd never let it, not even that first time in the back of that car in high school, with a guy whose name I couldn't even remember. Because I'd just wanted to do it. I'd wanted my virginity to be gone.

How weird. I'd had a lot of sex, but this was the first time I'd really felt it, really let it affect me. This was the first time it had touched my emotions, and in a good way...

And, yes, I was going to let that happen tonight.

Tonight, with him, I wanted to feel.

Trajan jerked his head to one side in an unspoken command and obediently I moved. He went over to the couch, then turned and sat down where I'd been sitting a moment or two earlier, right under the light.

Then he leaned back, spreading his long, powerful thighs arrogantly. 'Come here,' he ordered.

I couldn't move fast enough, kneeling between his legs and reaching for him. His cock felt smooth and hot and hard against my fingertips, his skin like velvet. The musky scent of salt and warm earth and pine surrounded me, and when his hands went lazily to my hair, his fingers burrowing into my curls, I trembled.

'Suck me, then, Maggie.' His voice was dark and deep and rough. 'Do what gives you pleasure. But, when I come, I want you to swallow me. Every last drop, understand?'

'Yes.' I could barely speak.

'Good.' His grip in my hair tightened and, slowly, he drew my head down.

I licked the smooth head of his cock, tasting salt and musk before running my tongue around it, swirling lightly. He made a deep, growling sound in his throat, his fingers pressing against my scalp making pleasure curl tightly inside me.

Squeezing him with one hand, I traced patterns with my tongue down the length of his shaft and then back up again, teasing him the way he'd teased me. Nipping at him, using my teeth to push him higher at the same time as I pumped him gently.

I loved the sounds he made, rough and hungry, his hips lifting in response to my touch. I stroked his hard, flat stomach with my free hand, glorying in the feel of him and how his breathing accelerated as I touched him.

But, as demanding as the sounds he made were, the hands in my hair were never rough or hard. They traced the shape of my skull, his fingertips pressing lightly against my scalp, massaging slowly and easily.

His touch felt so good, making everything more sensual, more erotic.

I took him in my mouth as deep as I could get, touching the back of my throat, and he gave a rough curse, his hips lifting. And then he began to thrust in a slow rhythm. I thought he might grip my hair tightly, holding my head still, but he didn't. He kept on with that slow, massaging touch while I began to suck him, too caught up in the taste of him to be aware of anything else.

I leaned into him, spreading my fingers out on his stomach, and he closed his thighs, holding me between them, the rhythmic thrust of his hips and the slide of his cock in my mouth making me feel as though I was surrounded in heat and hard, masculine arousal. He wasn't demanding, letting me set the pace, and there was something freeing about that. It felt as though there was no pressure on me at all; as if I was free to follow my own needs rather than his; as if he was content to let me kneel here for as long as I wanted.

I could feel him watching me and, when I flicked my gaze up, his blue eyes caught mine and held them fast. 'Yes,' he murmured. 'Just like that. Let me see you suck me.'

The light was shining on us both, his gaze was on my mouth, watching, and I could feel the change in his body—his muscles tensing, the slow undulation of his hips getting faster.

He was close now, I could tell, and I could feel his pleasure as if it were my own, a slow, building ache deep in my sex. I squeezed him harder, sucking him deeper, his hips moving faster in response.

And then his fingers abruptly fisted in my hair, his hips driving upwards into my mouth, a rough groan escaping him as he said my name.

And he came in my mouth, hot and hard against the back of my throat.

And I swallowed him down, every last, delicious drop.

Just as I promised I would.

CHAPTER TWELVE

Trajan

I STARED AT HER, unable to take my eyes off her, the effect of that stunning orgasm paralysing me. My breathing was fast, my heartbeat faster, the after-shocks hitting me in short, sharp, electrical bursts.

The light rendered everything in vivid detail: the silky golden curls that framed her face; her pouty mouth stretched around my cock; the red in her cheeks and the burn of hunger in her dark eyes that showed me how sucking me had aroused her.

I hadn't planned to get her to give me a blow job—or at least not until much later in the evening—but when she'd looked up at me and told me that she wanted me I hadn't been able to resist. I hadn't quite been able to see her face, which had frustrated me, but I could hear the longing in her voice; she'd given me the truth. She wanted me as badly as I wanted her and, if I'd wanted this night to be about her pleasure, then who was I to deny her?

Fuck, it had been phenomenally erotic to watch her kneel between my legs, lean forward and take me in her mouth. To feel the silky brush of her hair against my thighs and her hand squeeze around my aching dick. The soft press of her lips and the wet heat surrounding me, the promise of what she'd feel like when I was eventually inside her. And the pressure of her mouth, the gentle suck…

I'd had no idea how incredible it would feel.

Soft lips brushed my stomach, her hands stroking me, and I leaned down, gripping her and pulling her up into my lap, relishing the feel of her bare, warm skin sliding over mine. I settled her the way I'd had her before, in the crook of my arm, and then I gently tipped her head back again into the light so I could get a good look at her face.

Her mascara had run, her lipstick was smudged and she looked thoroughly and completely debauched. Sexy as hell.

I stared down into her dark eyes. 'Thank you, sweetheart. That was incredible.'

She gave me an almost shy smile, making something hot and tight shift in my chest. 'Actually, I think you're the incredible one.' Her hand lifted and I felt her fingers in my hair. 'And I'm also not the only one who tastes delicious.'

'And are you hungry for anything else?'

Her eyes glittered. 'You.'

The hot thing in my chest shifted again. God, I

loved that hunger for me in her eyes. 'I was think-ing of actual food, but I'll take that too.'

'Well, now you mention it…' She turned to rest her cheek against my shoulder. 'Actual food sounds good.' I couldn't see it, but I felt the brush of soft fingers trailing over my chest, the touch sending de-licious chills through me. 'Though you're going to need to give me a few minutes,' she added. 'Because I don't think I can walk.'

'Keep touching me like that and in a few minutes I might want more than food.' I lowered my head and nuzzled her pretty curls, enjoying the feel of her light caresses. It had been a long time since I'd been touched like this. Since I'd started to lose my sight, I'd preferred to keep my liaisons brief, and I hadn't thought I'd miss the simple pleasure of rest-ing, relaxed and easy after sex, a woman in my arms, with the prospect of yet more sex to look forward to.

Apparently I did miss it, though, because I was certainly enjoying it now.

The silence settled around us and there was no pressure in it. An easy silence. I allowed her fingers to trace patterns on my skin. My vision was full of golden curls, but I didn't mind that. I could feel the gentle weight of her in my arms, smell the delicious scent of musk and coconut, vanilla and orchids. Hear the soft sound of her breathing.

And there was a moment when the thought oc-curred to me that I didn't need more than this. That if I had all those sensations then I wouldn't need anything else. That what little sight I had left was just a bonus, not a requirement.

It wasn't a thought I should have had, since it implied I wasn't happy with what was happening to me—and, sure, I wasn't happy with it, but I'd accepted it. I had no choice, as there was no cure, and struggling against the inevitable was a wasted effort. Better to expend my energy learning to live with it, making sure it had no impact at all on my life, rather than dwell on what I couldn't change.

Have you accepted it, though? Have you really?

I ignored that snide little thought, preferring to focus on Maggie and how she felt in my arms. On the pleasure she'd given me and the pleasure I'd given her. Had she ever had this? Ever? I'd had pleasure with many women, it was true…but I had to admit, it had never been as intense with any of them as it had been with Maggie.

You don't want deeper, though.

I didn't. Yet sitting here on this couch, with her in my arms, made me feel as if deeper was something that could happen. And that it might not be such a bad thing after all.

'Why do you do this?' I asked idly, too caught up in the feel of satiny skin beneath my palm as I ran a hand down her thigh to pay attention to what I was saying.

'Do what?'

'Work for Strangers.'

I'd asked her about it before, a couple of weeks after we'd first started meeting. We'd been in the kitchen and I'd been cooking, and our conversation had drifted onto money for some reason. I'd been curious about what made a woman choose to hire herself out to men, and she'd told me it was quite simple: she needed the cash. But there had been a note in her voice that had made me sure there was more to it for her than that. I hadn't pushed her then. Perhaps she'd tell me now.

'Haven't we had this conversation?' she said. 'Gran is developing dementia and I'm going to need money for care—'

'I don't think it's just about your gran.' I toyed with her hair, wrapping a curl around my finger tip. 'Is it the money? Validation? What?'

She was silent a long time and I could feel a subtle tension coil in her body. Then slowly she let out a breath and tilted her head to look up at me. Her face swam into my central vision, her expression serious. 'Why do you want to know?'

Suddenly my idle question didn't feel quite as idle any more.

'Call it curiosity,' I said.

'Curiosity in general or—?'

'Curiosity about you,' I interrupted gently, wanting her to know that. 'You in particular.'

A fleeting expression I couldn't read crossed her

face, but I had the impression that the comment had pleased her.

'Well, okay. But, if I tell you, you can't laugh.'

I frowned. 'Why would you think I'd laugh?'

She shook her head. 'Just don't. Because if you do, I'm afraid I will have to kill you.'

The words were a joke, but her tone was not. She meant it.

I moved my hand to the back of her neck, clasping it gently in a reassuring grip. 'I won't laugh.'

Some of the tension left her body, as if my touch had soothed her, and I could feel her weight shift and a light pressure against my fingers as she leaned into my hand. Then she took a breath and gave me an oddly challenging look. 'I need money for college. I want to get into med school.'

She was smart—I'd always known that—and I'd sensed that she was a woman of determination, so the confession didn't surprise me in the least. What did surprise me was that she'd think I'd find it funny.

'Why would I laugh at that?' I asked. 'If that's what you want, then it sounds like a great idea. Tough, sure, but why not?'

A crease formed between her brows, as if she was studying me for signs that I was making fun of her. 'Don't you think it's a little weird, though? The whore who wants to be a doctor?'

I caught the undercurrent of anger in her voice— it was obvious, even if the word 'whore' hadn't been a complete giveaway—and instinctively I tightened my grip on the back of her neck, using the pressure to quiet her.

Then I realised she was trembling.

'Sweetheart?' I asked softly, unfamiliar concern constricting in my chest. 'What is it?'

She looked away from me, her curls falling over her face, hiding her expression completely. I wanted to turn her back again, to get the light back on those lovely features, but I could tell already from the tension in her body that perhaps that would be a mistake. That maybe I needed to give her a moment.

So I didn't move and I didn't speak. I kept my hand on the back of her neck, though, caressing the soft, vulnerable place with my thumb in reassurance.

'I always wanted to be a doctor,' she said after a very long moment. 'Ever since I was a kid. Gran told me not to be so stupid, that only smart people got to be doctors and I wasn't smart enough. And besides, where did I think money for college would come from? The sky? No, she said I needed to be practical. Kids who had a mom in jail didn't get to be doctors, and anyway, that was getting above myself. What was wrong with a good, honest, blue-collar job?'

I said nothing, just stroked her and let her say her piece.

'I was a serious kid,' she went on. 'I liked books and encyclopaedias and facts. I liked bugs and doing experiments. I liked mysteries. I wasn't much of a girly girl and I think my grandmother didn't like that. She made me help her out with cooking and cleaning, and learning how to "keep house", because that's what I needed to learn, not all this science nonsense. She took me in and brought me up after Mom went to jail, so I did what she said. And if she thought I wasn't smart enough to be a doctor then maybe I wasn't. But then I got to high school and I did well, got good grades, and I started to think that maybe I wasn't so stupid after all.'

'Well, you're not,' I said. 'Far from it.' She didn't need my validation but I wanted to say it all the same. For the record.

She lifted a shoulder. 'I told Gran that I was going to apply for college, try for a scholarship, and I showed her my grades. I thought she'd be surprised at them, that she'd be pleased for me, but she wasn't. She was only angry. She said I was ridiculous. That I wouldn't be able to do it. That I couldn't leave her, and what kind of repayment for taking care of me all these years was that? Especially when she hadn't even wanted me in the first place.'

The bleak words hung in the silence and the hot, shifting emotion in my chest clenched tighter. I felt anger on her behalf as well as a need to comfort her, to ease her obvious pain. And it was clear that she was in pain, and who wouldn't be, after being told that they'd never been wanted?

I let go of the back of her neck and eased my arms

around her, drawing her soft, curvy body against my chest. She resisted at first and then gradually let me cuddle her close, relaxing, her cheek hot against my chest, her breath warm on my skin.

'Sometimes I think her dementia was on purpose,' she said, her voice softer. 'That she was trying to find a way to make me stay with her. She didn't want to take care of me, but now she wants me to take care of her. And I have to, because there's no one else to do it, and I can't afford a retirement home for her. And so I work for Strangers because it pays fucking well, and so that one day I'll earn enough money to get Gran looked after and then I can go to college.'

There was steel in her voice, a determination that I found fascinating, not to mention unbearably attractive. I admired people who rose to a challenge, who didn't let it defeat them. Eli was one of those people. He'd gone through hell after he'd been burned, and yet he hadn't let it either defeat him nor define him.

My sister, Vesta, had also had her difficulties, yet she'd gone on to find her own success in the tattoo business she'd started up.

Are you sure you should be enjoying Maggie quite so much?

Why the hell shouldn't I? It wasn't as if we were in a relationship or anything. This was only for one night and then I was going to let her go. The end.

If you can let her go...

Almost reflexively I tightened my arms around her, holding her warmth close to me as if my body was determined to make a liar out of me.

'Determined,' I murmured, pushing away the other thoughts, 'and compassionate. Both excellent qualities for a doctor to have. You'll achieve it, sweetheart, of that I have no doubt.'

She sighed. 'I shouldn't be angry with Gran. It's not her fault she had to look after me when Mom got sent to prison.'

'Are you angry with her?'

'Yes,' Maggie said reluctantly. 'I didn't want to be, but I am.'

'Okay, so your gran looked after you and fed you and clothed you.' I ran one hand down her spine and back up again, stroking her gently. 'But she didn't have to make you feel like shit about it. You don't take that kind of thing out on a kid.'

'No, I suppose not.'

'And you don't need to beat yourself up for your own choices either,' I went on.

Maggie shifted uncomfortably. 'I'm not.'

'Yes, you are. Calling yourself a whore.'

A breath escaped her. 'That's what Gran would say. She doesn't know where I work. I haven't told her. She'd be...'

'It doesn't matter what she thinks.' And this time I did reach for her small, stubborn chin, tilting her face up again, not because I wanted to see it, but because I wanted her to see mine. To look into my eyes and see the truth of what I was trying to say.

She resisted but I forced her head back, her gaze meeting mine with obvious reluctance. I held it. 'Her opinion doesn't matter,' I reiterated. 'All that matters is how you feel about it. Are you okay with what you do? Are you ashamed of it?'

She blinked and a glint of that steely determination appeared in the depths of her dark eyes. 'No,' she said flatly. 'I'm not. It helps people. It gives them a connection that many of them have never had. Some of them just want to be held, to have someone listen to them, to feel like they're being heard and being cared for. It's not even about the sex most of the time.' She stared back at me, challenging. 'How can I be ashamed of helping people?'

My chest felt tight. Caring woman. Compassionate woman. I admired her for that, yet at the same time what she'd said made me uncomfortable. Because was that how she saw me? As some poor, lonely bastard who just wanted a connection? Who wanted to be held like a child in need of comforting?

I wasn't sure what was worse: her knowing about my sight and pitying me for it or her not knowing and me being an object of her pity anyway.

Who cares how she sees you? It's only one night, after all.

That was true. Besides, I'd make sure that pity was the last thing on her mind whenever she looked at me.

I leaned down and brushed my mouth over hers. 'You're going to make a fantastic doctor, you know that?'

The tense look on her face eased. 'I'm certainly martyr-ish enough to be one.'

I smiled. 'I meant that you're compassionate. You care a lot about people, even when you're angry with them. Even when they don't deserve it. It takes a big heart for that.'

She sighed. 'Maybe I'm just a door mat.'

'Seriously?' I laughed. 'A door mat would have meekly accepted whatever her grandmother said and taken that decent, honest, blue-collar job and put away her dreams of a career in medicine. A door mat would definitely *not* have taken a job providing company for strangers so she could earn money, not only to look after her grandmother, but so she could also go to med school.'

Maggie looked at me a second, though what she was searching for I had no clue. Then suddenly she smiled. 'I don't know why you'd want to make me feel better about this. But I really like that you do, because you have.'

I had no idea why I wanted to either, yet I liked that I had. I liked it very much. And I let myself have that as well—pleasure in the knowledge that I made a difference to her, that I could help her feel good not just physically, but emotionally as well.

I stroked her back again. 'I can make you feel better in other ways too. If you're feeling recovered, that is.'

Heat flamed in her eyes. 'That depends on what you had in mind.'

'This,' I said, and then I pushed her down onto the couch cushions on her back and stretched my-self over her, pushing her thighs apart with my hips, loving the feel of her warm skin sliding over mine. I put my hands down on either side of her head and looked down into the darkness of her eyes. 'Food now or after? And, just so you know, the correct answer is after...'

CHAPTER THIRTEEN

Magdalen

HE WAS SO stunningly attractive like this, but not because of how easily he'd handled me—his strength so obvious as he'd pushed me onto my back—or how glorious his bare flesh had felt against mine.

No, it was because of the teasing glitter in his eyes and the note of rough demand in his voice, despite the attempt at lightness. Because of the hungry way he was looking at me, as if I was all he wanted.

My heart thumped hard behind my breast bone, the warm, reassurance he'd given me before gradually getting hotter and more intense.

I'd told him my secret about med school, which wasn't something I told anyone these days, not after Gran had been so scathing about it. I hadn't even told Vesta. I wasn't even sure why I'd told him. Maybe I'd been orgasm-drunk or something, because I'd thought, *What the hell? Why not?* He'd asked me why I kept working for Strangers, so why shouldn't I tell him the truth?

When I'd mentioned my clients and how I viewed myself as helping them, I'd caught a flash of something sharp in his eyes—anger, maybe—and I had the sudden realisation that perhaps I shouldn't have said that they were lonely people searching for a connection. That perhaps Trajan would assume I thought the same about him.

But the truth was that, although Trajan was a client, I'd never seen him in quite the same way as I saw my other clients, and that was probably due to our intense attraction. He was so gorgeous, so confident, and not at all like the lonely businessmen I usually dealt with. I even wondered a couple of times why a man like him would pay for company, that surely he must have more than he knew what to do with, but then I'd dismissed the thought. It wasn't my place to wonder why and it presupposed things about a person that maybe weren't true. My job was to fill the need, not question why it was there in the first place.

Trajan hadn't laughed when I'd told him about med school, though. He'd seemed to find my desire for a career in medicine perfectly understandable, and not only that but achievable too. He didn't think it was a ridiculous thing for a whore to want more for herself, and he'd been far too sharp about that word.

He'd spotted my anger. He'd known that there was a part of me that judged myself for my choices.

The part of me that was probably my gran's voice telling me that I shouldn't get above myself, that I shouldn't want more. That I should be grateful for what I had. That selling myself for money was a terrible thing to do.

Except Trajan hadn't judged me and he'd seemed to understand that there was something profound I could give to lonely people. And that I liked that aspect of it. That there was no shame in wanting to give people a few hours of connection.

Even if you can never have that yourself.

Yet it was hard to think that what I was experiencing right now with him wasn't akin to that in some way. Because I certainly felt connected to him.

I lay beneath him, pinned to the couch cushions by his muscular body, and surrounded in the scent of pine and aroused male. His skin felt smooth and so hot, the muscles of his biceps and chest standing out as he held himself above me. He flexed his hips, sliding the ridge of his rapidly hardening cock along the slick flesh between my thighs in a slow, sensual movement. I shuddered as pleasure rippled through me, lifting my hands to the hard chest above me and stroking it.

His gaze was fixed intensely on mine and he watched me as he flexed his hips again, sending yet more shocks of pleasure through me as his shaft rubbed against my clit.

I gasped, arching up, closing my thighs around his

lean waist, rocking against him as I dug my nails into his skin. 'Don't stop,' I whispered. 'Please.'

'Just for that…' He pushed himself away from me, wickedness glinting in his eyes.

'Trajan,' I groaned. 'I wasn't trying to top from the bottom. I just wanted—'

'I know what you wanted. But first things first.' He leaned over the side of the couch, feeling around for something. And then he sat up, moving down one end of the couch as he flicked open his wallet and extracted a condom packet.

Oh. Okay, then. I, of course, carried some with me, but my bag was across the room and there was no way I was moving. I debated offering to put it on him, but watching his firm, decisive movements and the way he rolled the latex down over himself, one strong, capable hand curled around his cock, was so unspeakably sexy that I didn't.

He must look magnificent when he was giving himself pleasure. God, I wanted to watch him do it so badly.

'Come here,' he ordered in that peremptory way he had.

I shifted over to him, not even thinking of not obeying, and before I knew what was happening he'd flipped me over onto my back and was settling himself between my thighs once more. The light was above me, shining directly onto my face, and I had to half-close my eyes against the brightness. He definitely had a thing about making sure I was in the light. Why was that?

Then the question dissipated like smoke as he pushed one hand between my thighs, stroking my clit gently before sliding a finger through my slick flesh, testing the entrance to my body.

'Wet for me, sweetheart?' His voice had lowered in a deep purr. 'I like it. And so wet too.' His finger eased deeper and I gasped with growing pleasure, my hips lifting to his hand.

'More,' I gasped.

'Oh, yes, definitely.' His finger disappeared and I felt the head of his cock pushing against me, into me, stretching me until I groaned at the feel of him.

'Trajan,' I whispered, shuddering. 'Yes, my God, yes.'

He lowered his head, his mouth covering mine as he eased in further. One hand slid beneath my butt, lifting me, angling me so he could slide even deeper, making me shudder and shake.

His tongue was in my mouth, exploring me slowly and with care, even as he drove his cock deeper inside me. The combination was devastating.

I wrapped my legs around his waist, trying to get closer, my hands on his shoulders, gripping him tighter. The pleasure astonished me and I moaned in my throat, kissing him back with desperation.

He paused deep inside me, his weight pinning me to the cushions. He felt so good, and the pleasure was so acute and sharp as a knife. My nails dug into his skin, my thighs tightening around his waist. I'd never wanted anyone to move as badly as I wanted him to move right in this moment.

I bit his lower lip, arching my back, lifting my hips, but he just stayed there, a hot, heavy weight.

'Trajan,' I moaned desperately. 'Please.'

He lifted his head, his hands pushing my hair back from my face. 'Shh… Let me see you.' His voice sounded roughened and raw. 'Open your eyes for me.'

I obeyed, letting the light in. His compelling face was above me, the expression on it taut with hunger and something else I couldn't quite identify. His eyes had darkened to midnight again, a dark, depthless desire burning in them. He said nothing, only watched me as he flexed his hips, and I felt the drag of his cock sliding out and then back in, slow and sensual.

Ecstasy rippled through me like the Northern Lights in a dark sky, bright and glittering and magnificent.

I groaned with the intensity of it and he didn't stop. He kept on with that slow, sensual, dragging movement, building the pleasure layer by aching layer, watching me all the while.

I clawed at him, tried to urge him on, but all he did was whisper soothing things to me, quietening me with strokes of his hands, even as his cock kept up with that slow, merciless rhythm.

His control must have been insanely good, because I was steadily losing it. Especially when he adjusted his angle to hit my clit every time he thrust in, scattering hot, bright sparks of pleasure everywhere.

All I could do was lie there and take it, writhing in his grip as the tension inside me drew tighter and tighter.

Sobs collected in my throat and I put my head back on the couch cushions as the slow rhythm he set started to become unbearable. I was shaking so hard, I felt as if I was going to come apart, the pleasure so acute it was going to break me for sure. Yet I wanted to come apart, I wanted to dissolve, I wanted to break, and I wanted his arms around me when I did, holding me tight.

I moaned his name, pleading with him, begging him to give me what I was desperate for. His hands soothed and stroked, gentling me, even as the maddening flex of his hips drove me insane.

I was trembling, covered in perspiration, the slick slide of his flesh against mine making everything sharper. He kissed me, nipping and licking at my mouth, then further down my neck and my throat, making a meal out of me.

And I began to come apart, losing myself in the blinding heat of his mouth and the drift of his hands, in the relentless drive of his cock inside me. And, just when I thought I couldn't bear it any more, that it was all getting too much, he did something with his hips, his cock rubbing up against something deep inside me, and I felt the orgasm began to bear down. I fought it, half-afraid of being annihilated by it, crushed by the sheer intensity of all that sensation, yet it came for me all the same.

Except it wasn't annihilation in the end but something more, something purer and far more beautiful. It filled me like light, like the promise of heaven, like sunshine, filling me up and radiating out, and instead of shattering I dissolved into it, became one with it. A bright, shining ecstasy that made me open my eyes and look up into his. And hold him as he became one with it too.

I didn't know how long I lay there afterwards, his weight heavy on me, reassuring and hot. And I just wanted to lie there like that, my arms around him, the strangest thoughts running around in my head.

This must be how it would feel to be with someone, to be in a relationship. To hold them and have them hold you in return. And for sex to be more than just the easing of a physical desire but to provide something emotionally too. Closeness. Real intimacy.

This is what's missing from what you give to people—this feeling. And you can never give it to them. Because you don't feel this way with any of them and you never will.

He was so warm around me, his weight heavy and reassuring, and yet a cold thread wound through me.

He'd made everything different. He'd made sex different. And that was a problem because, now I knew how different it could be, how could I do my job? How could I be with clients when I knew how amazing it was to be with someone who mattered? With someone to whom I mattered? How could I do a good job for them when I knew how much better it could be?

I always wanted to provide the best experience for them, especially the loneliest ones. The ones who were desperate for what I'd just experienced with Trajan. I'd always felt as if I was giving them something real and that, apart from the money, was one of the reasons I did what I did. But it wasn't real, was it? It was closeness, but only physical. A human connection, but not an intimate one, and certainly not an emotional one. It was half measures. Second best.

You were right. He did ruin you.

'Hey.' Trajan's voice was soft and rumbling, the weight of him on me shifting, easing. 'Are you okay?' He stroked back a curl from my face, his blue gaze roaming over me, his mouth curving in a smile that looked a lot like tenderness.

Did he feel this too? Or was it just me? He'd wanted real, and I'd given it to him, but had he given me the same in return?

Does it matter? It's only a night.

The cold feeling tightened in my stomach. But that was all it took. Just a night.

A night to understand what I was missing out on. A night to realise that everything I'd told myself about what I gave to my clients was a lie. A night to finally understand that the emotional component to sex wasn't something I could ever give them.

It was something I could only give to Trajan.

Because you're falling for him.

My mouth dried, my throat tightening. This was going to ruin everything.

'Maggie?' His hands stroked the side of my face, his dark brows drawing down. 'What is it?'

I pushed at his shoulders, suddenly feeling as though I was suffocating. 'Please…let me up.'

His frown deepened but he shifted anyway, rolling off me and onto his side. His hand reached for me, but instantly I was up and off the couch, moving to the doorway that led to the kitchen, needing some space.

Only a couple of recessed lights were on in the kitchen, but it was enough light for me to go to one of the cupboards where I knew he kept the glasses and take one out. Then I went to the sink and turned on the tap, filling up my glass, desperate for some moisture in my dry mouth and throat.

Trajan appeared in the doorway a couple of seconds later, tall and gloriously naked. He moved around the counter, coming over to where I stood by the sink, then stopped not far away, folding his arms across his broad, bare chest.

God, he was beautiful—even more so when he looked concerned.

'What's going on?' he asked quietly, his gaze fixed on my face.

'I needed some water.' How could I tell him the truth? When a night was all we had? Turning back to the sink, I filled up the glass again. 'You want some?'

'Sure.'

I put the glass down on the counter near where he stood and tried to pull myself together.

Okay, so I needed this feeling inside me to mean nothing. Nothing at all. It might end up with the next few months being difficult when it came to clients, but time would get rid of it. Eventually it would fade. It did—all the time, if what my clients talked about was true.

'Want to tell me what's going on?' Trajan asked.

'Nothing.' My mouth still felt dry. I reached for the glass I'd poured him and drank it thirstily.

He dropped his arms, one hand making a grasping motion at the counter.

I noticed, but didn't take it in at first.

He made another motion, as if he was trying to take something that wasn't there. After a second, he laid his hand flat on the counter, unmoving.

I frowned. It looked as if he was grasping at the glass of water I'd poured for him, but that couldn't be right. He'd been looking right at me and would have seen me pick it up.

I stared at him, my heart beating very fast all of a sudden.

His gaze was dark and fathomless, staring into mine. '"Nothing" is not the correct answer,' he said. 'Not after sex.'

Hardly aware of what I was doing, I took a slow, silent step to the side, away from the counter.

He didn't turn his head and his gaze didn't track me. He continued to stare straight ahead, at the space where I'd been.

'Come on, Maggie,' he said softly. 'Talk to me. Did I do something wrong?'

My heartbeat was so loud, my pulse rocketing everywhere, little things I'd noticed but had dismissed slowly coming together like pieces in a jigsaw puzzle.

The meticulous way he picked things up and put them down, everything very precise. The lack of clutter. The careful way he cut up vegetables. The way he cocked his head when pouring a glass of wine, as if listening for something. All the lights in the living room tonight. The intense, focused way he studied my face...

I stepped back to my position in front of him and put the glass down carefully. 'When were you going to tell me that you're blind, Trajan?'

CHAPTER FOURTEEN

Trajan

I DIDN'T TAKE in what she'd said for a second. 'What?'

'I think you heard me.' Her voice was low, and full of something that wasn't anger precisely, but something akin to it.

A cold feeling washed over me. 'What are you talking about?'

'I'm holding a glass of water out to you, but you're not taking it. It's because you can't see it, can you?'

The cold became ice.

'Don't be ridiculous.' I reached for her and felt my hand brush something on the counter. Maggie made a soft noise and then came the sound of breaking glass, as if something had shattered on the kitchen's tiled floor.

'It wasn't in my hand,' Maggie said after a second. 'I put it on the counter and you knocked it off.'

Shock surged inside me along with a fury so intense I could barely breathe. Fury at myself and how

I'd exposed what I'd been so good at keeping secret for so long. Fury at my own distraction, too busy thinking of her to pay attention to where I was and my surroundings.

Fury at this fucking disease that wouldn't let me ignore it no matter how hard I tried.

'Don't move,' she went on. 'There's glass everywhere. I'll clean it up.'

I hadn't touched the lights in the kitchen; they were still on dim. Not that I could see. My night blindness was total. And now she knew, because I hadn't been thinking. I hadn't even thought not to follow her. Something had distressed her out there on the couch and I'd wanted to know what it was, so I'd come after her.

The kitchen wasn't uncharted territory—I knew every inch of it—so I hadn't even paused as the darkness had closed around me. I'd been with her like this for months after all, cooking for her while she sat at the counter drinking wine and chatting. She hadn't figured it out then, so there'd been no reason for me to think she'd figure it out now.

But I hadn't been thinking. I should have been aware of the movement of the air as she'd reached for the glass. I should have heard her drinking. Yet I hadn't. I'd just wanted to know what was wrong.

What will she think of you now she knows?

A wave of ice went through me and I'd turned before I knew what I was doing, heading for the doorway of the living room, not giving a shit about the glass on the floor.

'Trajan.' Maggie's voice was full of concern. 'Don't, you'll…'

I ignored her.

The light from the living room momentarily disoriented me and I stumbled against the coffee table. Fuck. The shock of running into something froze me in place, the ice winding tighter, the cold rising higher, my heartbeat pounding.

Who the fuck moved the coffee table? I'd never run into it before. She must have shifted it out of place. Perhaps it was a test…

She didn't move it and you need to get a fucking grip.

I stilled, breathing hard, fighting the wave of panic that had gripped me, trying to find my control. It was a familiar panic.

A thud of impact. The sound of smashing glass and tearing metal. The stunning silence, the complete and utter blackness. That was what I remembered most after the accident: not being able to see a thing. Feeling disorientated and dazed, hearing Susannah's whimpers of pain and not being able to help her because I was blind.

Blind and helpless.

I shoved the memories away hard. I wasn't helpless now, I was in complete control, and fuck, what did it matter if Maggie knew I was visually impaired? Why did I care?

When the car accident had resulted in my retinitis pigmentosa diagnosis, my father had greeted the news the same way he greeted all news he didn't like: he simply ignored it. And, following his lead, so had my mother. There was no cure for it anyway, so why bother making a fuss?

It was never mentioned again.

I'd tried once or twice, as my vision had deteriorated, to talk to them about it, but they'd refused to engage. Mom had patted me on the hand as if I were a child and told me that it would be fine, that I just had to think positively. And Dad had quietly dropped all his plans for me, giving the position at his firm to some other bright young spark who wasn't blind.

I had no support. No one to talk to. No one to help. I felt the same way I had the night of the accident— terrified and panicking, and no one coming to save me.

So I'd saved myself, using anger in the end. A clear and cold and utterly certain fury. I'd lost my peripheral vision entirely by that stage and, when I'd tried to update Dad about it, he'd simply changed the subject.

He didn't care. He didn't care about me. All my life he'd told me how proud he was of me, and how I was going to be such a big success; that together we would conquer the world. But it had all been a lie. It wasn't about me at all. It was only about him.

And if I couldn't help him achieve that success then he'd find someone else to do it.

So I'd decided that day, fuck him, I'd be an even bigger success than he'd ever dreamed, and I would do it on my own, blindness or not.

But he'd taught me one thing: if you had enough will you could ignore the things that didn't fit your vision of what you wanted for yourself. So, while I couldn't ignore the fact that I was losing my sight, I didn't let it get in the way of what I wanted either.

I managed it. I controlled it. I used my anger to get me where I wanted to go—a cold, controlled kind of anger. Because panic changed nothing. Fear changed nothing. Only focus and strength of will managed the situation, as did disregarding that my lack of sight made any difference to anything. Because if you treated it like nothing, it became nothing.

Yeah, so you're letting it becoming something now.

Fuck, yes, that was exactly what I was doing. I was letting myself get into panic mode and I couldn't do that.

Forcing away the steadily rising cold, I took a moment to breathe, to orient myself in the room. Coffee table on my left, couch on my right. I could only see the angled light over the couch—everything around it was a blur—so I shifted my foot slightly and encountered fabric. Denim, from the feel of it. My jeans. I bent and picked them up, breathing steadily as I pulled them on, finding my cool control once again.

Shit, that panic had been unnecessary. The whole reason I'd hired Maggie in the first place was to figure out how to handle social situations without my blindness getting in the way, and I'd done that. I'd successfully managed it for months without her being any the wiser, so really, I should be considering this a success, not a failure.

'Trajan?' Maggie's voice came from the direction of the doorway.

The concern in it scraped over my nerves, setting my teeth on edge. I hated the pity that came with people knowing. The sympathy. The not knowing what to do or what to say. The clumsy attempts to help that always ended up making things worse.

And she'd pity me, wouldn't she? Yeah, of course she would. She'd already told me how she viewed what she did as helping people, providing comfort to sad fucks who couldn't get it in their real lives. And, now she knew about my sight loss, no doubt she'd see me in the same way: a poor, lonely blind man desperate for a screw.

That was the one good thing about my father. There had been no pity in him. Because to pity me, he'd have to acknowledge what was happening to me, and he hadn't in any way. Which was all good from my perspective. I wasn't going to be that panicky, weepy boy he'd visited in hospital after the accident, afraid and desperate for reassurance.

My father didn't do reassurance, which made things a fuck load easier.

'Yes?' I kept my tone cool, my back to her as I tugged up the zipper on my jeans. My hands were still shaking. I steadied them.

'Are…we going to talk about this?'

'Talk about what?' I turned to face her.

She was leaning in the doorway to the kitchen, one of the spotlights above revealing her face. Her golden brows were drawn together, her dark eyes fixed on mine. The rest of her body was a blur, which irritated me. Because she was naked and I wanted to see that nakedness…

Jesus, why had I walked out of the kitchen? What I should have done was grab her and fuck her up against the counter or on the floor. Show her that my sight or lack of it didn't matter; that I wasn't like the other men she saw, desperate for some female attention. Why would I be when I had the power to make her scream my name the way she'd screamed it out on the couch earlier?

'Oh, I dunno… Maybe about the fact that you can't see?'

I left the button on my jeans undone because why the hell not? I shouldn't have put them back on again anyway. This night wasn't done, sight or not.

'Why should that matter?' I said coldly. 'I don't need sight to fuck you.'

'Can I ask—?'

'Do we really need to go through all of this? I don't have any peripheral vision and I'm night blind. That's all.'

'That's all? I think it's a little more than that.'

'It's whatever I say it is,' I said flatly. 'Come here. We have unfinished business.'

She ignored me. 'Sounds like retinitis pigmentosa. Is that right?'

I didn't want to have this discussion. I didn't want to sit around talking about my sight loss, not when there were better things to be doing.

'Yes,' I bit out. 'But you're not my doctor or my ophthalmologist or my therapist, and I'm not paying you for heart-to-heart chats about my sight. I'm paying you so I can fuck you. The end.'

Hurt rippled over her face and she looked down at the floor abruptly, her curls falling over her face like a curtain.

You asshole. So much for giving her something real. You just treated her exactly like a whore.

Fuck.

Shame threaded through me, along with guilt and regret. It was a shitty way to repay her for what she'd given me on the couch just before, with her body and her passion, with her pleasure and her trust. That had been a precious gift, not a sand castle I could kick over in a fit of petulance, like an angry little boy. And all because my pride had been threatened.

'I'm sorry,' I forced out. 'That was uncalled for.'

She was silent a moment. 'It's the truth, though, isn't it?'

There was a kind of weary acceptance in the words that made me ache, as if she'd had that flung at her too many times to count and so it had lost its power to hurt. Except, no, that wasn't true. It *had* hurt her. I'd seen it, and then she'd hid her face…

She has feelings for you, remember? Coming from you, it's always going to hurt worse.

The ache inside me, the ache that I didn't want to be there, tugged harder.

'No,' I said before I could think better of it. 'No, it's not true. Look, you want to know the reason I hired you? It wasn't for friendship or company. It was for practice. It was an experiment. I wanted to spend time with a woman to see if I could operate in a social situation without relying on my sight, and without anyone noticing I was blind.'

'Oh.' The word came out on a breath. 'You had to hire someone for that?'

'Those closest to me already know I have sight loss. I needed someone who didn't know. And, since I wasn't willing to deceive someone I met in a bar or anywhere else—not to mention that I wanted discretion—I thought hiring someone was the ideal solution.'

'I see.' Her tone was stripped bare of emotion. 'And was that why you kept the lighting in here dim?'

'Yes. I'm effectively blind in low light.'

She stayed quiet for a long moment. 'You hid it very well.'

Irritation rippled through me. 'The purpose wasn't to hide it. It was to see how well I could operate with no sight.'

'Right.' She didn't sound convinced.

'What?' I couldn't keep the annoyance from my voice. 'I'm not one of your usual clients, Maggie. I'm not some pitiful, lonely fuck so desperate for company he has to pay for it.'

Aren't you, though? Aren't you just like those pitiful, lonely fucks?

The snide thought whispered through me but I shoved it away. Hard.

'Some of my clients are pitiful, yes,' she said quietly. 'But not all of them. And I've never seen you as one of them anyway.'

I liked that. I liked that far too much. Because I hadn't realised until now how different I wanted to be for her. It was her desire and her passion that I wanted, not her pity. Not for her to heal me, give me comfort or save me.

I'd saved myself and I'd continue to do so.

'You didn't answer my question,' I said, changing the subject, abruptly sick of talking about myself and my failing vision. 'What happened before?'

She blinked. 'Before?'

'You got off the couch and just left. What was wrong?'

'I…' The shape of her shifted, moving to fold her arms. 'You really want to talk about that?'

'Why wouldn't I want to talk about that?'

'It's hardly important compared to—'

'Compared to what? Me losing my sight? I don't give a shit about that. It's handled.'

'If it's handled, then why did you turn away and walk out of the kitchen? And why don't you want to talk about it now?'

'Because it doesn't interest me.' Losing patience, I crossed the room to where she stood then stopped in front of her. 'You interest me, Maggie. And I want to know why you couldn't wait to get away from me just before. Did I hurt you?

CHAPTER FIFTEEN

Magdalen

TRAJAN STOOD IN front of me, radiating impatience
and intensity. There was no sign of the shock that
had rippled over his face back there in the kitchen
when he'd knocked over the glass. Or the shuttered
look that had followed it so quickly as he'd turned
on his heel and left, heedless of the broken glass.

It was weird, that response, and then this coldly
controlled dismissal…

He might not want to talk about the fact that he
couldn't see, or that he wasn't interested in it, but it
affected him all the same.

He was shocked that I'd found out. He hadn't
wanted me to know; I was sure of it. And I got why.
He was a proud man, a powerful man. A man in
control. And having a degenerative disease such as
retinitis pigmentosa, that had no cure and few treat-
ments, was the ultimate loss of that control.

So what did a man like Trajan do with when

faced with something like that? Of course he'd try and exert control over whatever he could. And it made what he'd said about why he'd hired me understandable. I wasn't angry about that. I got it. And I understood why he didn't want to talk about it. Perhaps he talked about it a lot to people. Perhaps he didn't want to be reminded of it, not now, here with me. Perhaps it was a weakness to him, or a loss he didn't want to contemplate, or any one of a number of things.

He didn't want to be pitied, though, that was clear, and he *really* didn't like the thought of me viewing him the way I viewed my other clients. Which, given how I'd talked about them, made sense. Yet I'd never seen him that way, because he wasn't like them.

He may not be sad, but he is lonely.

Was he? Was he just as lonely as I was?

My heart ached at that thought, just as it ached from the shock revelation of his sight loss.

Everywhere I looked now I could see the evidence I hadn't taken note of before. The exact way things were placed. No art on the walls. No knick-knacks. The coffee table had been pushed out of line, and I had a strong urge to go and push it back so it wouldn't trip him up.

'Don't think about it,' he said sharply. 'It's not relevant.'

I glanced away from the coffee table and looked at him.

He stood there in nothing but the soft, faded jeans that hung low on his lean hips, the light outlining every hard, chiselled muscle of him. The very epitome of male beauty, of power and control and strength...

What had it been like for him to lose his sight? Had he accepted it? Had he fought it? Had it been terrifying for him? Had he had anyone to help him adjust?

Why do you care? He's right; it's not relevant.

I shouldn't care. And I shouldn't be thinking about it. Yet... I couldn't stop. I wanted to know how he dealt with it, how he felt about it. I wanted to know what it had meant for him and why he was trying to hide it because, no matter what he said about experiments, he *was* trying to hide it.

But he didn't want to talk about it—not with me. And it wasn't my place to make him. As he'd already said, I wasn't his therapist or his doctor. I didn't have the right to his secrets, even if I wanted them.

You're not entitled to them. Not when you're only his whore.

That thought hurt, but I ignored it.

'Okay,' I said softly and stepped forward, closing the distance between us. I put my hands on his chest, loving the feeling of warm skin and hard muscle beneath my palms. 'No, you didn't hurt me. I just felt a bit...overwhelmed.'

His fingers caught my chin and he tipped my head

up so his gaze met mine, narrowing into splinters of midnight blue. Could he see my expression? He wanted to; that was obvious, given the intent way he stared at me.

In fact, I suspected that was why his stare was always intent. It wasn't because he wanted to see me in particular. It was because he just wanted to see. It felt wrong to be disappointed by that, but I was disappointed all the same.

'What were you overwhelmed by?' he asked.

I didn't want to do this, all of a sudden. I didn't want to stand there talking about me and my responses. If he didn't want to talk about his sight loss, then that was fine, but I wasn't going to have an in-depth discussion about my feelings for him either.

I had to keep something back. I couldn't give him everything.

I slid my hands up to his shoulders and around the back of his neck, arching against him, pressing my bare breasts to his chest. 'Stop thinking about that,' I said huskily, looking him in the eye. 'It's not relevant.'

His hands settled on my hips, warm and heavy, gripping me tight. But the expression on his face didn't change, his blue gaze burning into mine. 'You wanted real, Maggie.'

'And real is sharing things, Trajan.'

His black brows drew down in a fierce scowl.

'You're pissed I don't want to talk about my sight loss?'

'Of course not,' I snapped back, the ache in my heart settling deeper. 'You didn't hire me for that, did you? And you didn't hire me for discussions about our feelings. I'm just here to fuck you and that's all.'

It was wrong of me to fling back in his face what he'd said to me earlier. But I couldn't get rid of the disappointment that sat so heavily inside me. It shouldn't have mattered that I was just an experiment. A dupe. Someone to test himself on. While he'd been practising on me, pretending he was sighted, I'd been busily falling for him.

Okay, so it turned out I did mind about that. I minded *a lot*.

He went very still. Then, letting go of my hips, he cupped my face gently between his big, warm palms, that intent focus zeroing in on me. And, even though I knew it was only because he couldn't see properly, my heart swelled, because it looked as though it was me he wanted to see. Me he had to look at.

'I'm sorry I said that before,' he said fiercely. 'I didn't say it to hurt you. I just… You finding out about my sight was a shock and I didn't expect it. It's been years since I knocked something over and I thought… Well, what I thought doesn't matter. My pride was hurt, and I was angry about it, and I shouldn't have taken it out on you.'

My heart swelled even more, pressing painfully against my breastbone. He was sincere; I could see it in his eyes. A proud, controlled man, yet he wasn't too proud or controlled to apologise and mean it.

It made the ache inside me even more painful.

'It's okay,' I said.

'No, it's not okay. You're upset.' His thumbs stroked my face gently. 'Don't think I don't know that. I can actually see your expression, by the way.'

Damn him. Damn him for being so nice. For giving me another glimpse of the caring man he was under his cool reserve.

'I love the way you look at me,' I said in a rush, unable to stop myself. 'I've always loved it. You… focus on me as if I'm the most important thing in the world and you study me as if I'm the most interesting. And I thought it was because you actually did find me interesting, but…'

'But now it's because you think I was just squinting to see you,' he finished for me.

I could feel myself blushing. 'Look, I know. It's unfair of me to think that. I just…'

'Wanted to be special to me?'

The blush in my cheeks became fiery. I tried to pull away but he held me fast, kept me standing there, the tips of my bare breasts brushing against his warm, naked chest, the look in his eyes intensifying. 'You *are* special to me,' he said in a low, deep voice. 'And, yes, sometimes I do look at people that way and it's because I'm trying to see them. But it's also because I *want* to see them. I *want* to see you.' He paused a moment. 'Do you know why the lights are all on tonight?'

'Because you wanted to see me?'

'Because I wanted to see *you*. Maggie, I've never seen your face before—not clearly. Not until tonight. And I wanted to. I wanted to see all of you, every part of you. That's why I changed our contract. That's why all the lights are on. Not because I wanted to have sex while I could see, but because I wanted to see *you*. I wanted to see *your* pleasure. I wanted to see what *you* looked like when you came. I wanted to see what *you* looked like when you blushed. I wanted to see *your* skin and *your* hair and *your* sweet little pussy.'

His fingers tightened on me, my heart getting sorer and sorer. 'And I wanted to see your smile, sweetheart. I wanted to see you laugh.' His voice got rougher, deeper. 'My sight has been stable for a long time, but…a couple of months ago it started to deteriorate again. My ophthalmologist isn't sure if it's going to stabilise, or whether I'll lose it entirely, but I decided that if I didn't get to see you at least once I'd never forgive myself.'

He searched my face, his gaze full of nothing but truth. 'And if I woke up one morning and it had all gone, my biggest regret would have been that I never got to see your face.'

Tears pricked my eyes and I didn't know what to say. My heart ached and ached.

He'd wanted to see me. He'd wanted to see my face. He was going blind and he wanted to see me before he lost all his sight.

My throat closed up and I couldn't have spoken even if I'd wanted to. I'd never been that special, not to anyone. Not to my grandmother. Not to my mother. Strangers valued me, but there were plenty of beautiful women who could do what I did. I was replaceable.

But Trajan had wanted to see me before he lost his sight completely. *Me*.

I put my hands over his and I went up on my toes and pressed my mouth to his, letting my kiss say what I didn't have the words for. What I was afraid to say, my fear sitting deep in that aching heart of mine.

I'd wanted real, and this was starting to get more real than I'd ever thought it would. The kind of real that would hurt when tomorrow came and I had to walk away from him, because with every moment that passed it became clearer and clearer that that was the only option.

I knew nothing about him. Nothing beyond the things he'd told me. But it was clear that he had a lot to manage. He didn't need the woman he'd paid for to start putting her emotions onto him. To start asking him for things, for something that this was never supposed to have been about in the first place. That was why he'd spent money on me, after all. I was providing him with a service.

For tonight we might be real with each other, but tomorrow that would be all over. And then the actual real would start. And that didn't include him.

There was pain somewhere inside me, but I pushed that thought aside for the moment. Right now, there was only the feel of his mouth on mine as I kissed him and the hot press of his tongue against my lips.

I opened for him, letting him in, the kiss deepening, getting sweeter, hotter. Still kissing me, he pushed me gently up against the wall, pressing my sensitive nipples against the hard warmth of his bare chest. I shuddered with delight, squirming against him, sliding my arms up around his neck and arching into him.

He shifted, pushing one powerful, denim-clad thigh between my legs and up against my pussy, pressing on my clit. I gasped as bolts of pleasure pulsed everywhere, making me tremble. His hands dropped to my hips, urging me closer, the hard muscle of his thigh providing the most exquisite friction.

It was glorious. He was glorious.

But I didn't want this just to be about me now. I wanted to do something for him, to make him feel as good as he'd made me feel.

Sure, he'd told me tonight was about my pleasure, and that his own wants were about watching me and seeing me. But didn't he want something for himself? A fantasy of his own that had always turned him on?

He'd given me my fantasy; why couldn't I give him his?

I pulled my mouth away and leaned back against the wall. His lashes were lowered—long, thick, black and silky. His gaze glinted from beneath them, hot and blue. My face was in shadow; he probably couldn't see it clearly, but that didn't stop him from staring at me.

'What?' His voice was gravel and velvet. 'You want something in particular, sweetheart?'

'Yes,' I said huskily. 'I want to do something for you.'

'You are doing something for me. This whole night is for me.'

'But I told you my fantasy and you gave it to me.' I reached out, touching a finger to the smooth skin of his chest. 'So now I want to give you yours.'

The glint in his eyes became more pronounced. 'If you think I didn't get off on that, you can think again.'

I couldn't help smiling. 'Okay, true. But still. I want to give you something, Trajan. You've made me feel so good tonight and now I want to return the favour.'

He lifted a hand and put it down over mine where it rested on his chest, trapping it against his warm skin. 'You already have.'

I raised an eyebrow. 'Really? You don't have any other fantasies you're dying to try out?'

CHAPTER SIXTEEN

Trajan

I COULD FEEL the heat of her pussy against my thigh, could smell the scent of musky aroused woman mixed with light coconut and vanilla. Her face was indistinct in this light, but I stared at it anyway.

She didn't need to offer me this. It wasn't what I'd intended our night to be about. Her pleasure was about not having to be the one to give, but about receiving instead. That was why I'd told her that my sight was deteriorating.

There had been disappointment in her voice, and I'd seen it in the set lines of her face too. The fact that I hadn't wanted to talk about it had clearly upset her, though she hadn't pushed me. She'd snapped, though, throwing the stupid comment I'd made earlier, about paying her for sex, back in my face.

It was only what I deserved, but I hated that it had hurt her. Hated that I'd let my shock and anger at her finding out about my sight get to me.

No, I hadn't wanted to talk about it, but she deserved to know the reasons behind me hiring her for tonight. The real reasons. That it was about her. Seeing *her* pleasure. *Her* face. *Her* smile.

Real is sharing things, Trajan.

I'd never shared things with anyone before. I'd learned to keep my doubts and my fears to myself. My father had never wanted to hear them when I'd made the mistake of telling him about them when I was a kid, merely instructing me brusquely to shut up. Acknowledging a fear let it in, so if you were never afraid and never in doubt then you'd always triumph in the end.

He was full of so much fucking shit, but he was right about that one thing: never acknowledge a doubt or a fear, otherwise you gave it power over you.

I'd learned the truth of that the night of the accident as I'd hung upside down in the car, trapped by my seat belt, the only sound Susannah's whimpers of fear and pain beside me, and I'd gradually understood that the reason why I couldn't see a thing wasn't because it was very dark, or because I had something in front of my eyes, but because I was actually blind.

I'd panicked that night. I'd let my fear get to me and the sounds Susannah made had terrified me—because I hadn't been able to see her and she hadn't been able to answer me. Then she'd fallen silent and that had been even more terrifying.

I'd wasted precious seconds panicking, fumbling around for the catch of my seat belt and pressing it, then falling. There had been broken glass under my hands, the smell of spilled fuel in my nostrils and blackness pressing in all around me, suffocating me.

To this day I don't know how I managed to get out of that car. It certainly had been pure luck that my shaking fingers had found my phone, which had fallen out of my pocket and been thrown onto the road. I hadn't been able to see the buttons and I couldn't think. The blindness wouldn't lift and I'd wasted more time panicking, desperately mashing buttons on the phone to call the emergency services.

My panic had nearly cost Susannah her life.

If you'd acknowledged the loss of your peripheral vision earlier, though, you might never have been driving in the first place.

It was true. But that was another example of me letting fear get in the way. I should have admitted to myself that I was losing my vision. Instead I'd ignored it, too terrified at the thought even to acknowledge it.

Perhaps that would have been okay if it had only been myself who'd got hurt, but it hadn't been. My failure had extended to Susannah as well, and she'd had to spend months relearning how to walk.

Dad had been wrong about that one fear. Refusing to acknowledge that I was gradually losing my sight had given it power over me, rather than the opposite, so these days I picked and chose my fears and my doubts.

Ultimately, though, I preferred to handle them all myself and I did. And I didn't share them with anyone.

Except for now. Except with Maggie. Because, regardless of how sexy and beautiful she was, there was a vulnerability to her. A deep-seated need for reassurance. She didn't show it on the outside, but I knew it was there all the same. And, because she needed it and because she deserved it, I gave it to her.

I'd told her exactly how special she was to me, had seen the tears gleam in her eyes and had realised how much that meant to her.

Ah, God, she made my heart ache.

'You want to give me a fantasy?' I murmured. 'Isn't that Honey's line?'

'No,' she said patiently. 'You know that I can want to fulfil a fantasy for you without it having anything to do with being an escort, right? People in relationships do it all the time without being paid for it.'

There was the slightest thread of sarcasm in her voice, but I couldn't see her face well enough to see the expression on it.

I frowned. 'I've offended you.'

She let out a breath and then I felt my hand being taken and she drew it to her, letting my fingers trace her mouth and the curve in it. 'No, you didn't offend me. Feel my smile?'

I could, and it was so soft and so warm. My chest felt tight at the easy, familiar way she'd taken my hand and let me touch her face with no awkwardness at all. As if she'd been doing that for me a hundred times.

'Yes,' I said roughly. 'I feel it.'

'There. I was teasing. But, seriously, this isn't an escort thing. This is something I want to do for you, because...' She paused. 'Well, because you're special to me too.'

I stared into the pale blur that was her face, trying to see the darkness of her eyes, but they were lost to me. They would always be lost to me, and her smile too, regardless of my sight.

It hit me then, hard, like the quarrel from a crossbow, that tonight was all I'd have of her. That tomorrow she would be gone and all I'd have left would be the memories we created tonight.

It shouldn't hurt. There shouldn't be pain with that thought. So I ignored it, the way I ignored everything else.

'Okay,' I murmured. 'But, you know, all the fantasies I've had have been about you specifically.'

Her body shifted against mine, the scent of her filling my senses, making my breath catch. 'Hmm, I like the sound of that. What are they?'

I'd had them. Fuck, had I had them. 'Me, in absolute control of you. Getting you to do whatever I want.'

She gave a soft laugh. 'That's not unsurprising, Mr Control Freak.'

I let my fingers drift from her mouth to grip her chin, holding her firmly. 'No lights this time. I want you in the dark with me. I want you blind like me.'

A shudder went through her; I could feel the vibration of it in my hand. I felt it, too, in the trembling of her hips against my thighs. A thread of pure heat poured through me and my cock hardened. I pressed her more firmly against the wall, gripping her chin, my free hand finding the beat of her pulse in the hollow of her throat, measuring it. It was fast and getting faster.

'You like that?' I asked softly. 'Does it scare you to join me in the darkness?'

'A little.' Her voice was husky. 'But I want to.'

I stroked that fast little pulse, dragging my thumb over her soft mouth. 'It's not a fantasy if you're not into it, Maggie.'

'I know. But I like you being in control. It's a relief.'

'And the darkness part of it?'

She was silent a moment. 'I don't much like blindfolds. I never have. But... I think it would be different with you.'

The constriction in my chest became something deeper. She'd already given me her trust back there on the couch, and here I was essentially asking for it again.

What about you? Do you trust her?

Oh, yes, I certainly trusted her with my pleasure, no question. She'd already blown my mind on the couch and no doubt she'd blow it in my bed too.

That's not the kind of trust we're talking about...

I shoved away the thought, impatient now. Stepping away from the wall, I held out my hand to her, feeling her slim fingers entwine with mine. Then I turned and led the way to my bedroom.

'You know where everything is in the apartment, don't you?' she murmured. 'Exact locations, where everything is placed; distances.'

'Yes. I've never had any problems navigating around the apartment.'

We were in the hallway now, the ambient light dropping to zero for me as we moved out of the living area. It wasn't hard to find my way around as the apartment was fairly contained.

'You're kind of amazing,' she said, wonder tingeing the words. 'You cooked dinner for me and I never even realised.'

'That was the whole point.'

'How do you not cut yourself? Or burn yourself? How do you know where everything is? How do you remember?'

There was no judgement in her voice, only an intense curiosity, which was very much her. She'd often pepper me with questions during our meetings, especially if it concerned something she was interested in, and I'd never minded it then.

I found, rather to my surprise, that I didn't mind it now.

'I had some support from some independent living people.' I'd paid someone to teach me how to cook without sight. 'And after that it was all practice.' I glanced back at where I could sense her behind me and smiled. 'I cut myself a lot.'

'I can imagine.' There was a warmth in her voice that wrapped around me, holding me tight.

And I found myself going on. 'During the day it's not too bad, since I have my central vision. But I do find I rely on the map I have in my head of my apartment to get around, even when I can see. Sometimes it's easier at night when I can't see at all.'

'I get that,' she murmured. 'What about when you go out?'

'That's a little more problematic.' I could sense my bedroom doorway just ahead of me. 'But I know my office as well as I know my apartment and I can get around it.' I didn't add that the crowded spaces of the city with lots of people were difficult. That going to bars and restaurants was even more so. I didn't go out much any more. All the wining and dining of clients I left to Eli. My presence wasn't necessary for that kind of bullshit anyway, and besides, I'd never been much of a party animal.

You don't go out these days at all.

No, but that was my choice. I didn't want the white cane or to be led around like a fucking sheep. And, as it was getting harder and harder to go without those things, I stayed in places that were familiar to me. Places where I was in control.

'Do you go out anywhere else? Apart from the office, I mean?' Another one of her innocent questions. But I was done.

I pulled her into the bedroom, leading her to the bed, and didn't reply. There were windows directly ahead of me—large ones that looked out onto a beautiful view of Central Park during the day. The view would be of blackness and streetlights now, but of course I couldn't see it.

'Stay where you are,' I ordered, then stepped away, moving over to the dresser that stood against the opposite wall from the bed.

She obeyed me, the room filling with the soft, quickened sounds of her breathing. I opened the drawer that held my T-shirts and pulled one out. Then I turned and came back to where she stood, moving behind her.

Desire was rising inside me. I thought I'd got used to how badly I wanted her, but apparently not. The thought of having her in the darkness with me made me ache. Made my cock hard. Made the blood pump through my veins in a heedless rush.

It was a private world, my blindness. It was my cross to bear and I didn't want to share it with anyone else. Yet…the thought of her joining me in it made my hands shake.

I hadn't realised how badly I wanted that until now. Trusting me in the light was one thing, but trusting me in the dark, joining me in the dark, was another thing entirely.

The scent of her skin rose around me, the warmth of her naked body almost but not quite touching mine. She was breathing faster, harder, now.

'Are you ready?' I asked softly.

'Yes.' There was no hesitation in her at all.

I lifted the T-shirt and laid it gently over her eyes.

CHAPTER SEVENTEEN

Magdalen

I'D NEVER BEEN into blindfolds. I didn't like how it meant I couldn't see my client. It was a loss of control and, since every meeting I had with a client was about controlling it, that made me uncomfortable.

It had never been a hard limit, though, just something I endured because I did like to give my clients whatever they needed.

And I wanted to give Trajan this. The look on his face when he'd told me he wanted me in the darkness had conveyed everything I needed to know about how much this meant to him.

So I'd prepared myself to endure it, and yet the moment the soft cotton covered my eyes, I felt my heart shudder and shift in my chest, the dragging ache of desire intensifying between my thighs.

The cotton was soft and it smelled of him, and as it blocked out the light from the city beyond the windows I felt something inside me relax rather than tense, the way it normally did.

Blackness closed all around me, but I could feel the heat of his powerful body behind me, grounding me. This was the difference that trust made, I realised. Because it was all about trust, wasn't it? Me trusting him.

And him trusting you.

Yes, that was true. He might not think it himself but there was trust involved in this. He was trusting me with his private fantasy, trusting me to share his private world with him. And for such an intensely private man as Trajan to do that…

A pulse of some deep, intense emotion swept through me.

You aren't falling. You've already fallen.

His hands tightened the blindfold around my head and then moved to brush my shoulders before travelling down, stroking my sides lightly.

'All okay?' His voice was near my ear, a soft rumble of sound, his breath warm on my skin.

'Yes.' I touched the cotton covering my eyes. 'I don't normally like blindfolds but this is surprisingly okay.'

'And you call me the control freak.' His fingers made another glide down my sides and then up, soothing rather than inciting.

'Is this what it's like for you?' I stared into the blackness in front of me. 'At night? Just…black?'

'Yes.' Another soothing stroke, making me shudder. 'Does it frighten you?'

I swallowed, unable to give him anything else but the truth. 'Yes.'

'That's normal. I was frightened too. My father's an asshole, but he had one thing right: acknowledging a fear gives it power over you.'

A little thrill went through me. Another piece of the puzzle that was him. 'So, what—you just don't acknowledge the things that frighten you?'

'I don't acknowledge their power,' he corrected, his fingers pausing at my hips. 'I don't let being visually impaired stop me from doing anything I want. I have to adjust, of course, but I go on as normal. And that way I'm not at its mercy.'

That sounded very much like him.

I wanted to know more; the questions were tumbling around in my brain.

But then he said, 'Don't fixate on what you can't see. Focus on your other senses.' His fingers began to trace patterns on my skin, light and delicate.

It was very like something I would have said to one of my clients, and yet here, with him, with my eyes covered, it felt different.

Everything felt different with him.

I focused on his touch, on the slow drift of his fingers, my skin getting more and more sensitive. Heat prickled all over me as my awareness grew—of his tall, powerful presence behind me; of warmth and the scent of pine and salt.

The circles he traced grew bigger, turning into spirals along my sides and hips, rippling outward over my stomach, then going higher and higher, curving along the undersides of my breasts.

I shivered and leaned back against the hot wall of his body at my back.

His touch was unbelievably gentle and reassuring, and yet somehow I found my heart beginning to pound, the nagging ache between my thighs becoming more demanding.

The circling fingers moved to my breasts, tracing large circles that got smaller and smaller, narrowing in on my nipples that had now begun to throb. I couldn't stop the gasp that escaped as he circled the tips of my breasts, around and around, oh, so lightly. I couldn't stop the arch of my back, wanting more, wanting those teasing fingers to touch my nipples, pinch them, tug on them, intensify all the sensations.

'Trajan…' I murmured. 'Please…'

'Patience.' His mouth drifted down the side of my neck, trailing light kisses to my shoulder. 'You're so impatient, sweetheart.'

'I know, but…' His hands moved again, down over my stomach, brushing down over the sensitive skin of my pussy, tracing circles there, making every word I'd been going to say vanish from head.

'Relax.' His breath was warm against my shoulder. 'Let me handle it.'

And then his arms were around me and I was being lifted and carried, and I barely had enough time to understand what was happening before I felt the softness of a mattress and sheets under me, and I realised he'd put me down on the bed.

There was a moment or two when I heard the sound of a zipper and the rustle of fabric, then the mattress dipped and the warmth of his body was right next to mine, his hands on my shoulders pushing me firmly down on my back on the mattress.

Excitement gathered in the pit of my stomach, my breathing getting faster and faster. I couldn't see anything but darkness, yet I could sense him above me. He had one knee on either side of my hips—I could feel them pressing against me—and his hands were on either side of my head. He must be looking down at me, but I couldn't understand why, because surely he couldn't see me?

'What are you doing?' I asked breathlessly, reaching out to find him.

'Keep still,' he said, his voice full of authority. 'Arms by your sides.'

I obeyed, trembling with inexplicable excitement.

He shifted and I felt his hands run down my sides again, checking me. 'Good,' he murmured. 'As to what I'm doing, I want to get a sense of you. Smell your scent, feel your body beneath me. Listen to your breathing.'

'Oh. Well, I…' The words were cut off as a hot mouth covered my nipple, sucking strongly. I cried out, my fingers curling into the sheets beneath me, little points of light bursting in the darkness behind my blindfold.

Then I felt warm, exploring fingers between my thighs, parting my sensitive flesh, stroking and caressing. Teasing and pressing.

Sensations built, one after another, feeling more acute without sight, more intense.

I couldn't get a sense of where he was. My awareness had narrowed to his hands on my skin, his fingers moving inside me, his mouth on my breasts, neck, stomach and thighs. And then further, his tongue on my clit, his fingers moving in a relentless rhythm.

The pleasure was acute and the orgasm hit with incredible swiftness, making me cry out, clawing at the sheets as it swept over me. His touch gentled to long, sweeping strokes down my body as the aftershocks pulsed through every nerve ending.

I panted, my eyes closed, a little shocked by how quickly he'd made me come. And it was clear he wasn't done yet, because his stroking hands stilled and then gripped me, handling me with calm strength as he turned me over onto my stomach.

Then he began to stroke me again, his hands moving down my spine in long, luxurious caresses. I moaned with the simple pleasure of it, my muscles relaxing, the intensity of the first orgasm receding.

'That feels amazing,' I said croakily. 'What about you?'

'It feels amazing to me too.' Warm amusement threaded through his beautiful voice.

The pillow was cool beneath my forehead where the blindfold didn't cover my skin. By this stage I'd stopped trying to see through it, or even just trying to see. It was easier to close my eyes and concentrate, as he'd told me to, on my other senses. Especially where he was touching me. I felt as if I'd died and gone to heaven with his hands on me.

'You know what I mean.' I swallowed, my throat gone dry. 'Don't you want something for yourself?'

'Oh, believe me, I'm getting everything I want.' His hands drifted down my back to the curve of my butt, where he squeezed me. 'And I'll take it too.' He squeezed again, slipping his fingers between my thighs from behind and stroking the slick folds of my pussy. 'How does this feel?'

I shuddered as he slipped a couple of fingers inside me. 'Good. Oh… God…very good.' My hips lifted against his hand, pleasure beginning to build again.

He squeezed me again, his thumb sliding between my butt cheeks and pushing gently against the tight ring of muscle. 'That okay?'

I stiffened, my breath catching as a wave of heat blasted through me. 'I...' My breathing felt too fast, another wave of pleasure threatening to overwhelm me.

'Well?' He didn't take his thumb away, but he didn't push any harder.

'Yes,' I managed to force out. 'I mean, it's not my favourite, but...'

'My intention was to do everything to you tonight, Maggie.' There was a darker, rougher quality to his voice now, dangerous and seductive. 'Everything. I want every part of you to be mine. Will you let me?'

Anal sex had always been painful and unpleasant for me, but again, I never made it a hard limit because I hated to refuse my clients anything, especially if it was a special fantasy for them.

'And to be clear,' Trajan added. 'I'm asking Maggie, not Honey.'

Honey wouldn't have thought twice, and the fact that I was doing so now only proved how far she was from me in this moment. But that was good. That was what I wanted.

And I wanted to give him his fantasy too. If he'd made a blindfold okay, then maybe it would be different with this as well.

'Okay,' I said thickly. 'Yes.'

I felt him shift beside me, his fingers easing out of my pussy then back in again in a long, deep glide. At the same time, that thumb pressed harder, working its way inside me, making me groan into the pillow at the intrusion.

'Sweetheart,' he murmured, nothing but approval in his voice. 'Just say stop if you need me to.'

He worked me gently with his fingers and his thumb, until I was shaking, every sense I had focused on his touch and the intense, unbearable pleasure he was giving me. He pushed me and pushed me with gentle relentlessness, his rhythm more insistent until I was sobbing into the pillow as the climax swept over me, leaving me trembling and gasping.

He touched me soothingly after that for a few moments, easing me down from the peak, and then I felt him shift away, the mattress dipping once again as he got off it.

I wanted to ask him what was happening but I couldn't move. Couldn't speak. I lay there as a warm, sleepy lassitude crept over me. The sheets must have been expensive because they were soft and cool against my hot skin, and they smelled of laundry powder. There was something comforting about them, about the darkness around me. It was somehow full of sexual heat and soothing warmth, passion and relaxation, a strange mix of contrasting sensations that I found exciting and settling all at once.

Then the mattress dipped again and he was back, his hands on me again, authoritative, taking charge. He was stroking me again, my back, my sides, my thighs. And then his fingers slick and slippery, pushed between my butt cheeks again, caressing and rubbing with the glide of liquid against that sensitive opening.

I trembled, half with anticipation and half with a kind of dread, and of course he instantly picked up on it.

'You still okay?' He worked his thumb into me again, gentle but relentless.

'Yes,' I croaked. 'Just…' I bucked helplessly against his hand, the build-up of pleasure beginning again, dragged from me, making my breath catch.

'Shh,' he murmured. 'I'll go slow.'

His hand disappeared and there was cool air against my back for a second. I heard the sound of foil rustling, then he was touching me again, firmer this time, no longer soothing. Arranging me with a possessiveness that made something quiver deep inside me.

I felt him move behind me, and then came a shocking heat as he laid himself down on top of me, covering me completely, his weight pushing me down into the mattress.

A gasp ripped from my throat, the heat of his body on mine overwhelming. He surrounded me, the musky scent of aroused male and pine flooding my senses; the feel of hard muscle pressing into me was intensely arousing.

One hand slid beneath my hips, lifting me, and then I felt the press of his cock against my ass, hard and hot. He rocked against me a couple of times, a gentle rhythm, and then I felt him push against that tight ring of muscle.

Lights burst in the darkness behind my blindfold. 'Trajan…' I gasped.

His weight shifted and I felt one hand come down beside my head. His mouth brushed over the back of my nape and then my neck. 'It's okay,' he murmured. 'Hush.'

He pushed deeper, slow and relentless, and I felt myself give way before him, my tight flesh reluctantly parting for him.

It hurt, but there was pleasure with the pain. Deep and aching. So different from what I'd had before; but I already knew that, didn't I? Everything he did to me was different. And it wasn't so much what he did, as the feeling that swept through me when touched me.

It was the feeling that made it different.

I could feel tears prick the back of my eyes, which was stupid, and yet they wouldn't stop.

He was deep inside me now, rocking gently, slow and easy, his body curving around mine. And I realised I'd never felt so safe or protected or cared for. Here in the dark, with him inside me, surrounding me, nothing could touch me.

I murmured his name, a dark and deep pleasure winding through my body becoming more and more intense, building slowly. His breathing in my ear became rougher, more ragged, though his rhythm stayed steady, never getting wild or out of control.

It was so good. So very, very good. And it was him. All him.

His hand slipped beneath me again, his finger finding my clit, giving me extra friction, and suddenly I was twisting beneath him and writhing, unable to keep still.

But he didn't move any faster, just used every deep thrust to pin me harder into the mattress, keeping me in place, his movements causing my clit to jolt against his finger, sending hot, bright bolts of lightning everywhere.

I lost track of time. I lost track of myself.

There was only him. Only his cock in my ass and his hand on my clit. Only his body shielding me and protecting me.

Only the feeling in my heart, the long fall into a chasm I was never going to escape from. And I didn't want to. I didn't want to escape. Ever.

I screamed in the end, the sound buried in the pillow, and when I felt his teeth against my shoulder, and his big body shudder as he came too, I screamed again.

And then there was nothing but the velvet blackness that wrapped itself around me and held me tight.

CHAPTER EIGHTEEN

Trajan

THE ORGASM WAS the most intense I'd ever had and for long seconds I couldn't move. I lay there on her soft body, my cock still buried in her tight, hot flesh, the sounds of her screams still ringing in the air. The smell of musk and sex was everywhere, mixed with the sweet scent that was all Maggie.

She was trembling beneath me and, even after I'd come and come hard, all I wanted to do was ravage her all over again.

A wave of something primitive and raw caught at me. She'd given me this fantasy, of her with me in the darkness. Of her being mine. And now she was, every part of her. Her mouth, her ass, her pussy. All of her was mine. I'd put my stamp on her and, no matter who she was with after this, she would have me there.

And she will be with other men. From tomorrow morning she'll cease to be yours.

The possessiveness wrapped around my throat, choking me. The thought of her being with someone else...

You don't want her to be with anyone else but you.

I couldn't breathe. Trying to be gentle, I eased my cock from her ass and pushed myself away, desperately trying to get air into my lungs.

'Trajan?' Her voice was full of concern. 'Are you okay?'

'Yes,' I forced out. 'Just lie there. I'll go get something to clean you up with.'

I didn't wait for her to reply, slipping off the bed and finding my way to the *en suite* bathroom. There were cloths in a basket under the sink so I grabbed one and filled the sink with warm water, soaking the cloth gently before getting rid of the condom.

My heart was beating way too fast and all I could think about was the feel of her beneath me, warm and soft, and the hot grip of her flesh, the sounds she made and the way she moved. She made me feel strong and powerful. She made me feel in control.

She was in the darkness with me and I was in full command.

It eased something inside me—something that had been tense and angry for a long time and I hadn't even known it.

And I realised with a slight shock that, in bed with her, holding her, touching her, fucking her, I hadn't thought once about my sight. About what I was going to lose. What I couldn't do. And what I had to ignore in order to go on pretending that this was not going to impact my life in any way.

It was just such a fucking relief.

And tomorrow? When she leaves?

But that could look after itself. I didn't have to think about that now. I'd told myself I was going to enjoy the moment and so I would. Besides, if all it took to feel in control was anal sex with the lights off, then I could get that from any woman.

You don't want any woman, you fucking idiot. You never did.

But I didn't want that in my head. I didn't want the implications or the possibilities, so I shoved it away. Instead, I wrung out the cloth and took it back into the bedroom to where Maggie was lying.

She murmured softly as I lay down beside her, running the warm cloth between her ass cheeks and pressing gently. She gave the most delicious little shiver and moan as I did so, sending another rush of heat through me.

My cock was interested in another round, but she needed some recovery time, so I dealt with the cloth then came back to the bed and gathered her into my arms. She didn't protest, snuggling into my chest in a way that made my breath catch and my arms tighten around her. And I couldn't shake the sense that she fitted as though she was made to be there.

Perhaps I should have let her go at that thought, but I didn't. I couldn't bear to.

'Thank you,' I said into the silence. 'Thank you for giving that to me.'

'No, thank you.' She sounded sleepy and slurred. 'That was amazing. It's never been like that before for me.'

A hot pulse of satisfaction hit me at that. 'I didn't hurt you?'

'Not at all.' She sighed. 'I think you could make me like anything at all.'

I could feel her breath against my chest, her body lax and sated lying against me, and it was good. Too fucking good.

My chest ached, but I ignored it, as I ignored everything else. 'Well,' I said firmly. 'The night is still young. Plenty of time to test that theory.'

'Oh, dear,' she murmured. 'That sounds serious. Should I be worried?

'Unless you're worried about having too many orgasms, then no.'

She gave a soft laugh and her lips brushed my skin. 'You're funny. Having control is a big thing for you, isn't it?'

The question was asked in exactly the same tone, and for a second I was so distracted by the soft feel of her lips that I almost didn't hear it.

And then I did.

'And it isn't for you?' I asked idly.

'Of course. But that wasn't an accusation, you know. I was just interested.'

I still didn't want to talk about me but it felt wrong not to at least give her something, especially after she'd been so open with me before.

'Yes,' I said after a moment. 'It's important. You might not be able to control what happens to you, but you can control your response to it.'

'That's true.' She was silent a second. 'Is it really that important to you that no one knows about your vision?'

A flicker of discomfort hit me that I tried to fight off. 'It's not that it's important. I don't care what people think of me. It's that I don't want any aspect of RP to impact my life.'

There was a silence but I could feel her gaze on me, the slight change in pressure and the subtle shift of her muscles. But she still had that blindfold on so she wouldn't be able to see my face. She was as blind as I was.

And I felt something shift inside me—a need I'd buried for so long that I'd told myself I didn't feel it any more. I didn't talk about this with anyone, not even with Eli, my best friend. But here in the darkness, a darkness we shared, I suddenly wanted to talk, and to her.

'You remember I told you about that accident?' I said abruptly.

'The car accident with your girlfriend?'

'Yes.'

'What about it?' Her fingers had begun another slow circle on my chest, calming the restless and uncertain feeling inside me.

'The accident was caused by a car I didn't see. And I didn't see it because I didn't realise that I'd lost some of my peripheral vision. It was early evening, and the light was low, so there were a lot of things I didn't see and didn't realise that I didn't see. One minute I was talking to her, the next we were upside down.'

My heartbeat accelerated, a ghost of that old panic sweeping through me, tensing all my muscles, but I dismissed it. 'Susie was making these awful sounds and I realised I couldn't see a fucking thing. I…panicked. Lost precious time trying to work out what was happening. I'd lost my phone and I couldn't find it. Then Susie went silent and wouldn't answer me.'

A hand closed around my throat, making my breathing difficult. I wouldn't let it fucking get to me. I wouldn't. Not again. 'I was disorientated. I couldn't tell up from down. I didn't know where she was. There was just…blackness.'

Maggie said nothing, but then I realised I was concentrating on those small circles she was tracing on my chest, the warmth of her touch on my skin grounding me, calming that desperate thing inside me.

I felt myself relax, focusing on her touch. 'Somehow I found my way out of the car, but it was pure luck that I put my hand on my phone. I couldn't press the buttons—I was too panicked to think of using hands-free—and I wasted more time calling the emergency services.' I took another slow breath, focusing on her gentle, warm touch. 'I'd never been afraid of anything. I'd never doubted myself. I'd always been absolutely certain about the path my life would take and what I was going to do with it. But that night... I knew terror and doubt and uncertainty.'

'That must have been awful,' Maggie said softly, her voice full of concern. 'Poor boy.'

I tightened my arms around her, the warmth of her body seeping into mine, warming me through. 'I got my diagnosis a few days after that. And my dad...' I stopped, this part strangely difficult. A bitter anger I thought I'd long since got rid of turned over in my gut. 'Dad pretended that it didn't exist. He refused to acknowledge it. I couldn't talk to him about it, couldn't ask him for advice. Couldn't ask him what to do. He just wouldn't talk. I had to find out about it myself.'

'Oh, Trajan.' She sounded appalled.

'It was fine,' I said, though I knew the sound of my voice told the real truth. 'I figured it out. You can't rely on other people to help you get through things; you have to do it alone. But not only would he not talk to me about it, he changed all the plans we had for me to join his business. Without even mentioning it to me, he just cut me out.'

I'd become very tense, a remembered anger burning like a fire inside me, but then I felt Maggie's mouth on my chest pressing a gentle kiss there, and somehow the anger inside me lessened, the burn becoming less acute. It felt so distant now, with her mouth on me.

'What about your mom?' she asked. 'Didn't she help you?'

'No. She ignored it too. I think she was afraid. She didn't know how to deal with a blind son. Neither of them did.'

Maggie let out a soft breath. 'Oh, that's awful. I'm so sorry.'

I wanted to shrug and tell her that I'd dealt with it. That their failure to acknowledge what was happening to me hadn't impacted me in any way. But all that came out was, 'I decided that if they were going to pretend that my blindness didn't exist, all while making it clear that that they had no expectations of me doing anything worthwhile, then I'd show them what I could do. That I could succeed despite what they thought.

'And I did succeed. I built a fucking billion-dollar company based on body armour. My friend Eli and I deal with governments, with top business people, with the military, with research institutions. So you see, it didn't matter in the end that I had RP. It doesn't matter that I'm losing my vision. I am successful despite it.'

She pressed another kiss on my chest. 'That's incredibly inspiring, you know that? You're kind of amazing.'

Those kisses, the wonder in her voice... I hadn't realised how much I'd needed that until now.

Like you deserve it.

A whisper of cold washed through me.

'I'm not amazing,' I said flatly. 'I'm only successful because I refused to give in to fear. Because I learned how to take control of something rather than have it control me.'

'But—'

'I started losing my peripheral vision before the accident happened,' I interrupted. 'I knew I shouldn't have been driving that night but I ignored it.'

Maggie's hands didn't hesitate. She kept on stroking me gently. 'Why did you ignore it?'

'Why do you think?' My voice had got rough. 'Because I was afraid. I let fear get in the way and Susie got hurt. And then my panic delayed treatment for her. She survived, but she had to learn to walk again, and she has PTSD—'

I broke off all of a sudden as I felt Maggie's lips on my jaw, my cheek, my eyes, a rain of soft kisses on my face. 'It's okay,' she murmured gently. 'It's okay, Trajan.'

My soul ached at the tenderness in her voice, at the warmth.

'It was my fault,' I said hoarsely. 'I should have paid attention to the fact that I couldn't see at night. That I—'

'You were young,' she interrupted quietly. 'And that was the first time you realised that you weren't bulletproof. That you're human.' Another kiss on my cheek, another on my jaw. 'Realising that is always scary. But you're not alone, darling. You're not alone with it. I'm only human, too.'

I wasn't sure why that statement made such a difference. I didn't think I needed anyone with me in this hellhole. And it was a hellhole, even though I tried never to think of it like that, because nothing I could do would change it. All I could do was manage my response and my environment.

Yet…what would have sounded like platitudes and trite bullshit from anyone else was reassuring coming from her. Because I knew she meant it. And I knew she understood, because she'd had her own shit to handle.

And she'd joined me in the darkness.

I wasn't alone with her there. And being human when she was next to me… Well, maybe I could handle that after all.

I shifted, rolling over and taking her beneath me, pinning her into the mattress, letting the warmth of her body press against every part of mine. I lowered my head and found her mouth, letting my kiss speak for me. Letting her know how important those words had been for me, since I couldn't say it aloud.

Saying them aloud would have made them true and I couldn't allow that, not when she was leaving in the morning. Not when it would leave a crack inside me that I wouldn't be able to heal. A weakness I wouldn't be able to afford if I was to go on with not letting this thing ruin my life.

She shivered, her arms winding around my neck, her thighs spreading wide then closing around my hips. I could feel soft wetness and heat against my rapidly hardening cock, making me catch my breath.

'"Darling",' I said, nuzzling against her throat. 'Is that what you call all your clients?'

It was a gentle tease and she took it as such. 'Not at all,' she said primly. 'I sometimes call them other things. Like Daddy. And Hotshot. And My Lord and Master.'

I smiled against her sweet skin. 'I like the last one. I think you should call me that.'

She laughed. 'You would.'

I kissed her throat. 'Say it, sweetheart.'

She sighed, her body arching into mine, already hungry for me. 'Yes, my lord and master…'

CHAPTER NINETEEN

Magdalen

IT WAS THE daylight that woke me, shining full in my face and waking me up. I didn't want it, though, so I turned and rolled over, burying my face in the pillow, searching for the welcoming darkness again.

I lay there for a second, wanting to go back to sleep, before the realisation slowly worked its way through me that tiredness wasn't the only reason I wanted to be back in the dark.

It was morning. Which meant my night with Trajan was over. There was an ache in my heart, a tug of pain, but I forced it away.

I was the one who'd decided not to see him again and, despite the fact that I knew I'd fallen for him, I wasn't going to change my mind. It wasn't just because Strangers would frown on me having a relationship with a client outside of work, but because I had no idea how that relationship would even look.

He was such a very private man, and a proud one,

and he was dealing with a serious health issue. An issue, from what he'd told me last night, that he was determined to handle on his own. He didn't want to acknowledge it, he didn't want to let anyone in, and I could understand why. His father—his whole damn family—had let him down badly. He'd had to do this all on his own, and I got that. I'd had to handle my grandmother on my own too, and sometimes it was easier that way.

Sometimes you were stronger on your own.

You don't really believe that...

I let out a breath and rolled over, staring at the ceiling. Did I? Certainly when Trajan held me in his arms, when he listened to me talk and when he touched me, offered me reassurance and advice, I felt stronger. But of course I felt weaker too; the temptation to fall apart and let him handle things was too great to resist. And I couldn't do that. I wouldn't. He had so much other crap to deal with; he didn't need mine as well.

Besides, would someone like him really want someone like me? He was head of a billion-dollar company and I was...

Well, I was Honey. I made money from selling my 'company'. I had to take care of my gran and get into med school, and the money for that wasn't going to come from waitressing. Which meant I couldn't give up working for Strangers any time soon.

I turned my head, glancing at the empty pillow

beside me, feeling the ache in my heart deepen. Clearly he hadn't wanted to stay for any last-minute pleasure, which was his prerogative. And maybe it was for the best anyway. I didn't need this to be any harder than it already was.

Moving slowly, I slid out of bed.

My dress was out in the living area, along with my bag, and normally going out there naked wouldn't have bothered me but it did today. I felt vulnerable and fragile, and I wanted something to cover me.

After a hunt, I found the blindfold he'd used on me the night before, which turned out to be a soft T-shirt in black cotton. I put it on, shivering as the familiar scent of him surrounded me.

Perhaps it was a bad idea to wear something of his. Then again, I didn't have a choice. It was either that or use one of the sheets and I didn't want to do that.

I went out into the hallway and heard the deep rumble of his voice coming from the kitchen, so I followed it.

All the blinds had been drawn up and sunlight streamed through the glass. Trajan stood at the kitchen counter, leaning back against it as he talked on the phone. He wore jeans and nothing else, the sunlight gilding his magnificent torso, outlining hard muscle and smooth brown skin. It glossed his black hair too, lovingly outlining the stark planes and angles of his face.

A beautiful man.

But he wasn't mine and he never would be.

The pain in my heart became wrenching but I pushed it aside. It didn't matter. None of it did.

He must have sensed my presence because he suddenly turned his head and looked at me. And I knew he could see me because of all the sunlight and the way his gaze met mine in a collision of brilliant blue.

He didn't smile, just finished up his call, then disconnected and slipped the phone back into his pocket. 'Coffee?' he asked neutrally.

I went over to where he stood, strangely reluctant to get too close to him. He had a French press cafetière full of fresh coffee ready and a couple of mugs out.

'I'm going to cook breakfast,' he said. 'What would you like?'

Breakfast and coffee. More time in his company... No. It was going to make it too hard. I needed to go and I needed to go now.

'Thank you,' I said, trying not to sound husky. 'But don't worry about me. I have to go.'

'No, you don't.' His gaze caught mine, intent and fierce. 'We could have more than a night, Maggie. This doesn't have to end today.'

There was a wrenching feeling in my chest. 'I think it does.' I tried to sound calm. 'I told you why I can't see you again, Trajan. That hasn't changed.'

He searched my face. 'Hasn't it?'

I stared back, holding his gaze. 'No.' It was the truth. No matter what I felt for him, no matter how intense and perfect and wonderful our night had been, no matter how my world had shifted on its axis because of him, nothing had changed. My situation was still the same. 'Everything I told you about only wanting one night is still true.'

'What? About not getting involved with a client? Fuck that.' Trajan took a step towards me. 'I just won't be your client any more. We don't need a company to keep seeing each other.'

I hadn't expected it. I hadn't expected the fierce look in his eyes as he stared at me, or the note of possessiveness in his voice. And for a second a tendril of stupid hope fluttered in my chest.

'You really want to share me with my clients?' I stared back, trying not to let that tendril take root. Hope was one thing I couldn't afford. 'Because that's what you'll have to do, Trajan.'

A muscle jumped in the side of his perfect jaw, a flame of what looked like anger burning in his eyes. 'Why? Why can't I have you all to myself?'

My heart ached and I felt a raw throb in my chest. There was nothing I wanted more than to allow him that. To tell him I was all his. That I didn't want anyone else to touch me, anyone else to hold me. That I didn't want anyone else inside me, only him.

But I couldn't. 'Because I have bills to pay,' I said

as calmly as I could. 'I have college to save for and Gran needs—'

'I'll pay for it,' he cut me off brusquely. 'I'll pay for all of it. You won't need to go back to working for Strangers. You can be with me instead.'

'As what? Your paid whore?' I couldn't stop the words from spilling out of me. 'Or is "mistress" the more acceptable term these days? A little old-fashioned, though, isn't it?'

'There's no shame in it.' His stare was as uncompromising as he was. 'If it means you don't have to work for them, and it solves all the issues of—'

'No,' I said, cutting him off, a sudden anger rising up inside me. Because of course money would be how he viewed this. Payment for intimacy. Payment to have me all to himself. Payment so I could give him what he wanted.

The realisation hit me like a blow to the head, dizzying me. I didn't want to be paid. I didn't want to be paid for what was in my heart. It was precious, it was rare and it was fucking priceless.

I knew what the difference was now, the difference between paid intimacy and intimacy given out of caring. Intimacy given out of love. And you couldn't buy that. That could only be given freely and without expectation.

And maybe that was the fundamental issue. I wanted something in return. All my life I'd given freely—to my mother, to my grandmother, to my clients. And when I became a doctor I'd give freely to my patients. I'd give everything and get nothing back. Nothing to heal the ache in my heart.

The ache that had always been there. The ache that had driven me into working for Strangers, searching for the intimacy I'd always craved yet repeatedly been denied from the people who were supposed to care about me.

I'd been searching in the wrong places, though, and I knew that now. I couldn't get intimacy from the men who paid me, or from Gran, or from my mother. Trajan had given me a taste and I knew where it came from.

It came from love—because that was what this emotion was, wasn't it? The ache in my heart and the longing inside me. It was love. The need to give it and the need to have it returned.

And now I knew what it felt like nothing else would measure up. Nothing else would be good enough. And I wasn't going to settle for not good enough. Not any more.

'No?' he demanded. 'What do you mean, no?'

'I don't want you to pay me. That'll make you my client and I don't want you to be my client.'

'But if it'll solve the problem with your gran and college, then what's the big deal?' He took another step towards me. 'Don't you want this? Don't you want us to spend more time together?'

'Yes, I do,' I said helplessly, because I couldn't lie

about it. 'But you can't pay me for intimacy, Trajan. I don't want you to. I don't want you to be my client and I don't want to feel like I'm your kept whore.'

'That's not what I'm saying.' He reached for me. 'Maggie…'

I stepped away, not wanting him to touch me all of a sudden. Grief gathered in my throat. 'Don't,' I said hoarsely. 'Please don't touch me.'

He went still, searching my face. 'Why? What's so wrong with letting me take care of your money issues?'

I took a little breath. 'There's nothing wrong with it. And, maybe if I was Honey when I'm with you, that would be enough for me. It would certainly be enough for her. But it's not. Because I'm not Honey with you. I'm Maggie.' I took another shuddering breath. 'And Maggie is in love with you.'

Something flickered through his eyes, bright and shining, an intense blue flame. Then abruptly he turned away from me, his jaw rigid, his whole body gone stiff with tension. 'That was never supposed to be part of it.'

'No,' I said as the tendril of hope inside me curled up and died. 'It wasn't. But that's what happened. And I can't be with you, loving you, knowing that you're paying me by the hour.'

He said nothing, frozen in place, looking away at the wall. 'You can ignore it. We can pretend it doesn't exist. It doesn't have to change things between us.'

There was another wrenching ache and my eyes prickled with tears. But I blinked hard, forcing them away. 'You might be able to; you do so well with pretending you're not terrified of what's happening to you, after all. But I can't, Trajan. I can't tell myself this feeling in my heart isn't there, and I don't want to.'

He was silent, rigid and frozen with denial. And my heart contracted with a sudden aching pity. It was the worst thing I could have said, wasn't it? The most terrible crime—to love him. He was a man who valued control in all things and love was the ultimate surrender. The ultimate acceptance, too.

But Trajan hadn't accepted anything and he hadn't surrendered. He thought that by not acknowledging something he had power over it, but now I could see the truth. It was the opposite. His rigidity, his refusal to be vulnerable, had allowed it power over him.

He will never love you.

No. He wouldn't. I could accept that now. It broke my heart but I couldn't change it. I couldn't force it on him either.

This time I was the one who moved, going over to him, raising a hand to caress the smooth surface of his cheek, one last touch of his skin to take with me. 'It's okay,' I said. 'I'm not going to demand things from you that you can't give. Love requires acceptance and surrender, and I don't think you can do either of those things. But I get it. I know why you can't. You're afraid.'

He turned back to me, blue gaze pinning me in place. 'I'm not afraid.'

'Aren't you?' I looked back at him. 'Refusing to let your sight loss impact your life? Telling no one about it? Acting as if you can see just as well as anyone else?'

His face shuttered completely, becoming that blank, expressionless wall. 'That's got nothing to do with anything.'

'I know you think that's not true. It's all connected, Trajan. And this has nothing to do with me, not wanting to be yours, because I do. I can't think of anything I want more. But the problem is, you'll never be mine. You'll never give your heart to anyone, because you don't want to be afraid and you don't want to be vulnerable, and love is both of those things.'

He stepped back from me, as cold and reserved as he'd been the night we first met. 'You're right.' His voice was blank, stripped bare. 'Perhaps it's for the best that you leave, then.'

Of course he wouldn't give in. He was a man who never surrendered.

My heart broke clean through, but I was used to the pain by now.

'Goodbye, Honey,' he said tonelessly.

And then, without another word, he turned and walked out.

CHAPTER TWENTY

Trajan

I WALKED OUT of the kitchen, brushing against the doorway as I did so, then knocking against the table in the hallway that had somehow shifted out of position.

Anger burned in my gut, a formless, furious rage that I didn't know what to do with.

I forced it down, trying to be cold and clear as I staggered down the hallway, heading to the bedroom for reasons that eluded me right now. I just had to get away from her.

Something hit my shoulder, making me stumble, making the anger in my gut burn brighter, hotter.

What the fuck was happening? Had the cleaning staff moved all the furniture?

It's not the furniture, you fucking idiot.

I strode into the bedroom and, even though there was sun everywhere and I could see, I stumbled again, this time against the bed.

An odd panic gripped me and I stood there for a long moment, breathing fast and hard, trying to suppress it. Trying not to see Maggie's lovely face and the sadness in her dark eyes. The regret. The hurt.

It didn't matter. None of it mattered. I'd paid her for the night and now she was going. It didn't matter that she was in love with me either, because I hadn't asked for that. I hadn't wanted it either. I was fine with being alone.

Shit, if she didn't want more time with me then I'd hire another woman instead. There were always plenty of women who'd be more than happy to spend time in my bed.

You don't want another woman.

My heartbeat was loud in my head and I could smell her in the air, the lingering scent of coconut, vanilla and orchids…

I imagined myself in bed with another woman, holding another woman, fucking another woman… but I couldn't. For some reason I couldn't even picture it.

You can pretend that you're not terrified but that doesn't mean the feeling doesn't exist…

Sure it did. Pretending had worked for me for a long time and there was no reason to think it wouldn't work now. Fear was easy to overcome; you just didn't let it in.

Yet I found myself sitting down heavily on the bed, a cold thread of panic winding through me. I didn't want her to be right. I didn't want her in my head. I didn't want this feeling that pulled tight, but no amount of wishing I didn't feel it was going to change anything.

I wanted her. I wanted her desperately. I didn't want her to leave me.

I didn't want to be alone in the fucking dark with no one.

Love requires acceptance and surrender, and I don't think you can do either of those things.

And why the fuck should I? When had acceptance and surrender ever done anything for me? Fear had nearly let Susie die. Fear had made me deny what was happening to me.

And love? Fuck love. Love wasn't acceptance. Love was demanding nothing less than complete perfection, and the moment you were less than perfect, whether it was your own fault or not, that love was withdrawn. My father being a classic case in point.

That's not all love is and you know it.

I sat on the mattress, breathing hard, not wanting to think about this, yet the thoughts wouldn't stop flooding through my head. Memories of the night before when I'd knocked the glass off the counter and Maggie had found out I was blind. How she hadn't ignored it and hadn't pushed me away like my parents had.

No, she'd wanted to get closer. She'd come after me, asking questions and wanting answers. Then, later, she'd let me do everything I'd wanted to do to her in the dark. She'd never pulled away, never withdrawn her trust. No, she'd trusted me even more, her touch and her warmth grounding me in the blackness.

And even before then, before she'd known about my sight, in all those meetings we'd had, she'd simply taken me at face value, not expecting anything, not demanding anything. Giving freely and never asking for anything back…

She hadn't pitied me. She'd just accepted me in a way that even my own parents hadn't. And before, when she'd told me she loved me, she hadn't even asked for anything in return.

How can you treat her the way every other person in her life has treated her? As if she isn't good enough?

My heart gave a sudden, furious thump. She'd been abandoned and dismissed by the two people closest to her—her mother and grandmother. She'd been ignored and bullied by her peers at school. She'd had her intelligence minimised, her generous heart taken advantage of. And yet still she gave to everyone she could. To her grandmother and her mother. To her clients. To the company that employed her.

And to me. She'd given her very heart to me.

And you threw it back in her face.

A wave of heat went through me.

'Love requires acceptance and surrender,' she'd
said. *'And I don't think you can do either of those
things.'*

No, I never had. Because both of those things demanded a loss of control and a giving up of power
that I simply couldn't accept.

And yet, what were my options?

I could accept what she had to give me and surrender to the feeling I had in my own heart that I'd been
ignoring since the day she'd walked into my life.

Or I could let her walk out of it again, leaving me
alone in the dark.

No.

The denial came from deep inside me, so clear
and so strong that I caught my breath.

I couldn't bear the thought of it. I couldn't bear
the thought of not having her. Of being without her
and the difference she made to my life. Because she
did make a difference. She lit up the dark corners of
my soul. And if she could accept me, my blindness,
my control-freak nature and my arrogance and my
anger, how could I do anything less than accept her?

Fuck, I didn't need control. I just needed her.

I got to my feet and left the room, striding down
the hallway, searching. I searched the whole god-
damned penthouse but she wasn't there. While I'd
been sulking in the bedroom, she'd gone.

There was no thought in my mind except to find
her, so I went to the front door and pulled it open,

heading out into the hallway outside. Sunshine flooded through windows down one end, letting me see that it was empty. She'd clearly gone down in the elevator already.

I headed over to it, my hand hitting the button, propelled by a need so deep and so strong I couldn't even begin to find the words for it. It felt as if the elevator were taking years to come, the trip down to the lobby even longer.

I hated the big, echoing space of the lobby. There were always too many people in it during the day and I found it incredibly difficult to navigate. But right now I wasn't even conscious of the crowds or how the noise made it hard to figure out where I was. I was too busy scanning around, trying to catch a glimpse of her red dress in my narrow field of vision.

People cursed as I brushed against them, stumbling over things lying in my path that I hadn't seen, crashing into a set of armchairs near the door. I barely noticed. All I was conscious of was that I couldn't see her in the lobby. She must have already headed outside.

Shit.

My heartbeat hammered. If I wanted to catch her, I was going to have to leave the building. The thought made my mouth go dry, a familiar panic rising inside me, the need to turn round and head back to the safety of my apartment gripping me.

But the fear wasn't as strong as the other emo-

tion aching in my heart. The one that burned hot
and strong, that filled me with purpose. The one that
made me grit my teeth as I prepared to step outside
into the blurry stream of people.

And then someone behind me said, 'Trajan?'

I whirled around.

Red dress. Curly golden hair. Dark eyes. Cheeks
wet with tears.

She was right behind me.

'Maggie.' Her name burst out of me and I was
reaching for her, hauling her into my arms, burying
my face in her hair, closing my eyes and shutting out
the chaos of noise and light and colour, concentrating instead on her silky curls and the sweet scent
of her skin.

She didn't protest or pull away. Her arms wrapped
around me, her body moulding itself against mine as
if she'd been waiting for me all this time.

'I surrender,' I said hoarsely against her neck.
'I surrender, Maggie, sweetheart. I don't care what
happens; I don't care about your clients. I don't care
about having to share you. I'll do anything you want
if you'll stay with me.' It was so hard to get the words
out, so hard to accept them. After so long pretending I didn't need anyone, to admit the fact that I did
felt, even now, as if I was making myself far too
vulnerable.

Ah, but she'd been right about that. Love *was*
being vulnerable, and I hated that.

She stayed silent and gradually I realised that she was leaving a space for me to keep speaking. A space where she could hold my vulnerability close and protect it. Protect me.

Love is acceptance. Love is surrender.

So I accepted my vulnerability. I surrendered to the fear I'd been ignoring for so many years, letting it rise up to choke me. And this time I didn't ignore it. Because this time her arms were around me, holding me tight. Letting me know that I wasn't alone.

'You were right,' I went on in the silence, ignoring the fact that we were in a lobby full of people, because somehow it felt as if we were alone. 'I'm… fucking terrified. I'm terrified of losing what sight I have and I'm terrified of having to do that alone. But, more than either of those two things, I'm terrified of losing you.' I was shaking all of a sudden.

That was it, that was the last of my pride, the last of my armour. I was stripped bare, nothing left. It seemed that, in the end, I was just one of her lonely businessmen after all.

One of her hands moved to the back of my neck and then she ran it down my spine, a gentle, calming pressure. Last night I would have shaken that hand away, too proud to admit that I needed it, wanted it. But now… I felt every muscle in my body begin to relax, the shaking easing.

Still she didn't speak, just stroked my back silently, and I let the warmth of her body and her presence soak into me, seeping into my bones, my every cell, the very fabric of my soul.

An aeon passed, or it might only have been seconds, but finally I raised my head and stared down into her night-dark eyes. 'I'm sorry I walked away.' My voice was as cracked as an old pavement but I didn't care. 'I'm sorry I was such a fucking asshole to you. You were right: acceptance and surrender are difficult things for me, but you already have my surrender. And now you have my acceptance too.'

I took a breath, thinking I would have to force these words too, but as it turned out they were the easiest of all to say. 'My acceptance of the fact that I'm in love with you and have been from the moment you put your hand in mine that first night.'

There were tears on her cheeks, but the expression on her face glowed like the sun. 'What…what made you change your mind?'

I lifted my hands, cupped her face between them and kissed away the tears. 'You did. Your bravery. Your determination. Your acceptance and your surrender. My parents never accepted me the way you did, even before they found out about my sight loss, and so how could I give you anything less? It was a choice, sweetheart. A choice between being alone and being in control or having you. And, well…it wasn't even a choice. I had to have you.'

Her hands pressed against my chest, as if she couldn't get enough of the feel of me. 'So what does this mean?' There was hope in her eyes, and that warmth, that light I'd sensed in her right from the start. It was love; I knew that now. I could see it as clear as day. It was love that was at the very heart of her.

'I don't want to impose or demand anything from you, because I know—'

'No, please demand,' she interrupted huskily. 'I want you to be as demanding as possible, because I like your demands.'

Heat swept through me, and possessiveness, a ragged, raw feeling, and I let it come. I surrendered to it. I accepted it. 'Then what it means is that you're mine. You're mine completely and utterly—and I won't share you, Maggie. The only man you'll ever be with again will be me.'

Her throat moved in a convulsive swallow, her eyes full of fire. 'What else?'

'I insist that your grandmother goes into a care home and that you start doing whatever you need to do to get into med school immediately. I am absolutely going to demand that you become a doctor.' I paused, then added, to make it absolutely clear that what I wanted now was completely different from what I'd offered her just before, 'It's a partnership I want, sweetheart, not a transaction. I'm not paying for a care home or a college degree because I want you in my bed. I'm paying for them because I want to support you. Because you're important to me and I want to share your life and share mine with you.'

Her smile was the sweetest thing I'd ever seen in my entire life. 'I get it, I really do.' Something glinted in her eyes. 'Perhaps, when I get to be a world-renowned specialist, I might even let you have a small weekly allowance. Only if you don't spend it all at once, mind.'

My God. She was fucking delicious.

I kissed her hungrily, loving how she teased me. 'You will also stop working for Strangers,' I insisted, growling it out against her mouth, teasing her back in return. 'You won't have time anyway, since you'll be too busy studying or being in my bed.'

'Mmm. Those are indeed quite the demands.'

I lifted my head. 'But you don't know the most onerous one yet.'

'Oh?' She snuggled closer. 'And what's that?'

I smiled. 'All of the above will be for ever, Maggie.

Her eyes sparkled. 'Really?'

'Oh, yes. In fact, I'm going to have to insist.' I stroked her cheeks gently. 'Though, of course, all the demands in the world are meaningless if you don't want them too.'

'I want them,' she said without hesitation, her voice fierce. 'I want them all.'

'Are you sure? It won't be easy being with me. My sight is not going to get better. I might end up completely blind, and that's going to be hard on any partner I might have.'

'It might.' She lifted a hand and touched my

cheek, and her smile lit up the entire world. 'But then, I've always liked a challenge.'

She was so beautiful. And she was all mine.

'Then take me upstairs, sweetheart,' I said roughly. 'And I'll give you all the challenges you want.'

So she did. And, when we got upstairs, I made good on my promise. Then, much, much later, I made good on every single one of my demands too.

Because, when I was with her, there was no darkness. Love was the one light that never went out.

EPILOGUE

Magdalen

IT WASN'T UNTIL the morning after that I heard Trajan arguing loudly with someone on the phone. 'You fucking bastard!' he said with some feeling. 'What the hell did you do with my sister?'

I shouldn't have found it funny, but I did. Mainly because I'd already discovered that, not only was my best friend Vesta his sister, but that the client she'd taken on in my place was Eli Hart, Trajan's closest friend.

Vee had called me the evening before, after Trajan and I had spent most of the day in bed, to tell me that, not only had her night with the person who was supposed to have been my client gone well, but that he'd turned out to be the man she'd been in love with half her life. And they were now together.

That was my cue to tell her that it seemed that the man *I* was in love with turned out to be her brother. And that he felt the same, and was that okay?

Of course it was okay, and she'd be thrilled to have me as a sister-in-law.

Trajan eventually came round too, especially when he realised how happy his sister and his friend were.

Almost as happy as us.

We found Gran a care home she liked and, even though she was initially reluctant, on one of her visits she made a friend, which turned her reluctance into grudging acceptance. And by the time the last of her possessions had been moved in she'd settled quite happily.

I studied hard—got excellent grades at night school to make up for the schooling I'd missed caring for Gran. And I ended up getting accepted into medical school the following year. I even got a scholarship.

Trajan's sight stabilised and he got over himself, finally learning how to use a cane. At night when we went out, though, he didn't like to bring it. He said it got in the way. It didn't; we both knew he just liked me guiding him, as it gave him an excuse to hold on to me.

He was ridiculously proud of me, and when we got married the following year—not long after Eli and Vesta's first wedding anniversary—he gave the sweetest speech about how amazing I was, and what a wonderful doctor I'd make and how he couldn't believe his luck that he'd ended up marrying the woman of his dreams.

I cried, because I couldn't believe my own luck—that I'd ended up marrying the man of mine.

Because that was who he was—the man of my dreams. Who made me feel safe and special and wanted.

And, most important of all, he made me feel loved.

And that was one well that never ran dry.

* * * * *

GIVE ME MORE

A.C. ARTHUR

MILLS & BOON

CHAPTER ONE

UNPACK. SHOWER. MASTURBATE.

Those were the top three tasks on Grace Hopkins's agenda for her first night in Saint Lucia. She lifted her suitcase onto the bed and opened it, then got straight to business removing clothes she'd folded neatly and stacked inside three days ago.

Her thoughts went to the same replay reel that had been running through her mind for days now, prompting all kinds of memories: Ronald Martin Gold III, thirty-five years old, six feet three inches tall with a bodybuilder physique, rich umber-hued skin, velvety brown eyes, a deep voice that sent a warm tendril down her spine each time she heard it. Of course there was more about the man than that—he was ridiculously rich, heir to a fashion empire, one of the smartest men she'd ever met...and her ex-boyfriend.

She dropped a pile of tank tops and bras into the first dresser drawer and slammed it shut. RJ was going to be at this resort for the next two weeks. They would see each other again for the first time in ten years. To be clear, she'd seen him since their breakup, on television, in magazines and in the framed picture she still kept beneath her bed, which featured him posed in a very rare laid-back position. She'd left that photo back at her apartment in Harlem because it would've been ridiculous to pack it into her suitcase. RJ was no longer her man. In fact, as far as she could tell—even though she wasn't really making it her business—he hadn't been seriously involved with anyone in a very long time. Like since the night she turned down his marriage proposal.

Shaking her head, she walked back to the bed, grabbed more clothes, went to the dresser again and proceeded to open the drawer, dump clothes in, and close it again. She wandered back to her suitcase.

It was going to be fine. These next two weeks were about work, about finessing the final piece of her career goal with the story of a lifetime. A rough outline of the story was on her laptop and as soon as she settled in for the night, she'd pull out the additional notes she'd gathered and put in some work before going to sleep. That was on her list to do after the shower and the— Her hand closed over what was arguably one of her best investments. Just holding the vibrator sent sparks of desire zinging through her body.

She wasn't some horny sex addict. Sex wasn't something she craved or even needed on a regular basis, but when the mood hit she had to soothe it—immediately, or she turned into a cranky nightmare. That was the last thing she needed while she was here. Being around RJ and his family again was going to take all her people skills, smiles and endurance. Her pussy pulsated at that last word as a memory of RJ between her legs, moving as if he owned her body and its pleasure with every stroke, resurfaced.

Her fingers tightened around the wand, which was big and clunkier than some of the newer, more modern versions, but she liked this one. She liked its size and durability, the same traits she'd treasured during the year and a half that RJ was her lover. It didn't occur to her that she was now moving her hand up and down the length of the sex toy as if it were a real dick—*his* dick—until her phone rang.

She grabbed her phone off the bed with her free hand and pressed it to her ear.

"Grace Hopkins."

"Hey, Grace. It's Eddie, just checking in to see how it's going."

She rolled her eyes skyward at the sound of his voice. "Hey, Eddie. I'm just getting settled in at the resort."

"You wouldn't be getting settled in with RJ Gold, by chance? You know, the guy you neglected to tell me you dated." There was no missing the irritation in Eddie's tone or the instant alarm she felt at his words. She'd known it was not only wrong to leave out her past connection to RJ, but it was also highly unethical for her to even consider writing this story because of that connection. But she desperately wanted Eddie to accept her pitch and to tell this story.

"It was a very long time ago. We haven't seen or spoken to each other in ten years." She frowned, knowing he wasn't going to let that thin excuse stand.

"Don't give me that crap!" Eddie had a reputation as a yeller with a keen eye for detail. Right now, he was giving Grace her first taste of both. "You came to me pitching a story about the feud between Ron Gold and Tobias King. You said there was dirt there and you could dig it up, put it in black and white, and expose the dominating duo for their sordid backgrounds amid the impeccable designs that made them the best in the fashion industry. You said this was going to be the scoop that all fashion magazines, digital and print, wanted and would boost our print circulation. What you didn't say was that you'd be cuddling up with your ex at the same time!"

Grace was certain Eddie had taken her story pitch way out of context, but she wouldn't risk telling him that at the moment. The feud between RJ's father, Ron Gold, CEO and lead designer at RGFashions, and Tobias King, owner and designer at King Designs, was nothing new. It had been going on for more than thirty years and began with the two men working at RGF when Ron's father was still alive. Ron and Tobias grew up attending private schools and then college together, carrying their friendship into the fashion industry while being groomed by Ron's father. Then one day, that was over. Tobias left RGF and started King Designs. Before Tobias's first runway show, news surfaced that Ron had accused Tobias of stealing RGF designs to open his own fashion house. After his initial denial, Tobias never spoke of the design debacle again, until earlier this year when a similar situation occurred, only this time it was found to be true.

As Eddie continued to grumble, Grace thought back to the most recent development in the Gold/King feud.

A disgruntled designer from King Designs, Lenzo Fuchetti, coerced a receptionist from RGF to steal a design for a couture wedding gown. Once pictures of the King Designs gown were featured in a tabloid alongside RGF's gown with the headline accusing Ron Gold of stealing, Tobias and Ron went to the police to request a full investigation. When that was complete Tobias was the first to submit a public apology to Ron. Since that was also the time the men learned that Tobias's nephew Chaz was dating Ron's daughter, Riley, the two men decided it was time for the feud to end.

Grace wasn't convinced that was the whole story or that these two families were actually burying the hatchet they'd been swinging at each other for so long. Which was why she'd gone to Eddie with the idea for this in-depth exposé. Now Eddie knew she had a personal connection to the story as well, having dated Ron Gold's son. There was no need for her to ask how he'd found out. News was Eddie's business and the *Daily Gazette*, where he was editor in chief, had a big entertainment section. The Golds and figures in fashion often appeared there.

"Look, you're right I should've told you about being involved with RJ, regardless of how long ago it was. But I promise you I can be unbiased. I can get this story and the boost in your circulation, Eddie. And when I do, you're going to return the favor by giving me a byline and a permanent column because I'm a great investigative reporter and you know it." She'd graduated from the Columbia School of Journalism and had built her career so far writing freelance. It was all that mattered to her. She already had a couple interviews lined up for this story, and coming here to the island where Riley Gold was about to get married would put her in close proximity with all the players.

His frustrated huff was loud and he mumbled a few curses before continuing. "Hell, I don't even remember who I was sleeping with ten years ago, so I guess that could be considered a long time. But you listen here, if I let this slide and you stay on this story, I don't want a watered-down version of what Ron Gold's been peddling to the media for the last thirty years. I want the truth mixed with some juicy scandal. You think your boyfriend's going to give you that scoop?"

"First, he's not my boyfriend…anymore. RJ and I are incredibly old news and besides that, this is business. I'm dedicated to my career, just as RJ's dedicated to his. He'll respect that I have a job to do." At least that's how she hoped it would go down. For the past few days, thoughts of how RJ would react to seeing her after all this time had been mingling with memories of the deeply emotional relationship they'd shared. A relationship she'd walked away from and promised herself to never look back on—until now.

"Yeah, those are some nice words you're shooting me. Just like that pitch you sent me a couple weeks ago. But I need more. You've got twenty days to deliver that story or I'll make sure no syndication ever takes a pitch from you again. Got it?"

"Got it," she replied through clenched teeth, and disconnected the call.

How dare he speak to her that way? She wasn't some newbie in the field of journalism. She'd been building her portfolio with stories in a variety of industries, on blogs and in magazines, and she'd even done a review in the *New York Times* two years ago.

Of course, her name had been buried at the end of the article with more credit going to the new cosmetics product she'd been endorsing, but it was still a shining moment in her portfolio.

This story was going to be her crowning glory. Yes, the moment she'd thought of it, she'd immediately recognized the conflict of having once been involved with RJ. But what better way to prove how much she'd grown as a journalist than to write a story that she was close to, with integrity and honesty. This story was going to get her permanently on the staff at the *Daily Gazette* and she'd finally have proof that her career as a journalist was just as real and noteworthy as her sisters' careers as concert pianist, psychologist and obstetrician. Eddie Kane and his threats weren't going to throw her off track. To solidify that statement, Grace tossed the phone toward the bed but heard it roll across the floor.

Wait, roll?

A quick glance toward the sound had her looking back at the phone still in her hand. "Dammit!" She dropped the phone and hurried toward the vibrator on the move, hoping to get to it before it passed through the patio doors she'd opened upon first entering the room.

She chased it, another curse about to pass her lips, when to her horror the stupid thing picked up speed and eased under the railing, right over the edge of the balcony. "Great," she muttered. "Just great!"

Stomping back into the room, she grabbed the key card off the dresser, stuffed it into the back pocket of her denim shorts and yanked open the door. It was nearing eleven at night, but the last thing she wanted was for someone to come across her vibrator on the sidewalk first thing tomorrow morning.

The Marina Bay was a gorgeous luxury resort perched on a hilltop. The views would be stunning in the daylight. As it was getting late, there weren't many people out, at least not in the part of the resort where her room was located. The penthouses, suites and private villas were on the other side of the hill. Regular rooms for people uninterested or unable to cough up five-hundred-plus dollars per night were in the two buildings on her side.

She stepped outside. The tropical air mixed with the light scent of chlorine, as she'd noticed when she'd opened her balcony doors earlier. She suspected her room faced one of the resort's many outdoor pools. Cursing because she should've brought her phone so she could use the flashlight, but she headed towards where she thought the vibrator might've fallen. Stone pavers created a walkway amid plush green grass, and she inhaled deeply as she continued to move about in the dark.

The balmy evening breeze was soothing and the island scent was comforting. If only she were in her room, showered after her travels and lying on the queen-size bed. But no, her first night on the island couldn't go that well. Instead, she was walking around, dragging her feet over the grass and keeping her gaze down in search of her trusty sex toy.

"Ha! Maybe that's the story I should be writing. 'Woman on a twilight search for runaway vibrator.'"

And now she was talking to herself!

Wow. Grace hoped the rest of her trip turned out better than this.

Insomnia was his worst enemy and it apparently planned to stalk him even while he was on this forced vacation. RJ walked with assured steps. He pulled his phone out of the side pocket of the sweatpants he'd slipped on and made his way downstairs to explore the resort.

The brochure boasted five sections of Marina Bay, all situated amid the tropical hills of the very scenic Saint Lucia. He had to give it to Riley and Chaz—they'd definitely picked a gorgeous place to get married. It was also a great spot to insist their family spend the two weeks leading up to their wedding together. RJ had one of the many private villas at the top of the hills. The view from every angle of the space was nothing less than spectacular. Room service was phenomenal, and the bed was just the right amount of soft and firm. So why the hell wasn't he tucked into it drifting into a blissful slumber?

Because he rarely ever slept. If he was sleeping, he wasn't working and if he wasn't working, things weren't getting done. It was a simple enough equation.

Tonight, he was walking instead of sleeping, checking emails and trying like hell to push thoughts of couples, love and wedding vows to the furthest corner of his mind. As his sister had put it last week, when she'd been in his office giving him more information than he needed to know about her wedding, "love is in the air." Frowning, he swiped his thumb over his phone with a little more force than was necessary.

There was to be no working for the next fourteen days—that decree had come directly from his mother. RJ loved Marva Gold with every breath in his body, but he had no intention of totally refraining from work. Six months ago, Riley and Chaz had agreed to allow certain aspects of their wedding planning to be available for the media as part of their continuing marketing plan for the Golden Bride collection. So far, sales had been on an upswing as a result of two Gold siblings' weddings—Riley's and their brother Major's. Major had been first when he'd married Nina Fuller. The head of RGF's marketing department, Desta Henner, had created an ingenious strategy to plan a fake engagement to boost sales—and it had led to Nina and Major's actual wedding. Desta would be planning her own wedding soon. She was engaged to RJ's other brother, Maurice, after a ski trip last winter had brought them closer together. That left all his siblings paired up, and RGF sales—which was his department—shattering records during wedding season. A smile ghosted his lips as he silently congratulated his siblings on a job well done. Though he accepted that their newfound happiness had increased his workload.

As for him, the solitary life worked just fine. A fact that was helpful tonight as he continued walking along the property, lifting his gaze up from his phone every few seconds so he wouldn't trip and fall on his face. That or be scared by something going bump in the night. Another smile formed as he glanced at the time on his phone. Just after eleven and here he was—a relatively good-looking man—opting to entertain himself with a walk instead of cuddling in bed with a nice warm body, as all his siblings undoubtedly were.

He didn't even want to think about why his choice to remain single had begun to bother him lately. It was a decision he'd had to make, to protect not only his heart, but also his sanity. For the life of him, he still didn't understand how the one relationship he'd once cherished had gone so horribly wrong.

The pinging notification sound pulled him from his thoughts, and he watched as two new emails from reporters appeared. They were each looking for any family member who'd tell them the location and date of the wedding, or at the very least provide a Zoom link so they could offer their readership first-look snapshots. The answer was a resounding no, as he, his staff and his relatives had stated so many times before. While Riley and Chaz had given the media access to some of their wedding plans as part of RGF's ongoing marketing campaign, the wedding date and location was private. He deleted the emails. Seconds later, he nearly lost his footing as something rolled beneath his feet.

"Oh, no! Dammit!"

RJ heard the woman's voice but he was too busy trying to regain his balance to really look at her. She'd bent down and scooped something up from the ground—the object that had almost led to him busting his ass.

"I'm so sorry. That was my fault. I apologize," she continued, pushing her arms behind her back.

Shaking his head now, trying to hold on to all the curse words running rampant through his mind, he glared at her instead. "What the hell is th—" The rest of his words died in his throat as he stared into familiar whiskey-brown eyes.

He tried blinking repeatedly, hoping that when he focused his gaze again, he'd be mistaken, but that hadn't worked. Now the air froze in his lungs, causing his chest to constrict, and one strangled word tumbled from his lips. "Grace?"

She took a step back, her mouth opening slightly, then closing without a word. That's how they stood for the next…he didn't even know how many seconds had passed, and he didn't dare speak again. As if she'd figured that out, she cleared her throat and finally spoke. "Hello, RJ."

No, this couldn't be. Was he sleepwalking? Hadn't he just thought about his past relationship? Yes, and he'd pushed that memory way back to the place he'd buried it for the last ten years. Only now, it was right here, just a couple feet away from him.

Grace Hopkins. *His* Grace.

The first and only woman he'd ever loved, the woman he'd wanted to spend the rest of his life with. Dragging a hand down his face, RJ shook his head as if that were going to clear all this away. She was still standing there wearing very short shorts that showed off the rich mocha complexion of her long, gorgeous legs. A white T-shirt fit perfectly against the curve of her breasts and a gold heart pendant dangling from a choker necklace brushed over the hollow of her throat.

"It's good to see you again," she said when it seemed she might be the only one capable of speaking at this time.

Memories tangled and fought inside his mind. Grace had been his everything. She was the first and only woman to claim his heart. A heart she'd held so tightly in the palm of her hand that she'd been able to crush it with one, simple word—*no*. Muted pain rested in the center of his chest.

He hadn't seen her since that awful night years ago, but now she was here. It was Grace's voice he heard, her smile he saw as her lips tilted slowly. She eased an arm from behind her back to wave her hand at him as if they were long-lost friends. He didn't know what to say or do, which was uncharacteristically strange for him. Trying to get his mind right and act like he had some semblance of brain function, he gripped his phone tightly in one hand and nodded.

"What are you doing wandering around out here in the dark?" It wasn't the most pressing question at the moment, but he was still working up the nerve to ask the other one.

She shrugged, shifting her weight from one foot to the next, and dropped her arms to her side. "Going for a walk, which actually seems like the same thing you were doing." He should've expected the quick and snappy response. It was her signature and matched her ambitious and flirtatious personality perfectly. She loved to talk. Where some women might like cuddling after sex, Grace had been a talker. Those were the nights he'd learned so much about her. Unfortunately, the one time he'd needed her to be chatty, she'd clammed up and walked away from him for what he thought was going to be forever.

He had to ask her. It made the most sense that this next question come, he just didn't know how he was going to feel about her answer. "It's been a long time." He dodged the bullet again.

"Yeah. It has."

"You look…um…you look—" He noticed something else that made this entire scenario stranger. "Is that a vibrator?"

CHAPTER TWO

GRACE DID THE exact opposite of what he expected. She lifted her arms, extending them in front of her so the vibrator—he now had no doubt of what it was—was pointing directly at him. "This? Um, yeah. It is. But it's not what you think," she said in an obviously flustered tone.

This night couldn't possibly get any more confusing. Not only was he standing there staring at the woman who'd turned down his wedding proposal, but that woman was also holding a vibrator in a way that had his dick pulsing with need. If he weren't suffering from mild shock and experiencing a steady buzz of arousal, he might've laughed.

"Did you find that out here?" If she had, he was going to have some strong words for the management at Marina Bay.

"No." She huffed, this time reaching her free hand up to tuck strands of hair behind her ear. "Like I said, it's not what you think."

"What exactly do you think I think?" Every question he asked caused some level of anxiety because he wasn't sure if he really wanted to know the answer.

She tilted her head, giving him a knowing look. "That I'm out here looking for pleasure."

He lifted a brow in question, and he had to shift his stance a bit when his dick jumped at that salacious thought, but he wasn't going to state the obvious. "You're out here holding a vibrator." Okay, he'd just stated the obvious. "Is it yours? How'd it get out here?" *And can I please watch you use it?* Those words floated dangerously in the forefront of his mind.

"No. I mean, yes." She paused, shook her head and huffed again. "It is mine. It rolled off my balcony and I had to come get it."

Her arm moved as she spoke, and he was barely able to focus on her words because he was staring at that toy and the way her nipples were now pressing against the material of her T-shirt. "So you were gonna use the vibrator in your room, but somehow it rolled off your balcony. I stepped on it and almost busted my ass, now you're standing here holding it like—"

Like she was giving it a hand job, which made him uncharacteristically jealous.

"Yes," she replied, and squared her shoulders as if trying to find some semblance of control in this very awkward situation. She licked her lips and RJ couldn't help it—he groaned.

Her eyes widened and dammit, she licked her lips again. At least this time she figured out the error of her ways and dropped her gaze from him, looking down at the vibrator again. With a shake of her head she folded her arms across her chest. Now he could only see the globular top of the sex toy tucked between the warmth of her arms.

He swallowed, hard, and then cleared his throat.

"This is a crazy way for us to meet again." Her chuckle sounded nervous, but Grace was the most courageous woman he'd ever known. "It's good to see you."

It was great to see her, too. He hadn't realized how much he'd missed looking into her eyes until right this moment. When they lived together he'd spent his days at work looking forward to walking through the door into his penthouse and seeing her sitting at her desk typing, or lounging on the couch watching one of her favorite sitcoms, laughing heartily at some line she'd heard a billion times before.

"Yes. It's really nice to see you, too." After all this time…and after she walked out on him. He sighed. It was time to stop letting confusion rule this conversation. "Strange that we grew up in the same city, lived together for a year and now we're running into each other here, when we've managed not to see each other for the last ten years."

The memory of her walking away from him in that crowded restaurant was still so fresh in his mind. He gritted his teeth to keep the pain and irritation at bay. It annoyed him how quickly he could flip from heartwarming memories of their time together to simmering rage for the gaping hole she'd left in his heart.

She nodded. "You're right. It's been that long. And I'm still living in New York."

"Yet we haven't seen each other until now." He knew he was repeating himself. It was hard not to. He was still grappling with everything that had happened in the past few minutes.

"Well, that's not actually by chance." She cleared her throat and shifted so that her arms moved a little. The action pushed her breasts up higher and his throat tightened.

"What do you mean?" It occurred to him then that Grace was a journalist. "Did you find out from one of your colleagues in the press that we were here?" Although, no one in the media was supposed to have that information.

"Not exactly. I'm writing a story and when I reached out for an interview, I was told you'd be here."

Damn, this night just kept getting better. Standing a few feet away from his ex, who was still gripping a vibrator, wasn't going to be the worst part of this night. He could feel it in the lump that had just formed in the pit of his stomach. "You're writing a story about what or who? And who exactly told you I was here?"

"Well, not you, specifically." She tilted her head again, and strands of her hair brushed along the line of her neck, touching that soft spot just above her collarbone he used to love kissing. The jolt to his already burning desire wasn't enough to keep his mind from churning over each word she was saying.

"Why don't you just tell me *specifically* what you're talking about?" Even though he had a sinking suspicion he wasn't going to like it.

She dropped her arms to her sides and lifted her chin. This time his gaze focused on hers.

"I'm writing a story about the fashion house rivalry between RGF and King Designs." His fingers fisted the moment she named his company. "More precisely, it's a story about Ron Gold and Tobias King. I have an interview with Veronica King. She's the one who told me this is where I could find the entire family in one place. To make it easier to speak to everyone integrally involved in the feud."

RJ's nostrils flared and the temper he was typically good at holding at bay was on the brink of implosion. "Are you serious? Why would Veronica tell you we're here? She knows Chaz and Riley wanted the location of their wedding kept secret." She couldn't really mean what she'd just said. Of all the people in this world, Grace knew how he felt about the feud, and she knew how protective he was of his family. This had to be a cruel joke, like the manner in which they'd reunited.

"I'm very serious about this and I don't know why Veronica gave me the information instead of just granting me an interview back in New York. And listen, before you go off about this, I'm the best person to write this story and you know it. I know you and your family, and I—"

"You," he said in a tone that was deathly calm, but as lethal as he'd ever sounded in his life, "will go back to your room, pack your stuff and get the hell off this island. And there will be no story. I'll see to that."

If he had to burn down whichever newspaper, magazine or other outlet had authorized it, he would do just that. Nobody was going to write about his family's past for purposes of embarrassing or exploiting them in the media. Especially not the woman he used to love.

It was RJ's turn to walk away from her, and he'd turned so fast, Grace almost let him go without saying another word.

"I'm not leaving," she said before he could get too far away.

When he stopped, she knew this conversation was about to go as badly as was possible. RJ was not a man who took no for an answer, not easily, anyway.

Even though he'd surprised her when he'd let her walk out of that restaurant ten years ago and never tried to contact her again. She told herself it wouldn't have changed anything if he had come after her; she'd made up her mind, but for a while the realization that he hadn't even tried had stung. She'd gotten over that, just like she'd gotten over him.

His shoulders were broad and looked strong in the tight-fitted shirt he now wore. His sweatpants, hanging low on his waist, had done nothing to cover the semi-erection she'd glimpsed before he turned away. It had her mind wandering to all the passionate nights she'd spent in his arms.

"This is my job, RJ, and it's an important story, one that needs to be told." He didn't move, so she couldn't see his face, but it didn't matter—she'd never forget how he looked. His head was bald now, a new look from the last time she'd seen his photo in the media, but he still had the goatee, neatly maintained as always. He also still had thicker and fuller eyebrows than she could ever hope for, and his eyes were the deepest pools of dark brown she'd ever seen. Despite being an excellent swimmer, this was a place she'd drowned more times than she could count. She'd stared into RJ's eyes on so many occasions, and into his heart. Those glimpses had made her fall in love with him in the first place, that rare access he'd given her to the man beneath the gruff exterior.

Why that thought made her chest ache now, she didn't want to explore, so she continued, "What happened between Ron and Tobias set the stage for what the fashion industry is experiencing now for the first time. An intense rivalry and professional face-off between the top two designers in the game. The top two *Black* designers. You know that's groundbreaking."

"No!" he yelled, turning around, and she almost jumped back. It was exceedingly rare to see RJ this angry. He took his reputation and that of his family very seriously, so he always tried to maintain decorum, regardless of the situation. "That's my family and you know I don't tolerate any bullshit when it comes to them."

"This is my career" was her firm and resounding retort. He wasn't the only one who could be passionate about something. "Writing this story will give me the chance at a byline. I've worked extremely hard for this, and I'm not going to let you stop me from achieving it." The same way she hadn't let his marriage proposal deter her from going after her goals. It just wasn't in her to back down, even though watching him look at her with disdain in his eyes was breaking something deep inside her.

He closed the space between them quickly, and she momentarily considered stepping back. But no, if RJ wanted to go toe-to-toe with her that's what they'd do. She had just as much to lose here as he thought he did.

"That feud has been blown out of proportion for years and it's none of anybody's business how or why it started."

"It's everyone's business if it became a blueprint for their success. Don't you see that? What Ron and Tobias have done is historic and without that feud propelling the competitive edge that's formed two fashion empires, it might never have happened. You can't deny that."

"I can't condone anyone profiting from it and I'll never consent to my family's name being dragged through the mud." He clamped his lips down tight and gave her a stony expression. "How can you do this? You know my family. I thought you cared about them. You were so close to them at one time."

Oh no, he was not going to guilt her. Becoming part of his family back then had been easy and heartwarming. Knowing she'd been leaving them the night she walked away from RJ had been crushing. "Don't insult me like that. I did care about your family, and you—although now I'm wondering why, considering you're acting like a domineering brute right now."

He looked at her incredulously. "I'm acting like a man who's been blindsided. Again."

This was turning out to be more difficult than she'd thought. She knew reuniting here and under these circumstances wasn't going to be simple for either of them, but she had hoped for cordial and with the least amount of emotional impact as possible. That may have been too optimistic.

"You're acting like a guy not used to getting his way." And that wasn't as easy to say as it should've been. She didn't want this to be about their past, but there really was no way of doing this without walking that path. "If you're still angry with me about the proposal, that's one thing. But don't try to stand in the way of my career as retaliation."

He came even closer, his gaze following the strands of hair resting on her shoulder. Her body was a traitorous trickster, immediately forgetting the anger and instead letting the sneaky tendrils of need ease down her spine. She didn't want to yearn for RJ again, not for one second. But there was no denying the attraction was still there between them, as strong as ever. How was she supposed to get this job done if all he had to do was look at her and her mind filled with memories of how great things had been with him?

When his eyes moved from her hair to her lips, she sucked in a breath. Her breasts ached with need for him to touch them and her fingers tightened around the vibrator she still held. The memory of how she'd planned to use it was still fresh in her mind.

"You shouldn't have based your climb to success on my family." His gaze dropped and he stepped away before her mind could register that he was no longer near her. Unfortunately, her body had gotten the message and protested the loss of warmth with a shiver that made her teeth chatter. Before he turned to leave, he said, "You'd better come up with a plan B for your career, Grace, because I'm going to kill this story."

CHAPTER THREE ·

WELP, THE VIBRATOR was done.

She dropped it—along with her optimism about a polite reunion with RJ—into the trash can the moment she returned to her room. The base where the batteries were inserted was cracked—maybe from RJ stepping on it—so that the batteries wouldn't stay in. After closing the patio doors with a thud, she moved through the space, yanking off her clothes and tossing them into the bag she'd designated for her dirty laundry. It wasn't the patio's fault. It was Eddie's fault for calling her with that nonsense about her ability to write an unbiased story. Of course she could—that's precisely what she'd been doing her entire career. The audacity of him to think that just because she'd slept with RJ ten years ago…

Damn, even the thought of that man being inside her induced a reaction from her body. A flush of warmth spread throughout her as she recalled watching his eyes go dark while staring at the vibrator in her hand. She'd tried to convince herself it was the obvious erotic mood created by the presence of a sex toy, but the moment he'd stepped close to her, she'd known that was just an excuse. There'd never been another man who sparked the intense and immediate physical response in her that RJ did. It had been foolish to believe that the years they were separated might've proved that statement false.

Just as foolish as thinking that because she'd convinced herself she'd done the right thing by refusing to marry him, the deep emotion she'd felt for him would somehow vanish, the way she had from his life. She didn't call it love anymore; she couldn't. It wouldn't make sense for her to still be in love with the man she knew she couldn't have. Her career had to come first. She'd needed to become Grace Hopkins the journalist before she could ever accept being Grace Hopkins Gold, a member of the fabulous Gold family. RJ was an all-in kind of guy, and family was extremely important to him. She knew not only from witnessing him with his parents and siblings, but also because of the talks they'd had in the wee hours of the morning about the future home and family they'd create. Things Grace knew she wanted at some point in her life, just not when RJ had proposed. His proposal wasn't a total surprise to her, and it hadn't been totally unwanted. The timing had just been off. But she'd been sure that wasn't what RJ wanted to hear. His career had been decided and approved by his family; there was never any struggle to find his place. For her, it was the opposite, and he wouldn't have understood if she'd tried to offer her explanation. Now they were here.

The odds of RJ being out for a walk at the same time she was were phenomenally low, yet that scenario had played out like an episode of one of her favorite old shows, *Sex and the City*. Shaking her head, she entered the bathroom and immediately turned on the shower, then adjusted the water to lukewarm. For a brief moment earlier, when he'd moved closer to her, she'd thought RJ was going to kiss her. Would she have let him? After all this time? The mere thought had her sighing with pent-up need. What was it about his lips that used to make kissing him feel like she was being turned inside out? Was it the thickness of them, the way they could be soft and gentle one moment, hungry and persistent the next? No, it had to be a combination of skill and intention. RJ was intentionally sexy as hell, smooth in a dominating sort of way, and mouthwateringly handsome.

And she was out of her everlasting mind for thinking of him along these lines again. They were never getting back together. Ever. She'd made sure of that when she'd left him and tried her best to forget about him over the years. Of course, forgetting him completely hadn't worked, but she'd finally gotten to a point where she was at least comfortable with knowing he'd always have a place in her heart. As for

RJ, he wasn't a man who moved backward—he'd surely locked her and the life they once had firmly in his past.

She went back to the room and grabbed her toiletry bag, then returned to the bathroom to put her shampoo, conditioner and other personal items on the large built-in shelf inside the shower. The stall was huge, or at least it was bigger than the one in her apartment. In fact, the bathroom itself was bigger than two rooms of her apartment put together. She may have been staying in what they deemed the "regular" rooms at Marina Bay, but there was nothing regular about this bathroom. There was as much marble in here as was in the lobby at the only five-star hotel she'd ever visited in Manhattan. Dual vanities beneath a large mirror, freestanding tub, plush white towels in several locations so she wouldn't have to run around trying to find one. Rectangular light fixtures hung from silver cords in the ceiling, which matched all the chrome fittings throughout the space. It was elegant and lavish and exactly the type of place where the Golds would hold a wedding.

With a soft sigh, she opened the glass door again and stepped inside. Okay, there were two showerheads in here, one at the ceiling with dual recessed lighting and one on the wall in the usual spot. There was enough space in here for her to have at least four friends over and, thank all the deities, there was also a bench. After washing her body and hair she was tempted to get out and fall onto the bed—to possibly cry over the disaster the night had been—but thoughts of RJ held her still.

He used to love washing her, dragging the soapy loofah over her skin in movements so slow and decadent she thought she'd died and gone to the best spa in heaven. His big hands could provide such a gentle and soothing touch, and the way he stared at her while he was doing it… She sighed and dragged her tongue slowly across her bottom lip. The water was getting cool so she turned the nozzle until more hot water pounded against her skin. Lifting her face to the spray until it cascaded over her, she moaned at the warmth flooding her.

RJ always washed every other part of her body before easing his hands between her legs. On a ragged moan she resisted the urge to push her hands in that direction. Instead she reached up and grabbed the handheld showerhead from its base on the wall. Lifting her leg, she placed one foot on the bench and edged the shower head down between her thighs, letting the warm spray of water pelt her there.

A soft sigh slipped free at how good the water felt on her sensitive skin, and she let her head fall back, eyes closing. She recalled the many times RJ had rinsed her body free of all soap, moving his hands over her slick skin. His complexion was just a shade or two darker than hers, their melanin always shining bright in pictures they took, leaving her with snapshots of the Black love they celebrated so freely. She missed him.

She put her leg down and turned so she could sit on the bench, then leaned back against the marble wall, lifting the showerhead to her breasts now. She missed everything about RJ, from his tongue on her nipples to the way his thick fingers pushed possessively inside her pussy. Both her legs came up this time, feet planted on the bench as she let her knees fall to the side. With one hand she aimed the showerhead at her clit; with the other she pressed a finger to the same tightened bud and began to rub.

She moaned loudly, the sound echoing throughout the stall as she worked herself into a fevered frenzy. He'd looked good tonight, even in simple sweats and a T-shirt. His arms were still strong and muscled, and his thighs—damn that man had thick, sexy thighs and those sweatpants did nothing to hide that fact. Something else the pants didn't hide was the impression of what she knew was a long, heavy dick. On that memory she slid her fingers over the slick flesh of her pussy, easing two into her opening. Crying out with the pleasure, she then bit down gently on her bottom lip and began to pump her fingers inside while the hot water rained down over her skin.

RJ used to go so deep inside her she felt like they were connected. And that's exactly what he'd whisper to her: "You're a part of me now." Over and over

he'd say those words, and she'd believed them. She'd
wanted to be a part of him, a part of the love that had
blossomed so wildly between them. She'd wanted it
all. Until it became clear that she couldn't have it.

With that last thought her fingers moved faster,
pressing her body to find the release she needed so
desperately. Circling her hips, she matched her own
rhythm, chest heaving, breasts jiggling with the motion. Water still rained down from the showerhead
in the ceiling, pelting the floor of the shower like
background music to this personal seduction. Her
body tingled as pleasure surged through every crevice, edging her closer to the precipice. Sliding her
fingers out of her opening, she went back to working her clit, circling it frantically, panting, waiting,
wanting, needing this release like she needed to live.
When her climax came it was strong, seizing her entire body and snatching her breath for the seconds it
took for her to fall.

Moments later she was sated, tired, pissed about
her broken vibrator and still totally confused as to
what her next steps with RJ would be.

The first thing RJ did upon returning to his suite
was boot up his laptop and search: *Grace Hopkins,
journalist, New York*. He'd tried not to keep close
tabs on her over the years, figuring it was counterproductive to continue longing for a woman who
didn't want him. Now, since that woman had decided

to step back into his—or rather, his family's life—he wanted to know everything.

Pictures of her appeared on the screen and he sat back in the chair rubbing a finger over his chin. She was still fine as ever. Her skin was like the smoothest chocolate covering her svelte body, with curvy hips and more than ample breasts. She'd always worn her hair long, and tonight it had hung in waves past her shoulders. Her breasts had looked amazing in the tight T-shirt, nipples so hard he'd wanted desperately to rub his fingers over them. He licked his lips, knowing he'd never get that image of her looking so damn alluring out of his head. From the laptop screen her whiskey-brown eyes stared back at him, tauntingly, seductively. One hand curled into a fist while the other fingers continued to worry over the hair on his chin.

High cheekbones, slender nose, plump lips. Need pulsated through his body like a sickness, and he furrowed his brow. Closing his eyes, he hoped for more restrained thoughts. He had to think about this clearly, to see beyond the face he'd once thought he would look at every day of his life. But with his eyes closed, memories of her laugh—the light giggle that inevitably morphed into a throaty chuckle—made him want to repeat whatever he used to do to bring it out, again and again. The way her hair always tickled his face and chest when she leaned over while riding him. The straightness of her back and the way her glasses slid down on her nose whenever she was sitting at her desk typing on her computer. How she chewed spoonfuls of Raisin Bran as if it were the best cereal in the world—which it was not. Her scent, soft and sweet like honey. The feel of her fingers as she massaged his shoulders after a long day at the office.

"Dammit!" His eyes shot open and he pounded his fists on the desk, shaking the laptop. Why'd she have to come back, and why now of all times?

He released his fingers, put them over the keyboard and began scrolling through articles she'd written. There were pictures of her at charity functions, one with the ASPCA. She'd always had a soft spot for dogs but had said she wanted a house in the suburbs with a large yard and kids before owning one. Hadn't he tried to give her that house, kids and a dog? Anything. He would've given her anything she wanted as long as he could go home to her every night and wake up beside her each morning.

Apparently, she hadn't wanted those things with him. It'd felt as if she'd ripped his heart from his chest and carried it out the door as she'd left the restaurant that night. The velvet blue Tiffany box open with a Soleste cushion-cut diamond engagement ring had sparkled up at him from the table where she'd left it. He didn't recall how long he'd sat there—twenty, forty, another sixty minutes, perhaps. He'd been unable to move, every part of his body shocked into stillness, covered in embarrassment. Eventually he'd left and taken the ring with him, carrying it home to his penthouse in Manhattan and throwing it across the room. Anger, heartbreak, betrayal all soared through his body that night and in the days that followed. Major said he'd been as mean as a rattlesnake for the following month. His mother had been a little easier with her words, declaring him sullen and temporarily displaced. He'd just wanted to break something, anything, everything in his house for starters. Everything Grace touched, from the door handles to the pots in the kitchen. On a rage one night he'd ripped the sheets from his bed and tossed out every set he had, only to have to go through the annoying task of ordering new ones the next day. But eventually, he'd gotten over her.

At least he'd thought he had.

Staring at her on the screen now, seeing the accolades she'd garnered over the years, he noted her smile, the flecks of deep amber in her eyes, that little scar on her chin where she'd fallen down the steps at eight while trying to be a majorette.

She shouldn't be here, and she definitely shouldn't be writing about his family. Dragging his hands down his face now, he wondered what to do. How could he handle this so that no one in his family had to know what was going on? Bringing up this feud now, days before Riley and Chaz's marriage, would ruin everything. His sister had fought long and hard for her happiness, and Chaz was the one for her. Ron and Tobias had put that grudge to rest, deciding that their children—Tobias had raised Chaz after his sister died in a car accident—deserved to be happy and unhampered by mistakes of the past. It had been a valiant stance for both men to take, and RJ had been extremely proud of his father for giving Riley his blessing. Not that Riley needed it—she was going to be with Chaz whether or not anyone in either family approved. RJ loved his sister's tenacity.

He loved his family, period. His parents would celebrate their thirty-sixth wedding anniversary in four months. His father was retiring and the new plaque on RJ's office door would soon read Ronald Gold III, Chief Executive Officer. The position he'd been groomed for his entire life was in arm's reach, and he was eager to step into the big, impressive shoes his father would be leaving.

What he wasn't about to do was let Grace and whatever words she planned to write hurt them. If that meant he had to go head-to-head with the woman who'd crushed his heart and made it impossible for him to ever love again, then so be it. First thing tomorrow morning he was going to find Grace Hopkins and send her on her way. If she protested—which she would because Grace was as ambitious and ruthless as him when it came to her career—then he'd resort to other measures. Pulling up his email, he started a message to his assistant instructing her to find out who Grace was working for and whom she'd already contacted within the fashion industry in the last few weeks. He wanted to know everything she'd done in the last decade, everywhere she'd been, every guy she'd been with…gritting his teeth, he took that last part back. He didn't need to know who Grace had been involved with. Even ten years later, his heart couldn't take that pain.

CHAPTER FOUR

RJ AWOKE THE next morning to thoughts of Grace. Aside from the obvious physical attraction—as noted by the semi-erection he'd returned to his hotel room with last night—memories circled in his mind. After dating for a year and a half, RJ had weighed all his options, he'd listed the pros and cons, and considered every possible factor of proposing to Grace, except the one where her answer was no. They were in love, of that he'd never had a moment's doubt. Nine months after their first date, they'd moved in together. He knew everything about her, and she knew everything about him. They meshed well with the other's family. Everything was in sync, and yet she'd still walked away without explanation.

To be fair, he hadn't asked for one. Not that night or any time after. If she could walk away without looking back, he'd decided he could, too. And in not looking back, he'd never allowed himself to trust or seek out love again. He wasn't giving another woman the opportunity to break his heart. Besides, he'd known there was never going to be another woman like Grace. Not for him, anyway.

Now, after a restless night's sleep, he still had no idea how he was going to deal with her arrival on the island. As the upcoming CEO of RGF he had to consider how this story would ultimately affect the company. The feud was no secret. In fact, RJ was certain that a portion of the media coverage RGF and King Designs had received over the years was a direct result of the known conflict between them. Since the initial whispers of the feud—which had come from Ron's accusing Tobias of stealing and someone in the office overhearing that argument and leaking it to the media—reporters had taken every opportunity they could to ask Ron and Tobias about it. Whenever a new line was launched by one company all eyes would immediately turn to the other to see what they would do to up the competition. Ron and Tobias never had to speak another word about the feud because the media and those in the fashion industry did enough talking and speculating about it to keep it afloat year after year. To RJ's way of thinking, his father and Tobias had simply sat back and let it work to their advantage. When he became CEO, RJ planned to take a more preemptive approach. And since the time for him to take over was in the near future, he decided he might as well get started now.

Grace was back.

At this resort, which had been reserved for fam-

ily and one hundred wedding guests—close friends
and business associates—for the next two weeks.
So how had she gotten a reservation? Veronica. He
needed to speak to Chaz's aunt as soon as possible
and as discreetly as he could manage. He didn't want
Chaz or Riley to find out about this.

And he wanted Grace gone.

She'd been gone for so long already, and he'd told
himself that was fine, that he'd built an even better
life without her. Sure, he'd known all along that was
a lie, but nobody else had to know that. Keeping his
private life private, even from his family, was something RJ had always done well. While Maurice and
Major were media favorites, Riley spent her time
dodging reporters and the like. RJ could go about his
business without too much fanfare because his siblings provided enough conversation about their personal lives to keep the attention off him. That suited
him and his preference of retaining all his intimate
feelings, fears and desires to himself.

Grace was leaving this island today, no matter
how much he'd been turned on by seeing her again.
It was as simple as that.

As if to solidify those words and cut off any further thought about the situation, his phone chimed
from the nightstand where he'd plugged it into the
charger last night.

"Yeah?" he answered gruffly and immediately, as
if whoever was calling might somehow know that

he'd been thinking about how to get his ex-girlfriend away from here.

"Mornin', sunshine," Maurice's all-too-chipper voice sounded through the phone.

"Make it fast," he told his jovial younger brother. "It's barely seven."

Maurice's response was a hearty chuckle. "Hey, man, I get it. You and I aren't the morning people in the family. But Riley is and she has this crazy itinerary we're all supposed to be following."

RJ closed his eyes, bringing his free hand up to squeeze the bridge of his nose. "Let me guess, your highly organized and punctual fiancée told you to call me. But we all know that I'm better at staying on schedule than you are."

"Truth. However, we've never all been on vacation at the same time, so assuming the rules that apply in the city are now tossed out the window, I'm doing what my lovely Desta asked, and reminding you that we're scheduled for lunch and a hike up the mountain at noon. This means we all need to meet at whatever destination is printed on the itinerary, which you also have as an email attachment, at eleven thirty."

This was insane, or cruel, or whatever the word was for something he couldn't believe he was involved in. His mother had mandated this a vacation and yet he still felt like he was on the clock. His life was normally dictated by his Outlook calendar, which was carefully coordinated with his assistant and linked to the company executives' schedules. He'd planned to do work while he was here anyway; he just didn't like that work being traded for social outings he was sure he could do without.

"I'll be there," RJ grumbled, because what else was he going to say.

"Cool. Don't be late," Maurice joked before disconnecting the call.

RJ frowned, but his irritation quickly dissipated as he put his phone back on the nightstand. He loved hearing his brother sound so relaxed and happy. Even though Maurice had always been the jokester of the siblings—certainly more outgoing than his twin, Major—he'd had a traumatic experience during his early college years and had only recently moved past the guilt it had left with him. Part of that moving on had come from Desta, who'd worked for their family for years but had just claimed Maurice's heart a little over six months ago.

And just like that his mind went back to couples, love, happiness. All things he'd reached for at one time but had lost just the same. Tossing the sheets to the side, he eased his naked body out of the bed and went directly to the bathroom to shower, shave, brush his teeth and otherwise get his mind right for the task to come.

An hour later, after he'd dressed and checked his emails, RJ was once again walking around the resort. His conversation with Grace last night hadn't led to her telling him what room she was in and while he could've easily asked registration, he felt that was walking a very thin line toward creepy. Instead, he went back to the spot he'd found her last night. Her room had to be close, considering her story about her vibrator falling off the balcony. He hadn't even let himself think about how or why that could've possibly happened.

RJ walked behind the same building again. This time, in daylight—and without the distraction of his ex and her infamous sex toy—he noticed the expansive pool area cluttered with lounge chairs on one side and cabanas on the other. There was a bar and light island music playing. As he walked toward the bar with the singular focus of grabbing a drink, regardless of what time it was, his phone vibrated in his pocket. He didn't reach for it but kept walking because he'd just spotted the only person he'd let distract him right now.

Grace was sitting at the bar. Veronica King had been seated beside her but was just slipping off her stool. Veronica smiled at Grace, said something and walked away. RJ gritted his teeth but didn't speed up toward her. He didn't want to speak to Grace with Veronica close by. What he needed to say was private.

"We need to talk." He leaned over to whisper in Grace's ear the moment he was close enough. "Now."

She hesitated only briefly before picking up the

tablet sitting on the bar and dropping it into the large blue plaid tote bag hanging on her stool. He waited while she eased off the seat with much slower movements than Veronica.

Even though RJ had seen her from a distance and had chosen to come up close behind her, he hadn't been prepared to come face-to-face with her again. When she turned, the air was knocked from his lungs as he stared at her once again.

Her hair was styled differently today, pulled up into a messy bun, leaving her neck and shoulders bare. She wore a strapless high-low dress with a black-and-white paisley print. Bangles circled her left wrist, and long silver earrings in an abstract geometric shape dangled from her ears. There was nothing spectacular about her wardrobe choice or the light makeup she wore. In his business he was accustomed to seeing women dressed more fashionably or sexy. He was certain Grace's goal wasn't to attain that look—it never had been. And yet she'd always been the best-looking woman in the room—or, in this case, at the pool—without a doubt.

"Well, good morning to you, too, RJ." Her tone was easy, the smile that followed cordial as she slipped the straps of the tote onto her shoulder. "Shall we take this discussion someplace a little quieter?"

"Gladly," he replied tersely before reaching out to touch her elbow.

To anyone looking at them the action seemed

normal, probably inconsequential, but he'd seen the quick flash of light in her eyes and the way her easy smile had faltered just a bit. He had his own reaction to touching her again, a fierce punch of lust that almost had him gasping, but for a quick clearing of his throat. She didn't pull away but fell into step beside him as he began walking them toward the private cabanas. There were six of them lined in a row about twenty feet from the bar. A second row stood at the other end of the pool. He directed them to the center one, then untied the sashes at each of the four corners. The beige-and-white curtains fell around them, enclosing them in the space. They were completely blocked from view.

"I want you off this island," he said.

"Well, tell me how you really feel." Her derisive reply came as he turned to face her.

She dropped her bag onto the light gray cushion of the sectional sofa and stood with one hand on her hip, a prickly expression on her face.

"I told you last night," he snapped, and moved across the spacious area. If he were here under different circumstances, he'd certainly compliment the resort on the calming color scheme that traveled from the draping fabric that surrounded them to the sofa and the rug beneath their feet. Exquisitely designed lanterns were on each of the three glass-topped tables, while a matching one hung from the ceiling. An ice bucket and complementary water bottles—still and sparkling—sat in the center of a longer table, and a television was mounted to the thick column above it.

"You need to leave and drop this story, Grace. I'm giving you a chance to do it on your own before I make the call to your newspaper and have it pulled."

Her one hand fisted at her side. "You wouldn't dare," she said through gritted teeth, but the look in her eyes said she knew he would.

"Whatever it takes to protect my family," he replied. "You know that's how I roll."

"I know you're being unnecessarily unrelenting in this matter." She sighed, dropping her hand from her hip. "You know me, RJ. I know you and your family. I would never intentionally harm any of you."

"But your words could harm us all and I'm not willing to take that risk." Especially not since he was soon to be running the company. The personal consequences aside, RGF may be at the top of the industry presently, but he knew all too well how easily the tide could shift. Scandal, whether based in truth or manufactured, was one of the top game changers.

She opened her mouth to say something else, but then clapped her lips shut and took a deep breath. Releasing it slowly through her nose, he watched her shoulders relax as she tried to gather her emotions. Grace didn't play games. A person always knew where they stood with her because she was often brutally honest. Right now, she was trying to remain calm, likely trying to think of a way to convince him she could write this story without damaging his family's reputation. He should probably tell her right now it was a futile mission.

"I'm not going to leave," she said, her voice as calm as the soothing colors in this space. "I have a job to do and I know you can relate to that. All your life you've done nothing but work toward the goals you set for yourself, and now the position your father groomed you for is waiting for you to claim." She nodded. "Yeah, I've heard the whispers about Ron possibly retiring this year. That's not news—your father alluded to it in one of his press conferences about the wedding a few months ago."

"That has nothing to do with this." He had no idea why he bothered with the denial. Grace knew him just as well as he knew her.

"It has everything to do with this, and I'm here to reassure you there's nothing to worry about. The story I plan to write will only shed light on the past and uplift two powerful men for the generations coming after them. For Black professionals like you and the generation after that, to show that despite the odds they can succeed. *We* can overcome the odds and shine just as bright as anyone else." She sounded like a motivational speaker, her tone uplifting and poignant.

"They're already trailblazers in the fashion industry, role models for others coming up in the trenches.

You bringing up the past can only hurt them now."
He was positive of that, because while other reporters had mentioned the feud, he knew Grace. She
worked better than that. She wasn't going to write
a snippet about the feud; she'd dive deep, add every
detail she could find and print a thought-provoking
story that he feared might harm his family more than
help them this time around.

"Why won't you just leave?" he implored, frustration and lingering pain etched in his tone. "You
did it before, you can do it again."

His words were meant to sting, to anger her and
push her away.

Instead of acknowledging the momentary slap
of irritation, Grace took a step closer to him. She
squared her shoulders and tilted her chin, holding
his gaze. "This isn't like before. And I'm not leaving.
If you call my editor, I can assure you he'll buckle
down on this story. He might even print something
about your threat to stop it, spinning that to sug-
gest some type of guilt or cover-up on behalf of the
Golds."

Eddie would also undoubtedly have something
to say about her personal relationship with RJ already interfering with her job. The very thing he'd
warned her about.

When RJ lifted his hands and dragged them down
the back of his head in the way that told her he was

frustrated but listening, she pressed on. "This is an important story and you're too good at what you do to not consider the positive implications it could have on your company. Any exposure is good exposure."

"Don't do that." He moved closer so that only one of the square tables stood between them. "Don't try to put a sales spin on this."

"Why not? You know it's a proven tactic. Just like Riley and her fiancé allowed the media into certain aspects of their wedding planning. And Major and Nina were part of that fake engagement promotion before actually falling in love. It all increased your bottom line, putting RGF well ahead of King Designs for the last two quarters."

Yeah, she'd kept tabs on RGF and the family she'd once been a part of, because she cared about them almost as much as her own family. She'd grown up the youngest of four sisters. Hope, the newly engaged concert pianist, was the oldest; Charity, the happily married psychologist with four children, was second; and Trinity, the obstetrician who'd been married for three and a half years, had yet to give their parents, Milton and Videtta Hopkins, any grandchildren. Trinity was just two years older than Grace at thirty-six. Grace had come from a big, loving family, but there'd always been sibling rivalry. Her relationship with Riley Gold had been totally different from what she'd experienced growing up in Westchester. With Riley, there'd been no competition, just a normal friendship with the young introverted Gold daughter who would go on to become one of the most talented and influential women in the fashion industry.

"Why did you keep track of what was happening in my family?" RJ's gaze was pointed, his proximity suddenly intense.

RJ stepped around that table to stand just a couple feet away from her, and suddenly the space felt small. "I'm a reporter," she said with a shrug. "And our no longer being a couple didn't mean I stopped caring about them."

If her tone was a little huskier than it had been, she totally planned to ignore it. Writing this story was her goal, and getting past RJ's gatekeeping was an obstacle she had to overcome. Neither of those things could afford the interruption of her body's immediate response to his.

He looked way too good standing there with a suspicious expression on his beautiful face. Today he wore khaki shorts and a crisp white polo, like a *GQ* cover model at the beach. Her breasts immediately felt fuller, her pussy aching with need even after that shattering orgasm she'd had last night. Nothing about this situation was simple, but the past wasn't something she wanted to keep dwelling on.

She could write this story with or without RJ, but because of the past she should've known would be this prevalent between them, the small measure of guilt she still felt from walking away from him, and the love he'd so freely offered her long ago, she wanted his approval.

That thought had occurred to her late last night as she'd lain in bed thinking of their impromptu re-union. She'd left him to pursue her goals on her own. To be here now, in this place, wanting him to accept her as a journalist, was a bit ironic.

"Keep your enemies close. Remember you used to say that?" She knew he not only recalled one of his favorite quotes, but that he'd probably already been thinking it. "Since you already know who my sources for the story will be, what if I give you a summary of my meetings with them so you have some idea of what's being said?"

It was an olive branch, one she didn't have to offer. One she probably shouldn't have offered be-cause it could be construed as showing bias and if Eddie found out he'd definitely yank her off this story and probably never hire her again. Yet she wanted RJ to believe that she'd protect his family with the same fervor and loyalty as him. She wanted to make amends.

He tilted his head, contemplating her words. RJ considered a situation from every angle before mak-ing a decision. He possessed a brilliant analytical mind that some overlooked because they were too in awe of his handsome features, deep umber-toned skin and muscled physique.

"You expect me to trust you?"

"I expect you to remember." Even though she kept telling herself not to focus on the past. "To reach deep down inside to that time when we both trusted each other implicitly. You knew back then when I was covering some of the Fashion Week shows that I'd never write anything false or harmful about your family."

Of course, that had also been the time they'd been sleeping together every night, cuddling in each other's arms in the early morning and promising to love each other forever.

"You sure you want me to remember, Gracie?"

He closed the space between them with one quick movement, standing only a breath away from her now as he lifted a strong hand and cupped her neck. She moved with the action, didn't have much choice over her faithless body, stepping into him and the intense partial embrace. He'd begun calling her Gracie a few months after they'd started dating and she'd taken it as an endearment, her heart fluttering each time she heard it. Today was no different.

"I want you to…" She paused, the next words lodging in her throat. What the hell did she want at this moment? So many things were flying through her mind. Snippets from their past, touches, kisses, declarations of feelings she hadn't felt in far too long. She couldn't concentrate.

"You want me to what?" His question was a mere

whisper as he lowered his face to hers. "To kiss you? To touch you?"

His lips were only inches away when she opened her mouth to speak, their gazes locked, bodies touching. "Trust me." The two words were a breathy whisper.

He brushed his lips over hers and she gasped, needing more than just that teasing touch and hating how clear that thought was in her mind now.

"You trust me, Gracie?" he asked while lacing his other arm around her back, pressing her to him. "Say you do."

Right now she'd say about anything if he'd just kiss her. Urgency, that's all she could think about. The feel of her breasts pressed against his hard chest, the strength of his touch engulfing her, the throbbing of his dick against her, they were all taking center stage. With that knowledge it occurred to her that this may not be such a good idea, that mixing business with what she was certain would be fantastic pleasure held the potential to go horribly wrong. Grace didn't give a damn; she'd never been one to deny herself pleasure. "I do," she whispered before cursing and closing that breath of space between their lips.

CHAPTER FIVE

IT ONLY TOOK seconds for the years they'd been apart to melt away. They were right back in his penthouse, on one of the many evenings he'd come home from work and they'd been unable to keep their hands off each other. But something told RJ this was going to be different.

His mouth slanted over hers; she leaned into him, touching her tongue to his. Every cell in his body came alive again, filling him from the inside out with warmth, need and satisfaction. He moaned into her, keeping his eyes closed, because if this was a dream he didn't want to wake up. She felt just like she used to, fitting into his embrace as if they'd been specially made for each other. Moving his hand down her back, he crushed her against him until they both moaned. She'd lifted her arms, wrapping them around his neck, and now her hands were pressed to the back of his head.

Tongues and teeth, gasps and groans, mingled fiercely. All he could think was that he wanted more.

It only took one step forward from him, one back from her, and she was near the sofa again. He eased his hands down past her plump ass to the backs of her thighs so he could lift her legs and wrap them around his waist. He used to love entering her this way, pumping deep and fast inside her until she cried out his name. As if he were taking that memory seriously, his hips were thrusting, his thick erection pressing against her like they'd already removed their clothes and decided to have sex.

But they hadn't. It wasn't even something he'd considered when he found her at the bar a while ago. He'd only searched her out to tell her that she had to leave, because that's what he wanted, for Grace to go away. Again…didn't he?

She tore her mouth from his, and both of them breathed heavily at the temporary respite. He continued nibbling along her chin, dragging his tongue down the line of her throat when she tilted her head back. Last night that heart pendant had been right there, at this hollow spot. He licked there feverishly, loving the faint hint of the floral-scented perfume she'd no doubt sprayed on her neck after showering this morning. Her ass was so soft beneath his hands, and he squeezed each cheek loving the way she pressed her pussy into him as if she was as hungry for him as he was for her.

As if she wanted him again. When she hadn't before. That thought had him going still. The sound of their heavy breathing almost beat out the sound of his thumping heart as every word she'd spoken to him last night and just moments ago circled like a brewing storm in his mind. Grace was back, but not for him. She'd come to this island to write a story about his family, not to pick up where they left off. She was a journalist, so that made sense. This—his hands on her ass, mouth on her skin, the same pulsing need for her he'd always had—did not.

She must've been thinking the same thing because as he slowly released his hold on her, she hurried to put distance between them, smoothing down her dress as he turned away, trying desperately to calm the rage of emotion soaring through him.

Nowhere in her planner did it say "kiss RJ," or rather, "let RJ make you weak with need." No, Grace was absolutely certain she'd never written any such thing.

She was meticulous about her schedule, jotting down every step of her day in one of her many planners. She scheduled everything from the time she would wake up to how many USB drives she packed as backups for her backups. She could, admittedly, be a little intense about planning and more than a little wanton when it came to RJ Gold.

He had his back to her now as he stood across the room opening a bottle of water. She felt like a schoolgirl who'd been sneaking around, hoping the principal wouldn't open the door and catch her. Because she'd been caught skipping class more times than she could remember during high school, there was real mortification to the thought that someone could have come into the cabana while RJ's very clever mouth had been making her moan.

"I've gotta get going. Riley has us scheduled for a lunch and hiking thing." He didn't turn to face her but took a deep swallow from the water bottle.

Okay, so they weren't going to talk about what just happened. Cool. Great. That worked for her.

"Yeah, I should get going, too. I have another interview scheduled with Veronica later this afternoon, just before dinner with the family, I guess. And I need to go back to my room to do some more research."

"What did she tell you?" He did turn to face her then.

She'd been about to lift a hand to check her hair but now that he was staring at her, she changed her mind. "We only had a short time to speak this morning because Tobias woke up early and wanted to have breakfast with her. So we just talked about how she and Tobias met."

"How did you link up with her? Do you two know each other?" RJ looked pretty perplexed as he questioned her, and she wondered if his confusion was solely related to meeting with Veronica.

"Her stepson from a previous marriage is a freelance photographer I've worked with on stories a couple times. He gave me her number and I called her."

"And she agreed to tell you all of her husband's business, just like that?" He sounded incredulous, and she had to admit it did seem unbelievable, but it was true.

"I told her exactly what I wanted and she agreed. She said it was high time people knew what they were talking about when they referred to the feud." And Grace had been elated at having the close, personal insight into Tobias King.

"I'm gonna talk to her," he said, and Grace eyed him cautiously.

"If I don't write this story, RJ, someone else will. And if Veronica has something to say, she'll say it to me or the next person."

He didn't immediately respond.

"You know I'm right," she said after a few seconds of silence.

The heated glare he'd given her just before that kiss was gone. Now he was giving her the look he most often carried during business hours. The scrutinizing facial expression that said he was determined to be in control and there was nothing she could do about it. But Grace had already offered RJ all the control she could give him. He could either take it or leave it.

With that thought she grabbed her bag and pushed the straps up onto her shoulder. "I'd gladly show you my work, let you in on this story every step of the way, but if you don't want that, it's fine. Just know that I'm not backing down. No matter how good that kiss felt."

She started toward the front of the cabana, but his hand on her arm stopped her from reaching for the material to let herself out.

"It felt good for me, too."

It was a quiet admission that sent a flush of warmth over her skin. Telling her that wasn't easy for him. RJ didn't like admitting any weakness—and kissing her when he was angry with her for being here in the first place was definitely a weakness. One she hadn't counted on.

Maybe it was time for her to make a partial admission as well. "I don't want to hurt you. I never did."

He shook his head with a quick jerking motion. "I don't want to talk about the past anymore." She was happy to hear him say that. "And I don't want you writing this story. But—" he turned her slowly until she faced him again "—I know how much your career means to you. I also know how tenacious you can be, and while I'm certain I could shut this down even if it cost us a little backlash in the press, I'm not going to do that." He shook his head again. "I'm no stranger to ambition."

That was an understatement. She didn't say that, but simply gave him a tentative smile. "We can meet tomorrow morning and go over my notes from Veronica." There—she was putting the offer out there again. She told herself this was how she'd deal with any possible source in a story, giving them a little so that they'd eventually offer her a lot. But it was probably a big fat lie. A part of her had always wanted to give RJ everything, just not at the risk of losing herself and all she wanted to become. She told herself that was then and this was now. Could she give him everything now? Was there a place in his life for her after all they'd been through? Of course not. They weren't the same people, too much time had passed, he was about to become CEO of RGF, an even bigger and more high-profile position than he'd had before. And she was writing a story that would undoubtedly expose some of his family's deepest and darkest secrets. Ambition had once been their biggest commonality; now it was probably their greatest obstacle.

His hand still touched her arm lightly. "I have to check my schedule."

"Me, too." Moving her free arm, she reached into her bag and found the business cards she'd tucked in the side pocket.

"We're quite a pair," he said.

She looked up at him again just as he clapped his mouth shut.

"I mean, what other two people would come to a beautiful island like this and still keep scheduled appointments." He finished the statement with an uneasy look.

"You're right about that. But I definitely plan to take some R & R time while I'm here. I mean, who knows when I'll be back here again?"

Probably never, since traveling alone wasn't high on her list of things to do and after walking away from RJ. The extent of her dating life since had been dinner-and-a-movie dates, and occasionally sex before getting in her car and driving home. Work was her priority and it created an easy excuse for those parameters. An excuse that didn't allow her to admit she didn't want to do any fun social activities without RJ in her life.

"Yeah, well, at least you're not being forced to do that. Riley's got us booked mostly every day up until the wedding." He pulled his hand from her arm to look at his watch. "Speaking of which, I really have to get going."

"Sure, no problem. Here, take my card." She pushed it at him and he accepted it. "I'll be around tomorrow if you want to hear about my interview. Just call or text me and we can set up a place and time to meet."

He nodded, glanced down at the card he now held and then back up at her. "I'd like that," he said. "I'd like to hear what Veronica says."

"Good." She almost said "it's a date" but wisely kept her mouth shut. She and RJ weren't dating.

"I'll see you tomorrow then," he said after a few more uncomfortably silent moments.

"Right. Tomorrow." Then, because she couldn't stand this awkwardness that had replaced the desire brewing between them, she turned and lifted the curtain before stepping out of the cabana.

Nobody paid attention to her as she walked toward the building where her room was located, and she didn't look back to see RJ again. It was smarter to play this as a business dealing, not any type of rebooted affair. She and RJ as a couple were over. No matter how much her body wanted that statement to be false.

CHAPTER SIX

It was a little after ten the next morning when RJ knocked on the door of Grace's room. While waiting for her to answer, he adjusted the tray containing two cups of coffee he held in one hand and clenched his fingers over the bag of doughnuts in the other.

"Hey," Grace said brightly when she opened the door. "Oh, wow, you brought coffee. Bless you!"

She stepped back out of the way before he could respond, so RJ walked into the room saying, "Yeah, I was hungry so I figured you might be, too."

"I thought you might've had something on the schedule for today, so I was surprised when you texted me a while ago."

Today she wore another pair of those barely-there shorts, the ones that seemed to make her legs appear miles longer than normal, giving him way too many ideas about traveling up and between those legs. Yesterday's kiss had rattled him. It had felt like they'd never parted ways and yet, things were drastically different now. With a shake of his head to rid his mind of the thoughts of Grace that'd plagued him during the hike yesterday afternoon and well into the evening, he walked through her room, toward the table near the open patio door. She had her laptop set up on the table. Two spiral books and a handful of pens were scattered around as well.

"Nah, I got out of it. Well, to be fair, the women are having dress fittings."

Grace was already lifting one of the coffee cups to her mouth, pausing only to say, "And you don't need to try on your tux?"

He shrugged. "I've tried that tux on three times already. If it doesn't fit by now it never will."

She chuckled and then sipped from the coffee. "Still the defiant one."

He watched the way her lips pressed over the lid of the cup, then forced himself to stop being a horny fool and reached for his own cup. "No, that's still Maurice. He's the one who suggested we all skip the fitting and go do something fun."

She'd taken a seat in the chair near her laptop, so RJ sat in the one across from her.

"And this is your idea of something fun? Bringing doughnuts and coffee to my room while I work?"

For a second, he could only stare at her. She had no idea how lovely she looked with her hair in a messy ponytail, her oversize T-shirt hanging off one shoulder and her face scrubbed totally free of makeup. "Maurice's idea of fun was scuba diving, which interested me even less than trying on that tux. Besides, you love doughnuts."

She sat back in the chair, both hands wrapped around the cup she now held close to her face. "Coffee and doughnuts are the breakfast of champions," she said, her tone a little more wistful than it had been just seconds ago.

"So you always said." He grinned because he couldn't help it. There'd been so many mornings when they'd had this discussion.

Where RJ preferred something from a more traditional breakfast menu—eggs, bacon, pancakes—Grace wasn't as formal with the meal and claimed the caffeine and sugar mixture she loved worked much better for her throughout the day. He could never vouch for how the combo improved her productivity, but it never failed to bring about that glorious grin on her face. The one that almost matched her look of being well-pleased in bed. How many times had he lost himself in that particular look? The one where she was heavy-lidded, a slow smile spreading across her face just before she'd drag her tongue over her teeth and say something sexy like how much she loved being with him.

"RJ?"

"Huh?" he responded to the raised tone of her voice, clearing his throat in hope that the thoughts he'd just had would dissipate. He felt like a total ass for thinking about getting her in bed at ten in the morning.

"I asked if you and the family had a good time on the hike yesterday."

He sipped his coffee and watched as she reached for the bag of doughnuts, taking the Bavarian cream–filled one that had been dusted with powdered sugar. Deciding it was smarter not to watch her bite into it, he fished into the bag for one of his own. He grabbed a chocolate frosted one and a napkin, then set his coffee on the table.

"I'm not a hiking kind of guy," he started. The memory of yesterday afternoon with the rest of the bridal party was still a hilarious scene in his mind.

"Oh no, what'd you do? You're on an island, not at some snowcapped mountain. From what I can see of the resort it's beautiful up there."

Chewing the bite he'd taken only allowed him to shrug initially. "It's a big rock. A steep rock. And it was about two hundred degrees outside by the time we finished lunch at the beachside café and started walking." He left out the part about Nina and Desta being attacked by a bug and Major and Maurice bumping into each other trying to swat it away until they looked like a scene from a comedy sketch. They'd eventually tumbled into the waterfall they'd been exploring.

"Yeah, it was pretty warm out yesterday. I'd been hoping to get a chance to go for a swim, but I fell down so many rabbit holes while doing my research." She was taking another bite of her doughnut, licking the cream from her finger.

The second he caught himself groaning he stuffed the last bite of his doughnut into his mouth. "You still enjoy swimming," he said when he was finished chewing. It was a statement, not a question, because when they were dating, Grace had used the pool in his apartment building more than he had.

"You know it." She reached for a napkin after finishing her doughnut. "And whenever I get around to buying a house, that's going to be a prerequisite."

A pool and at least four bathrooms because she didn't want to have to share a bathroom with guests or anyone else. There'd been a few discussions about what type of home they might like to have together. Those conversations about their future had seemed so natural after the first year of their relationship, leading him to believe that they'd been on the same page about their trajectory.

"Your parents have a pool at their house. I'm sure they wouldn't mind you moving back just to use it on a daily basis." He liked Grace's parents, Milton and Videtta. They were both professors of Black studies at a local college and he'd had the pleasure of meeting them multiple times during the year and a half he'd dated their daughter. He'd even called Milton and asked for his blessing before proposing to Grace.

"Yeah, they do, and so do Charity and her family

of five, who're still in Westchester with my parents. They have a house on an acre of land with a massive pool that I'm in each summer when I go home for vacation." She grinned like an excited child just talking about swimming. It was her favorite hobby.

"That's right, Charity and Bret, that's his name, right? They'd just gotten engaged when—" He couldn't finish that sentence. "You said she has a family of five, so she's got three kids now?"

"That's right." Her hand was already in the bag for another doughnut—powdered and cream-filled again. He knew exactly what she liked. "Two girls and a boy. Trinity and her husband, Randall, don't have any kids yet, to my mother's dismay. But they've got a huge aquarium full of brilliantly colored fish."

He nodded and smiled. Major just had a custom aquarium built in the basement of the house he and Nina purchased a few months ago. RJ thought it was a clever addition to the space but he wasn't a pet person, at least not after the idea of having a dog with Grace had fizzled.

"And how's Hope?" The oldest Hopkins sister had a chilly personality.

Grace's raised brow and half smile hinted that she knew exactly what he was thinking about her sister. "Just got engaged three weeks ago," she said with a smirk that surprised him almost as much her announcement.

"Really?"

So Grace was the last single sister. Did that bother her? During the time they were together she'd shared with him the pressure she'd always felt to be just as good as her parents and sisters were in their careers. The weight of that task had sparked her competitive and tenacious nature. He'd been able to relate as the oldest Gold sibling—it was expected that he'd one day helm the company and he'd strived to prove he was up to the task. As he was also the last single sibling in his family, it occurred to him that while successful in business, he and Grace had fallen short in the area of love.

"Yeah, somebody finally cracked that stiff exterior of hers." She laughed. "And my mom's ecstatic that the majority of her daughters are about to be married. 'Cause you know, the more who're married, the greater the possibility of that houseful of grandchildren she wants."

There was a hint of something in her tone, irritation, sarcasm. The relationship among the Hopkins women had been a close-knit but still strained one, if he recalled correctly. From the sound of Grace's voice and the look on her face, it still was. What if problems with her family dynamic had influenced her decision to not accept his proposal? Frustration threatened to push to the surface. If anyone knew about juggling different personalities and expectations within a family, it was RJ, and Grace knew that.

"Well, I guess you can't blame her. My mom

hasn't said anything yet but I know she's waiting very impatiently for her first grandchild." RJ obviously wouldn't be giving her any since that was another idea that had drifted away when Grace left. He hadn't imagined how much that realization bothered him until this very moment.

Grace wiped her hands against each other, sending remnants of powdered sugar floating in the air. As if she hadn't thought that would happen, she reached for a napkin.

"At least your mom isn't sending text messages to you, the only unattached child, saying things like 'the clock's ticking.' I got one just a couple days ago saying 'maybe you'll meet a hot guy on the beach. You don't need a marriage certificate to have a baby.' Can you believe that? Now she's even telling me to get pregnant before I get married. What parent does that?"

Obviously, Videtta Hopkins did. And apparently, Grace didn't like it. RJ didn't like how this conversation was going. The tendrils of resentment mixed with unsettling desire created an enormous weight in his chest. He took a gulp of his significantly cooled-down coffee and prayed it would relieve some of the pressure. It had been an awfully long time since he'd thought about children, or rather the ones he wouldn't have because he'd decided not to ever let another woman into his heart again. And unlike Grace's mother's stance on reproducing, if the woman wasn't in his heart, she certainly wasn't having his baby.

"How'd you respond to her?" Again, this wasn't the question RJ really wanted to ask.

What he wanted to know was so simple—why the hell had she walked away from him and the love he thought they'd shared? But really, what did it matter now? He knew that some people needed closure for things like this, but not him. Nothing she said was going to change the fact that his heart had been broken and he could never trust giving it to anyone, especially Grace, again. Nobody knew how much strength it had taken for him to move past her leaving before; if it happened again, he wasn't certain he'd survive.

She shrugged. "I ignored the text. Which I know really pisses her off and maybe borders on disrespect or some other parental rule, but I just can't think about any of that right now. I've got other stuff on my mind." She put her hands on her keyboard then and tapped a few keys. "Speaking of which, I know you really came here to talk about my meeting with Veronica, so let's get to it."

He sat there for a few moments while he presumed she pulled up her notes up. The war going on within him—one side warning he keep a safe distance, the other edging him toward her like a magnet, drawing them together in spite of everything that made sense—continued until he finally sighed wearily.

Then he stood and walked over to her. She jumped when he touched a finger to the corner of her lip.

"You missed a spot," he said softly, and wiped the powdered sugar away.

Well, damn. Moments after that very intimate touch, Grace's voice was surprisingly steady as she briefed him on her notes. She silently commended herself for not leaping across the table to straddle him. She'd wanted to. Oh man, had she wanted to.

She'd spent the twenty minutes after he'd sent her that text in the bathroom, brushing her teeth and running her fingers through her hair. She'd slept in a tank top and panties and hadn't yet decided what her outfit for the day was going to be. The shorts and T-shirt were on the top of the pile in the drawer so they were it. And he still hadn't mentioned yesterday's kiss.

Neither had she, for that matter. The memory was startlingly clear in her mind and the desire between them was very much still a real thing. Case in point, the way her pussy had throbbed the second his finger touched her lip and the subsequent dampness of her panties thereafter. It was insane, yet undeniable— she still wanted RJ.

At least, she wanted to have sex with him. Anything beyond that was out of the question. That ship had long since sailed and there was no going back. Not that she wanted to anyway. This current situation reminded her that walking away from RJ had been the right decision. The Gold and King families had rented an entire resort for a wedding. Reporters and fashion bloggers all over the world were clamoring for any clue about this very event because they desperately wanted to be the ones reporting on what promised to be a glamourous spectacle. Not because they wanted to see Riley and Chaz commit to their love and each other. No, that was buried beneath the prestige of being in this family, the same way she knew she would've been.

"So Veronica wants you to write her book?" RJ's brow wrinkled, his eyes narrowed.

"Is that all you got from my notes?"

He angled his head and frowned. "It was the biggest bullet point, yeah. Are you kidding me?"

Now the cursing came.

"What's she thinking?"

"If you ask me, she's thinking that it's just a matter of time before she becomes the ex-Mrs. Tobias King number eight and she's trying to get her ducks in a row."

In addition to the feud with Ron, Tobias was known for his many marriages. And Veronica, who'd been married twice before herself, was known for burying her husbands and keeping control of their estate. So Grace figured the two were in a standoff of sorts and in the meantime having "hot monkey sex," as Veronica had described it.

"It's unacceptable, and she definitely left that little detail out of the conversation I had with her last night after dinner," RJ said.

This piqued Grace's interest because she hadn't really thought RJ was going to discuss the article with Veronica. She probably should've, though. RJ wasn't known to mince words with anyone, for any reason. And as ticked off as he'd been about this story combined with Veronica's open invitation to Grace, it made sense that he'd want a confrontation with the woman.

"What'd she say to you?" Grace opened a new document and kept her fingers poised over the keys, ready to take notes.

RJ's brief hesitation and the leery look on his face she spied when she lifted her gaze from the screen said he noticed her actions and wasn't sure about proceeding.

"Look, last night I had a thought." She cleared her throat and sat up straighter. "What if I tell the story of Ron and Tobias, pioneers and visionaries reshaping the fashion industry. I start from the beginning—the best friends throughout grade school and college, the grooming of two dynamic leaders at the hand of Ronald Gold Sr. There's a stumble in their path that ultimately spurs them on to the top of their industry. What were the steps they took to get there?" She'd started toying with the idea after she'd thought about what happened between her and RJ in the cabana for the billionth time yesterday.

He rubbed a finger over his chin, the hair of his goatee causing a rasping sound. "Focus more on everything they did to get where they are instead of the cause of the feud."

Well, put that way it sounded like she'd gloss right over the feud, which wasn't totally her goal. "The feud wouldn't be the focus of the story. Your father and Tobias would be. The families they both built and oftentimes put before their fashion houses. The secret to their success. How these two, who were once best friends, became enemies and competitors, the best of the best, and now are becoming family once again."

That sounded really good. She hurried to type it before she forgot the exact wording.

"Veronica said she didn't see a problem inviting you here because the media would write what they wanted about us otherwise. This way, we had a semblance of control over the dialogue." He made a sound that had her looking up at him. "I guess what she said makes sense."

Grace agreed. "I mean, you're sitting here right now sharing your conversation with her and I'm sharing my ideas for the story with you."

"That doesn't mean I have control over what you write."

"Why would I go through all this if I planned to lie to you?"

She could see the moment his mind took that question in a completely different direction. The slow lifting of his brow said he probably believed she'd lied to him before about loving him when she had no intention of marrying him. That had always been her fear, that he'd believe everything they had together was a lie just because she refused his proposal.

"This is about business for me," she hurriedly said. "It's about me getting to the next step in my career. I'm going to write the very best story I can, revealing things about the families that no other journalist has revealed before while remaining in the parameters I've set. That's all that matters to me."

Not the past or the feeling that there was something totally new buzzing between them now.

"Yeah," he said with a nod. "I know that's all that matters to you. And all that matters to me is that my family doesn't get hurt in the process of you tending to your goals. So we'll keep checking in while you're here."

"Great!" She wasn't able to hide her excitement at the agreement they'd come to.

"But first, answer this question for me," he said.

"Sure, what is it?" She typed a note of his agreement but looked up when he hadn't spoken for a few seconds.

"What's the plan for dealing with this other thing between us?"

The way his gaze had grown darker, causing her heart to immediately thump wildly, told her the *other thing* was that scorching hot kiss from yesterday.

"It's in the past," she said quickly. Too quickly.

The blank expression he now wore didn't tell her if he was okay with that or not, but she wasn't going to elaborate on her answer. She couldn't.

Not only had she and RJ moved on with their lives; there was still another bit of contention she'd just broached in their conversation about her family. While Grace was achieving her goal of being just as successful in her career as her sisters were in theirs, being a wife and mother was still a bit daunting, and her mother's persistence wasn't helping. Videtta and Charity had made having a career and a family seem so easy. Trinity didn't have kids yet but she was married, and Hope never failed at anything. Grace knew the minute they both had children, the bar of Hopkins perfection would be even higher and even more unobtainable for her.

Sitting here like this with him—as if nothing had happened between them ten years ago or even twenty-four hours ago—was one of the hardest things she'd ever had to do. It ranked right up there with the day she'd walked out of his life, because this morning she'd had to reconcile with herself that she still had feelings for RJ Gold. Really significant feelings that she feared could easily carry her down a path she couldn't afford to venture on again.

She had no idea why she'd shared the content of her mother's text messages with him, or any of the specifics about her sisters and their families. Well, he'd actually asked her about the latter, but still, she needed to keep this as cordial and emotion-free as possible.

"We're having dinner at the Sienne Club tonight. You should come. It'll give you a chance to see the family again." He was already standing before he finished.

She cleared her throat and stood as well, rubbing her now slightly shaking hands down the front of her clothes. "You want me to come to dinner with you and your family?"

If she sounded shocked and confused it was because she was. RJ wasn't down for this story, and while she'd been ready to interview as many people in the family as she could, sitting at a table and having dinner with them was a totally different ball game. She knew this because she recalled the Gold family dinners and how close their family was. That was the part she wasn't ready for.

He shrugged. "You're the one hell-bent on doing this. The least you can do is sit down and have a meal with the people you plan to write about."

His words made her seem ungrateful or rude, neither of which she wanted to be considered. "Sure. I can come to dinner," she said as she followed him to the door.

He opened it and stepped into the hallway.

"Thanks for the doughnuts and coffee."

"No problem. You needed breakfast and I needed

to catch up with you. So, as we agreed, we'll meet daily after your interviews for an update on what you've been told and what you're writing. We're here for another twelve days, so you have that time to wrap this up because I don't want any of my family disturbed on the day of Riley's wedding."

"I'd never do that," she replied, getting a little annoyed that he felt it necessary to remind her not to be a jerk.

"Good to know. I'll see you tonight." He walked away before she could say anything else.

That was fine; she didn't have anything else to say to him. After closing and locking the door, Grace moved back to the table. She sat in the chair again and stared at the coffee cup for what felt like an eternity. When her phone chimed with a text she checked it and read yet another message from her mother, this one giving her the link to an IVF clinic. She groaned and rolled her eyes.

CHAPTER SEVEN

"GRACE IS BACK." RJ said the words quickly, knowing that whoever heard him would immediately command the rest of them already seated at the table to ditch their current conversation and turn all their attention to him.

Everyone at the table went silent in less than three seconds. That worked better than he'd planned.

"Excuse me?" Riley asked, resting her elbows on the table across from him.

"Grace as in Grace Hopkins?" was his mother's follow-up question. She was seated at the end of the table with his father at the head beside her.

Major was apparently up next. "Can you clarify 'back'? Is she back from a trip? Back in your life?" He moved his hands to indicate he could go on but would rather RJ just tell them more.

RJ decided to do that. "She's here on the island because Veronica invited her." He'd timed his announcement just right because so far on this trip, Veronica and Tobias had been late to dinner every night. The only one currently at the table who wasn't part of the Gold family was Chaz, who was glaring at RJ with a frown on his face.

"I'm gonna have to echo Major and ask for clarification," Chaz said.

RJ could totally relate to the irritation he saw building in his future brother-in-law. "I ran into Grace the night before last and she told me the reason she's here is to write a story about Dad and your uncle and the feud between them. When I asked how she knew where we were and was able to book a room, she said Veronica had given her the information."

Chaz leaned back in his chair. "Dammit!"

Riley rubbed a hand over his arm.

"So, wait," Nina started, "you're saying that your ex-girlfriend is here to write a story about our families and his aunt is responsible?"

The basis of that statement was true, but the minute RJ noticed his father frowning in Chaz's direction he knew he definitely needed to say more. "Grace was already set to write the story. She had a contact who put her in touch with Veronica." And before anyone else could speak, he added, "She's agreed to focus the story on Dad and Tobias and how they've built their empires and not the details of the feud. I'll be paying close attention to her progress."

"You negotiated a way for her to write the story?" Maurice asked. "And you're going to be, for lack of a better word, *working* with her on this?"

While Major looked almost as peeved as Chaz, Maurice's tone was light. His question was definitely aimed more at RJ on a personal level than the impact of this story on the family.

"Calling the paper insisting that the story be dropped could've backfired on us. Eddie Kane, her editor, is known for his exposés and he's meticulous with details. Fighting him would've no doubt been very public and even if we'd won on that front, Grace is a freelance journalist—she could've easily taken the story to another paper." And she would've. RJ had no doubt about that. Grace thought this story was going to get her a full-time position, and she was probably right. It was a huge story and if she pulled it off, she'd definitely reap amazing accolades. He wasn't prepared to take that from her, but his family didn't need to know that.

"I think it's a fine idea," Marva said.

RJ's attention immediately went to his mother. She wore a white dress with a bold fuchsia floral print tonight, her hair pulled back into a neat bun. She was the epitome of style and grace to RJ, a college graduate and an esteemed philanthropist. When his mother caught his gaze, she smiled and his chest warmed. There was nothing like his mother's smile—her happiness meant the world to him. Always had.

"Grace is a wonderful journalist," Marva continued. "She's always handled her stories with tact and decorum that too many in the media lack. If she's here to write a story about us, then we should be sure to give her all the facts. It may be our only chance to have a story told the way we want it."

"Those were my exact thoughts," Veronica said as she and Tobias arrived.

Tobias King was a tall man who commanded attention with his deep, raspy voice and snow-white beard against a sepia complexion. He was the same age as Ron, who'd decided to go bald and completely shaved his face when his gray had started growing in. Veronica was twelve years younger than Tobias, and the purple dress she wore tonight was a little tighter than the one she'd worn last night. Her golden-hued skin tone complemented the honey-blond curls that fell over her left shoulder.

"I figured it's good to know what people are saying about you, but it's even better when you can put the words in their mouth." Veronica smiled around the table at everyone.

"You should've asked me before inviting someone to my wedding," Chaz snapped, and then turned his attention to his uncle. "Did you know about this?"

Tobias looked grim but added a half-hearted smile to Chaz. "Not until last night, and believe me I told her exactly what I thought about her duplicity."

"It's not duplicitous if I came clean." Veronica signaled for the server.

RJ wasn't sure where the conversation was about

to go but it didn't matter, because Grace walked up to the table at that moment.

"Good evening," she said, her tone clear and even, her gaze immediately finding his.

She wore a boho-style maxi dress tonight in a royal blue tone that made her deep mocha skin glisten. He'd always loved jewel tones on her, and she looked amazing tonight with her hair held back behind her ear with a sparkly clip, the rest left flowing in deep waves. He suddenly wished that this was a dinner for two and that there was no story as the topic of conversation, just the two of them having a normal reunion. That thought was interrupted by the sound of his mother's voice.

"Grace." Marva immediately rose from her seat. "It's wonderful to see you again."

RJ stood and watched his ex-girlfriend walk past him to greet his mother. The hug they shared was genuine. He could tell by the way his mother closed her eyes the moment Grace was locked in her embrace, and how Grace held on to Marva as if she'd been waiting forever for that moment. The sight caused in him an uneasy flicker of sorrow, and he breathed a sigh of relief when they finally pulled away from each other.

"Here, Grace, I'll move down a seat." Nina also stood, and RJ's attention went from the hug to his sister-in-law, who'd been sitting next to him and was now doing the unexpected.

When Grace passed him again it was to smile at Nina. "Thank you."

"No problem. I'm Nina, by the way. Major's wife."

Grace shook Nina's offered hand and took the seat beside RJ. "Oh yes, I've seen a few pictures of the two of you. On your website, of course." Nina and Major ran the Gold Service, a company geared toward app integration and tech development for the fashion industry. They had amazing new ventures on the horizon. "Congratulations to you and to you, too, Major," she said.

Major smiled at her. "Thanks, Grace. It's good to see you again."

Eventually RJ sat down and more pleasantries ensued as Grace was introduced to Chaz and Tobias King. Ron remained quiet through the ordering of their meal, but as they all sipped their drinks, he finally settled his gaze on Grace to ask his first question of her.

"Why now?" He sat back in his chair.

The senior member of the Gold family wore a tan linen suit tonight, which fit expertly over his expansive build. RJ and his father shared not only the same body type, but their skin tone and deep voices were almost identical, as well.

Desta and Riley had been discussing something while his mother and Veronica were sharing a strained but cordial conversation. All of that stopped with Ron's question and everyone at the table waited expectantly for Grace's reply.

RJ waited for some sign that Grace was in distress or felt uncomfortable in any way. The instinctive spurt of protectiveness startled him. He was prepared to jump in and say whatever was necessary to smooth things over between her and his family, but when he glanced at her she was just setting her wineglass on the table. Turning her attention to his father, she met Ron's gaze and smiled.

"Why not now, sir? What better time than now to focus on a success story, when Black people and so many other marginalized groups are feeling the repeated sting of racism and baseless disdain in this country and oftentimes abroad as well." Her brows arched as she spoke. "This story has the potential to build hope by showing how you and Mr. King were able to overcome adversity both within your inner circle and from the outside to build two of the most influential empires in the fashion industry."

Across the table, Tobias took a breadstick, tearing a small piece from its corner before stuffing it into his mouth. He stared at Grace while he chewed.

"I think she's right," Riley said while Ron remained silent. "Chaz and I were determined not to carry the brunt of a feud that didn't involve us and yet it still hung over us until the moment you and Tobias stepped up and called a truce. Both companies have experienced a steady bump in sales since that announcement, and I know it's partially because of the unity the two of you showed within the industry when it mattered most."

"What do you need from us?" Marva asked Grace while placing a hand over her husband's.

RJ watched as his father glanced down at his wife's hand. When Ron looked up again there was an expression of calm on his face that hadn't been there moments ago.

"I'd like to interview each of you to get your thoughts on not only the feud but how you think it's influenced who you are personally." She paused and looked at Desta and Nina. "Or in your case, Desta and Nina, how you believe it shaped those you ultimately decided to love and commit to," Grace said.

Grace believed that Desta and Nina *decided* to love and commit to Maurice and Major, the way she'd decided *not* to do those things with him. RJ hated that her walking away from him still bothered him so much. It was taking more strength than he thought he had to not confront her with all the questions that circled his mind about that long-ago night. He just wasn't certain he was ready to hear the answers. "Be careful what you wish for" was a very real mantra in his mind, and if Grace told him something like she'd wanted to be with someone else or she'd fallen out of love with him, he didn't know how he'd respond to that.

Desta gave a light chuckle. "Well, I don't know about the deciding to love part. I'm not sure any of us made the decision to love, rather than having love find us and basically beat us over the head until we came to our senses."

While Nina and Riley nodded their agreement, Tobias spoke up. "I don't know about that. Once love is in the picture it can influence many decisions, good and bad."

Now Grace did tense. RJ sensed it in her silence and when he glanced at her, the slight falter of her smile. The servers arrived with their food then, and the meal proceeded with much lighter topics of conversation. RJ appreciated the interruption. Love wasn't something he wanted to hear about, especially not when the woman he'd considered the love of his life was sitting right beside him, *not* wearing his wedding ring. They survived the meal and were just finishing dessert when the next blow to the precarious state of his and Grace's personal life came.

"So why'd you two break up?" Veronica asked. "You're so lovely together."

This time Grace visibly stiffened. There was no smile on her face and her wineglass was empty, so she couldn't reach for it as a refuge—which RJ knew she wanted to do because he wanted to grab his glass and ask for another shot of vodka. Without hesitation he eased a hand beneath the table to where she'd dropped hers into her lap. He clasped her wrist and she relaxed enough that he could lace his fingers with hers.

"Let's keep the past in the past," Ron intervened. "And instead we can talk about this volleyball game that's scheduled for tomorrow."

Chatter around them began again and RJ leaned over to whisper in Grace's ear. "Sorry about that."

"No. Don't be. I expected it," she replied.

She was lying. He knew from the crinkle in her nose when she attempted to smile afterward.

"Oh, volleyball is going to be so much fun," Riley said. "And now that Grace is here, we'll be evenly matched."

"What?" RJ blurted. He'd been hoping the uncomfortable part of this evening was nearing an end.

"She's right," Maurice chimed in. "Now it all works out, we'll be evenly matched with Grace joining us tomorrow."

"But Grace isn't joining us tomorrow," RJ replied, releasing Grace as if their entwined hands were the cause of his siblings' suggestion.

"Why not?" Riley asked.

"It does make sense," Desta said. "She evens out the women versus the men and if she's here to interview all of us, it stands to reason that she'd also hang out with all of us."

No, that definitely didn't make sense. RJ had spent the better part of the day kicking himself for letting the "keep your enemies close" philosophy goad him into making this arrangement with Grace. He'd been especially annoyed with himself for kissing her because in the end—i.e., this morning—she'd simply turned him down again. She'd brushed off what had happened between them in the cabana as being "in the past." Each time he saw Grace he felt as if he were locked into a front-row seat on a roller coaster of emotions. One minute he couldn't resist remembering how good they'd been together, leading to the persistent need to touch her, kiss her and protect her from all harm. And the next minute, fresh anger churned in the pit of his stomach at the confusion that still plagued him over her abrupt departure. Now they had an agreement and he couldn't back out. Though he wanted access to her story, he'd planned to check in with her during quick coffee breaks, not spend every second together doing every insane item on Riley's itinerary.

"I played a little volleyball in high school," Grace replied. "I'd love to join you tomorrow."

His head whipped around so fast it was a wonder he didn't injure himself. What the hell was she doing? This morning she hadn't made a move to stop him from leaving her room, but now she was suddenly keen on spending a few hours out of her day with him tomorrow. Or had the chance to spend time with his family in order to gain more info for her story prompted the change?

"Maybe I could schedule some time to meet with Desta and Nina a little before the game?" Grace asked by way of follow-up. "That way I'll be totally focused on playing later."

RJ hated the spike of hope he experienced with her suggestion to handle business first, as if she'd somehow heard his question about her true motivation for participating in the game.

"Sure," Nina replied, and Desta also agreed.

"Well, tomorrow sounds like it'll be fun," Ron said. "But tonight, I'd like to walk along the beach with my wife."

RJ watched his father get up from the table and stand by his mother while she did the same. Ron's hand went to the small of his wife's back and Marva smiled at him, the love they still shared obvious in their expressions.

"Awww, that's so romantic," Nina said to Major after Marva and Ron had bid their good-nights and walked away. "When we've been married for thirty-six years, I hope we still look like that.".

"They're definitely relationship goals," Riley told Chaz, who lifted her hand to his lips for a soft kiss.

Tobias stood then, taking Veronica's hand. "Well, that's the cue for the other set of old heads at this table to also say good-night."

Veronica waved at Grace before leaving.

"They're going on three years in case anyone was wondering," Chaz said.

Nobody at the table commented, even though they were all probably trying to figure out how much longer Tobias's latest union was going to last. Chaz had shared his uncle's philosophy on being married so many times—"never be afraid of falling in love"—with the Gold brothers months ago. RJ begged to differ with Tobias's words. Love was definitely something to be afraid of, which was why he'd steered clear of it since getting burned the first time.

"Nightcaps by the pool?" Maurice suggested. "Which building are you staying in, Grace? Well, it doesn't matter, I'm sure RJ will escort you to your room so you can change into your bathing suit and then bring you back to the pool with us."

RJ couldn't go to the other side of the table and slap Maurice against the back of his head like he'd often done when they were younger and his brother said something foolish. Like he so desperately wanted to do now.

"You're still the clever one, Maurice," Grace said lightheartedly. "But I can walk myself back to my room."

She was standing and moving away from the table before he had a chance to catch her. Probably because he was too busy sending Maurice a sour look. Moments later he caught up with her just as she was about to walk out of the restaurant.

"So you're coming to nightcaps by the pool, too?"

He didn't know what else to say but noted that his tone was a mixture of surprise and irritation.

Grace kept going through the doorway, stepping out into the evening with its balmy breeze. He followed and stopped when she did the same.

"Yes, I'm going to change and then join you and your family at the pool because, like Desta said, I'll get a much better idea of how everyone was affected by Ron and Tobias if I'm spending a lot of time with them. Is that a problem for you?"

Words didn't immediately come as RJ realized the real problem here was staring him directly in the face. He *wanted* to spend a lot of time with Grace. Whether or not it made sense, or if it was smart, didn't really matter. What he discovered after sitting beside her and hearing her talk to his family as if she hadn't been gone for the last ten years, after holding her hand when he thought she needed support, was that he really wanted to be with her. Despite the story and even if it was temporary.

"No. It's no problem at all." He cleared his throat. "I'll walk you back to your room."

Her face remained blank, so he couldn't tell if she was relieved or worried about his response. "I wasn't joking when I told Maurice I'll be fine walking by myself."

He nodded and started moving. "Yeah, well, I know Maurice is the jokester of our family, but he was spot-on when he said I'd want to walk you to your room and back. C'mon, let's go."

She fell into step beside him without argument, and marveled at how differently this night was turning out to be.

CHAPTER EIGHT

THIS WAS A shocking change from how Grace thought she'd spend her evening. She'd planned to enjoy the pool at the resort when she had a chance, had even said as much to RJ when they'd talked about it this morning, but she hadn't imagined visiting the massive pool available to guests in the private villas.

During the walk over, RJ had explained the layout of the resort, as if she'd needed to know this was where the people with the big bucks stayed. It was the exclusive area of the resort—not for those like her who'd put a slight dent in her savings to afford the airfare and two-week room stay. The pool outside her building was a nice size, and the cabanas around the bar area were large, as well. But this pool, with its cabanas the size of her apartment, was phenomenal.

"You sure you're gonna be okay doing this?" RJ asked as they came to stand at the edge of the gated swimming area.

They'd stopped at his suite after hers, and he'd

changed out of the navy-blue slacks and button-front shirt he'd worn at dinner. Now he wore light gray board shorts and a loose-fitting white tank top. On his feet were leather flip-flops, and he carried a black travel kit she'd watched him drop his phone, wallet and room key into.

She'd dumped the contents of the small clutch purse she'd carried at dinner into her tote bag and tossed in a pair of shorts in case the sarong she was wearing got too wet. "I'll be fine. You don't have to worry about me, you know. I've been around your family before."

This was something she'd repeated to herself throughout the day in preparation for tonight's dinner. But as it turned out, being around the Golds again had been easier than she'd thought it would be. While she'd expected anger and demands for her to explain what happened between her and RJ, none of that had occurred. Instead, Marva had been her wonderfully warm self and Maurice, Major and Riley had talked to her as if she hadn't been away all this time. Desta and Nina had also been welcoming. Chaz and Tobias hadn't said a lot to her directly, but they'd both seemed comfortable by the middle of dinner. Veronica had been her normal chatty self, annoying Grace only when she'd asked what happened between her and RJ.

Grace suspected they'd all been thinking that, but no one except Veronica had the guts to ask. She would be forever grateful to Ron for circumventing that question and changing the subject.

Things were different between her and RJ now, but that didn't mean her mind never slipped back to a time when they'd been a couple, too.

As they'd all sat paired up at dinner, it had been so easy to let herself believe it was once again true. Good food, easy conversation—even when RJ reached for her hand in a way he often used to while they were out—she'd accepted and let herself believe, if only for that brief time.

"There they are. We were wondering what was taking you two so long," Maurice said, winking at RJ when he looked Maurice's way.

They'd taken the cabana at the farthest end of the pool. The one that was only about twenty feet away from the hot tub she was dying to get into.

"We saved you the two lounge chairs over here." Desta directed Grace to the seat beside her.

It was strategic placement, she immediately noted. The four guys were sitting on the outside of the square setup while the women were in the center. Easier for them to talk to her without interruption. She might've been a little concerned if it didn't work to her advantage as well. For as many questions as she was certain Riley, Nina and Desta were planning to ask her, she'd decided to ask them plenty more.

Grace put her bag beside the designated lounge chair and RJ dropped his on the one behind hers.

"Let's get a drink," he said, and waited while she walked around her chair to join him.

There'd been a larger bar when they first entered the pool area, but it was closed. The one a couple feet from their cabana was smaller, completely stocked and self-serve. No doubt something the Golds had arranged.

"What can I get you?" Chaz asked as she approached. "I'm the designated bartender for the moment, so keep it simple." His smile came quick, giving her the impression that his ire during dinner hadn't been directed at her after all.

"She prefers a martini, but keeping it simple, watermelon vodka or a glass of pinot noir," RJ said before Grace could speak.

This morning he'd remembered she liked doughnuts and coffee for breakfast. Now he was recalling her favorite drinks. How she managed to smile when something like a billion butterflies fluttered in the pit of her stomach, she had no idea. "He's right," she told Chaz, and shrugged when Riley's fiancé raised a brow in question.

"Okay, here you go," Chaz said after pouring the watermelon-infused vodka into a glass over crushed ice.

"I'll grab my own," RJ said, stepping behind the bar with Chaz.

"Cranberry and vodka's your comfort drink, but

I saw you drinking it straight at dinner." She had memories, too.

Chaz looked at RJ, who'd already grabbed the bottle of cranberry juice, then back to Grace. "You two are really something."

We were. The wistful thought fluttered through her mind as Chaz walked away, leaving her and RJ alone at the bar.

"We've got good memories." RJ finished fixing his drink.

"Yeah, glad the good ones stuck around."

"Did we have bad memories?" He came back around to her side of the bar.

"Everybody's got bad memories." She lifted her drink for a sip.

"True," he said. "But tonight, can we just talk about the good ones?"

Her every instinct said to scream no. They couldn't talk about anything that involved their past. It had to stay off-limits, just like Ron had said earlier. But if that were true, she wouldn't be here. Wanting to leave her time with RJ in the past but coming here to dig back through the years of Ron and Tobias's early life was more than hypocritical of her. She had to make a choice.

"You used to enjoy sitting in the hot tub first, before going for a swim." And in the years since they'd been apart, she'd grown accustomed to doing the same whenever possible.

He nodded in the direction they were walking. "Exactly where I'm headed now," he said, looking over at her with a grin.

"Oh, we aren't going back to the cabana with the others?" She'd been so busy trying to ignore the jitters in her stomach, hold on to this drink and keep her composure while being near RJ on a casual basis again, she hadn't even noticed they'd changed course.

"They're not going anywhere. Besides, I'd like a few minutes alone before we have to be part of the couples' corner."

She silently agreed. When they were at the hot tub, she placed her drink near the edge and stood to remove her sarong and flip-flops. He rounded the tub and did the same with his drink, then lifted his shirt over his head before kicking off his own sandals. They both stepped into the hot tub from opposite sides and eased down onto the bench.

"You still give those killer massages?" RJ asked, spreading his arms over the lip of the tub like wings.

Damn he looked good. Like really sexy delicious good lounging there with his naked chest and smoldering dark brown eyes.

"Haven't given anyone a massage in a very long time." She reached for her drink. She should've gotten it straight, or better yet, asked for whiskey instead. Brown liquor hit her harder and usually knocked her on her ass pretty quickly, which was why she didn't have it while out in public. But tonight, she probably needed to be knocked out. Otherwise she had no idea how she was going to get through the rest of this night with RJ so close and so damn alluring.

"No boyfriend?" he asked.

She tilted her head and eyed him sarcastically. "Fine time to ask that question, don't you think?" He'd been the one to bring up yesterday's cabana tryst earlier this morning; now it was her turn.

"Touché," he said with a sly grin. "So no boyfriend at the moment. That's good."

"Why's that good? Because you don't have a girlfriend at the moment?" She hadn't recalled any tabloids saying RJ had a girlfriend.

"That, and because I don't poach on another man's property."

She tossed her head back and laughed. "Now you know damn well I'd never allow myself to be considered someone's property."

"You know what I mean. If you're seeing someone, you're not doing anything with me. Period."

She sobered. "I wasn't aware that I was doing something with you now?"

Silence. As sure as the water bubbling around them was warm and the night was dark.

He reached for his glass, wrapped his long fingers around it and brought it to his lips. "I meant what I said about enjoying our kiss in the cabana," he said after taking a drink.

She'd enjoyed it, too, which was why she was still staring at his fingers on that glass instead of responding to his comment immediately. Remembering the feel of his hands on her was taking a quick and potent toll on her body.

"Did you like when I kissed you?"

First, she had to take another drink herself—a gulp was more like it—and she really wished for that whiskey now. Surely the dark liquor would've been strong enough to wash away the feeling that her body was more than a little prepared to totally betray her once again. "I wouldn't have said I did if it wasn't true. I always like when you kiss me." She looked down into her glass. Her drink was half gone and she already wanted another. Anything to stop this burning need from attacking her.

"I liked how you tasted." He took another drink before placing his glass on the rim of the pool again. "Smooth and sweet just like that drink." When he nodded toward the glass, she followed the action with her gaze.

He was just about finished with his drink as well; just a few cubes of ice and barely a finger of red liquid was left.

"Your mouth was so warm and welcoming," he continued. "I remember all the sweet, sexy things you used to do with your lips on me. So that quick, hot taste of you again made me feel drunker than I ever have from consuming any amount of alcohol."

As she'd thought a few minutes ago, Grace had memories, too. Of the impromptu blow jobs she'd given him while he'd been driving, which could've easily ended with them veering off the road. Of kissing over each hardened nipple of his pecs, tangling her tongue in his mouth until they both moaned for more. She licked her lips and crossed one leg over the other, pressing one thigh down tightly over the other. "Why're you doing this?" Her voice sounded low, quiet, pitiful.

"I want to kiss you again," he said simply. "And more. How do you feel about that?"

RJ wanted to kiss her again. Her gaze flew to his mouth. His bottom lip was heavier than the top. She used to like sucking on it, dragging her tongue along the soft plumpness of his skin. That mouth, neatly framed by his goatee, was the most dangerous part of this beautiful man. His hands were another enticing feature, followed by the thick long dick that she knew from experience would rival any vibrator ever created.

Grace finished her drink, put her glass down and looked him directly in the eye. "I feel like that's probably inevitable." That was the damn truth. It would've been nice to say "Hell no, we're not going there. We're going to keep this just business and that's all." But every word of that would've been a lie, and if there was one thing Grace had never done, it was lie to RJ.

The next move was on him. Sure, she could simply stand up, cross the hot tub and straddle him, but he'd initiated this conversation. She wanted to see where exactly he planned to take it.

Before that could happen, someone called to RJ from the pool and just like that, the thick haze of desire that had cocooned them in the warmth of the bubbling water was cracked.

RJ didn't speak right away but the immediate furrow of his brow said he was irritated. Well, good, 'cause now thanks to him she was hornier than she'd been in she didn't know how long. If she had to suffer, so the hell did he. With that thought she stood and climbed out of the tub, knowing he watched the sway of her ass as she made her retreat.

"C'mon, you don't want to miss nightcaps by the pool, do you?" She said over her shoulder, knowing she was playing with fire, teasing him and alluding to what was to come. It was something she'd always done well, something he'd always made sure she paid for later. A slither of excitement inched down her spine at the memory.

RJ got out of the water, too, grabbing his shirt and shoes in one hand before catching up with her. His gaze was hot and intent when he said, "They get half an hour, then you're coming with me."

CHAPTER NINE

RJ WAS TRUE to his word. Thirty minutes and another drink later, they were walking away from the pool and heading toward the villas. From what she could see through the darkness, there were at least four in this area, some a little larger, which she presumed meant they had more than one bedroom. RJ's, she recalled, was on the far left and looked to be a smaller unit.

When they'd come here so he could change earlier, she'd opted not to go inside, instead sitting on one of the lounge chairs outside the floor-to-ceiling wall of glass patio doors. Now he was using his room card to swipe over the security panel, and she watched those doors slide open. He'd left the light on and the drapes partially drawn.

Her flip-flops were still a little wet as she stepped onto the natural-colored wood flooring. The room was bathed in golden light, the walls and furniture a pretty neutral tone. For her, the most intriguing part of this space was the high ceiling, accented with thick beams painted a rich chocolate brown.

"Do you want another drink?" he asked from behind her.

She could hear him moving about as she walked farther into what she presumed was the living room. He'd closed the door and then she heard a swishing sound she assumed was the curtains being closed. Turning slightly, she saw a table with four cushioned chairs surrounding it. A bottle of wine with four wineglasses was in the center.

"Not if you want me to remain coherent," she said before turning to face him.

He startled her with how close he was, and his arms immediately went around her waist to pull her up to him. "Oh, you definitely want to be wide awake for this."

There wasn't a moment to respond before he came in for a kiss, his mouth taking hers in a fierce sweep of lips and tongues. The action took her breath away but she was quick to fall into the groove, lifting her arms to place her hands at the back of his head. His hands were everywhere, up and down her back, cupping her ass, pressing her into his already-hardened dick.

She'd known it was going to be like this. As they'd frolicked in the pool with his family, playing an impromptu game of water volleyball, the sexual tension between them had been ratcheted up to an almost explosive level. Each time he'd brushed past her in the water, his palms moving over her ass or down her

spine, she'd felt a little more breathless with desire.
When she'd lost her footing and gone underwater un-
expectedly, he'd been right there, arms around her
waist as they both floated, bodies pressed together.
She'd wrapped her legs around him that time and
he'd slid a finger between her legs and beneath her
bikini bottom for a quick touch to her pussy. Already
on the edge of need, Grace had almost come right
that second. Luckily for them they weren't alone in
the pool, and the women had a point to prove by
beating the men.

But that was over now.

With his palms planted on the cheeks of her ass,
he hoisted her up until she was again wrapping her
legs around his waist. He broke the kiss and she let
her head fall back while he used his teeth to nip along
the line of her jaw and down her neck.

"How many bathing suits did you pack?"

The question floated through the haze of heavy
arousal in her mind as he began walking.

"Three, no, four, I think." Truthfully, Grace
couldn't think. Not beyond how good his mouth felt
on her skin, or how badly she wanted him inside her
at this moment.

"I'll replace this one," he grumbled, and seconds later when they were in the bedroom, he set
her down.

The sarong and bikini bottom went first. He
yanked at both until she heard a tearing sound and

all the material fell from her body. To be fair, the sa-rong was nothing more than a gauzy strip of fabric, and the bikini bottom was even less—two triangles and ties at her hips. She'd picked the sexiest one to wear tonight when she realized RJ would be seeing her in it. The ones remaining in her suitcase were pretty basic one-pieces, because this trip hadn't been planned to catch a guy and get laid.

His hands were busy on her top now, yanking at the strings until it fell from her breasts to join its companions on the floor. He lifted her again, this time dropping her onto the bed where she did a lit-tle bounce before scooting to the center of the king-size mattress.

The bed was in the center of the room facing an-other wall of windows with the curtains already drawn. More beams adorned the ceiling but she didn't look at them long. Not when RJ was pushing his board shorts down past his thighs to step out of them. He hadn't bothered putting his tank top on as they'd walked from the hot tub, so she'd had an un-fettered view of his muscled chest for the past hour. She hadn't realized how much she missed seeing him up close and naked, not until he climbed onto the bed with her.

She pulled him to her so she could get her mouth on his again. This kiss was hotter, slower, wetter as feelings of familiarity engulfed her. Kissing RJ had always been like a journey for her. Whether it was a small kiss or a full-mouth exploration, her body and her soul had always delved deep into it, as if she were made only to kiss him. At first, she'd thought that was a weird thing to consider—one woman, one man, one kiss, forever. But that's precisely how it felt. He knew just how to drag his tongue over hers until she moaned with longing. With her eyes closed, it always felt as if the moment their lips met, she stepped into another place, a smaller space where there was only room for the two of them.

He came down with her, covering her body with his as she lay against the mattress once more. Lacing his arms around her back, he held her close in an embrace not so much constricting as possessive, as if he had no plans to let her go. That worked well because she had no plans to go anywhere. The kiss went on for what seemed like forever and then, the second he pulled back, leaving both of them breathless, it didn't seem like long enough.

For endless moments he just stared down at her and she stared up at him, their gazes locked, some silent communication hovering between them. She rubbed her palms against the back of his head, gliding over the smooth skin. Their chests remained melded together, both rising and falling quickly with the intense pattern of their breathing. His hands were in her still damp hair and she lifted a leg to wrap around his waist.

The groan rumbled deep in his chest as the action opened her wider, so that the length of his dick pressed against the warm folds of her pussy.

"You love teasing me, don't you?" The question was a rough growl that sent waves of pleasure along her skin.

"I love feeling you against me," she replied, and lifted her ass a little to thrust into his hardness.

He sucked air through his clenched teeth, closing his eyes as she continued to rub against him. The friction, the heat, his dick sliding along her already slick core, was tantalizing and she couldn't stop. She enjoyed pushing him to edge, taking them both there until they could barely think, or breathe, before coming together. Pulling his face down to hers again, she licked his lips. Tucking her tongue against the corners of his mouth, dragging it along the outline of his lips, feeling the crisp edges of his mustache.

She could hear him breathing, a heavy rumble starting from the center of his chest and rolling up until it was released in a barely restrained huff. She continued to move her tongue along his lips, stopping at the bottom one only seconds before sucking it into her mouth. He leaned into the action, moving his hips now to maintain the rhythm of his dick against her pussy. She was so wet his thickness simply slid along the path, creating a sound that was driving her insane.

Holding his head in her hands, his lip in her mouth, it was all so familiar. Memories of so many nights like this flooded her like a tidal wave and she shuddered with their intensity.

Helpless. That's how he'd said he felt when she was sucking on his lips, helplessly drawn to her in a way he could never explain with any other word. Well, tonight it was her turn to feel that way. She couldn't stop this if she wanted to, if her career, hell, if her life depended on it.

When he groaned the next time, he moved to take her into another kiss, this one painfully slow and deep. She couldn't hold him any tighter against her, couldn't whisper his name in her mind any louder. His hands moving in her hair, fingers grazing her scalp, body moving with infinite slowness over hers. She was drowning.

He pulled away, breaking the kiss and her hold on him as he moved from the bed. She watched him walk, his taut ass, his muscled thighs and his gorgeous hard dick jutting out from his body. Her mouth watered and her pussy pulsated. He pulled a box of condoms out of a bag sitting on the floor, ripped it open and took out a packet. Her gaze was trained on his every movement as he tore that packet open and pulled out the latex.

"You still love to watch." It was a statement spoken as he put the latex to the tip of his dick and rolled it slowly down his length.

There wasn't an ounce of shame to her truth. "Hell yeah, when you're the show."

He grinned, that sexy-as-hell RJ grin that she'd like to think was meant only for her. Then he was on the bed again, lifting her legs until her ankles rested on his shoulders. Turning his face from side to side, he kissed each ankle, brushed his hands down her calves and looked at her.

"You sure?" he asked quietly.

She lifted her hands to her breasts, cupping them before touching her fingers to each nipple. "I need."

It was all the permission required, and in the next moment he was pressing his dick into her, stretching her, filling her, completing her.

Dying.

That was RJ's new word for how he felt when he was inside Grace.

It was like dying and being reborn into something he knew he could never be without her.

Grasping her ankles, he spread her legs and continued to move in and out of her, his teeth clenching, eyes closing with the pleasure ripping through him with each stroke. The sound of her whispering his name had his eyes gradually opening. She was gorgeous with her damp hair spread out around her face, hands slipping slowly from her breasts to grasp the comforter beneath her. The dark tone of her skin was luminous against the pale hue of the bedding. Her deep brown nipples were taut as her breasts jiggled with the force of his thrusts.

It took concerted effort—and the fact that he didn't want to pass out from lack of oxygen and miss this glorious pleasure—to remind himself to breathe. "Damn." The one word came out in a whoosh when his gaze fell lower and he watched his dick sinking deep inside her.

How had he gone so long without feeling the tightness of her muscles grasping him, sucking him back in the moment he dared to pull away?

"Ronald." She sighed his name. His full name, as she always did during sex.

Nobody called him that, not even his parents. In fact, no Gold with that name had ever been called that—his grandfather had gone by Ronnie. So hearing her say it always made him feel like he was special to her. But that couldn't be, not anymore.

The thought spurred a need to stake his claim, even if only in this bedroom. Tonight she would be his, and he would show her once again how it felt when they were together. Pulling out of her, he ignored her moans of protest and eased off the bed. The way she shot up told him she thought he was finished and she wasn't happy about it. Her eyes widened and she opened her mouth to speak.

"Shhhhh." He noted the instant rise of her brow, a look that clearly asked if he was out of his mind for basically telling her to shut up.

Grace was a beauty, there was no doubt. She was also confident, brilliant and feisty as hell when provoked. He didn't verbally respond to her expression but stood at the end of the bed and reached for her legs again, easing her to the end of the bed as well. When she was there, he took her hands and pulled her to her feet. With a hand to the back of her head and one slipping behind her to cup her ass, he kissed her again.

This time the hungry exchange included his teeth running over the line of her jaw when they gasped for breath, only to return to dueling tongues again when her arms came up to wrap around his neck. That hand on her ass moved until he touched her tight sphincter and she jumped in his arms. He wouldn't break the kiss, but took in her pleasured moans and joined with a guttural groan of his own.

It'd been a very long time since he'd taken her in that place. Too damn long by his estimation, and he knew he wouldn't go there tonight, but he would remind her how it'd felt when they'd both explored something they'd never done with anyone else before. She clung to him as he applied more pressure, not enough to enter her but just enough to drive them both crazy with need.

"Now who's teasing?" She breathed the question as her head fell back and he licked along the line of her jaw.

"Oh, I'm not teasing," he groaned. "I definitely plan to deliver."

And with that statement he eased his hand from

between her legs and turned her away from him. With a hand to the small of her back he pushed her over until her palms were flat on the bed. "Arch your back, babe," he instructed, and she complied until her legs were spread, ass lifted up to him in offering.

He smacked each plump mound, the sound echoing throughout the room and sending spikes of desire straight to his dick. Gripping her ass cheeks then, he spread them slowly until he could drive into her core with one quick thrust. She screamed and he almost came right then and there. Fueled by their shared desire he pumped fiercely in and out of her until her legs shook and she yelled his name. The warmth of her essence covering him as she came was enough to push him straight over the edge, and in the next seconds he was gripping her hips as his body shook with his release.

In another time, once their breathing had returned to normal and he was certain he wasn't going to collapse over her, RJ would've carried her to the shower or run them a warm bath. Tonight, they each moved in and out of the bathroom solo. He'd let her go first so when he came out of the bathroom she was standing with a pair of shorts on and her sarong tied around her upper body like a tube top.

"I had to improvise," she said with a shrug when he was obviously staring at her in question.

He grinned. "Maybe you should come work for us at RGF as a designer."

She smiled back, but the easy conversation between them had dissipated. Now there was an uncomfortable tension that he sensed neither of them knew how to deal with. Did she think this was a mistake? Did he? She'd said it was inevitable. After yesterday's kiss and the hours spent thinking about taking that kiss further, which had plagued him all day and night, he wholeheartedly agreed with her. Just like yesterday in the cabana, being alone with her tonight had been great. He was starkly aware of the fact that he'd thought he and Grace were great together before, too.

Despite their obvious history, there was a part of him—a very big part that he was having a hell of a time battling with—that wanted to ask her to stay. That part of him wanted to lie and cuddle with her the way they often had after sex, in the comfort of his penthouse in Manhattan. That part had never wanted to let her go, and while RJ had respected those feelings all this time, the look of determination on Grace's face dictated he keep a tight lid on those emotions.

"I'll walk you back to your room," he said, and moved to the dresser to grab fresh clothes.

She was quiet as he pulled out basketball shorts and a T-shirt, slipping them both on and then going to find his flip-flops. When he faced her again, he wanted desperately to take her in his arms and tell her that he…what? What would he say? How did he feel now? Was he still in love with her?

"You don't have to," she said when they'd stood in silence for a while.

He gave her a "don't be ridiculous" look and headed out of the room. They walked along the property in silence and minutes later, when they arrived at the front of her building, she turned to him.

"We can do this here," she said, and he looked at her quizzically.

His thoughts had been all over the place as they'd walked. Reminiscing on their time together, searching for when and where it could've gone wrong, just as he'd done for weeks after she'd first left him. This current effort was just as futile as the others, because he still had no clue what had happened between them. And yes, he could've just asked the question and let her tell him, but there was a very real part of him that wanted her to trust him enough to open up to him. She hadn't before so it was probably foolish to want that now, but he did.

"We can do what here?" he asked.

"Say good-night," she said with a shrug. "I mean, we don't have to feel like it's that uncomfortable moment of a first date."

That wasn't how he felt at all. He was so beyond the nervous expectation of a first date with Grace, but he was also tired of the emotional back-and-forth tonight had brought.

"Well then, good night," he said.

"Good night, RJ," she whispered.

And neither of them moved.

Their gazes remained locked as he inhaled the tropical air mixed with the scent of chlorine they both carried from their time in the pool. A light breeze blew, lifting the ends of her hair, sending a few strands into her face. She tucked them behind one ear.

She stepped close to him then, coming up on the tips of her toes to kiss him lightly on the lips. "I'll see you tomorrow."

He wrapped one arm around her waist and held her close, kissing her again, dipping his tongue into her mouth to tangle with hers. There'd been no consideration of making this move, no weighing options, just the persistent need to act. A need he suspected he was going to feel for the rest of their time on this island. With that resolution, he finally broke the kiss, said, "See you tomorrow, Gracie," and walked away.

CHAPTER TEN

SHE'D HAD SEX with RJ. The man she'd once loved with all her heart.

Standing beneath the shower spray at just after nine the next morning, she let that resonate in her mind. The physical act had already taken its toll on her body, leaving her limbs languid and relaxed, her lips still tingling from all the hungry kisses, a dull ache deep in her center as she anticipated it happening again.

There'd never been any issues for her and RJ when it came to the physical. She could safely say that remained true. Another truth glaring in the forefront of her mind was anxiety. The spikes of uncertainty that had barreled into her with a rampage when RJ had proposed years ago.

Marry me, Gracie. That's what he'd said that night at the restaurant. He came around to her side of the table, went down on one knee and opened that lovely blue box.

She'd looked into his face, familiar with his every

expression, and noted the hope and love filling his smile. If she'd said yes, that smile would've grown bigger, excitement lighting his eyes. He would've hugged her close before putting the ring on her finger and whispering how much he loved her. And she would've whispered how much she loved him back. If she hadn't felt as if her chest would explode from the assault of questions and concerns that assailed her in those moments.

"No." The softly spoken word had come quick. It was knee-jerk and for days afterward she'd wished she could take it back, say it in a different way, something. Anything to erase the broken and rejected look that instantly followed on his face. That memory had been more painful than anything she'd ever experienced.

He hadn't spoken after her reply and she couldn't find the words to follow up that solemn answer. He wanted to know why; she could tell by the way his eyes continued to search her, silently begging for explanation. She had words. Her career was based on finding the right words to present the best story. So of course she knew the words to say. Yet she hadn't said them. Would he have believed her? Would he have thought she was out of her mind, afraid, a coward?

No matter how many words she'd thought she had, no explanation had come that night. Instead, she'd stood, grabbed her purse and walked away.

With a heavy sigh at the memory, Grace dropped her head, letting the warm water trickle down her back. Tears stung her eyes as regret lodged in her throat.

What if she'd had the guts to explain to him that night? What if he'd said, "I still love you and want to be with you, Gracie"? What if she'd made a big mistake walking away?

And why did any of that matter now? It was years ago, water under the bridge, a closed chapter of their past. Except everything that did and didn't happen that night stood between them each time they were together now. Even last night as they'd enjoyed each other physically, the questions had been there. The what-ifs and whys lingering in the air around them.

What if she'd just said yes? Would they have children by now? Probably. And would she have failed at both motherhood and being a wife by now?

That had always been the deeper issue, even beyond her desire to stand firm in her career. That niggling doubt that had lived with her every second of her life as the youngest sister, the baby of the family, the one with all those big shoes ahead of her to fill. The one who'd failed at filling those big shoes so many times before. Sure, she'd only been eight when her teacher had made a comment about Grace not reading at the same level as Trinity had when she'd been in that class. And she'd only been fifteen with short arms and legs when she'd been cut from the high school majorette squad that each of her sisters had been on. But by the time she'd entered college and decided on a career in journalism—only to have her mother scoff as if that were nothing compared to being a scholar or any of the occupations her sisters had chosen—the seeds of doubt had been firmly planted in her mind. She'd decided then that she'd prove herself to them by succeeding in her career no matter what.

Not that any of that made a difference now. Grace didn't have any more answers today than she had ten years ago. And because that was a hard truth to face, she did what she always did—pushed it aside.

An hour later, when she was dressed in blue shorts, a white T-shirt and white sandals, Grace walked into the café where she, Nina and Desta had planned to meet. She'd styled her hair in a simple ponytail and packed a notepad, pens and her tablet into her bag. As she was the first to arrive, she grabbed a table near the window and ordered a cup of coffee and another one of those great doughnuts RJ had brought her yesterday. She checked her phone while she waited, reading text messages from her sisters' group chat. Hope wanted to know what they thought about a fall wedding and Charity announced that Skye, her oldest daughter, had lost one of her front teeth. The picture of her niece missing that one tooth made Grace smile. She hadn't been home since her mother's birthday celebration in March, and she missed seeing her family. The immediate longing to be with them now had to be spurred by what had happened between her and RJ last night and all the thoughts it brought to mind this morning. Thoughts of what might've been if she hadn't turned down RJ's proposal.

"Hey, what're you in such deep thought about?" Nina asked when she appeared. She pulled out the chair across from Grace and took a seat.

Nina was absolutely lovely, with her cinnamon-hued complexion and alluring curves in the hot pink romper she wore.

"Oh, hey, nothing. Just checking text messages," Grace said, and closed the screen on her phone, pushing it to the side.

Nina frowned. "You sure?"

Graced nodded. "Positive. Where's Desta?"

"Oh, she's coming. She and Riley wanted daiquiris so they stopped at the bar by the pool." Nina signaled the server and when the young lady appeared, she ordered water and a fruit bowl.

"Taking the healthy route, I see," Grace noted. Nina had also opted for bottled water over alcoholic beverages last night at the pool.

"Trying," Nina replied with a shrug.

"Did you say Riley was coming?"

"Yes. We just figured we'd help save you time

with the interviews and that way you could spend more time doing…other things."

Before Grace could ask about the "other things," Desta and Riley joined them. Desta wore black Bermuda shorts and a yellow tank top, her dark hair styled in two braids that hung down her back. Riley wore her hair in a ponytail, her entrancing hazel eyes highlighted with a nude eyeshadow that matched the color of her shorts and the stripes in her halter top.

"Mornin'!" Desta said cheerfully while taking a seat next to Nina.

Riley pulled out the chair beside Grace and sat. "Hey. How're you feeling this morning? You and RJ were taking those vodka drinks down last night."

Yeah, they had been drinking but not enough that either of them was drunk, which she thought could've been an excuse for what they'd done after the pool party. But Grace definitely didn't want to think about that right now.

"Oh, that was nothing. I'm fine. Shall we get started?" They were scheduled to play volleyball at eleven thirty and since she was now interviewing three people, Grace wanted to make sure she had enough time to get everything in.

"Sure," Riley said. "But first, if you don't mind, I wanted to ask you something."

Grace had been digging her notepad and pen out of her bag and looked up to see that all three women were staring at her.

"Ah, no, ask away," Grace said, trying to hide the fact that she was more than a little leery about what Riley wanted to know.

It didn't escape her that she was sitting next to RJ's younger sister, a woman whom she'd been close to a long time ago and who undoubtedly wanted answers to the same questions her brother probably had.

"I know you don't know Desta and Nina as well as you used to know me, but since we're all related by marriage, and outside of that we're all women, I figure it's okay to speak candidly." Riley didn't wait for Grace to agree or disagree. "What happened between you and RJ? I thought you two were the perfect couple. I mean, coming from me, who at the time wasn't even considering being in a relationship, I thought next to my parents, you and RJ were exactly what love was supposed to look like. And then you were just gone."

Riley sipped from her straw when she was finished. Her expression was one of innocent curiosity, while Grace grappled with whether to speak just as candidly around this group of women.

The server returned with Grace's coffee and doughnut and Nina's water and fruit. Grace reached for the cream and poured it into her coffee, then added sugar, all while knowing they waited for her response.

"Nothing happened," she replied, figuring if she

expected these women to be honest with her, she owed them the same courtesy. "I needed something different in my life at the time, so I left to find it."

"Did you find it?" Desta asked. "What you went looking for?"

Well, if this story did what she was hoping it would, the answer to that question would be yes. "I think so. Which leads me to this interview."

"But you did love him, right?" Riley asked. "I mean the two of you seemed so perfect together. I just remember wondering if you loved him, how could you have left him?" She clearly didn't want to let this topic go. "I guess what I'm really concerned about now is that you're not here to hurt my brother again."

There was no heat to Riley's words, but an air of tension settled over them and Nina acted quickly to resolve it. "Well, I can kinda see walking away from someone you love, if you have a good enough reason," she said. "I mean, I loved Major but when I thought he'd used me and my company for his benefit and was then trying to take over everything I'd worked hard to build, I had to get away from him."

Grace didn't have all the details, but she suspected these were the events that led up to Nina and Major's fake engagement turning into the real thing.

Desta nodded. "She's speaking the truth. Sometimes walking away is what you need to get things straight in your mind, to make sure what you're feeling is the best thing for you. Despite what people say, love isn't always the only answer."

Grace wanted to high-five Desta for saying almost exactly what she'd been thinking so long ago.

"I know," Riley started. "Don't get me wrong, Chaz and I definitely went through some things before we got it right and my first inclination was to let it all go. But you and RJ didn't seem to be having any problems. Like, I really thought things were perfect between you guys."

It was clear that her breakup with RJ had hit Riley hard. When she'd walked away back then, Grace had thought a clean break was best. And as certain as she'd been that she was making the right decision about leaving, there'd been many times in the past years that the guilt over not saying goodbye to his family had assailed her.

"I never meant to hurt RJ or any of you." Grace sighed and shook her head. "And I'm not here to cause any more pain. But you should know that 'perfect' can be misleading." Nothing in her life had ever been perfect. Not when she always felt like she was fighting to find her place. Her relationship with RJ hadn't made her feel that way in the beginning, but the moment he mentioned marriage, she'd seen all the possibilities run through her mind like a movie trailer and she'd known she had to go. "Sort of like Ron and Tobias working together at RGF. They were seemingly the perfect duo of fresh new talent, set to take the fashion world by storm. Then something happened and it all fell apart."

The conversation, thankfully, took a turn with her words and the interview questions she'd planned were asked and answered. The three women gave her insight into so many aspects of the two men and their impact on the fashion industry. Nina spoke of how she'd wanted desperately to work with one of the two top fashion houses to build on the app she'd created. Desta talked about working at RGF and learning from Ron's work ethic and dedication to his family. She didn't know much about Tobias except for how his company was positioned as RGF's biggest competitor, but she liked Chaz and thought he was bringing a dynamic edge to King Designs and their new branding.

It was Riley who pricked Grace's heart with the story of her parents and how they'd met at a party sponsored by RGF and fallen in love. From Riley's perspective her father had been driven by Tobias's betrayal, pushed to work harder to make RGF bigger and better than any other company. She spoke of how everything RJ did was in his father's image and how much RJ was looking forward to taking over the company in just a few months.

"He'll be the CEO at around the same age my father was at his peak in the industry. My parents were newly married and my mother was about to have RJ. My father says that's when he first realized he had everything he needed to succeed in life. When he had his wife beside him, a baby about to be born, and he sat in the CEO's chair for the first time."

Riley's words resonated with Grace well into the time they walked along the beach in preparation for the volleyball game. Ron Gold ran his company and built a family. Now his children were doing the same thing—Riley and Chaz, Nina and Major, Desta and Maurice. RJ was the only one who wasn't married. Just as she was the only one in her family who wasn't. What did that mean? Nothing, and then again, to Grace, everything.

It reinforced the pressure she'd already felt about what her life should and shouldn't be. Could she have been the wife that Marva Gold was to Ron? Or that her mother was to her father? Could she be a wife, period? All the fears that had lain dormant these past ten years were bubbling to the surface now, until the next question she had to ask was: What if coming here was a mistake?

The answer came the moment she saw RJ walking toward her. The sun was at his back, framing his muscled body in golden light. He wore black shorts and a white T-shirt. His feet were bare and dark sunglasses covered his eyes. But she knew he was watching her; she could feel the warmth of his gaze as it filled her body, circling around to clench her chest.

A mixture of anxiety and need settled there as he

came closer. No, coming here hadn't been a mistake. She'd needed to see RJ again, to touch him and hold him in her arms as a reminder that she had loved him and he had loved her. Where those past emotions were taking them now, she had no idea.

The way Grace was looking at him had RJ's heart racing. She'd been on his mind all night, starting from the second he watched her walk into her building until just about an hour ago, when some of his family had barged into his villa demanding answers to their questions.

"Did you really think it was better to strike some sort of deal with her instead of coming to me and discussing this beforehand?" His father had spoken first, while Major, Maurice and Chaz had found seats in the living area.

RJ had just gotten out of bed and was on his way to take a shower when he'd heard them at the door. He'd pulled on a pair of shorts but was otherwise undressed for what turned out to be an intervention of sorts.

"You're turning the company over to me in a few months. Don't you think I'm capable of dealing with issues on my own?" He'd asked his father that question, even though he knew this situation was different from anything RGF was liable to face in the future. Still, he needed his father to understand his position.

"I don't doubt your abilities, son. But I know you realize this is a sensitive subject," Ron had replied.

"Which is exactly why I decided to handle it the way I did. Keep her close, keep my eye on what's being discussed. Having control of the situation cuts down on the chances that it'll cause more harm than good." With all that said, the "keep her close" part was what resonated with him most this morning.

"Are you sure you're the right one to try to control Grace, considering your history?" Major asked.

RJ had sent his brother a death glare for that remark. "Don't go there."

"We kinda have to go there, man. She's writing a story about us. She knows us better than any other reporter out there. She broke your heart." Leave it to Maurice to put that last nail in the coffin.

"All that might be true but our relationship is in the past. I can handle this." He'd told them that a few more times during the exchange, but now seeing Grace at this moment on the beach, he wasn't quite sure.

He stopped walking toward her and she closed the rest of the distance between them. "Hey." She spoke with a light cheeriness to her tone.

"Hey."

"You ready for part two of the butt-whoopin' we served y'all last night?" Desta asked as she walked past them.

"Oh, she's talking smack already," Major said. "Mo, come get your lady!"

RJ couldn't help it—he chuckled. His brothers were just as competitive as he was, but it was pretty comical to see them this way with the women they loved. It was fun watching them straddle the fence between being full-on obnoxious about winning and distractingly apologetic to their significant others at the same time.

"Guess we better get ready to play," Grace said.

He shrugged. "I guess we better." He watched her walk away, staring at her legs and remembering them being wrapped around him last night.

"You gonna be able to play without drooling?" Chaz asked him.

RJ frowned at his soon-to-be brother-in-law. "I'm not the one who just finished kissing and groping all over the competition." He'd watched his sister greet Chaz as he'd been walking toward Grace. Months ago the site of his sister hugging and kissing any guy disturbed the hell out of him. Now that he'd gotten to know Chaz and trusted the guy wasn't going to break Riley's heart like the last asshole she'd been engaged to, he was sort of okay with them touching.

"Yeah, that's because I'm marrying her next week and we're getting in all the practice we can leading up to our honeymoon."

RJ frowned. "TMI, man! TMI!"

The second game of volleyball between the guys

and the girls went a lot better than last night's water version. The guys claimed victory and boasted about it all the way through lunch. After that Chaz wanted the guys to join him for a few rounds of golf, and since RJ had already bailed on the fitting yesterday, he figured he should go, even though he really wanted to spend more time with Grace.

"I'm meeting with Tobias this afternoon," she'd told him when he asked what she was doing for the duration of the day. "Then I'll probably write for the rest of the evening. I have a lot I want to get done."

"Cool, then I guess we'll figure out another time to check in." He hadn't bothered to try to hide the disappointment in his tone.

Watching her run back and forth during the game, hearing her laughter, seeing the genuine fun she was having, had touched something in him. To be honest, it enhanced the same something he'd felt when he was inside her last night. The feeling of incompletion that he knew was only assuaged when they were together.

"Sure, ah, breakfast tomorrow?" she suggested.

Tomorrow seemed like a decade away, and he didn't want to wait another decade to see her. "Yeah, that's fine."

He wasn't desperate and he wasn't going to allow her to think he was. They were on this island together for just under two weeks—certainly he'd see her again. In the meantime, he needed to get himself together. Acting like a lovesick puppy wasn't his thing. It felt odd and demoralizing and he didn't like it. Still, when Grace walked away, he stared at her until she was out of sight, missing her the second she was gone.

CHAPTER ELEVEN

"Okay, we've gotta build a better sandcastle than them, or I'm never gonna live this down," RJ said. Three days later, they were on their knees on the beach for another family activity.

They'd been divided up as couples this time, so Grace was on his team. He'd convinced himself that it did make sense for Grace to participate in Riley's itinerary, as had been pointed out the other night at dinner. As a result, he'd seen her every day for the past few days. Often that was due to their story status updates, but on other occasions Riley and his mother had invited her to join in whatever they were doing. And he was okay with all of that. He could be around her and not want what they used to have. Or at least he was trying his best not to.

She wore a coral one-piece bathing suit today, as evidenced by her low-riding denim shorts. Her sandals had been dropped into that mammoth bag she always carried, and she was now barefoot as she unhooked the stack of buckets they'd been given.

"Let's get started," she said. "What type of design do you want to make?"

He frowned. "It's a sandcastle. We're making it look like a sandcastle."

She glared at him then with her lips turned up. "Are you serious? That's not gonna work. We have to have a game plan. Are we going for a real royal castle, or something brooding and creepy?"

Each team was spaced about ten feet apart down the beach and the others were already packing sand and getting started with their structure. "We're doing whatever's going to win," he replied. He wasn't prepared when she scooped up a handful of sand and threw it at him.

Stunned for a few seconds, he contemplated what his next move should be. Yet his teammate had just done the unspeakable so really there was only one option. He tossed a handful of sand back. She frowned and then brushed the sand off the front of her. Bits of it had fallen between the lovely cleavage she was sporting today.

"Need me to help you get that?" he asked with a sexy grin.

The way her eyes cut over at him after that question was a cross between hilarious and deadly, so he held his hands up in defeat just in case.

"What I need is for you to get out of my way. I can do this," she said after brushing away the rest of the sand and picking up a bucket.

"Wait, we're a team. We're both supposed to be doing this."

"Then you need to get yourself together and stop fooling around," she said sternly.

He nodded. "Okay, well, for the record, you started it."

She cut another raised-brow look at him and turned over the bucket she'd just filled with sand. He'd better get started doing the same—so he did. In no time they had a semblance of a castle under way. When Grace leaned over to use a tool that looked like a spatula to carve into one of the mounds they'd created, he couldn't help but follow her movements.

Her shorts weren't just low riding, they were also very short. After seeing her these past few days, he wondered if she had any shorts that came below her upper thigh. Probably not, and for that he should definitely thank every deity there was. But the way she was leaning over today he could see a bit more of her cheeks than he suspected anybody else could. More like, he hoped nobody else could. The thought of another man looking at her and thinking the things he was thinking right now didn't sit well with him.

"Taking another break?" she asked without moving from her spot.

"Nah, just enjoying the view." It was the truth.

"You're incorrigible."

"I think the correct word is horny."

With that Grace turned to look over her shoulder

at him. He winked at her and grinned. They hadn't
been physical since the night of the pool party. Considering how awkwardly that had ended, they seemed
to have made a conscious effort not to touch each
other since then. Not that he didn't want Grace—he
did, there was no doubt about that. He just wasn't
sure what sleeping with her now would mean once
this island trip was over.

"I'm really confused," she said, and continued her
work on what he now saw was going to be a fin. "You
want to win this competition. You want to win every
competition, actually, yet you haven't been working
very hard over here."

He reluctantly grabbed another bucket. "Something's distracting me," he told her as he stuffed more
sand into it. He really didn't like this activity and
planned to share those thoughts with Riley when
it was done. She wouldn't care—she'd just laugh at
him as she'd been doing a lot these days.

He knew his sister had spoken to Grace but when
he asked Grace about their conversation, she'd only
told him about the parts that were related to the feud
or his family. Nothing about their breakup, even
though RJ was certain that would've been one of
the first questions Riley asked. His sister had been
really upset when he'd announced that Grace was
gone. So much so that he'd been tempted to reach
out to Grace just for the purpose of telling her she
needed to talk to Riley, but he hadn't. And in time,

just like him, Riley had moved on without Grace. Now his sister looked almost elated anytime she saw the two of them together.

"Are you calling me a distraction?" she asked without even looking at him.

The way she was able to control her feelings, whether it was desire to have sex or tension about their past, was unnerving to him. He was certain she was feeling the pain of withdrawal the same way he was. Last night when he'd been sitting on the balcony in her room, he'd caught her staring at his crotch. His dick had never gotten so hard so fast, but as soon as it did, she looked away.

"No, I'm calling this weird sexual truce we seem to have initiated a distraction."

She paused then and pushed up from the sand to sit back on her legs. "What are you talking about?"

"I think you know."

She shook her head.

"Okay, look, neither of us was ever known to give in to our circumstances. So why are we tiptoeing around each other now?"

"What would happen when it ends?" she asked.

He had and hadn't come up with an answer, or rather he hadn't come up with an answer he wanted to accept.

"Let's have dinner tonight," he said. "Not a meeting to discuss the story. Just dinner at seven, you and me. I'll make all the arrangements."

She looked skeptical. "Are we going to talk about this at dinner?"

He shook his head. "We're going to have a nice meal like we used to do. I miss that." He'd also missed times like this, when they were just doing stuff together. Sure, he wasn't going to like the sand that was already sneaking into places he didn't want to think about, but he wasn't going to lie about enjoying being with her.

"Yeah," she said with a slow nod. "I do, too. But I'd really like to win this sandcastle contest first."

They both grinned. Competitiveness, ambition, tenacity—all traits they shared. "You're right. Let's do this."

And do it they did. An hour later they were being crowned the winners for their underwater castle with all the intricate aquatic life that Grace had managed to design. RJ let her take the gift shop sandcastle they were awarded as a prize. When she went off to an interview with Major and Maurice, he returned to his room to make plans for tonight.

Grace stepped up onto the yacht, the balmy evening breeze blowing her hair and the light material of her full skirt.

"Good evening," RJ said as he stood from the table at the far end of the deck.

"Good evening," she replied. "We're having dinner here?"

"Yes." He came closer and took her hand, leading her toward the table. "Dinner and a sunset sail. You still like to watch the sunset, don't you?"

"I love to," she answered softly. She'd dated RJ for a year and a half and in that time, she'd been on the Gold private jet and had attended numerous A-list parties, from LA to Milan. RJ had given her pearls for her birthday, couture gowns for Christmas, and commissioned artwork for their first anniversary. She'd been privy to fine things, but she'd never been on a private yacht to watch the sun set in Saint Lucia.

"I heard it was beautiful out here on the water, so I wanted to make sure you had a chance to see it before you leave." He held out a chair for her and she sat down.

It was silly—her legs were a little wobbly and butterflies danced in her stomach as if this were her first date. Not just with RJ, but ever.

"You look really nice," she said, fighting for some semblance of calm. And it was true. He'd changed from the swim trunks and tank top and now wore dark brown linen pants and a matching button-front shirt.

"Not nearly as nice as you," he replied.

She glanced down at the hunter-green wrap dress she wore. A good portion of her leg was visible through the side slit and she eased the material over to cover it, suddenly feeling more than a little exposed.

"What are you doing?" she asked when she looked at him again. "This seems like more than just dinner."

The table was covered with a white cloth, and plates with gold rims were set next to sparkling silverware and crystal glasses. A bottle of wine was sitting inside a silver ice bucket; two long white candles were lit and centered.

Everything was set almost identically to the way it had been the night he'd proposed to her.

"What is this? Why'd you do all this?" She was already standing to leave, but RJ stood, too, touching a hand to her arm to hold her still.

"It's just dinner," he said. "I wanted it to be special, but if you don't like it, all you have to do is say the word and we can go back to the café or order something to your room. I really just wanted to have some time with you tonight, away from everyone else."

He sounded earnest and his hand on her arm loosened so that if she did really want to leave, she knew he wouldn't stop her. "I'm fine with an evening sail." Over RJ's shoulder she glimpsed a guy dressed in all white. He gave a hand signal to someone she couldn't see and the yacht began to move.

After a few seconds, she said, "You created this to look like that night at the restaurant. The night you proposed."

He dropped his hand from her arm and slipped it into his front pocket. "You're right," he said.

"Why?"

"Because I haven't been able to move forward since that night, Grace." He shook his head. "Yeah, I've gotten up every day and I've gone about my business doing my job, and being with my family, but that's it."

She took a step back from him, realizing now that in addition to wanting to do something special, this dinner was an attempt to find closure. "Don't say you haven't moved on, because you've dated, RJ. I've seen pictures of you in the tabloids with dates." But not girlfriends. There'd only been about three or four times that she could recall that there'd ever been any mention of RJ with a date, and those few times were usually during some big high-profile function on the company's behalf. She'd told herself to let it go at the time, but now, tonight, it felt like they were both still holding on to everything that did or didn't happen in the last ten years.

"And I'm sure you've dated, too, although thank all that's holy I didn't have to see any pictures of that."

His tone was grim and she knew why. RJ wasn't a jealous man, but he did protect what he deemed to be his, and those he cared for deeply. Seeing him in pictures with those women, despite how few, hadn't been a joyful experience for her, either.

"Okay, so we did move on."

"I want to know why we had to, Grace." He walked

to the railing and stared out at the water. "I told my-self I wasn't going to ask you this question and so far I've resisted the urge over a dozen times. But then we were together the other night and it felt like no time had passed between us. It felt good and right."

She didn't respond because there was truth to his words. That night every touch, every kiss and stroke between them, had felt more than good and better than right.

Truth was, she'd wanted to be with him in any way she could for any amount of time possible. If that was wrong, then she was definitely guilty.

"Why didn't you accept my proposal?" He asked the question she knew had been on his mind all this time.

"I couldn't," she said simply. He wanted to hear more; he deserved to hear it all. She cleared her throat and continued. "I couldn't marry you and be-come Mrs. Ronald Gold III, when Grace Hopkins hadn't made a name for herself yet. Can you under-stand that?"

He ran a hand over his beard and then folded his arms across his chest. "You didn't want to marry me because you thought my name would overshadow yours? You could've kept your last name, Grace."

"No, RJ. It's not that simple." She took a step to-ward him. "I could've kept my last name but the world still would've known me only as your wife. Another member of the Gold family. Part of the fashion industry. I would've been all those things and somewhere in the footnotes it would've said, 'Oh yeah, and she writes stories sometimes.' That's not what I wanted my life to be."

"I thought you wanted your life to be with me." His voice was bereft and a tiny part of her crumbled at the sound. "We'd talked so many times about where we'd live, the kids, the dog. All of it. We'd planned our whole future together and then when I thought I was giving it to you, you threw it back in my face and left without a word."

And the hurt from that night filled every word he'd just spoken. She wanted to cry or better yet, to scream in frustration. "I handled that badly, I know. There were so many times in those first few weeks that I thought about coming back to tell you how sorry I was for not being honest with you."

"Why didn't you?"

She shrugged. "I thought it was too late."

"I loved you," he said quietly. "I never stopped loving you."

If words could totally demolish a person's spirit, RJ would get an award for casting a death blow right now. "I never stopped loving you, either." She spoke a lot softer than he did and with much more doubt than she'd heard in his tone. But that wasn't because she doubted that she loved him—that was the truest thing she'd ever known in her life—but that also didn't seem like enough.

"Then tell me why, Grace. Because your last name, my last name, what was printed about you in the tabloids, I don't give a damn about any of that and I know you don't either. Now I'm not saying that I don't respect you wanting to make your mark in your career, you know I understand that better than anybody, but you had to know I'd always support you and your career. Always."

She walked to railing now, standing there next to him and staring out at the water. The sun was just beginning to lower in the distance. The sky was a brilliant mix of orange, blue and golden-yellow stripes, shimmering over the water.

"I wanted to be a good investigative journalist and I knew I could do that. I just needed a little more time." She sighed. "I didn't know if I could be a wife and mother. Not like my mother and my sisters planned to be. My mother had her career and her family and she made it all look so easy. And my sisters were eager to do the same, but I couldn't stop thinking about my career. So didn't that mean I couldn't do the same? Or at least not at that time. Hope, Charity and Trinity, they'd all made marks in their careers by the time they started thinking about having it all. I needed to do the same. I needed to make my mark first and then perhaps I would've been ready for the family."

When he didn't speak, she was certain he thought she'd lost her mind. He came to stand closer to her, until their arms touched but they both continued to stare out at the water.

"Why didn't you tell me that's what was going on? You threw away everything we had because you were afraid?"

She'd never, not once in ten years, said it that way. It had always been a choice for her—career over family. Establish who and what she was before becoming the other half of someone else. Admitting she was afraid would've been just like accepting that she'd always been the least accomplished of the Hopkins sisters, a burden she'd carried on her shoulders all her life.

"I threw it all away because I didn't think it was for me at the time." Her chest ached with the realization that she'd succumbed to her fear of not being enough. Again.

"And now...how do you feel about us now?"

She didn't know how to answer that question. How could she explain that she still loved and cared for him, but she hadn't yet done the most important thing in her life? How did she admit that the fear still gnawed at her?

"I don't know," she whispered, wishing like hell that wasn't the truth.

CHAPTER TWELVE

RJ HAD NO IDEA how to deal with what she'd just told him. After a few minutes of silence he finally decided on leading her to the table and telling the chef on board to serve their dinner. A flurry of emotions filled him—anger, hurt, confusion, longing—and he couldn't focus on just one. He didn't want to focus on any of them. What he really wanted, and what seemed like the most important thing right now, was to just be with Grace.

"You even told them to fix my favorite, spaghetti and meatballs," she said when he sat across from her.

"With extra meat sauce of course." He liked doing things for her. Recalling all the things she liked and what made her smile had come naturally from the moment he saw her on the island.

"I told you, I remember things about you, too," she said, and removed the silver ring from her napkin. "Like, you prefer a mixed drink with dinner over wine and that you hog the TV remote."

RJ tossed his head back and chuckled, he couldn't help it. The TV remote had been an ongoing debate in the penthouse. "You don't even watch television in bed. You usually have something to read."

"I like the background noise."

"Right, so it shouldn't matter if I change the channel or not."

"It matters when you change it to that sports channel. It's noisy and distracting."

He shook his head slowly. "Isn't that considered background noise?"

She paused and then frowned. "You're not funny."

RJ laughed again, this time feeling the joy deep down in his soul. Why couldn't it always be like this? The carefree ease that was between them right now. Why couldn't they have this forever? Probably because she hadn't trusted him with her truth ten years ago, and now he wasn't certain he could trust her to not choose something over them again. And yet he couldn't bring himself to stay away from her.

"This is delicious," she said after she'd tasted her first bite.

It was, but he enjoyed watching her much more than he did the taste of the food.

They were halfway through the meal when she said, "Riley mentioned you'd be taking over the company in a few months. I know you're excited about that."

"I wouldn't say excited," he told her before taking a gulp of his rum and Coke. "It's like I've been anticipating this for so long, now that it's getting closer I'm a little numb."

"You're going to be great as CEO. You were born for this job."

"More than that," he said. "I really want this job. My grandfather and my father have done a phenomenal job carving out a space for us, but I'm ready to take it to the next level. I'm looking forward to working with our designers on creating new and exciting pieces that tell our full story. We have such a diverse and rich history and I want to see it flourish into everything we touch from clothes to handbags, jewelry and even as far as the philanthropy efforts we take on. Even though that's creeping into my mom's domain."

"That sounds amazing," she said with a look of admiration on her face, and his chest swelled with pride. "Your family is so rooted in this company. I was shocked when I read about Major and Nina starting their own. Not just because he was stepping away from RGF but also because he was taking a partner. It just seemed so out of character from the Major I knew," she told him.

The reminder that she'd had a relationship with everyone in his family warmed him.

"I think that decision surprised him, too. But Nina's a great developer. Her app was amazing before Major ever came along and since he'd already been planning his own business, I guess it made sense for them to be partners. Especially since they'd fallen in love and decided to get married."

That word brought down a veil of silence and they finished dinner before having their drinks refilled. Grace picked up her glass of wine and stood. He took a gulp from his own glass and left it on the table before following her to the railing once more.

"This is an amazing place to have a wedding," she said.

"Riley wanted it private and my mom suggested someplace tropical. Dad said he's just signing the checks." They both laughed at that.

"Hope wants a fall wedding. Fifty guests, outside venue and candy corn instead of wedding cake for dessert." She shook her head and sipped her wine while RJ grinned.

"Sounds like Hope." She was her most eccentric sister. But none of the Hopkins sisters were like Grace. He could see that from the first time he'd been to Westchester to meet her family. It was no wonder she'd always felt like she was different.

"We would've had a nice wedding," she said quietly, and finished the wine.

RJ had no doubt that was true, and while his goal tonight had been to talk about their past, he was through with the regret and sadness now.

"Dance with me." He took the glass from her and put it on the table.

When he turned back, she had a hand on one hip and a quizzical look on her face. "There's no music."

He shrugged and took her hand, pulling her to him. "We'll make our own music." With that he wrapped his other arm around her waist and started singing the lyrics to Bruno Mars's "Just the Way You Are." It was her favorite song and even though he was singing horribly off-key, he moved his body to the melody.

Grace laughed at his efforts but joined in with him until they were dancing around the deck, singing as loud as they could. In the distance the sunlight faded, dropping down into the water, and a deep magenta and blue color filled the sky. Their movements slowed as they came to the end of the song until they were both still staring into each other's eyes as they'd done so many times before. Only this was different, and they both knew it.

It seemed as natural as breathing to lean in and touch his lips to hers, and when she tilted her head and joined in the kiss everything that happened in the past, every obstacle, every worry, disappeared. There was only him and Grace now, the sweet tenderness of their kiss, the powerful yearning in their embrace.

Breaking the kiss was difficult, but when he twined his fingers in hers and began walking them toward the stairs that would take them below deck, she followed. He led her down to the master bedroom and closed the door behind them. Earlier he'd been in awe of this space himself. He'd rented the yacht so it'd been his first time touring it, but this bedroom had been amazing. The king-size bed was against one wall facing windows that brought the ocean inside with unfettered panoramic views.

She walked to the bed and sat, patting the space beside her.

"I've got something for you," he said.

"I know. That's why I'm telling you to come here." Her smile was sexy and alluring and his heart thumped wildly in his chest.

The dress she wore was sexy as hell, that slit up the side a dangerous threat to his senses. But he could restrain himself, at least for a little while longer. He went to the nightstand and pulled out the top drawer. In it was a black velvet box, too big to be another engagement ring, so her smile remained in place when he carried it toward her.

"You know I love presents," she said, her expression changing from teasing to giddy with excitement. She even lifted her hands to do a quick clap.

He couldn't help it; he chuckled. "You're such a kid when it comes to gifts."

"I know. My mom used to say I acted like it was Christmas whenever somebody gave me a gift."

"She's right," he told her, and walked closer, still holding the box just out of her reach.

She was practically bouncing on the edge of the

bed and when that became too much for her she just reached out and grabbed it. RJ laughed, enjoying the authentically happy look on her face more than she would ever know.

She opened the box quickly and then stopped to stare up at him. "When did you get this?"

His words almost faltered when she reached her hand into the box. "I ordered it when I went back to my room the first night I saw you here. I requested express delivery." Because he'd needed to see her with it.

She lifted the new vibrator out of the box, her fingers wrapped securely around the apparatus in a way that made his dick jump.

"I want to watch you this time," he said, and began unbuttoning his shirt.

"You sure you're just gonna watch?" she asked as she rubbed the tip of the vibrator over her cleavage.

He struggled to breathe but managed to keep his fingers on the buttons instead of reaching to pull the straps of her dress down so he could see her breasts completely. "Absolutely. I'm going to enjoy the show."

With a smirk, she set the vibrator down and stood to remove her clothes. When she was done, she leaned over to pull some of the pillows together and set them up at the head of the bed. It was an elaborate act, giving him an unfettered view of her delectable ass.

True to his word, RJ removed the rest of his clothing and pulled one of the cushioned chairs from the corner closer to the bed. He sat and waited for the performance to begin.

"Show me what you planned to do with the one that got away from you the other night."

"You mean the one you broke," she said as she lay back on the bed.

He figured it had broken after he stepped on it, even though she hadn't given him an update. "This replacement's better."

She adjusted herself on the bed and switched the vibrator on. "We'll see."

RJ swore he'd died and gone to heaven. The sight of Grace lying gorgeously naked on that bed, legs lifted so that her feet were planted on the mattress, knees spread, was more than he'd ever imagined. When he expected her to slide the apparatus between her legs, she lifted it to her lips instead, licking it up and down until his fingers gripped the arms of the chair.

He recalled her tongue moving over his dick just like that in the past, and he dropped one hand down to soothe his aching erection. She took the toy deep into her mouth and he began jerking his dick, wanting to be inside her mouth the same way that vibrator was. She removed it from her mouth with a plopping sound that had him moaning. Then she rubbed it over her breasts, circling her nipples and going down

her torso to her stomach. He licked his lips when he
knew what would happen next.

Grace glanced at him before switching the vibrator on, the low buzzing sound much louder in the
otherwise quiet room.

"Now," he whispered, his throat hoarse with need.
It was possible he hadn't quite thought this through,
because now watching her seemed like torture.

She obliged, slipping the vibrator down until it
eased inside her. On a long deep moan, she arched
her back from the bed, her head sinking into the pillows. With one hand she moved the vibrator in and
out of her pussy, while the other hand toyed with her
breasts. RJ jerked his dick like he was ready to come
at any moment—which he probably was.

He was entranced by her moaning, the thrusting
of her hips that matched the motion of her hand, the
sound of that vibrator and the jiggle of her breasts.
And then he was done. Done with the watching
part.

He stood from the chair, grabbed a condom from
his wallet and hurriedly rolled it on. Climbing onto
the bed, he grabbed her wrist and eased the vibrator out of her. He took it from her hand and turned
it off. Then he was between those long legs, lifting them onto his shoulders and glancing up at her
once more.

"Do you trust me?" When she only blinked at the
question, he hurried to make himself clear. "Trust

me to make you feel good," he whispered. He saw her nod just before he lowered his head.

His mouth touched her warm folds and he moaned. On a deep inhale he let her scent permeate every part of his body, and as she shook with the intensity of the pleasure ripping through him, he licked her. Tender strokes over her pussy, a quick, clever flick to tease her hardened clit. She bucked beneath him and he gripped her bare ass in his hands, lifting her lower half off the bed so she was closer to his face, feeding him.

"Dammit." The one clipped word from her spurred him on.

"So sweet. Just like I remember." It was the truth—she tasted heavenly. With each caress of his tongue over her soft flesh, he could think of nothing in his life that had ever tasted better. And it was just like he remembered. The feel of her thighs against his cheeks, the throbbing of his dick each time his tongue stroked along her damp skin. It was all as good as before, a part of the memories he'd cherished and secretly longed for again.

"I want more," he groaned. "More of you."

She was pumping into his mouth now, trying to give him what he wanted so he'd provide the release he knew she so desperately needed. He planned to give it to her. Easing two fingers between the crease of her ass, he let one linger momentarily over her anus before continuing on to sink inside her entrance.

She bucked again, a mixture of curses and moans softly filling the air.

He slid another finger inside her, feeling the contraction of her body around him. This was it right here. The silken honey that seeped onto his fingers and eventually his tongue as he continued to lick her pussy was addictive. So much so he had no idea what he was going to do from this moment on. The need for her was going to be too great to watch her walk away again. Not this time. Even if all he got from her was this physical gratification, that's what he wanted. What he'd needed for far too long.

Pumping his fingers in and out of her while flicking his tongue over her clit had her body jerking wildly beneath him. She whispered his name.

"Ronald," she said again and again and he thrust his hips, wishing it was his dick buried to the hilt inside her instead.

"Gracie." He said her name softly when he let his mouth leave her, his fingers still moving. "My sweet Gracie."

Her body tensed the second her climax hit and he hungrily put his mouth over her once more to catch every drop of her release. Moments later he was easing away from her, lifting his body so he could drop a tender kiss on her mouth. She clapped her hands to the back of his neck and dragged him down for a deeper kiss, one that fused them together in a thick haze of longing, need and something more, something he wasn't sure either of them was ready to name.

Instead of thinking too much on that, RJ positioned himself between her legs, sliding easily into her. She gasped when he entered her, bowing up off the bed. He massaged her breasts and began moving inside her, losing himself in the glorious warmth that always welcomed him. This is where he belonged, there was no longer any doubt in his mind. It was only Grace for him, now and forever.

He couldn't get enough, and he totally lost himself in the feel of her muscles holding him tight, the sound of her voice whispering his name. When she wrapped her legs around his waist, he leaned forward, putting his arms around her back before changing their position. He sat on the edge of the bed while she straddled him, bouncing up and down over his dick until her name ripped from his throat. "Grace. My sweet Gracie."

"Yes." It was the smallest whisper from her that played over and over again as she moved her hips to match his upward thrusts. "Yes, Ronald. Yes."

And that's what RJ continued to hear in the next seconds when she arched in his arms, her second climax causing her body to tremble around him. He came right behind her, shuddering not only with the pleasure tearing through him, but with the love that followed that brilliant explosion. That was it, that was the name of the emotion he'd felt earlier. Love.

It was what had been pulling him toward her from the moment he'd first seen her on this island. The love that hadn't died in the ten years they'd been apart. The love he prayed she wanted to accept this time around.

CHAPTER THIRTEEN

FOUR DAYS LATER, Grace rolled over in the bed, going still the moment she realized she was alone. Lying on her stomach, she extended her arm over the rumpled sheets where RJ had lain for a while last night. It had been just a little while longer than the previous nights, and she'd thought he might stay until morning. He hadn't done that on any of the nights he'd come to her room.

After their tryst on the yacht, they'd returned to the shore much later that evening. He'd taken her to her room and stepped inside for just long enough to take her in his arms one more time. The embrace had been long, each of them holding on to the other as if they thought it might be their last opportunity.

"I wish you'd trusted me ten years ago," he'd whispered just before pulling back slightly. "Part of the reason I admired you so much was because of your work ethic and your tenacity to pursue your goals no matter what. There's no way I would've ever asked you to give that up."

She'd let her forehead rest on his chest as regret filled every crevice of her being. "I should've told you that night. I don't know why I didn't." Or rather she had known. Fear was a cruel bastard that she wholeheartedly despised.

He'd lifted his hands to cup her cheeks, tilting her face up to him. "Everything I just said is still true. I still admire you and wholly support your career goals."

Grace knew that; otherwise his father and possibly the rest of his family wouldn't have been so open to her being here and writing the story. "I appreciate that, RJ. I really do."

He'd kissed her again, a very soft and lingering kiss that had left her dreamy-eyed and hopeful. In the days that followed she'd continued with her interviews, speaking to Chaz and then conducting a third interview with Veronica. She and RJ had also continued with their evening trysts, most times after the family dinner that Grace no longer needed an invitation to attend. During the days when she wasn't writing, she had an unspoken invite to everything on Riley's itinerary. In fact, Riley had taken to texting Grace daily reminders so she wouldn't forget and stay in her room working. But Grace liked being in her room, especially during the time that RJ was there with her.

That's what scared her.

After talking about what happened that long-ago

night, she and RJ seemed to be of one accord, just like they'd been before. In Manhattan, their private space had been RJ's penthouse, because it was away from the RGF offices and his parents' palatial home. It was where RJ could relax and be himself instead of being one of the top executives at the company, or the oldest son of the family. It was the one place where Grace could feel comfortable and not like she was in constant competition with her sisters.

Here, on the island, the villas that RJ and his family were staying in were much larger than Grace's room, but in her room they had privacy. For all intents and purposes, her room was now like his penthouse had been, all except for RJ spending the night. She never asked him why he didn't. She hated the thought that she was once again allowing fear to take up space in her life.

Her vibrating phone disrupted her thoughts and she rolled over in the bed again, catching herself before she tumbled over the edge. With a shake of her head, she reached for the phone on the nightstand and removed it from the charger. The notification was a text message from Riley.

Truth or dare at 2 p.m. in the café.

Grace groaned and buried her head in the pillow. Did she really want to play truth or dare with Riley and the gang, which was the name Maurice had given the group of four couples? Were she and RJ a couple again? Another groan escaped at the question because she was so confused. She was beginning to believe that was her natural state of being now—at least it had been since setting foot on this island.

Her phone vibrated and chimed in her hand. She startled and then lifted her head from the pillow to stare at the screen. "Dammit."

She answered it with a bland, "Hi, Eddie." Eddie's gravelly voice was the last thing she wanted to hear this morning.

"What's going on? Is the story almost done? I was thinking of sending Tiege down to get some pictures of the wedding. He says he has a connection that could get him onto the property without any detection," he rattled off without pause.

She bolted up in the bed. "Absolutely not!" Shaking her head as if she thought he could see her, Grace frowned. "I mean, why would I need Tiege here if I'm just doing interviews?"

Tiege was Veronica's former stepson, so Grace knew exactly how the guy would get in undetected. Veronica really was planning her exit strategy if she'd told him about the wedding being here this week.

"Don't try that stunt with me," he replied. "The only reason I'm sitting on the fact that Riley Gold's wedding is taking place this week is because this story is a lot bigger."

"Look, I'm getting a lot of good material. The story is coming along nicely and will be in your inbox early next week."

The wedding was Saturday, three days away, and her flight out was already booked for early Sunday morning. She planned to give the story one final pass on Monday and send it off to Eddie that afternoon.

"Send me what you've got so far. I want to make sure you're on the right track."

"Not a chance. That's not how I work. I'll send you the complete story when it's done and *no* pictures."

"Do you have any idea how much circulation we'd get if we landed the first and only wedding photos?"

"Do you have any idea how powerful both these families are? You sneak into this venue to get pictures and they'll come after you. I mean, they'll go over your head to the owner of the paper and they'll make his life a living hell as payback. How do you think he's gonna react when he finds out you're the one who brought that type of heat to his doorstep?" She was bluffing, sort of.

Grace really had no idea how RJ, his family or Tobias dealt with the media when they overstepped boundaries. That wasn't a conversation she and RJ ever needed to have, because up until this point she'd represented his family and their business with the utmost respect on the few occasions she'd written about them. Sure, this story was a totally different ball game, and she'd taken a very calculated risk in coming here to do it in the first place. But she did know that after several recent debacles—the blogger who'd printed those designs from King Designs and insinuated Riley had stolen them from Chaz, the reporter who'd revealed Nina and Major's business connection, and the woman who'd made a fake video depicting Maurice as an absentee dad—the Golds had met their quota of dealing peacefully with the media. Any intrusion into Riley's wedding wasn't going to go over well, Grace knew that for certain.

"Look, I'll meet my deadline. That's all you need to worry about."

"You'd better, or you're through. Not only will I never work with you again, but if I'm ever asked about you—"

"Okay, I get it, Eddie. Like I said, the story will be in your inbox by close of business on Monday." She didn't wait for Eddie to say another word, but disconnected the call on her own terms. Having him threaten her when the sun was barely up wasn't her idea of good morning conversation.

She fell back onto the bed, feeling the urge to toss her phone again. But recalling how that had turned out last time, she simply dropped it onto the mattress and closed her eyes. She was definitely going to have a story for Eddie come Monday morning. Unfortunately, it wasn't the story she'd pitched to him. Well, not exactly. The new angle she'd told RJ

she would take on the story had turned out to be a
great call. What she'd written so far was informa-
tive and enlightening; it was inspirational and touching. Not surprisingly each of the Gold siblings and
Chaz spoke not only highly of Ron and Tobias, but
also of what the two companies meant to them, to
the people they'd ultimately become. She'd felt mo-
tivated just writing it, pressed to take everything her
parents had taught her about resilience and courage
to be the very best reporter she could be. She didn't
want to toss that aside.

She climbed off the bed, went to the table where
her laptop was and opened it. Plopping down into
the chair, she waited for it to boot up and clicked on
the file with her story draft. After reading over what
she had so far, Grace knew she couldn't change it.
Not just because she really liked it, but also because
it was exactly what she'd promised RJ she would
write. It wasn't the juicy exposé she'd promised the
Daily Gazette. It was a story about how RJ's family
had broken the mold of all fashion houses and become number one all while facing adversity. No, she
wasn't going to change a word, not even if it meant
Eddie would probably try to ruin her career.

"I dare you to kiss RJ." Maurice chuckled heartily
after saying those words.

Grace froze, obviously regretting choosing a dare
over the truth. RJ didn't move either, but not for

the same reason. He'd come into this game knowing exactly what his siblings would try to do. They'd
each been on him about what happened in the past
between him and Grace. Riley had been especially
emotional, which he totally chalked up to her im-
pending nuptials and new outlook on love.

"I don't think she's here by mistake," she'd said
a couple nights ago when they were the last two at
the table after dinner.

"She's not. She's writing a story about our family, remember?" he'd replied, and Riley had smirked.

"You're a goof, but you're not stupid. She could've
stayed in New York and written that story."

"We're all here—what better time to come and
interview us?" he'd countered.

"There's such a thing as a phone. Zoom, Skype,
email. Besides those other options, she wasn't guar-
anteed an interview with any of us. She had no idea
we would agree to this story. Yet she used money
from her savings to pay for the room and airfare just
to spend two weeks on this island."

"How do you know she used her savings?" Because of everything Riley had just said, that was the
most important part to RJ. Grace hadn't cared that
she didn't make a lot of money being a reporter. Even
when her parents had compared her salary range to
that of her sisters', she'd argued that she made enough
to live comfortably and that she was following her
passion, doing what she was meant to do. And he'd

championed her courage and determination. But the thought of her taking any type of financial hit because of this trip didn't sit well with him.

"She mentioned it the other day when we were having drinks," Riley had said with a wave of her hand. "But what I'm really saying is that I don't think she's here just to write this story and I'm hoping my big brother is smart enough to figure that out himself."

Riley had left him to stew over that information and he'd been letting it ruminate in his mind since. On more than one occasion when he'd been with Grace at night, he'd thought about bringing it up, but since the night on the yacht, he'd liked the new low-stress caliber of their relationship. They'd been simply enjoying themselves, rekindling the things they enjoyed most about being together. Rocking the boat with questions and talk of where this was or wasn't going was something he'd decided not to do.

Today, this truth-or-dare game that was meant to pass the time and entertain them may just be propelling them in another direction entirely. It made what they were doing much more public than either of them had probably considered.

"Well, alrighty then," Grace said and stood from her seat.

She wore white capri pants and a yellow top. Her hair was out today, wavy and hanging past her shoulders. When she walked over to him he wanted to jump up and say something, do something that might take them out of the spotlight. But that would've been counterproductive.

Riley and Nina clapped while Major whistled and Maurice stood pumping a fist in the air. They were being ridiculous, and RJ looked at Grace with what he hoped she'd take as his apology for his wacky family. He made a move to stand when she was closer, but she stopped him by putting her hands on his shoulders.

"You don't have to do this. We can leave," he said.

She shook her head. "I'm not a sore loser," she told him. "Besides, they want a show, I'll definitely give them one."

And with that she shocked them all, but mostly RJ, by straddling him and wrapping her arms around his neck.

"Yeaaahh!" Maurice yelled.

"Get 'em, Grace!" Nina followed with a whooping laugh.

Riley whistled this time and he heard Chaz chuckling as well.

RJ couldn't take his eyes off Grace, or his hands—which had a mind of their own and were now cupping her ass. "You sure you know what you're doing?"

She sucked her bottom lip between her teeth and nodded. In the next seconds she was moving in, tilting her head before touching her lips gently to his. RJ was sure this was supposed to be just a peck. Maurice hadn't specified what type of kiss she needed to give him in his dare, but to hell with that. Like Grace had said, if they wanted a show, they were going to get one. Especially since pulling away from kissing Grace wasn't something RJ was able to do.

His hands moved up her back as he took the kiss deeper. She followed his lead, hugging him tighter and pressing her body into his. For a moment he almost forgot his family was there staring at them and cheering them on. All he could think about was how good she felt in his arms, how perfect and right it felt kissing her and holding her.

Grace broke the kiss—he was positive he wouldn't have been able to do it. The cheers and comments in the room grew loud again, reminding him that they weren't alone. Yet their gazes remained locked. Something was happening, some form of communication passed between them, which RJ didn't think either of them had expected. It was a silent acknowledgment of sorts, but now was neither the time nor place to explore.

Grace apparently realized that as well because she pulled back from him, easing off his lap to stand and look at him for a few seconds before turning away. When she walked back to her seat it was with her arms raised in triumph, like she'd just run a marathon instead of kissed him senseless. As for RJ, he couldn't get out of that chair if somebody paid him. His legs felt weak, his chest full of heat and emotion. All he could do was clear his throat to try to get himself together. When his brothers responded to that with more crude comments and guffaws, he replied by giving each of them the middle finger.

Later that evening, after the dinner Grace had decided to skip, RJ walked along the pathway that had taken him to her room so many nights before. The first time he'd walked this way, over a week ago, he'd had no idea what—or rather, who—he was going to find. His lips tilted into a smile as he recalled stepping on the vibrator she'd been looking for, even though at the time, laughter had been the furthest thing from his mind.

There'd been an instant mixture of confusion and elation at seeing her again after so long. Of course that'd been combined with a potent punch of lust once she held the sex toy in her hand. That lust hadn't abated in the days since that night and the many times he'd slept with her. It never would, apparently. Neither would the feelings he'd been harboring all this time.

His mother had tried to talk to him about it; even his brothers had tried to broach the subject with him over the years, and RJ had shot each of them down, not wanting to admit what was definitely still there. He was still in love with Grace.

What did that even mean now? In the past he'd thought those feelings meant the next step was marriage. Now, after all that had happened, all that he'd learned, did it make sense to hope for a second chance?

"Hey," Grace said when she opened the door.

He'd been so caught up in his thoughts that he didn't remember knocking.

"Hey," he replied. "Missed you at dinner." He punctuated that statement by stepping toward her, slipping a hand around to the nape of her neck. "I missed you a lot." He pulled her closer, sweeping his tongue along her lips before diving in for a deep kiss right there in her doorway.

When he was finally able to release her, she blinked up at him. His ego inflated at the obvious staggering effects of his kiss on her. RJ grinned and said, "Hello."

She cleared her throat and shook her head. "Hello, yourself." Moving out of the way, she let him into her room, then closed and locked the door behind him.

"I have a lot of writing to get done," she started as he moved farther into the room. "I met with your mother this afternoon and tomorrow I'm meeting with your father and Tobias. Both before the bachelor and bachelorette parties are scheduled to start."

Stopping near the table where she had her laptop and notepads scattered, he turned back to face her. "The last three interviews."

She nodded. "And then it'll be done."

He stuffed his hands into the front pockets of his shorts. "You didn't interview me." Truth be told he hadn't wanted to be interviewed. After agreeing to this story and spending more time with Grace, he hadn't wanted to be bothered with any of its details. He'd only wanted to focus on her, but he had a job to do.

She came closer to where he stood, lifting her hands to tuck wayward strands of her hair behind her ears. She wore a nightshirt, legs and feet bare, hair pulled back into a messy ponytail.

"I didn't think you'd want to be interviewed. Besides, I know how everything your father did affected your life. And I know you've always had a distaste for the feud between him and Tobias."

It was an inherited distaste, he could admit, since he'd never asked questions about what his father said had happened. Those were the facts, and as Ron's son RJ had acted accordingly. That meant keeping a close eye on their competition. RJ could follow his parents' decree that there was now a truce between the families, but he still intended to pay close attention to Tobias and his fashion house. Starting with Veronica and this book she planned to write.

"I might have something new to add," he told Grace, even though he really didn't. He just wanted her to interview him, or at least say she'd stop working to interview him, and then he could easily maneuver that into something else.

He closed the distance between them, pushing his hands under her nightshirt to run along her hips.

"You can start by asking me whatever questions you want to ask."

She let him pull her to him, already shaking her head. "Nah, buddy. Not yet anyway. Just let me get these notes typed up and then you'll have my undivided attention."

That last word was followed by her hand cupping his burgeoning erection, and he grinned at her to keep from moaning. "I can respect that," he said, dropping a quick kiss on her lips. "I'll just be over here waiting."

When he didn't move but kept his hands on her delectable body, she pushed him away, laughing. He chuckled, too, going over to sit on the bed. He took off his shoes and reached for the television remote. There wasn't usually much on these hotel televisions with limited satellite channels, but he wasn't really watching anyway. No, when RJ lay back against the pillows, one arm tucked behind his head, his gaze shifted over to the table where Grace sat.

He had no idea how long he watched her staring at the laptop screen, fingers moving over the keyboard. Every now and then she'd turn her attention to the notes on the many pads laid out, and then she'd go right back to typing again. He loved to see her work, enjoyed wondering how her brilliant mind came up with so many words. Her stories were always meaningful and poignant in some way. Even when she was talking about makeup comparisons, upcoming style changes, the lack of books in a public library. Regardless of what she wrote he could always find the heart and empathy she'd put into each word. While they were dating, he'd read every one of her articles, had even saved many of them on his home computer. She was the love of his life and everything about her was important to him.

So when he dozed off, it was to thoughts of how she would work in the home office of the house they'd purchase together one day. He'd stand in the doorway watching her until he was too tired. Then he'd head to their bedroom and wait for her to finish and join him. He wouldn't sleep soundly until the moment she was lying in bed beside him, where she belonged.

CHAPTER FOURTEEN

THE NEXT MORNING when Grace awoke and rolled over in bed, she again went immediately still. This time, it was because she'd bumped into something, or she should say someone. Opening her eyes very slowly, she saw RJ lying on his back, one arm on the pillow above his head, the other hand buried beneath the sheet that straddled his waist. A smile ghosted her lips and she propped herself up on an elbow to stare at him.

Sunlight poured in from the partially closed drapes at the patio door, a slash of gold cutting across his deep umber-hued skin. Tucking her bottom lip between her teeth, she stared at his muscled biceps and chest. There was no part of this man that wasn't heavenly to look at. If he turned over on his stomach, which he often did when he slept, she'd have a view of his firm ass and strong shoulders. As it stood now, she dragged her gaze back up to his face. He looked so peaceful in his sleep. No concerns about the company marring his forehead with lines, no private jokes from his brothers ruffling his mood, no worries about the wedding going perfectly for Riley. In the past few days, she and RJ had talked about a lot of things—his family, hers, his job and hers. Those conversations coupled with this morning wake-up view was just another reminder of old times.

Last night after she'd finished writing, her thoughts had begun to focus on what the future held not just for the two fashion houses, but also for her and RJ. For whatever reason, she'd been able to keep what they were doing here on the island compartmentalized, or at least that had been her goal. But that was before truth or dare, and it was before her conversation with Marva Gold.

"Why did you really want to write this story?" That had been the first question Marva asked after Grace was seated in the living room area of their villa.

There'd been a level of comfort in all the interviews she'd conducted up to this point. She used to have a really good relationship with Marva but this was the first time she'd been in a room alone with the woman after turning down her son's proposal.

"Because it'll be good for my career," Grace had replied.

Marva had seemed to accept that response by giving a slight nod. "Or was it because you knew it would bring you back to RJ? You wanted to right the wrong you knew you'd done by leaving all those years ago."

Well, clearly, Marva had some things she wanted to say about their breakup. Grace had figured this was fair. In fact, she'd given each of the Gold siblings a chance to voice their feelings about that situation during their interviews. For the way she'd left everyone high and dry, she figured she owed them that much. "I wasn't wrong for making a decision to follow my dreams. Men do it every day. They sacrifice it all for their careers and they're given a pat on the back. Why was I supposed to do something different?"

"So that's the reason you decided not to marry my son?" Marva nodded after she spoke again. "I see. You thought you wouldn't be able to continue on your career path while being married to such a high-profile man. Oh, I definitely see now."

While Grace wanted to tell Marva that she couldn't possibly know what Grace had been feeling then or what was motivating her now, she didn't. The irony of the situation was, if anyone in the Gold family could relate to what she'd gone through with RJ, Marva was the one. She'd attended college and worked briefly as an educator before marrying Ron and becoming the legendary man's partner. In the years she'd been a Gold, she'd also become a very notable philanthropist, starting several initiatives to aid schools specifically in underrepresented communities.

"Ron was that man for me," Marva went on. "His big personality, the company, the fortune, even that fancy Rolls-Royce he rode around in, was a lot for a girl like me who'd come from much humbler beginnings in Baltimore."

"I know you were able to build a separate life and identity for yourself within the marriage," Grace said in the hope that they could speed past this part of the conversation. She knew Marva's backstory, had done all her research prior to this interview. They didn't need to rehash any of it.

"Then why didn't you believe you could do the same?"

"I didn't want to," Grace immediately replied, realizing then that it had boiled down to that simple fact. Grace hadn't wanted to re-create herself under the Gold name; she'd wanted to have her own name personified first and was certain there was nothing wrong with that.

"That makes sense. But how do you feel now? Are you certain you became fixated on doing this story because you believe you're the one to tell it, or was it partially because you knew it would bring you face-to-face with RJ again?"

Hours after that very long conversation with his mother, Grace stared down at RJ next to her, wondering if some of Marva's observations might be accurate.

"If you keep staring at me like that, you're never

gonna make it to your last interviews and I'll be late for a call I have scheduled with the office." He didn't open his eyes when he spoke, and she wondered if he knew she used to stare at him every morning like this.

With a grin, she shook her head, figuring he probably did know and had enjoyed it. RJ may not seem interested in the personal attention the media always wanted to offer the Golds, but he enjoyed any attention she gave him. The thought warmed her heart.

"I can't believe you're here. That you stayed." That wasn't what she'd planned to say to him, but the words had tumbled free anyway. "I mean, when I finished working it was really late and I just climbed into bed." She'd known he was there, had even cuddled up to him for a while, intending her touch to initiate foreplay. Then they'd get to the business of sex like they'd been doing each night and afterward he would return to his villa. But the sex hadn't happened and he hadn't left.

His eyes were open now, holding her gaze intently. "You were sleeping pretty soundly when I woke up. I didn't want to disturb you."

"So you undressed and joined me in the bed instead of leaving?" It was obvious that's what happened, but she wanted to him to tell her why he'd done it.

He reached over to take her free hand, weaving his fingers through hers. "I didn't want to leave last night." He looked at their hands and then returned his gaze to hers. "I didn't want to be without you again. For ten extremely long years I vowed to sleep alone and I intended to honor that decree forever. I wasn't going to let anybody else in, Grace. Not into the space that was reserved solely for you."

In that moment her heart felt like it was breaking again, but this time for the sadness so easily detected in his tone. "I never meant to hurt you."

With an easy smile, RJ brought her hand up to his lips, kissing each of her fingers. "I know. I understand what you did and why you did it."

"I'm so sorry," she said, because she was. She was sorry that she hadn't talked to him about what she was feeling, sorry that she hadn't given their relationship the respect it deserved by ending it better.

He reached for her then, pulling her until she was on top of him. He hugged her close, whispering, "Don't apologize, baby. It's in the past. We're here now and that's all that matters."

Grace held on to him for what felt like hours. She inhaled the fading remnants of his cologne, felt the steady strength of his body beneath her. This wasn't a memory. She felt everything—the overwhelming sense of remorse mixed with the undeniable push of hope. Easing away slowly, she placed her palms on his chest and adjusted herself until she was sitting over him, her legs spread, her pussy flush against his dick.

His arms had fallen to his side but he continued to look up at her, not speaking, just watching and, she suspected, waiting to see what she would do next. She grabbed the hem of her nightshirt, pulling it up and over her head before tossing it onto the floor. He waited a beat before lifting his hands to cup her breasts, kneading them gently. She leaned into the touch, arching her back to give him better access. Then she lifted slightly off him, just enough so she could reach a hand behind her, lowering it to rub along his dick.

He didn't make a sound, but in the early morning light she could see a muscle tightening in his jaw. She eased her hand into the slit of his boxers and touched his dick skin to skin. His hands stiffened on her breasts until she wanted to scream with the mixture of pleasure and pain. When he lowered one hand to push beneath the band of her panties and down further until he was rubbing her clit, she bucked over him and gasped.

A tidal wave of desire washed over her and she shook her head to try to find some clarity, but there was none. There was only her and RJ.

"More," she whispered as she moved. "Give me more."

Grace wanted it all. Every inch of him, every part of his soul, every emotion he possessed. She needed it desperately. The sheet went first when she pushed at it until it his legs were free. Then she attacked his boxers, yanking them down his legs until they were flying across the room to land wherever. Her hands were on his dick again, this time holding and stroking it until she could close her mouth over the tip.

RJ sucked in a breath, his hands immediately going to the back of her head, gripping her hair as he spoke through clenched teeth.

Grace obliged, lowering her head until the better portion of his length was in her mouth, touching the back of her throat. She pulled up slightly and began to suck while he guided her head, lifting his hips slightly off the bed to meet her.

There was nothing else, not here on this island and not in New York, that could ever compare to this, to him. The taste of him, the feel of his hands in her hair, the sound of her name in his voice.

"Gracie, baby," he whispered.

Yes, she wanted to reply, she was his Gracie and only his. Even after years apart there was no denying a part of her still belonged to this man.

He was the one to move fast this time, easing her away, then hurriedly sliding off the bed to find a condom and put it on. The second he was sheathed he reached for her, turning her over and then pulling her up onto her knees.

"I thought about you every day," he said as he positioned himself behind her, then thrust deep inside her.

Grace arched her back and yelled with the explosive pressure of his quick entrance. He didn't waste another moment but began pumping into her fiercely. "Every. Damn. Day. Gracie. I couldn't stop thinking about you."

"I know," she breathed, her fingers clenching the sheets. "I thought about you, too. All the time. So much. I missed you so much."

She could say that now and not feel as if she were going back on her word. The decision to walk away from him had been made, and they'd both served that ten-year sentence of being apart. Now was no time for regrets.

"Missed you more," he declared. "More and more."

There was no use holding back; he felt too good inside her and she'd needed this too much. Her legs trembled and her arms shook until she had no choice but to lower the top half of her body to the bed, moaning into the mattress as her release took her.

He stayed deep inside her while her muscles gripped him, rubbing a hand up and down her back and over her ass while his other hand still held her hip.

"I need more, Gracie."

The second she heard him whisper those words she knew what he was asking. "Yes," she immediately whispered. "Yes."

When he eased out of her she felt an immediate sense of loss but she knew it wouldn't last long. During one of their many nights together, he'd come across her toiletry bag where she'd stored the new vibrator and a few other pleasure items. It was in the bathroom in plain sight and she wasn't the least bit embarrassed by him seeing it. Most of the items in that bag they'd explored when they were together. So she knew he'd gone into the bathroom to grab the lube and when he returned, touching his fingers to her anus with the cool product, she felt desire bubbling deep in the pit of her stomach once more.

"Gracie," he moaned while moving his finger over the tight area, pressing inside slowly.

Her nipples were pebble hard, her pussy clenching with need. She wanted to tell him to hurry and to take it slow and to give her more all at once. Instead she bit down on her bottom lip, closing her eyes to the delightful sensations rippling through her at his touch. The moment he moved his hand and pressed his dick there she let her hips relax and breathed in deep. His hands were on her ass now, holding her open.

"I missed this," he whispered. "Missed it so much."

She had, too. There was never going to be another man she allowed to have her this way, never going to be anyone she trusted the way she trusted RJ. He eased into her slowly until she felt full and on fire with need.

"Please," she moaned. "Now."

He gave her what she wanted, pumping in and out of her with slow measured strokes, until they were both gasping with satisfaction, breathing hard and loud as the need built into a crescendo between them.

Now was exactly what RJ wanted to give her. Except there was even more to it. He wanted to give Grace now *and* forever.

Leaning over her slightly, he reached a hand around between her legs until he found her clit and rubbed simultaneously with his thrusts into her. She moaned long and deep and he felt her body shaking beneath him. He was so tightly embedded in her he could hardly think straight. This connection they had when they were together like this was deeper than anything he'd ever experienced with anyone before, and more than he ever wanted to give anyone else.

This was for them only; it was their shared moment, the time when they were the most connected intimately and emotionally, and he'd thought he would never experience it again.

"I love you, Gracie." The words came before his mind could process whether or not it was wise to say them. "I love you so damn much."

She made a sound that was too close to a whimper and he paused.

"Please, don't stop, Ronald. Please."

He continued, loving the sound of his name on her lips, the feel of his dick being gripped by her muscles, the warm dampness of her pussy. It was everything and still on some level not enough. Until she bucked beneath him, her body going still, his name a litany on her lips.

"Never stopped loving you, Ronald." She gasped and shook her head. "Only you. I only love you."

As if that was what he needed to take that leap into pleasure, he pumped into her a couple times more before his body jerked, his release coming with such force he lost his breath.

The moments felt like hours before he could ease out of her and fall flat on his back on the bed. She collapsed onto her stomach and he reached out to take her hand, bringing her fingers to his lips once more. "I love you, Grace."

She turned her head toward him, touching her lips to his biceps before whispering, "I love you, RJ."

CHAPTER FIFTEEN

THE AIR WAS warm even though the sun had already set. It was the night before the wedding. The family was gathered outside on a grassy area, with the magnificent mountains and water as a backdrop. The ceremony would take place here tomorrow morning at eleven.

Grace stood off to the side, admiring the work Riley's event planner and her massive team had created. A gazebo covered in peach, orange and white roses was at the end of a twenty-foot aisle flanked by rows of white chairs. White silk was draped from one chair to the next, and gold lanterns with peach ribbons hung from iron shepherd's hooks at the end of every other row. Tomorrow the floor of the aisle would be covered in fresh white rose petals.

She'd seen the gowns that Nina, Desta, Marva and Veronica would be wearing. While Marva and Veronica would don original designs by their husbands, made of the same cream-colored fabric, Nina and Desta had signature dresses from the RGold line in the palest peach hue. Riley's wedding gown consisted of over seventy yards of pure white bias-cut organza tiers that hung beneath a tight bodice, creating a gorgeous fantasy-looking piece that Ron Gold was more than a little proud of designing. They were all going to look amazing. Even the guys, who would wear specially designed cream-colored tuxedos.

When Veronica had invited Grace to the island, Grace knew it was going to be for Riley's wedding, but she hadn't given any thought to whether or not she'd be invited to attend. For tonight's dress rehearsal, she'd been asked to stand in for Riley, as the family believed it was bad luck for the bride to walk down the aisle before her wedding day. Grace's family believed that same superstition, so this wasn't Grace's first time as a fill-in. It was, however, the first time she would walk down an aisle and see RJ standing at the altar. The implications of that were huge and not easily ignored.

"You all right?" She jumped at the voice and turned to see Riley standing next to her.

Grace knew she'd never seen a happier smile. Riley was ecstatic to be marrying Chaz. There was no doubt the two of them were madly in love, and if there had been a doubt, they'd both dispelled it during their separate interviews with Grace. Riley and Chaz had fallen in love against all odds and under the scrutiny of the media. Yet each day Grace watched them in this tropical setting surrounded by family, she saw how tight their bond truly was.

"I'm fine. Just daydreaming, I guess." Grace shrugged in the hope that it would help downplay the surge of longing she felt when thinking about walking down that aisle toward RJ.

"Daydreaming of a wedding possibly?"

Obviously, she hadn't convinced either Riley or herself.

Grace shook her head. "No. We're not ready for that." Which was exactly what she would've said ten years ago. She'd really had no clue that RJ had been ready to propose to her. Sure, they'd talked about their future, but that was just talk. Conversations they'd had in the middle of the night, ideas for a shared life she'd thought was further away than RJ did.

"I don't know," Riley said. "RJ really wants to be married. And I'm not just saying that because I'm getting married tomorrow. He never talked of not getting married or not committing to one woman for the rest of his life until after you left. Now he's not frowning whenever one of us holds hands or kisses or says anything about being a couple. He's been doing that for the last decade and we were all wondering when he'd snap out of it." Riley touched Grace's shoulder. "The minute he saw you again, he did. How amazing is that, that even after all this time the two of you are still in love."

The event planner arrived with her clipboard and two assistants by her side. "Let's get started. We want to be at the rehearsal dinner on time," she said.

From that point on, everybody followed her directions, until the moment it was time for Grace to walk down the aisle.

Ron stepped up and extended his arm to her. Their interview had gone as well as could be expected, but she knew he still wasn't happy about the story. When she only stared at him, the edge of his mouth tilted up in a smile that looked so much like RJ's she couldn't help but smile back. She linked her arm in his, and when the event planner gave the signal they started walking slowly down the aisle.

"You've put a smile back on my son's face," Ron said to her.

He hadn't spoken about her and RJ during their interview yesterday morning. He'd only answered her questions and made sure to tell her what he didn't want to see in the story. She'd agreed to not print the personal stuff about him and Marva.

"I missed him, too," she admitted.

Ron reached his other hand over to place it on top of hers. "Don't waste any more time," he told her. "Life's too short."

Grace looked at Ron and then because they were still walking, she looked straight ahead toward the altar, where RJ was smiling at her.

* * *

Ten years ago, he'd asked her to be his wife. Tonight, RJ wanted to ask her again. He wanted this trip to be the beginning of their future. But how could he tell her that here, in the middle of Riley's rehearsal dinner? He couldn't, that was the bottom line. This was Riley's time, and his sister deserved every bit of happiness in the spotlight that she'd created for herself. He wasn't going to upstage that or even interrupt it with an impromptu proposal of his own.

"She looks happy," his mother said when she came to sit beside him.

They'd finished dinner and dessert about fifteen minutes ago. Grace had been called over to take pictures near the fireplace with Nina, Desta and Riley.

"Yeah, Riley can't wait to be married tomorrow," he said, keeping his eye on the photo session.

"I wasn't talking about Riley," Marva said. She touched RJ's hand. "You look happy, too."

He glanced down at his mother's hand covering his and then over to her. "I am," he admitted and then took a deep breath. "I didn't realize how unhappy I was until she was back."

"I told you to go after her."

"I know you did," he said, remembering his mother had come to visit him the week after Grace had left. "I didn't because of my pride. But as it turns out, I think the space was exactly what Grace needed to do the things she wanted to do."

"I told her she could've done those things while being married to you."

He grinned. "I told her that, too. She's stubborn."

Marva chuckled. "Like somebody else I know. My grandchildren are going to be a handful if they take after you and her."

Two hours later, RJ was still thinking about his mother's words. He was also thinking that, before he jumped the gun and went shopping for another engagement ring, he wanted to talk to Grace, to see where her head was with all this. They'd admitted their love for each other again and weren't opposed to showing it in public, but that had been the extent of their new relationship. Day after tomorrow they'd be heading back to New York and to their normal lives; he wanted to get some things straight before then.

That was one of the reasons he was on his way to her room again—the other was that they'd already arranged to meet at ten. She'd volunteered to help decorate Riley's room with Desta and Nina so they hadn't left the restaurant together after dinner. He'd gone to his room first and changed into shorts and a T-shirt. He'd also wanted some time alone to think about what he was going to say to her. Now he was almost to her suite and his phone was vibrating. He pulled it out of his pocket and read the text from Grace.

Got a little sweaty so I'm grabbing a shower. Door's open.

Wishing she'd waited for him to get in the shower, RJ smiled as he entered her room. He locked the door behind him and walked to the small refrigerator where he knew there were bottled waters and a couple vodka and rum miniatures, which he'd put there a few nights ago. He took one out, opened it and went to the table where room service had left a clean set of glasses and coffee cups. He poured his vodka into one and he took a seat, waiting for Grace to get out of the shower.

Her laptop was open and he glanced at it while taking his first sip. His mother's name caught his attention and in that second he realized this must be Grace's story. He turned away slowly, setting his glass on the table. *Don't read it.* The words floated into his mind and he kept his gaze averted. There was no reason to read it; he and Grace had talked about all her interviews, he knew what everyone was going to say. Still, he was going to read it eventually. He used to always read Grace's work and he'd enjoyed that. So all he had to do was turn his attention back to the laptop and read. And when he did, fury deep and red-hot boiled in the pit of his gut.

The Golds and the Kings have come full circle. From a feud that started with a love triangle featuring the major players, Ron Gold Jr., Tobias King and Marva Gold, to these powerhouse men taking the fashion industry by storm.

RJ had to set his cup on the table. His fingers

immediately clenched into a fist as he continued to read.

Marva Gold recalls meeting Tobias first and marveling at how focused and talented he was. It was a totally different feeling when Tobias introduced Marva to Ron at an RGF holiday party. "I knew Ron was the man I would marry from the first moment I saw him," Marva said.

That night Marva had no idea that meeting the man who would turn out to be the love of her life would destroy a friendship and create a second fashion house. That's precisely what happened when Tobias saw Ron and Marva kissing weeks after the party.

"Hey," Grace said from behind him.

RJ stood, whirling around until he faced her. "What the hell is this?"

"What—"

"I thought we discussed this. You said you weren't going to write anything but the truth. That you weren't interested in slandering my family." His temples throbbed and his heart raced. She was standing there with a towel wrapped around her looking as if she'd just been caught with her hand in the cookie jar.

"Wait a minute, just calm down and let me explain."

"There's nothing to explain, Grace! I told you what I expected and you lied to me. I specifically said what would be allowed and what wouldn't, and you went against our agreement and wrote this crap! What the hell is wrong with you?"

He was yelling, his hands were clenched into fists, and for the life of him he couldn't find the strength to calm down. How could she do this? How could she lie to him every day of this trip, every night that they'd lain together, when he'd held her in his arms and told her he loved her, how had she been able to do all that knowing she'd planned to betray him with this story all along?

"I think you should calm down," she said, and took a step toward him.

"I'm not gonna calm down while you destroy my family. How dare you create this lie about my mother! She had nothing to do with this feud. You promised me you wouldn't do this and I trusted you, Grace." He huffed and ran a hand down the back of his head. "After everything we've been through I trusted you to write a story that focused more on the companies, not the personal trials of my family. And you did it all just to get a promotion!"

She jerked back as if he'd made a move toward her, and RJ felt like crap. He'd never put his hands on a woman, had never even yelled at one the way he was yelling at Grace now.

"It's not what you think," she said before clearing her throat. "If you would just sit down and let me explain."

He didn't sit, nor did his anger abate, but he did

lower his voice. "Explain what? That you're not telling lies to glorify a feud that I told you was quashed months ago? I read it right there on your computer, Grace. That's the story you're planning to send to your editor. It'll end up on the fashion page of some newspaper."

"Lies? RJ, everything I write is factual. I'm meticulous about fact-checking everything. I've conducted lengthy interviews and transcribed my notes myself."

"You never shared this with me during any of our meetings!" He pointed to the laptop. "I never heard about any of this, and I never would've approved of it if I had. So you have to delete it. You shut this whole story down, Grace, or I swear you'll never work on another article for any paper again."

Grace walked away. She went back into the bathroom and shut the door. Leaning against it, she closed her eyes and counted to ten. When she opened her eyes again, she dared a single tear to fall. She could feel that they'd welled up in her eyes but she wouldn't let any fall. She couldn't. Instead she picked up her robe from the duffel bag she kept in the bathroom and pushed her arms through it. She removed the towel wrapped around her, belted the robe and took a deep breath before reaching for the doorknob.

RJ was upset. Given what he thought the circumstances were, he had a right to be upset. He didn't, however, have a right to read her unpublished story without her permission, and, in turn, threaten her job. And that's exactly what she would've said if he were anyone else.

She opened the door and went back into the room where he was still standing near the table. He had both arms up, hands on the back of his head, and when he saw her return the look on his face said he was still angry. But he was still there, which meant he either wanted her to explain or he wanted her to tell him she was pulling the story. He wasn't going to like what she had to say.

"Everything you read on that screen is the absolute truth. Your mother told me how the feud started. She dated Tobias first, then she met your father and fell in love with him. Tobias was pissed and that's why he left RGF and refused to speak to your father or mother again." RJ took a couple steps back, until the back of his legs bumped against a chair. "The design that it was said Tobias stole back then, that sketch belonged to Tobias. He'd worked on it while he was at RGF, but it was all his work. So there was some question as to whether the sketch was RGF's work product or if Tobias as the creator owned the IP rights. But the real issue was that love triangle." She paused, took a breath and folded her arms over her chest. "Your father and Tobias corroborated the story."

RJ sat down with a thump and dropped his head. "All this time," he said softly.

"Yes," she replied. "All this time your parents and Tobias let the world believe the reason for the feud was the stolen dress. That's how they protected their privacy. Despite her breaking his heart, Tobias loved your mother and he didn't want her name dragged through the mud for dating best friends."

"And that's why my father never spoke of the details of the feud. But he harbored it. He told us that King Designs was the enemy." RJ was visibly shaken, his voice rough as he tried to come to terms with what she was saying.

"Because Tobias left. He broke the pact that he and your father made to run RGF together. Tobias couldn't work with the man who he felt had stolen his girl. And your mother, she swore she never had romantic feelings for Tobias and they'd only gone out on three dates. She admits she should've handled the situation better, especially since Tobias and Ron were friends, but she never meant to hurt Tobias." Grace recalled feeling the overwhelming sorrow and regret in every one of Marva's words as she'd shared that story with her.

"You can't put this story out there, Grace. I'm begging you," RJ said.

"Stop." She held up a hand. "That's not the story that's going to my editor. I always start with an outline and from there I work in a draft mode. That's what you just read. I was checking it earlier to make sure I didn't leave out anything important in the final copy."

There was no turning back now. So many rules had already been broken. She went to the laptop and pulled up another document before turning the screen to face RJ. "Here's the real story."

After staring at her a few seconds more, he reluctantly shifted his attention to the screen. Grace took the seat across from him at the table. Moments later, when he looked up at her again, it was with a look of sadness and regret.

"I didn't know there were two stories," he said quietly.

She shook her head. "And you didn't trust me. I told you I wouldn't write anything to hurt you or your family and I meant it. But you didn't believe me. You didn't trust that I'd protect you and the ones you love."

"Grace—"

"No, let me finish. I'm not angry that you didn't trust me. A long time ago I didn't trust you." She sighed. "I guess that's our shortcoming, RJ. We have this amazing sexual connection and all these emotions for each other that we can't seem to turn off. But we don't have that one basic thing—trust."

"Look, I'm sorry about my outburst. I thought you were betraying my family. But you can't compare this to what happened to us before. They're two entirely different scenarios," he argued.

"I know what you thought, RJ. But I'd already promised you I wouldn't write anything detrimental.

I shouldn't even have been writing this story because of our previous connection, I could've lost this job and possibly any future hope of being a respected journalist. I even changed the scope of the story and shared some of my interview notes with you. Yet you still stood here and jumped to the worst conclusion possible, which tells me you never trusted me to do what I said I would." She used both hands to cover her face and breathe in and out deeply. "That night you proposed, I said no. Then I got up from that table and walked away. I never trusted you to understand my reasons for not wanting to marry you at that time."

When he didn't speak right away, she shrugged and lifted her hands as if in surrender. "The lack of trust between us is obvious."

He sat back in the chair, shaking his head. "It was right there on the screen, Grace. What'd you expect me to think?"

She didn't break eye contact. "I would've expected you to ask me for an explanation and then wait until I provided it to decide how you were going to react."

He dragged a hand down the back of his head. "Well, it's done. I apologized and we can move on."

"Yes, we can," she said. "We can move on." Grace stood from the chair and went to the door. "I'm really tired now and I told Nina that I'd meet the girls in Riley's room by seven tomorrow."

RJ didn't stand immediately, but he did look

at her. For an instant she thought it was the same shocked and confused look he'd given her that night at the restaurant, but no, this look was different. It was disappointment and despondence. She wasn't sure how much of that was attributed to her or what he'd just found out about his parents, but the fact still remained that everything between them was different now.

"You're angry," he said when he finally came to stand in front of her.

"No," she said, and to prove her point she smiled. "I just don't want to make the same mistakes I made before, so I'm telling you how I feel this time." Against the incessant pounding of her heart, and the panic of losing what just hours ago she'd been ecstatic to find with him again, her brain insisted she keep going. "We should take some time to figure out if this is what we really want. This forever love the people around us seem to have. Because I don't know, RJ. I don't feel like I know anything about this anymore."

He stepped closer to her. "You're afraid."

Irritated that he continued to blame everything she did or said on fear, she snapped, "And so are you! Which is why you could so quickly jump to the wrong conclusions about me. You're afraid that what we've been doing these last two weeks and all that it's made you feel might've been a mistake. You want what your brothers and sister have, but you're afraid it won't work out that way for you again. So yelling at me and threatening me came as your natural defense."

And it had cut through her like a hot blade, leaving her to deal with the hurt she supposed she'd inflicted on him all those years ago.

His eyes glittered with intensity, his lips forming a tight line. "I wasn't lying about how I feel about you and that has nothing to do with two weeks or ten damn years. I loved you then and I love you now."

He was standing close, so close she could reach up and touch his face, put her finger on that muscle in his jaw that jumped as he clenched his teeth.

"I didn't lie about my feelings, either. But you know what, RJ? We were in love before. And that wasn't enough."

"Grace—"

"This time, before we go any further, we should make sure we have what it takes to make it work. Because if not, we shouldn't put each other through another ten years of heartbreak."

He looked like he didn't know how to respond to that. She didn't really know what else to say, either. There was a dull ache in her chest and she was still feeling like a breakdown was imminent. She needed to get him out of here because the last thing she wanted was for RJ to see how badly he'd hurt her.

"I don't want to lose you, Grace. Not again." His words were so sincere, and Grace wanted nothing more than to fall into his arms and say that all was well, but it wasn't.

When he was gone, she locked the door and sat on the couch, dropping her head into her hands. She hadn't trusted him with her feelings about her career in the past, and tonight he hadn't trusted her to keep her word. Did that mean they shouldn't be together? She didn't know. Was she overreacting? She wasn't sure. Was everything she was feeling in this place, amid all the wedding excitement, wreaking havoc with her emotions and the commitment she'd made to her career? Possibly.

It was all so confusing and exhausting. All Grace knew for certain was that the man she loved had just walked out that door and she was sitting here feeling like he probably had years ago—that love was a cruel joke and she no longer wanted any part of it.

CHAPTER SIXTEEN

Four months later
Manhattan, New York

"I CAN'T BELIEVE you're still acting like this," Maurice said. He was standing near the door of the suite RJ had reserved at the Park Lane Hotel, where Ron and Marva's anniversary party was being held.

RJ looked in the mirror one last time, adjusting his bow tie and then smoothing his hand over his beard. "I got this," he told his brother.

Major, who was lounging in the chair across the room, laughed. "You always say that."

RJ turned to face both of them. "And I always mean it."

"Yeah, but we haven't seen Grace since Saint Lucia and we know the two of you are in love, so what gives? Are you getting her back or are you just gonna sit on your ass like you did before and let her get away again?" Maurice wasn't known to mince words.

"My love life is none of your business," RJ said, enjoying the perplexed look on Maurice's face.

"I mean, you can't still be upset with her," Major interjected. "The story that appeared in the paper was touching and painted Dad and Tobias as trailblazers and role models. It even spotlighted how much influence Mom had on the business in the early years. We've received nothing but good press behind it."

That was true. The week after Riley's wedding, the story had been printed in the *Daily Gazette* and posted on all digital media outlets. The Golds and the Kings were making headlines once more, but this time it was in a way that would ensure their story would go down in history. To RJ and the rest of the family's surprise, a few photos from their outings in Saint Lucia and one photo of both families together at the wedding were also released with the story. Riley had called from her honeymoon in Venice to tell them she and Chaz had approved the pictures and worked out an agreement with Grace to have them released with her story.

"The good press made up for that mind-blowing admission Mom gave just before the wedding," Maurice added with a rare frown on his face.

Major sat up in the chair then, leaning forward to rest his elbows on his knees. "Yeah, I'm still trying to wrap my mind around the fact that Mom dated Tobias first."

RJ agreed with his brothers; that part of the story had been a shock to his system and had also taught him one of the most important lessons of his life—to fight for love, no matter the circumstances. "I'm glad she told us," he said, even though a part of him wished Marva and Ron had told them the full story a long time ago. Preferably before he blew up at Grace about it.

"And I don't blame Tobias for being pissed," RJ continued. "If I were in his position I would've been angry enough to quit as well."

"Yeah," Maurice agreed. "Me, too. If Major had dated Desta after me and then ended up marrying her, I'd be ready to strangle him."

Major smirked. "I beat your fiancée at poker last week and you were ready to bite my head off, so believe me, man, I know."

The brothers shared a laugh at the memory of their monthly poker game. Desta was still the only woman who attended and she routinely beat the brakes off each of them, so Major had really celebrated his win last week. Until Maurice had threatened to stuff him in the closet if he didn't pipe down. RJ had enjoyed seeing his family happy.

Riley and Chaz had bought another house, this one in the country as a getaway for when they wanted to leave all the hustle and bustle of the city. Maurice and Desta were now planning their upcoming winter wedding at the ski resort where they'd learned they'd been email pen pals. Major and Nina were over the moon with excitement in anticipation of their son, who was expected in December. And RJ, well, he was doing just fine, too, despite what his brothers thought.

"We should get downstairs. The party's about to start and you know how Mom is about being late." RJ walked toward the door and Major stood from his chair to follow him.

"You really aren't going to go after her, man? You two are meant to be together," Major said when the three Gold brothers walked out of the suite.

They each wore RGold black tuxedos with gold satin vests and ties. Tonight, Ron and Marva were celebrating their thirty-sixth wedding anniversary and the announcement of Ron's retirement at a lavish gold-and-white-themed party.

"I know Grace and I are meant to be together," RJ said when they were finally in the elevator.

Maurice punched him in the shoulder. "Then why isn't she here? Why hasn't she moved back into your penthouse so the two of you can start making wedding plans?"

RJ laughed. "You just want to share the misery you're going through with Desta, her mother, her grandmother and Mom planning your big day."

Major chuckled. "Yeah, he is."

The brothers stepped off the elevator and walked down the white marble hallway toward the ballroom.

Guests had already begun to arrive, and music from the band hired to play for the first half of the event flowed out into the hallway. After dinner and the big announcement, the DJ would facilitate his parents' plan to dance the night away.

RJ hoped his intentions for this evening would go off without a hitch as well.

Grace traced the embossed gold letters on the white invitation, reading the words one more time. *You are cordially invited to share in the celebration of thirty-six years of love between Ronald Gold Jr. and Marva Westing Gold.*

"He's gonna die when he sees you in that dress," Hope said from her perch on Grace's bed. She'd been sitting there, with her legs crossed at the ankle and pillows propped at her back, for the last hour watching Grace get ready.

"It's just a dress," Grace replied. She stood in front of the full-length mirror on the inside of her closet door surveying the final product.

She'd lied. The rose-gold-sequined two-piece gown was stunning. The halter-style top hugged her bodice before stopping to leave her midriff bare, and the skirt fit her tightly from her waist to mid-thigh on the right where it opened into a split. The soft and elegant material fell to the floor with a short train behind her. She'd worked on her hair all day and was now thoroughly pleased with the shorter length and bouncy spiral curls that rested on her shoulders.

"Are you sure you're supposed to be eating like that?" Grace asked her older sister when Hope put yet another chocolate frosted doughnut hole into her mouth. Grace bought those especially for when she wasn't able to get to a bakery to buy her favorite whole doughnut.

Hope was seven months pregnant, hence the reason she'd wanted a very quick fall wedding. The nuptials were scheduled to take place next weekend at their parents' house, and Hope seemed to be eating away all her nerves.

"This may be the only time I can eat guilt-free, and I plan to take full advantage of it." Hope grinned after she finished chewing. "And don't get off topic. You and RJ have been writing letters and having long phone conversations like teenagers for the past four months. I sure hope tonight he's gonna put a ring on it."

Grace's stomach churned at the thought.

"Oh, and I hope you keep the ring on it this time," her sister added.

"We really don't have to talk about this again." She moved from the mirror and grabbed her purse.

After her return from Saint Lucia, Grace had gone directly to her parents' house in need of a safe haven. Of course, she hadn't found it there. Videtta had been beside herself once Grace explained that she and RJ had rekindled and then snuffed out their chances at love during the trip. Her sisters had come to her rescue, taking her on a girls' trip where they let her confess about all the competitiveness and validation issues she'd harbored all her life. And then they'd promptly read her the riot act for assuming she was less than anything but brilliant and competent just like they were.

With her new job at the paper and a newfound bond between her and her sisters, Grace had begun to feel better about herself and in doing so, she'd been better able to deal with RJ. Which turned out to be a good thing because when she returned to her apartment after the girls' trip it was to find two letters from him. She'd read each letter a dozen times before deciding to respond, and since then they'd been communicating either by old-school snail mail or telephone calls at least four times a week. She'd made the mistake of sharing all those details with her sisters.

"I'm just sayin', you've had the great sex and now you've done the—what did Grandma used to call it—the 'courtin' thing'? So there's only one obvious next step," Hope said.

"Well, that might be obvious for some people, but for others, it might take a while to get to that point." Grace left her sister in her apartment then. Hope had a key since she was the only relative of Grace's who lived in the city. When her sister was done eating she'd let herself out.

An hour later, Grace walked into the ballroom at the Park Lane Hotel. Marva had sent her an invitation and RJ had confirmed she'd received it, so if there'd been any doubt in attending tonight, she'd pushed it aside. She didn't want either of them calling her to find out why she hadn't shown up. And truth be told there'd been no doubt. Tonight, Grace was feeling more in control and focused than she'd ever felt before.

She was late. After taking the time to get ready and chatting with Hope, she'd left her apartment a lot later than she'd planned and then, of course, there'd been traffic. She'd arrived just in time to hear Ron's retirement announcement and to see RJ stepping up behind the lectern.

"It's an honor," he began after the lengthy applause from the room full of what looked to be three hundred guests. "Not only to stand here and accept this position, but to share in this momentous evening with my parents. Mom, Dad." He paused and looked over to where Ron and Marva sat at a private table draped in white linen with a gold candelabra at its center.

The entire room was decorated with white table coverings and gold pots full of white flowers. Candlelight illuminated the place, along with the one dark-painted wall that was alight with tiny white lights.

"I've learned so much from you," RJ went on,

"and not just about the business. But about love and tolerance. And compromise. You've shown Riley, Major, Maurice and me what it means to be a couple, to cherish someone and to hold their heart as tenderly as if it were precious as gold. For that I thank you from the bottom of my heart. I love you both and wish you nothing but happiness for the next thirty-six years and beyond."

Tears filled Grace's eyes as the crowd came to their feet, lifting their glasses in a toast to Ron and Marva. Her chest felt full and she struggled to breathe as emotion overwhelmed her. She needed air. Turning, she started to move toward the door when she bumped into Chaz.

"Hey, there. You okay?" he asked.

She nodded. "Yeah. I mean, yes, I'm fine. Just need to get a little air. I'll be right back."

And then she was on the move again, not stopping until she was in the hallway, her fingers clenching her purse tightly. She didn't know how long she stood there staring at the marble walls, trying to get her thoughts together, but the moment she felt a hand on her shoulder she knew who it was. Chaz had no doubt hurried to tell him she was there.

"Hi," RJ said when she turned to face him.

"Hi. Sorry I was late."

"No. I'm just glad you made it." He laced his fingers with hers. "Let's go over here and sit down."

She followed him to a row of red velvet benches.

"It's really good to see you," he said when they were seated.

Grace took a deep breath and let it out slowly. "Yes, it's good to see you again, too. I have something I want to say to you and I'm just gonna say it now before I lose my nerve." Because she was in danger of totally losing it right now. Hearing RJ's words, the sound of undeniable love in his voice as he spoke of his parents and all they'd taught him, had triggered something in her that she'd been waiting to feel for a very long time.

"Okay," he said. "I have something I want to say to you, too, but I'll let you go first."

"Good. Thanks." She smiled nervously and stared into his beautiful brown eyes. "I love you. I've loved you for longer than I can remember and it's still here." She reached up and rubbed her fingers over her heart. "I didn't know before. I didn't believe I was ready to be a wife and a journalist at the same time. I really believed I had to make a choice, and I made the right choice for me at that time."

"Grace—"

"No," she shook her head earnestly. "Let me finish. After we returned from the island, I still wasn't sure. I thought, 'See, you were right not to marry him,' after our last argument and the realization that we didn't trust each other."

"I know, baby, and that was my fault. I should've

trusted you. I just thought about my parents and I reacted."

She lifted two fingers to touch to his lips. "Your love and dedication to your family is one of the many things I adore about you, Ronald Gold III. I also love the way you never asked me to be anything but myself. The way you supported my goal as a journalist, reading all my articles and even keeping some of them." She was filled with awe and complete reverence remembering the times he'd done that.

"I know that I can be myself whenever I'm with you and that's enough. It's enough for you and for me. And in the end, that's all that matters, isn't it? What you and I feel and what we have together?" She let her hand fall from his lips and pressed it to her purse, which was sitting in her lap. "I knew what I wanted to say to you when I came here tonight but then when I heard you talking, I actually felt it. I felt that thing that I think has sustained your parents and my parents in their marriages all these years." Hurriedly, she opened her purse and pulled out a black velvet box before lifting her gaze up to him again. "I love you, RJ, and I need to know if you'd still like to marry me."

RJ glanced down at the box and back up to her, his expression perplexed and then animated as he shook his head.

Her heart sank. "You're turning me down?"

He reached into the inside pocket of his tuxedo

jacket and pulled out another black velvet box. "No, baby. I was gonna ask you to marry me again."

Grace stared at the ring box he held and then pushed hers until the boxes clinked together like champagne glasses. "Then I guess we're getting married."

RJ smiled and leaned in closer to her. "I guess we are," he said before taking her mouth in a soft kiss.

* * * * *